PRAISE FOR
A Lady's Guide to Ruin:

"A wonderful story, with a heroine who finds her true self through love and friendship. Kimmel's debut adds a new star to the romance galaxy. I loved this book."
—Madeline Hunter, *New York Times* bestselling author

"Kimmel demonstrates a talent for storytelling."
—*RT Romance Reviews*

"Excellent character development." —*Publishers Weekly*

"A very fine start to a promising writing career for this new author." —*Romance Reviews Today*

"Kimmel writes characters that leap off the page and adventures that leave you breathless."
—Anna Randol, author of *Sins of a Wicked Princess*

A
Gentleman's Guide
to Scandal

Kathleen Kimmel

BERKLEY SENSATION, NEW YORK

BERKLEY SENSATION

An imprint of Penguin Random House LLC
375 Hudson Street, New York, New York 10014

A GENTLEMAN'S GUIDE TO SCANDAL

A Berkley Sensation Book / published by arrangement with the author

ISBN: 978-1-101-98681-3

PUBLISHING HISTORY
Berkley Sensation mass-market edition / June 2016

PRINTED IN THE UNITED STATES OF AMERICA

10 9 8 7 6 5 4 3 2 1

Cover design by Colleen Reinhart.
Interior text design by Laura K. Corless.

Penguin
Random
House

To my parents.
(Please skip the naughty bits.)

Acknowledgments

I am deeply grateful to everyone who helped make this book a reality. Thank you to my agent, Lisa Rodgers, my editor, Julie Mianecki, and the team at Berkley, for all their hard work. Many thanks to Rhiannon Held and Jennifer Canada, who read early drafts and made all the right soothing noises when plot holes were discovered, and to Madeline Hunter, for providing a fabulous blurb. And as always, a huge thank-you to my family: Mom and Dad; my siblings, Helen and Thomas; and my very favorite husband, Mike.

Prologue

~

SUMMER, 1812, BIRCH HALL

Colin Spenser, Marquess of Farleigh, paced. It was, he allowed, a cliché, but he felt he undertook the task with style. He had chosen the library for his pacing, surrounded by weighty books and furniture of a deep mahogany, which lent a dignity to the endeavor he did not feel himself. He was a man in love, helplessly so, and any moment now—the next circuit, or the one after that—he would stride out, declare his affections, make the requisite proposal, and be done with this discomfort.

Colin considered himself a man of great certainty. He knew on instinct, without the aid of a compass, which direction he faced at any given moment; he knew the time without glancing at a clock; he knew Latin and Greek, mathematics, the precise distance between New York and London, and the rules for fifty-seven separate card games. He *knew* that Elinor Hargrove was an irritating, nosy twig of a girl, her only redeeming quality being her relation to his closest friend.

The problem was, he'd been so very *certain* of that fact, and the image of her as a young woman—blotchy-skinned, gawky, in poorly fitting gowns, constantly ill—had been so fixed in his mind that he had not seen the gradual transformation she had undergone. He had missed, too, the incrementally longer moments he had lingered near her, the more extensive conversations they had engaged in. He had missed that her no-longer pimpled skin was a soft, pale shade that bordered on luminous, her hair effortlessly swept up off her long neck, her body slender and gracefully curved. He had missed that when she laughed across the room, his thoughts faltered, and his conversation fell to silence so he could listen.

Somehow, through all of that, he had insisted to himself that he did not care for her one whit. Until now. Until this summer, in her family's home at Birch Hall. There had been no sudden flash of insight; he could not give himself that kind of credit. No, the evidence had accumulated over months and years, a slow accretion, like snow on a roof. Each flake inconsequential, until the roof bowed and broke.

For all its discomfort, it came as a relief. He had spent the last several months in a state of numbness, ever since word arrived—months after the fact—that his elder sister had died in India. Months after she'd left England, he'd found himself turning as if to ask her advice, straining his ear to catch the light fall of her laughter again. By the time she died, he was accustomed to her absence, and that made it hurt all the more. It was only on his mother's insistence that he'd dragged himself to this party. And then he'd seen Elinor, and it was as if he'd remembered at last how to breathe.

He could not go back to that half death. He had to act.

He stopped, straightening, his hands clasped behind his back. He was a logical man, and he could recognize his failure in this circumstance. He had allowed himself to be blinded by his adolescent prejudices. It was time to correct his mistakes, and all of this pacing would not change the situation. Nor did it appear to be supplying him with the correct words to convince a girl—a woman—whom he'd studiously ignored for two decades to marry him.

He'd extemporize. Women liked that, didn't they? Spontaneity?

He cleared his throat and strode out into the hall. He took a sharp right, proceeded thirty-one steps down the hallway, and turned toward the door to the Blue Room. Elinor spent every afternoon in the Blue Room, reading or sewing, alone with her thoughts. It was the perfect time to approach her without interruption.

Except—

Except the door was ajar, and he had arrived not in the midst of a long silence, but a short one. A pause, one might say, and now the conversation within resumed.

"You needn't give me an answer now."

The voice belonged to Matthew Newburne, a fellow guest at Birch Hall for the summer. Colin frowned. Newburne and Elinor despised one another. They had fought all summer, trading jabs and burning glares from the time the carriages pulled up in the drive. What was Newburne doing there?

"Needn't I?" Elinor asked. She didn't sound angry. She sounded . . .

Oh, God. Not this.

"You can take as long as you require. I do not mean to pressure you."

Colin tensed. He could burst in. Fall down on his knees. Or stand. Loom. He was tall; he was good at looming. Dear Lord, Newburne was shorter than Elinor!

"Though . . . how long do you suppose you might require?" Newburne managed a chuckle, but the strain in his voice was obvious. Colin balled his hands into fists. He recognized that strain. Good God, he should have seen what hid behind that bickering.

"Oh, Matthew. I don't need any more time. My answer is yes."

Colin closed his eyes, jaw tensing at Newburne's startled laugh, Elinor's inhalation of—surprise? Delight? Laughter again, and the unmistakable sound of a kiss. And then, footsteps. They were coming for the door. Colin's eyes flew open. He stepped back, mouth parting, eyes widening as he frantically considered what he might say.

The door opened. Elinor stood, flushed, her hand

stretched back and Newburne dragged along merrily behind her. She halted, eyes shining and a smile lighting her elegant features. Colin stood gaping, breathless, feeling as if someone had just punched him in the stomach.

"Lord Farleigh," Elinor said, after the pause had grown distinctly uncomfortable.

"Ah. Lady Elinor. Mr. Newburne. Good afternoon."

"We've just—" Elinor trailed off, laughed breathily, glanced back at Newburne. The man had a sheepish grin on his face. Colin contemplated sinking a fist into it.

"I overheard," Colin said. "Not that I was listening, mind. I happened to walk by." He tilted up his chin. His heartbeat seemed to have deserted him; certainly the blood had ceased to flow through him, and vertigo swept in to take its place. "My congratulations," he said, light and airy. He was going to faint. Or commit murder. "It is a surprise, of course. You do seem mismatched. In height, in temperament . . . but I suppose that differences do a lively match make. And certainly it is high time you were wed, Elinor. You are what, twenty-five years of age? We had begun to worry." He cursed every word as it came out of his mouth, and yet he could not stop himself. He wanted to fling all the helpless hurt back at them, to watch someone else's face crumple with the despair that compressed his lungs.

Elinor gaped at him. Newburne had turned red, but when he made to step forward, Elinor tightened her grip on his hand. "Thank you for your well wishes," she said. Her voice was just as tight as her hold on Newburne. "Now, if you will excuse me, I must find my brother."

"In the garden, I believe," Colin said. "Again, my congratulations." He turned on his heel and strode back the way he had come. Thirty-one steps. A left turn. He shut the door to the library behind him and stood with his hand on the knob, his brow inches from the solid wood. Perhaps he should slam them together a few times. Which of the two methods might be more efficacious, he wondered: ramming his head forward into the door, or yanking the door into his forehead? The latter might attract more attention, but as he rather hoped he would be unconscious at the end of the procedure, it didn't particularly matter.

Matthew Newburne. *Mr.* Matthew Newburne. The son of an earl, yes, but the *third* son. And his brothers were *quite* healthy.

He turned, abandoning the quick release of a concussion. Perhaps there was something in the room he could tear apart. Some of the books looked heavy enough to throw through the windows, and if Martin got upset, he'd simply explain . . .

Under no circumstances could he explain this to Martin, he realized. The man must never know; not if their friendship was to continue unaltered. He'd simply claim to have been drunk, then.

Which, come to think of it, was a marvelous idea. He stalked to the table beneath the window, on which rested brandy and sturdy glasses. He filled the glass halfway and downed a large swallow. Ah, yes. That would do.

He would drink. As plans went, it had the advantage of simplicity.

He threw himself into the nearest chair. He'd spent two decades ignoring the woman. He could certainly manage a few more.

Chapter 1

~~

The Earl of Levenbane was a frightening man. Everyone said so. It was one of the rare points of agreement across the whole of the peerage. Colin, of course, was not intimidated. Admittedly, he was thirty years the man's junior, and currently the recipient of a scowl that would down a pheasant at a hundred paces. But Colin had one advantage. Lord Levenbane had thirty more years of multi-course meals and idle days to expand his person to an impressive girth, along with a bad knee that necessitated a cane. In short, Colin was fairly certain he could outrun the man, if things turned sour.

Nonetheless, when the earl settled back in his seat and pierced Colin with that infamous stare, Colin experienced a definite prickling at the back of his neck.

"We've edged around this thing long enough. I think it is well past time we made it official," Levenbane said. "Don't you?"

Colin gave a languid wave of his hand. "I have no particular timetable," he said. "And thus I bow to yours. As long as Lady Penelope is agreeable, of course."

Levenbane grunted and reached for the wine at his side. Colin reached for his own wine. He'd never gotten a nose for the stuff, but even he could tell it was expensive. Light, lighter than he preferred, though he supposed it was early in the day.

Levenbane's drawing room was steeped in opulence. The cushions were a rich burgundy, the arms of the chairs intricately carved. Gold leaf had been applied to the wallpaper in curlicues, with wild and mythical creatures sketched in miniature at the edges, all of them seeming to peer at Colin with appraising expressions.

Colin's own father had been an austere man, not fond of excess, and the style of his homes reflected that. Colin had seen no reason to change it, and while his mother clotted up her private rooms with decadent flourishes, she had preserved his father's tastes wherever she could, leaving every residence a mausoleum in the man's memory. Colin supposed that Penelope would want to change that.

Well, good. Lack of change was stagnation, and stagnation might as well be death. He'd been worse than stagnant the last few years. He'd refused to even entertain the notion of marriage since the disastrous interlude with Elinor, and it was well past time he put aside his sentiment and took care of the task in a logical manner.

Even if it meant marrying a woman with whom he'd never had an entire conversation.

"My daughter is a sensible girl," Levenbane was saying. "Most of the time. Every girl has a fairy tale knocking around her mind, of course. But proper breeding and education teaches them to ignore it when reality comes to call."

"Lord Levenbane—"

"Levenbane, please," the man said. Colin paused. He did not particularly want to establish casual intimacy with his soon-to-be father-in-law. He had always imagined the role as one of a dragon on a nearby hill, watching him with narrowed eyes and smoke trailing out of his (rather wide, it must be said) nostrils. One did not befriend the dragon; it only made it more awkward when conflict inevitably arose.

"Levenbane," Colin corrected himself. "I intend to make your daughter quite happy."

"Not at first," Levenbane said. Colin found himself at a loss for words. "She will be happy with the life you give her, certainly. And happy with you for a protector in time. And happy to be a bride, certainly; what woman can resist being at the center of attention so thoroughly? But the first year will be difficult. Perhaps even the second. It is one thing to throw a party, and another to look ahead to a long lifetime in each other's company. More wine?"

At some point Colin had finished the glass. He nodded.

"Or something stronger, perhaps," Levenbane suggested.

"If you have it."

Levenbane gave him a look like Colin had inquired about the religious affiliation of the Pope and fetched a decanter of brandy from a side table.

"It is superior to a love match, of course," Levenbane said as he poured. "In a love match, the first year is bliss and the rest is hell. In the more civilized mode, the first year is awkward and the rest have the ease and efficiency of practice, without the disorienting addition of strong emotion."

"I should think passion has its place in either mode," Colin said.

Levenbane settled back into his chair. "Passion? If you want passion, get a mistress. Wait until you've got your wife with child, of course, that's safest. But it will keep you sane, and keep her from needing to bear the burden of your 'passion' along with the management of your household. A mistress, a wife, a set of children, and enough residences that the three don't have to see one another. That is the recipe for a perfect marriage."

"I see," Colin said. It was not at all the model of his parents' marriage. They'd adored each other, though they'd not spent five minutes alone together before their wedding. Up until the day he died, his father was forever darting off the street because he spotted some treasure he wished to present to his wife, and serenading her behind closed doors. Colin had spent so many years hearing how rare, how spectacular their love was, that he had never believed it could be replicated. He had assumed he would, at best, marry a woman he had a moderate amount of affection for. He had allowed for the possibility of this bloodless type of match, and it had not troubled him.

Until Elinor.

Damn it all. It had been five years. It was well past time for that foolishness to be forgotten. It was undoubtedly preferable to enter a marriage of equals, with no strong affection on either side, than to be left longing after a woman who didn't return his feelings. He had done a thorough job of scrubbing his soul of its pathetic, moping regard for Elinor Hargrove.

And then this summer she had the gall to come and spend the Season in his household, gadding about London with his youngest sister and wafting through his presence every hour of the day. He would say it was driving him to drink, but that was too mild a statement. Instead, it had driven him to an engagement, which was a far more drastic step. And hopefully far more effective.

"You're a smart man," Levenbane said. "You'll see. And now I think you'd better spend a little time with the girl, eh? Make her feel like she's got something to do with the whole business." He chuckled.

Colin murmured assent and finished his drink quickly so that it could be cleared away. Lady Penelope appeared in short order, looking very charming and very young in a pale blue frock. She had the most remarkable curls, he noted, perfect ringlets that shone in the light. She was adorable. He was marrying a woman who could be described as adorable. God help him. God help *her*.

Levenbane was saying something about an official announcement and Lady Copeland's ball—the last of any note that season.

"The Copeland ball," Colin repeated dully.

"Is there a problem?" Levenbane asked, in a tone that allowed only one answer.

"I do not usually attend," Colin said. Though he was, of course, invited. The ill blood between their families was not the sort one could speak of, nor act on; they'd spent years smiling and nodding to each other in passing and simply ignoring each other the rest of the time.

Levenbane's expression darkened.

"I will have to make an exception," Colin said, with a roguish smile to Penelope, who blushed scarlet. She had a good complexion for blushing, he noted. When his sisters blushed they turned all blotchy; Penelope bloomed like a rose. He wondered if she'd practiced.

"Very good," Levenbane said. "And October for the wedding, then?"

"If that is enough time for Lady Penelope," Colin said graciously.

"Oh, yes," Penelope said. It was the first she'd spoken. "It needn't be extravagant."

Her father's expression suggested that it would be, if he had anything to say about it. Since Colin would be only minimally involved in the planning, he didn't see how it affected him. Levenbane extended his hand. Colin shook it. And that was that.

In three months, he'd be a married man.

He exited Levenbane's town house with a curious numbness in his limbs. It was taken care of, then. It was done, and he could finally put Elinor out of his mind.

He paused as he reached his carriage, frowning. A thin figure was puffing its way up the street toward him. William, he realized, the youngest footman.

"Lord Farleigh," the boy squeaked as he came within wheezing distance. "I came—you said—"

"Deep breaths, William," Colin said. The boy was far too excitable. His cheeks were so red now that Colin feared he would pitch over in the street. "What is it?"

"You told me to tell you if Lady Phoebe got into any trouble," William said between panting breaths. He leaned over, bracing a hand on his thigh.

Colin stifled a sigh. Of course the boy had taken his offhand jest about watching the youngest Spenser sister as a sacred mission. He accepted every order—from fetching lemonade to straightening his cuffs—with the gravity of a holy crusade. "I take it my sister has found some mischief to get into, then. You really didn't have to run all the way here."

"Oh," William said, crestfallen. He straightened up. "My apologies, my lord."

"Don't worry about it. I did say to tell me," Colin said, rubbing his temples. "So what's she done now?"

"Lady Phoebe and Lady Elinor have gone out," William said. "To the East End. Whitechapel. My lord."

Colin scowled. What the devil were Elinor and his sister doing there? No doubt chasing some harebrained adventure Phoebe had concocted. It was one thing when she darted off in search of excitement, but Elinor ought to have known better. He looked William in the eye. The boy straightened up, setting his jaw and no doubt channeling every ancestor who'd ever lifted musket or sword in service of his country. He looked ready to charge Napoleon's armies single-handed.

"You did well," Colin said. "Now. Tell me exactly where they've gone."

Elinor Hargrove did not believe in ghosts. The dead stayed dead. Their voices did not echo back to the living, and anyone who claimed to hear them must be mad—or a cheat. In the case of Madame Vesta, it was almost certainly the latter. And Elinor intended to prove it, even if it meant a trip to a thoroughly dubious neighborhood of London.

The streets were narrow and filthy, and the buildings seemed to lean against one another like drunken friends. A mangy cat and a mangier child ambled down the street, unperturbed by the clatter of the carriage's wheels or the slowing clop of the horse's hooves. As the carriage pulled reluctantly to a stop, Elinor turned her skeptical gaze on her companion.

Phoebe Spenser sat, perched at the very limit of her seat, on the far side of the carriage. She buzzed with energy, her fingers fidgeting in her lap and her teeth nibbling at the inside of her lip.

Elinor could not claim to be close to Phoebe. They were a full decade apart in age, and Elinor had spent far more time with her elder sisters, Kitty and Marie. After all the kindness Phoebe's mother had shown her over the years, though, it had been impossible to decline her request that Elinor serve as Phoebe's unofficial companion and escort during the London Season. The dowager marchioness herself was indisposed with a bout of existential despair regarding her youngest child's marriageability, and had decamped to Kitty's estate to fawn over her young grandson. And of course Elinor had nothing better to do, having no spouse or children or social obligations of her own, so *obviously* she ought to be the one to grapple with Phoebe Spenser's overinflated sense of adventure and try to steer her toward an eligible man at last.

"We are here," Phoebe declared, drawing Elinor's attention back to the present. "That's it, just down the way." She had flung open the door and hopped onto the street before the coachman had the chance to clamber down to assist. Elinor hurried after, nearly tripping on her skirts.

She was beginning to sympathize a great deal more with Lady Farleigh. Phoebe was positively manic; no wonder the woman had engineered an escape from her. It was like trying to keep up with an excitable terrier. At least the Season was nearly over. She could manage a few more weeks.

The narrow house Phoebe now hurried toward stood crushed between two brutish tenements, its windows masked with gray curtains. A sign hung outside, creaking ostentatiously in the breeze. Faded paint in a jagged script declared it the home of Madame Vesta. A crudely painted eye glared beneath the words.

"Are you certain this is where you want to be, m'lady?" the coachman asked. Judging by the tremor in his voice, he was thinking of what Lord Farleigh would do if he discovered the location of their afternoon errand.

"Apparently so. Wait here," Elinor said firmly. The coachman touched his cap in acknowledgment, but concern still wrinkled his brow.

Her moment's hesitation had attracted the small, grubby child, who took hold of Elinor's skirt and looked up at her with wide eyes. "Hello," Elinor said, startled. She held her hands awkwardly at her sides and cast a quick look around for the child's keeper. It appeared to have none. "Er. I have to go, child." She started to move away, but the child clung fast.

Elinor sighed and rummaged in her reticule until she found a small sweet. She had taken to carrying them since her

sister-in-law began to increase, as a form of defense against
the sudden changes in her moods. It worked far better on the
child than on Joan; pressing the sweet into the child's palm
earned her skirt an immediate reprieve, and she left the child
struggling to extricate the treat from its paper wrapping. Elinor hurried to join Phoebe, who was dancing foot-to-foot in
impatience.

"You must watch what you say around this woman," Elinor said as she reached the front steps. "She will try to
deceive you."

"She has a true gift," Phoebe said. "You'll see, Elinor. She's
the most incredible thing. You will be entirely convinced, I
promise." Phoebe knocked lightly on the door. Her whole body
seemed to quiver, and her eyes were fever-bright.

"Are you certain this is a good idea?" Elinor asked.

"You will understand as soon as you speak with her,"
Phoebe said, a touch breathless. Elinor stifled a sigh. Phoebe
had apparently been coming here for some weeks now, and
handing over a considerable amount of money for the priv-
ilege.

The door opened with an ominous groan. Despite herself,
Elinor gave a startled hop. No one stood beyond; only a long,
darkened hallway. A single door stood open at the end, oozing
candlelight.

"This way," Phoebe whispered, and drifted inside.

Elinor stepped over the threshold reluctantly. She did not
believe in spirits, or in the ability of mediums to conjure
them. She believed in people, and their capacity for trickery.
And so when she stepped inside, she did not shudder in
dread or anticipation. She looked up and back, and squinted
into the shadows. There. A fine cord was knotted around a
nail at the corner of the door, and threaded carefully along
the wall, down the hallway. She tried the latch on the door.
Loose. A good tug on that cord would open it.

"Oh, Phoebe," Elinor whispered. The dusty hallway
swallowed the sound, and turned her footsteps dull and van-
ishing. The light at the end of the hall seemed to press
against her, oily and unpleasantly warm. The air was thick

with burnt incense. Elinor took a deep breath and immediately felt a wave of dizziness sweep over her. With distrust beetling in her belly, she followed Phoebe into Madame Vesta's chamber.

The woman herself was a spindly thing, though younger than she wished to appear. Even in the shadows Elinor could make out the smudge of something smoky dabbed around her eyes, to make them appear sunken. Her hair she had grayed, perhaps with a powder—not quite reaching the roots. Her hands gave her away: smooth and lithe as they shuffled a deck of cards in a rhythmic susurrus.

Two chairs sat on the opposite side of Vesta's table. Phoebe looked again at Elinor, as if the appearance of the correct number of chairs proved something. Perhaps the previous clients had come in a pair. Perhaps Vesta had guessed that Phoebe would bring her visiting friend. And if Phoebe had come alone, the extra chair would be easy to excuse. It was a calculated guess, Elinor decided, meant to immediately instill in her a sense that Vesta knew more than she ought.

Nonetheless, Elinor did her best to keep her face clear of judgment.

"Madame Vesta. I have brought my friend, Elinor, to see you," Phoebe said. The worshipful tone in her voice made Elinor wince, even leaving aside the blatant disregard for proper forms of address.

"Of course," Madame Vesta said, and waved a hand at the chairs. "Please, sit. You are welcome in my house."

Elinor eased herself into the chair, wondering if it would wobble to make her feel off-balance—but it was a sturdy thing, and quite comfortable. She cast a cynical eye about the room. The windows were covered, leaving the candles as the only illumination. They were arranged such that Elinor and Phoebe were well-lit, while light flickered indistinctly over Madame Vesta's features. Elinor had always had a knack for reading people. She suspected Madame Vesta had the same talent, and wished to observe their faces as she spoke. The twitch of a lip, the slight furrow of a brow—tiny signs could spell the truth.

"You have come today to speak to me about . . ." Madame Vesta trailed off, briefly enough that she might have only been pausing for breath.

"It is not the usual thing, no," Phoebe said, leaning forward, and Elinor resisted the urge to groan. The trailing off bit was Joan's favorite trick. In general, people could not abide silence. They were eager to fill it, and rarely remembered that it was they who had finished the sentence.

"Of course. You have come to speak to a particular spirit," Madame Vesta said, eyes fixed on Phoebe's face. She must have seen some sign of agreement there, for she did not immediately correct herself. "Someone close to you. Ah, but not close. Is it distance . . . ? Time . . . ?"

"She died far away, and years ago," Phoebe said.

Elinor bit the inside of her lip. If it had been someone dead two days the next street over, Madame Vesta would have claimed some metaphorical distance. And there was only one person Phoebe could be speaking of.

"Marie," Elinor said softly. Phoebe glanced at her in surprise. Elinor shook her head. Of course it was Marie. Phoebe's life did not offer many ghosts to choose from, and Marie's memory held a near-mythical sway over the girl. She had been gone for six years, but she haunted all of them—the dowager marchioness, Lord Farleigh, Kitty, Phoebe. And Elinor, too.

"Yes. Your sister," Madame Vesta said. The hint of a frown flitted across her face. She wasn't pleased at having her guessing game preempted. "She is here. She is listening."

Elinor curled her hand in her lap, digging her nails against her palm. Even if Marie had found herself in possession of a spectral form, she never would have come to this place. Elinor would have sooner expected her to appear at the foot of her bed, laughing at how thoroughly wrong she had been proved after years of dedicated skepticism.

The question was not whether Marie's spirit was truly present. The question was why Phoebe should seek her out now.

Apparently Madame Vesta wondered the same thing. "Something has changed," she said. "You are disquieted."

Her accent was thick. Thick and inconsistent. It had started out Slavic and was veering into French, but underneath . . .

"I see a man. Family? No, not connected by blood. But he knew your sister. I do not see him among the spirits . . . yes, he still lives. His name swirls around you. I see a letter. A J? No, an E . . . Edward?"

"Edward Foyle," Phoebe declared, and cast another look of triumph at Elinor, who had been watching the youngest Spenser's features. A faint widening of Phoebe's eyes at the suggestion of a man, a downward twitch of the corner of her mouth at the *J*, a sudden tightening of her jaw at *E*. At times Elinor felt there were only a half dozen names in rotation among the men of England; it was not such a startling thing that Madame Vesta had hit upon the right one. And she had started with J, of course. One could not spit without striking a John.

That accent still bothered her. Its drunken wandering between foreign locales covered something familiar.

"Shropshire?" Elinor guessed aloud.

Madame Vesta was a professional, Elinor gave her that. The only hint that Elinor had guessed right was a flaring of her nostrils and a slight twitch of her eyelid. "Pardon me, I am not sure I follow," she said. She'd taken a left into Italian with that. Elinor let out an unladylike snort.

"You should pick an accent and stick with it," she said. "Phoebe, this woman is a fraud."

"Elinor," Phoebe said, half reproachful, half pleading. "She knows things. Things she couldn't—"

"She's reading you, not listening to the spirits. You have an expressive face, Phoebe. I could do the same, if I had the desire to swindle you out of your coin. I guessed about Marie, didn't I?"

"You know me," Phoebe said. "That's different."

"And how much have you told her about yourself? A fair bit, and I doubt you realized half of what you revealed." Elinor stood, pushing back her chair.

"I cannot reach the departed with such a person in the room," Madame Vesta declared. "You must leave, or the spirits will not speak." Madame Vesta had a red tinge in her cheeks. Elinor suppressed the urge to slap a bit more color into them.

"I am leaving. We both are," Elinor declared.

"No, we aren't," Phoebe said. "Elinor, please."

Elinor was accustomed to pity. She had been ill most of her life. She was used to being treated like a small, hapless child. And so she did not allow pity to cross her face. Instead, she spoke in a quiet, steady tone, a tone meant for an equal who has momentarily stumbled.

"Phoebe, this woman is a fraud. She is trying to take advantage of you and your trusting, loving heart. Whatever answers you are searching for, you will not find them here."

Madame Vesta hissed between her teeth. "You call yourself her friend, but vile air swirls about you. The spirits shy from your very presence! Ah, all but one. A man. I see him, clearly. He reaches for you. His name . . . I see an M. Matthew." She paused, triumphant. Perhaps she read Elinor's silence as shock, as awe at her insight. Which only showed that she was not as good at this game as she believed. Elinor heard her pulse in her ears like a drumbeat, fury rising in her breast.

She leaned toward the woman. She rested the fingertips of one hand against the wood, focusing on the five points of pressure, forcing herself to take steady breaths. If she let emotion sweep her up, she would begin to breathe too quickly. She could not succumb to her anger; it would only drive her to an attack, as she'd suffered so many times before. With the incense in the air, her chest was already tight. And so she did not shout. She lowered her voice, calm and sweet.

"Marie Spenser was my dearest friend," she said. "Matthew was the best man I have ever known. You are not fit to speak their names. They would have nothing but contempt for you. If their spirits had truly returned, they would not come to you if every other man, woman, and child in England had perished," she said. "Do not speak to Phoebe again." She did not spell out a threat. Madame Vesta clearly knew who she was; she knew the heads that would bend at Elinor's whisper. She could likely imagine the kind of power that could be brought to bear against her, at Elinor's request. Elinor was not proud of using that sort of influence—it always made her feel a bully. But in this case, she was willing to make an exception.

Madame Vesta had the sense to fall silent, at least, but settled back in her chair with a defiant glint in her eye.

Phoebe looked ready to cry. She stood, eyes downcast, and set a single coin on the table. "I'm sorry," she said. Elinor couldn't tell which of them she addressed. Guilt added to the pressure in Elinor's chest. She hadn't meant to humiliate Phoebe, only protect her.

"Let's go," she said gently, and took Phoebe's arm.

Outside, the air was fetid but cool, and Elinor gulped down a grateful breath. The incense clung to her skin and her hair. Phoebe pulled free of her and stood, hands cupping her elbows and eyes fixed on nothing.

"Forgive me," Elinor said. "I handled that brutishly."

"I knew she wasn't real," Phoebe said. "I did." She lifted her chin. She'd known no such thing, but like her brother, she was a creature of pride.

"She was very convincing," Elinor said.

"I *hoped* she was real," Phoebe said.

It shouldn't have surprised Elinor that Phoebe would long for her eldest sister's counsel. Elinor longed for it as well. When her mother had died and her brother went away to school, the Spenser women had taken her in as one of their own. She was between Kitty and Marie in age, but it was Marie she always gravitated toward. The older girl would brush her hair out and tell her fairy tales, stories of knights and dragons and princesses—who always seemed to be the ones with the clever idea to solve all the kingdom's worries.

And it was Marie who had lain with her when her world dissolved into the unbearable pain of her frequent headaches and who stroked her back and held her when her breath came in a strangled wheeze. Those stories had kept her calm, had kept her taking in one breath after another.

She was never Elinor's sister, but Elinor had longed for her to be.

"I am sorry," Elinor said, and touched Phoebe's arm softly.

At that moment, a commotion at the end of the street drew them all around. There was a great clatter of wheels and hooves, and the excited whicker of a horse pulled up suddenly. A hired hack lurched to a halt at the end of the lane, Lord Farleigh already half out of it.

"Oh, drat," Phoebe said.

Elinor might have chosen more emphatic language. Even from this distance, Lord Farleigh's expression was one of deep anger. He strode to them, eating up the distance with his long legs. Tension darkened his eyes, leaving them the dark gray of a roiling storm.

Elinor flinched. Colin had a unique ability to make her feel gawky, awkward, and perpetually half a second from some grand faux pas. He was not a lovely man; his features were too severe for that. His narrow jaw gave his face a lean, almost hungry cast, and the nearly colorless blond of his hair lent him an otherworldly air that drew women more surely than *lovely* ever could. Even as a lanky teenager, he'd had a way of glancing at you out of the corner of his eye, his smile halfway between indulgent and contemptuous, that lured in young ladies like kittens to catnip—and made Elinor feel rooted in place, with all the wit of a damp potato.

She drew herself up as he approached, interposing herself between Lord Farleigh and Phoebe. But he never glanced at his sister. He halted directly in front of her and fixed her with his other *look*, one she had a far more intimate acquaintance with—the ever-so-slightly upturned chin, the downward angle of his gaze (and few men could manage to look *down* at Elinor Hargrove). A familiar quiver started up in the vicinity of her stomach, and she suddenly felt very much like the thirteen-year-old girl who had gotten mud on his favorite jacket.

"What," he said, slowly and deliberately, "have you dragged my sister into?"

Chapter 2

Colin folded his hands behind his back and waited for Elinor to speak. She stared at him, silent, lips slightly parted. Five years of training had taught him to ignore the coral shade of her lips, the faint sprinkling of freckles across her nose that he knew she hated, and the stray curl of rich auburn hair that hung beside her slender neck. If he lingered on any of these things for long, his gaze inevitably found its way to the graceful bend of her shoulders, the swell of her bosom, the feminine flare of her hips. And then he might overcorrect, and sweep his eyes back up to hers, and find himself caught there.

They were nothing remarkable, really. Dark brown eyes, one with a golden fleck just below the pupil. The dark sweep of her lashes framed them in such a way that made them appear impossibly deep, but it was not their beauty that concerned him. It was that every time he met her eyes, he had the uncomfortable feeling that she saw him, saw him stripped of title and fashion and arrogance and pretense— and found him deeply wanting.

So he looked at none of these things. He focused instead on what he considered her least becoming feature: her left earlobe. It had a mole just along its edge that rather ruined her symmetry.

She still had not spoken.

"Well?" he prompted.

"I beg your pardon, Lord Farleigh," she said. "I had thought to give you the opportunity to rephrase your question in a more civil manner."

He blinked. Had it been that bad? Certainly not how he would speak to a stranger, but this was Elinor. She was used to him. "I see," he said. "Perhaps you can understand my distress in learning that my youngest sibling had undertaken to visit a part of the city that normally requires armed escort."

"You exaggerate," Elinor said. "We have yet to be accosted by anything more dangerous than a six-year-old in need of a bath. And as for our purpose, we were seeking diversion."

"It was my idea," Phoebe said. She tilted her chin up, trying, he imagined, to look imperious. The effect was somewhat spoiled by her need to squint. He really would have to convince her to start wearing her spectacles in public; she was going to squint her way in front of a carriage someday.

"I am well aware that it was your idea," Colin said. It always was. "But you ought to have had more sense than to allow it," he continued, returning his scrutiny to Elinor.

"As if she could stop me," Phoebe said with a toss of her head. "We were having a bit of fun."

"Honestly, Lady Elinor," he continued. "You are the sensible sort. You are not *fun*."

Her eyebrow arched. "Is that so?"

Upon review, he entirely regretted his choice of words. Another man might have stammered a retraction, but Colin could never stand moving backward in a conversation. He was done with being a leaf buffeted by the wind of this woman's every action, after all. Done watching her movements and straining to catch every word that she spoke.

"I've always thought of you as entirely reliable," he said. Forward momentum, that was the thing. "And I regret being disappointed in this instance. Now, what *were* you doing here?" He looked up at the sign hanging above the door. "Is this some sort of palm reader?"

"It is unimportant," Elinor said. "As we were on our way home." Her voice was cold.

He looked between the two of them. Phoebe studiously avoided his gaze, choosing instead to inspect the ground. Elinor's expression shifted swiftly from icy displeasure into a bland combination of annoyance and resignation, a clear symptom of overlong acquaintance and his complete failure to charm her. It was this benign expression she wore whenever they were part of the same group. She spoke warmly enough of him to others. But he wished she would go back to anger. At least that communicated something other than indifference.

"Hmm," he said. "It would seem I have encountered a conspiracy of silence. If I were to ask"—he glanced at the sign—"Madame Vesta what you discussed, would I learn something interesting?"

"I wished to contact Marie," Phoebe said softly.

It was like a physical blow. His mouth went dry. Phoebe had not spoken Marie's name in years. Nor had he, to anyone but his closest friends. Marie's death was a toxin in their family's blood. A foul air that he breathed every day, but could do nothing to banish. They did not speak of it. He had tried very hard not to think of her at all.

"Can you blame me?" Phoebe asked. She lifted her eyes to his; it seemed to take a great effort. "When we act as if she never existed? I had to search for answers somewhere."

"There are no answers," Colin said. "She's gone."

"For some more than others," Phoebe said. He accepted the accusation with only a slight nod. He knew the depth of his own grief. He didn't need to prove it.

"I trust that you will return to the house promptly," he said. "I have an errand to run, but afterward I expect to see you there. And I beg you, no more diversions like this one. We do have a family name to uphold."

Phoebe rolled her eyes, back to impetuous in a blink. She wafted by without another word, angling for the carriage, and Colin was left with only Elinor before him.

"There is something troubling you, lately," Elinor said, startling him.

"Nothing more than the usual," he said. *Apart from you.*

Her head tilted slightly to the side, and he was treated to the slow, layer-by-layer dissection that he had watched her engage in countless times before. He swallowed, and did his best to close his expression. He did not need her scrutiny. He certainly did not need her reporting any findings of distress to her brother. Martin would have no choice but to ask him about it, and what could he say? *Oh, I've only been in love with your sister for half a decade. Nothing to fret about.*

He shuddered at the thought.

Apparently his engagement had not made him immune to her. Damn it. The announcement, that was it. The trouble was that he was the only one who *knew* he was engaged. Once it was public, surely his mind would be able to focus on something other than the way her eyes met his or the way her lips pursed ever so slightly as she considered him.

"You shouldn't be so hard on Phoebe," she said at last. "She's at a difficult age."

"She has been at a difficult age since she learned to grab at whatever was dangled in front of her," he said. "She has never been anything *but* difficult."

"I wonder where she learned that from," Elinor said distantly, and he almost thought he detected a smile at the corner of her mouth. Which he was not supposed to be looking at, damn it. And no, he saw, it wasn't a smile. It was definitely a frown, albeit a well-concealed one. "I'll see you at the house, then," she said.

"Yes. Right. The house," he agreed. She turned from him, and he allowed himself to relax, just a fraction.

If the announcement didn't cure him of this, he was going to have to flee the bloody country.

It was clear to Elinor that Lord Farleigh had no intention of telling her what was troubling him. She was not certain what had possessed her to ask. Farleigh might be honest to the point of bluntness when it came to his opinions of others, but he used that bluntness to hide his own feelings adroitly. She abandoned the effort with relief and made her way swiftly to the carriage. The truth was, she did not wish to know what occupied Lord Farleigh's thoughts. He disoriented her. He made her feel dull, and she was accustomed to being the most clever person in the room. Her lack of humility in that regard was, she knew, a failing. But with so little else to cling to that was her own, her wit was a treasure she did not enjoy being tarnished.

She did her best to maintain a dignified gait back to the carriage, where Phoebe was waiting. She felt his eyes on her all the way. Her cheeks were hot by the time the driver handed her up into the carriage, and when she caught Lord Farleigh still standing, watching her, she looked away quickly.

Honestly. If he were not her brother's dearest and oldest friend, if she did not have such habitual affection for him herself, she would find him entirely unlikeable. She could not believe there were so many women who *enjoyed* this feeling of being knocked off-center. Or perhaps he had a different effect on the girls who flocked to him. She'd asked Marie about it once, actually, but his sister had been as mystified as she was.

Whatever you do, marry a man who's nice *to you*, Marie had told her once, when they had been speculating on the matter. Shortly thereafter, she followed her own advice. She might not have loved Lord Hayes, but he had offered kindness and affection enough to entice her to India, and away from her family. Permanently, as it turned out.

"Are you quite all right?" Phoebe asked. Elinor shot her a glare. The girl sat back in her seat. "It's only, you're a bit red," she said, voice trailing off.

Elinor drew a deep breath through her nose and set her shoulders. "Your brother is occasionally impossible," she said.

"Isn't he just?" Phoebe said. "But you should have seen him when I put a toad under his sheets. It makes it harder to take his whole *oh, look, I'm so tall and intimidating and marquess-ish* act quite so seriously."

"You were such a handful as a child," Elinor said.

"As a child?" Phoebe said. "That was two months ago."

"Phoebe."

"He squawked like a chicken getting its tail feathers tugged," Phoebe said solemnly, her eyes sparkling.

Elinor shook her head. She had a hard time imagining that. She didn't care to, either; she wanted to put Lord Farleigh as thoroughly out of her head as she could manage. And there was another Spenser she was far more interested in at the moment.

The carriage had started forward. When she was certain that the noise of their passage was enough to conceal their conversation from the driver's ears, she leaned forward. "You are keeping something from me," she said.

Phoebe immediately looked guilty. It was a wonder she ever got away with anything.

"Edward Foyle," Elinor said. "Who is he? And what does he have to do with Marie?"

Phoebe rolled her lips between her teeth.

"Come on, now. You trusted me enough to bring me along. You can trust me enough to tell me outright," Elinor said, trying to conceal the sting she felt. However graciously she'd been welcomed into their home, however close she and Marie had been, she was not quite family. That had been made all the clearer when Marie died, and Elinor was shut out of their grieving entirely. It was a private thing, that grief, and she did not rate high enough to share in it. Martin, her brother, hadn't known Marie well at all—hadn't known how much she'd meant to Elinor, when he was away. And so she hadn't tried to explain.

Phoebe let out a soft sigh. "The fact is, Marie remarried after Lord Hayes's death."

Elinor stared. "What?" No. Marie would have written to her. She'd written every week before Lord Hayes died, though the letters took months to arrive. After his death she'd only written once—but the letter had made no mention of a suitor, much less a husband.

"We only found out when we learned of her death," Phoebe said.

"Why wouldn't you tell me?" Elinor asked, numbness creeping through her limbs.

"It was a family matter," Phoebe said. "We told no one. They were only married for a few months, you see."

"They who? This Edward Foyle?" Elinor asked.

"Yes," Phoebe confirmed.

"She never said anything about him," Elinor said. The name had no meaning to her.

"He's Lady Copeland's cousin," Phoebe explained. "And Lord Copeland was Lord Hayes's partner in the mines."

Elinor frowned. The diamond mines had been Marie's idea, and they had proved extremely successful—but after Marie's death, Elinor had heard nothing more of them. She hadn't realized that Lord Copeland was involved.

"Lord Hayes owned the bulk of the shares in the mines," Phoebe said, nodding. "When he died, Marie got the shares. She was thrilled."

"I remember," Elinor said. Lord Copeland and his diamonds . . . She blinked. "Wait. Were these *the* diamonds?" London had been abuzz two years ago with the news that Lady Copeland's famous diamonds had been stolen.

"Three invaluable diamonds were mined and cut. Lord Hayes presented them to Marie on her birthday," Phoebe said. "The next time we heard of or saw them, they were hanging around Lady Copeland's neck. Apparently after Foyle married Marie, he sold the mines and the diamonds to Lord Copeland. For a pittance."

"Then Lady Copeland's diamonds belonged to Marie?" Elinor said, eyebrows raised. "I suppose I don't feel so bad that they were stolen, then."

"Do thank your sister-in-law for us," Phoebe said with a glint in her eye.

"Joan will be thrilled to hear it," Elinor said. Phoebe was one of a very select club of those who knew that Diana Hargrove, Elinor's sister-in-law and supposed American heiress, was in fact Joan Price, London thief and fugitive. Lady Copeland's diamonds had financed that transformation. "I remember how excited Marie was with the mine," Elinor said. "She wrote of little else. She wouldn't have given up on it so easily, for so small a price."

"I don't believe it was her choice," Phoebe said.

"When did Marie marry Mr. Foyle?"

"Four months after Lord Hayes died. And he sold the mines a week after that."

"I see," Elinor said, though she didn't yet. She gazed out the window, trying to put the information in some semblance of order. Outside, row after row of drab gray buildings slid past. A line of girls in drab gray capes marched up the steps of Mrs. Fincher's School for Girls, and a chimney sweep slouched his way down an alley. It was always so strange, how the world refused to acknowledge when it had been turned on its head. "So Foyle somehow coerced or tricked Marie into marrying him, so that he could gain control of the mines. And then he took away the one thing she had left in that distant place."

"He kept her from us. He kept her alone. And that's how she died. Alone and afraid, and far from home. And I want him punished."

Chapter 3

Elinor had never seen Phoebe's eyes light with such intensity. "You're certain, then, that there were misdeeds in play?" She hoped that Phoebe would say that she wasn't; that Elinor would be allowed to hold onto the possibility that her friend had been happy, had passed from the world unafraid.

"There was a letter," Phoebe said. "Marie sent it before she died. She referred to other letters—letters we never saw. She said that Foyle had taken something from her. She said he knew something that could ruin her, ruin us, and that was why she had to marry him. She said she was afraid."

Elinor's hands curled to fists in her lap. She had never seen Marie afraid of anything. That strength had been like a beacon to Elinor and to Marie's younger sisters. It was a promise that they could prevail against the world, if only they could find the strength that Marie so effortlessly possessed.

"Colin and Mother pressed for answers. They contacted everyone they could in India, but no one would tell them anything. Those who would speak with them claimed she'd been delirious."

"You don't believe that."

"Marie wasn't mad!" Phoebe declared. "You knew her. She was the sanest woman in the world."

When Marie had died, the only thing that brought Elinor through it was finding Matthew. His death, mere months later, had nearly destroyed her. But she had survived. She had recovered. Now it felt as though the wounds were opening afresh. She pressed the palm of her hand to her stomach and shut her eyes. She could feel the familiar prickle of needles against her brow, a sure sign of an oncoming headache. She needed silence and solitude. She needed to not hear this hideousness.

"There was nothing anyone could do," Phoebe said. "Edward Foyle had already vanished. No one has heard from him since. He might as well have been dead, for all we knew."

"I hope he is," Elinor said fiercely.

"But he isn't," Phoebe said. She bit her lip. "That's why I wanted to speak with Marie. Mr. Foyle isn't dead. He's back in England. He has been for two weeks."

"And you've kept this information to yourself?" Elinor asked.

"I only found out because I was talking to Lady Copeland's daughter, and I couldn't very well admit that. Colin would have my head for it. Which is entirely unfair, as she is nothing like her parents and quite sensibly eloped with a botanist two years ago, which I have tried to explain to him."

"You might have told me," Elinor said.

"I was going to. After I'd spoken with Madame Vesta about it," Phoebe said, and Elinor stifled a groan. "I planned to ask her what Marie wanted us to do."

"Marie would want us to take thumbscrews to him," Elinor said. Her headache was advancing. It had become pressure, like a cap fitted snugly over her skull. Not pain, not yet, but that would come.

Phoebe peered at her. "Thumbscrews, Elinor? That seems a bit . . . barbaric."

"Marie was not one for forgiveness," Elinor said, and Phoebe nodded, forced to agree. Marie held a grudge. It was generally agreed upon as her only fault, and the creativity of her vengeance provided enough entertainment to make up for the flaw.

"Unfortunately, we don't have any thumbscrews," Phoebe said. "Though from what I've heard, Monsieur Beauchene might."

Elinor looked at her askance. "Beauchene? Of the parties?"

"The ones we, as proper ladies, have never, ever heard of?" Phoebe said. "The very same."

"Good Lord. That's where Foyle is staying?"

"Apparently so. And no surprise. You just know he has to be some kind of degenerate."

"We should tell your brother," Elinor said.

"No!" Phoebe exclaimed. Elinor was taken aback. "He'll kill Foyle. Think about it. You know he would. And then he'd hang."

"Don't be dramatic. The last time a peer was hung for murder was before either of us was born." But Phoebe was right about one thing. Lord Farleigh was not one to stand idly by when there was a threat against his family. He could not know about this. He would surely take matters into his own hands. Which meant a duel. And even a marquess would have difficulty allaying the scandal of a fatal duel—or avoiding prosecution. "There must be something we can do," Elinor said. "The authorities—"

"It's been six years," Phoebe said. "What could they do now? And Marie said that what he had could destroy her," Phoebe said. "He had *evidence* of something. If we went after him, he would surely make it public."

"But what is it that he has?" Elinor said. "What could Marie possibly have done to warrant that kind of fear?"

"I don't know," Phoebe said. "But whatever it was, it was enough to force her to marry him."

"Then there's nothing we can do," Elinor said softly.

The carriage pulled to a halt. "We're here," Phoebe said.

They regarded each other in silence for a moment. "We can't speak of this again," Elinor said. Her skull felt as if it were splitting in two, but the pain was almost welcome. She could lose herself in it, and not have to think of this horror. "We must try to forget."

"How?" Phoebe asked.

Elinor shook her head. "I don't know. I only know that we must."

Colin had an appointment to keep, and his ill-considered excursion threatened his punctuality—and he was never late. Though given the habits of the *ton*, that was more a vice than a virtue. He stalked to his room and changed, with the assistance of his valet—a process which took a positively ungodly amount of time. He enjoyed the effect of proper fashion, but the accomplishment of it would drive him mad.

"They visited a *medium*," he said, and his valet grunted. "I thought even Phoebe had better sense than that."

The valet, for his part, had better sense than to respond. He brushed Colin's shoulders and stepped back, wordlessly declaring him ready for the public eye. Colin adjusted his cravat with a frown. He could not imagine what had prompted his sister to try to contact Marie's spirit now, after all these years. They never spoke of her. Phoebe accused him of forgetting her, but the truth was that the silence on the subject was by agreement—unspoken for the most part, except for a single, fevered conversation months after Marie's death.

No one must know, his mother had said. *No one must know of this.*

He glanced toward his wardrobe. It had been over a year since he'd removed the long, flat box from the back of the wardrobe; years since he had examined its contents piece by piece, as if he could find an answer within that he had missed on every previous occasion. He tore his eyes away. There were no answers to be found in that box, or in tarot cards, or the mutterings of a fraud. If there were any hope of discovering the truth of Marie's death, it lay with Edward Foyle. And he had vanished as thoroughly as if he were a ghost himself.

"Will you be needing the carriage again, my lord?" the valet asked. Richards was his name; Colin didn't know him well. His old valet had been a friend, a confidante. Then he'd abandoned Colin to marry a lovely girl and run a lovely country inn, damn the man. Nowadays Colin found himself in need of a sympathetic ear. Luckily, brandy was very sympathetic indeed.

"Yes," Colin confirmed. "Have it brought 'round, will you? And I won't be needing supper."

"I will inform the cook, my lord, and have her leave something out for you."

Eight months and the man was already familiar with Colin's late-night meals. He at least tried to time them so that he was stumbling into the kitchen a bit too early to frighten the scullery maid. The last time that had happened, the poor girl had actually fainted. He'd had to stand four feet away, frantically fanning her with a dishcloth, in an attempt to revive her without further alarming her as to his intentions.

"Very good, very good," Colin remembered to say, and then Richards was gone. Alone, Colin found his gaze tracking to the wardrobe once again. The great majority of what lay in the box would come as no surprise to his family. Letters from solicitors and from those who had known Marie in India, recounting the tale of her illness and death. But there was one thing that he had taken pains would never appear before his sisters' or his mother's eyes. It was beneath all the other letters, sealed in an envelope and hidden beneath the cloth that lined the wooden box.

And there it would remain.

Colin tugged at his collar and tore his eyes from the wardrobe. He strode out into the hall with his jaw set and his shoulders stiff. Whatever had provoked Phoebe's sudden interest in the afterlife was no concern of his. He had a future to worry about—his own. It involved Penelope Layton and a happily married life, not ghosts from his past.

Which would be a great deal easier to convince himself of if one of those ghosts was not standing in the hall before him.

Elinor stood with one hand against the wall, only her fingertips braced against the wallpaper. Her head was bowed, her eyes closed.

"Lady Elinor," he said stiffly, meaning to pass by with only a curt nod. But at his voice an odd shiver went through her, and she jerked around quickly—and just as quickly winced, making an abortive gesture as if to touch her fingers to her temples. "Are you all right?" he asked in alarm.

"Everyone always asks me that," she said. "I'm only tired."

"Ah," he said. "Of course."

A frown pulled at the corner of her mouth. "Of course," she repeated, voice prickly as a burr.

He suppressed a scowl. He ought to have remembered that she was sensitive about her spells. There were a select few people allowed to comment on them; he was not on the list. He opened his mouth to offer a defense, or perhaps a rejoinder, but something in her expression stopped him. She was more than tired. Her eyes were bright with tears, her features pinched with pain. He started to ask her if she really was all right—and stopped himself just short of it.

He realized they had been standing there for several seconds without speaking.

"Is there something I can help you with, Lord Farleigh?" she asked.

That was too dangerous a question to answer truthfully. "I . . ." He trailed off. "I had forgotten to ask you," he said, trying his best to sound breezy and unconcerned. "Mother's fixed on a new man for Phoebe. Randall's second son, what's-his-name."

Elinor's brow furrowed. "John?" she supplied.

He nodded vigorously. "That's the one." It was true—his mother *was* rather fixed on the young man. And it was a far safer subject than any of the alternatives that had presented themselves. Colin himself had only spoken to the young man once. He was a bit young for marriage—though Phoebe would do better with a man her own age anyway. He was a retiring fellow, and when Colin had spoken to him he'd had to coax out conversation, like talking a recalcitrant horse out of its stall. He was a terrible match for Phoebe.

"He is not unkind," she said. "But I think Phoebe would run circles around him, and go mad with boredom."

"That's about what I said," Colin agreed. "He's not the sort of shy that needs a boisterous wife to liven him up. He ought to find a bluestocking, content to stay home and read with him. Like Miss Eugenie Marlowe, come to think of it."

Elinor tilted her head, considering him. "Perhaps you should lend out your services as a matchmaker," she suggested.

He laughed. "Can you imagine that? It does have a certain ring to it—'The Matchmaker Marquess.' It sounds like the dreadful novels Phoebe is always reading." He offered her a smile, a soft one, hoping she might return it.

Instead she frowned slightly. "Is this meant to be an apology?" she asked.

"What?"

"Asking my opinion. Is this your version of an apology?"

"I don't apologize," Colin said, truthfully. "There's no point in retreading what's been said. Better to make a new effort entirely."

"It's hard to make a new effort without knowing that the old one won't repeat itself," Elinor said. He tugged at his cuffs distractedly. Elinor tsked. "Does your valet know you're undoing his hard work?" she asked.

He halted in his adjustments. "They were crooked."

"*Now* they are," she said. She flicked her gaze up and down. "You know, you are the worst sort of perfectionist."

"Which sort is that?" he asked, irritation sparking along with a traitorous note of curiosity.

"The sort that thinks he isn't one," she said.

"Oh, no. I am well aware that I am a perfectionist, if a selective one," Colin answered, earning himself an arched eyebrow. She was so very good at that. "Is this *your* version of an apology?"

"What on earth would I be apologizing for?" she asked.

"Your terrible influence on my poor innocent sister, of course," he said, and grinned. That, at last, got a smile out of her, even if it was tinged with familiar annoyance.

"I'm afraid that if you refuse to apologize, I must do the same," she said.

"As long as we're agreed."

"You have an odd definition of agreement." She took another look at him, seeming to note his change of clothing. "You're going out?" she asked.

"I am. I likely won't be back until quite late," he said. Idling here meant that he was at serious risk of arriving after the appointed hour, but he found himself unconcerned. "I will be whiling away the hours in the company of that most degenerate of species, the gentleman." He sounded almost as though he were trying to justify himself to her, which was ridiculous. It was practically required for a well-bred gentleman to have bouts of degeneracy.

That arched eyebrow had returned, though. "Ah. I expect there will be a great deal of drinking and card-playing, then."

"But of course," he said. "It is a universal law that where three or more gentlemen gather, cards appear."

Elinor looked disappointed. Anger he could handle, but he did so hate to disappoint her. "Try to come home with your fortune intact?" she suggested, with a not-that-I-care tone that made his gut clench more than heated words ever could.

"Fortune, yes. Dignity, perhaps not."

She chuckled, and then came the wince again, her hand flitting up to touch her brow.

"Are you sure you are all right?" he asked.

"I have one of my headaches, if you must know," she said.

"Do you need anything?" he asked, alarmed. At their worst, her headaches could cripple her for days.

"It is not one of the terrible ones. I need only a few hours of darkness," she said. "Silence. Cool cloths."

"I'll send a maid."

"It's been handled," she told him. They stood in awkward

silence for several seconds. "I should rest. And you should be going," she reminded him.

"Of course. I hope you recover swiftly, Lady Elinor." He executed a neat bow, and she made a passing reference to a curtsy. Then, to his relief, she moved past him and down the hall. He looked back to watch her as she made her way to her room.

"Lady Elinor?" he called to her suddenly.

She paused, turned. "Yes, Lord Farleigh?"

"If you need anything, anything at all—you need only ask."

"Of course, Lord Farleigh," she said. "I know."

You don't, he wanted to tell her, but she had already gone, rounding the corner and disappearing from his sight.

Anything at all, he said, forming the words on his lips without speaking them, and turned to go.

Chapter 4

❧

The crowd at Luke Gibson's table was growing distressingly thin. They had staked out their corner of the club as usual, men too rich for their own good dedicating themselves to an evening of redistributing their wealth amongst one another, but tonight there were only four men in evidence, including Colin. Martin had been a rare commodity since his marriage. Lord Grey, Colin's waste of a brother-in-law, was playing the degenerate on the continent, far from his wife and child. Nor did Colin see any sign of Lord Kushner, nor the wheat-haired man he never did catch the name of and had been calling "dear chap" for three years out of sheer embarrassment.

"No Kushner?" Colin asked as he settled into his seat beside Captain Harken, a powerfully built man with the distinctive swagger of a sailor.

"Another victim of Cupid's bow, I'm afraid," Gibson said. He was a small, precise man, neither the wealthiest man at the table nor the best titled, being the son of a baron, but he had taken charge of their regular game all the way back at Eton, and held onto the dubious honor through a combination of morose looks and bared teeth. "Off courting."

"He'll be married inside a month," Harken forecast, a

touch of gloom in his voice. Harken wore gloom and serious-ness like a favorite cravat these days. The man didn't know what to do with himself without a war on. "And we're down to three."

"Four," Weathersby piped up. They all glanced momen-tarily at him as if they had failed to notice him on their arrival, which Colin nearly had. He was a plump young man, soft-spoken, whom Colin didn't know terribly well. He'd simply appeared at the table some time last year. Colin had a vague recollection that he was some friend of Gibson's. Or maybe it was his father who knew Kushner from parliament. He'd probably be told at some point. In any case, it was pos-sible that he was the nicest man Colin had ever met, and certainly one of the smartest, and he won or lost depending on how deeply one managed to engage him on one of his favorite subjects. Distraction was the only defense against his cheerfully methodical strategies.

"How are those bees doing?" Colin asked, with an eye toward winning back some of what he'd lost the week before.

"Splendidly," Weathersby said, a smile splitting his face and making his cheeks go round as apples. No grown man should be that adorable, Colin thought; it left him feeling old and rough-edged.

"And you, Farleigh?" Gibson asked. "When will you be leaving us, hm?"

"Does everyone in London know my business? The engagement hasn't even been announced," Colin said. He waved at a waiter, who was either ignoring him or blinded by the ever-present smoke. Colin gestured to Harken, who produced a pair of cigars so that they could make their contribution to the haze.

"Damn," Gibson said. "I owe you a pound, Harken. You were right."

"I can't believe I fell for that," Colin said, scowling. Gib-son had just been guessing.

Gibson grinned around his cigar and rapped his knuckles on the table. "Come on, then. Are we here to listen to Far-leigh moon about his bride-to-be, or lose some money?"

"Who is she?" Weathersby asked. "She must be quite a woman, if she's convinced you to succumb to matrimony."

Colin peered at Weathersby, wondering if he detected the hint of an insult in his words. But Weathersby had probably never insulted anyone in his life.

"It's merely time," Colin said. "I must produce an heir, after all." He scowled at Gibson, who was being overly leisurely in his movements as he extracted a deck of cards from his pocket.

"Oh, that's right, boys," Harken said drily. "I'd nearly forgot Farleigh here was a marquess."

"Oh, come on now. You didn't even know me back then," Colin said, reddening. He'd been a bit too proud of his title, back in school. To the point of referring to it roughly every third time he opened his mouth. He needed a drink if they were going to traipse down the lane of those particular memories. Where the hell was . . . ?

Ah, there. Slow in arrival, but exactly what he needed. Brandy, spicy and sharp, downed quickly and just as quickly replaced. Evenings like this were best launched with determination, not tentative sipping.

"The girl, Farleigh," Gibson said. "Her name?"

"I couldn't possibly tell you," Colin rumbled.

"Doesn't know," Harken said wisely, and Colin took a more moderate swallow.

"I think it's splendid," Weathersby said. "I myself am going to be engaged quite soon. As soon as I make a few arrangements. Yes, things in place, all of that. Any day, though. Any day." He nodded to himself.

"Don't wait too long," Colin advised. "Women have a bad habit of marrying other men, you know."

"Aye," Harken said into his drink. "That they do."

"And what about you, Harken?" Colin said. "Anyone catch your eye?"

"Harken dedicates himself to impossible love," Gibson said. "When I met him, it was the girl outside the village with hair the color of gold, and then it was his captain's daughter, and then—"

"Have we really come to the one place in London guaranteed to repel all manner of womenfolk to discuss love?" Harken asked.

"Not love," Colin said. "Not in my case. Merely a business arrangement." Had he already finished his second drink? No matter; now that his presence had been properly noted, the staff were quick to replace it. He'd savor this one more slowly. Wouldn't do to finish three drinks in his first quarter hour; he meant to improve his fortunes tonight.

"How dull," Gibson said. "I always figured you for the one of us to have some grand love story."

"Hargrove's taken care of that," Harken said.

"Yes, you really must tell me about this mysterious Mrs. Hargrove someday," Gibson said, with a good-natured annoyance that indicated he was quite resigned to his ignorance. "No one even knows how they met."

"It's not that interesting," Colin said quickly. "The mysterious Mrs. Hargrove" was in fact a wanted fugitive named Joan Price, a secret known by very few—Colin and Harken among them. "I'm with Harken. Let's choose a new subject."

"Like how Edward Foyle's back in England?" Gibson said.

Colin froze. He stared at Gibson, his lips parted to just bare his teeth. "What did you say?"

"Edward Foyle. He's back. Or so I heard," Gibson said.

"Who?" Weathersby said.

"Damn." Harken leaned back in his chair and regarded Colin with narrowed eyes. "You want me to help you find him?"

"Who?" Weathersby said again.

Colin deftly swapped drink for cigar and back again, letting the flavor of the smoke and brandy roil over his tongue in a dark dance. Foyle was back. And Phoebe had been asking about Marie. It could be a coincidence—but that strained the imagination.

"Where is he?" he asked.

Gibson grinned. "What is it they always said about the man? Find a pint and a pair of tits, and Foyle won't be far. Beauchene's taken him in, so he'll have plenty of both."

"You're joking," Colin said.

"Who's Beauchene?" Weathersby asked. They cast him brief looks of mingled admiration and pity.

"He is truly the most pure among us," Gibson intoned, then clapped the man on the shoulder to show he didn't mean anything by it. "Beauchene's a Frenchman. Obviously. He throws these parties every summer, to mark the end of the Season. Like a Hellfire club, but less religion. Gentlemen, ladies of ill-repute, and a solid week without consequences."

"Not that Gibson would know," Colin said darkly.

Gibson laughed. "I prefer my debauchery in private. Can't say I've never been invited, but it's all a bit theatrical for me."

"So then. Should we pay Foyle a visit?" Harken asked, casual as could be. "A social call."

"We could welcome him back to England with a friendly thrashing," Gibson suggested.

"I'm confused," Weathersby said. "Who is this man?"

"Foyle seduced Farleigh's sister, right," Gibson said, emphasizing his words with precise jabs of his fingers. He'd finally got round to dealing, Colin noted, and retrieved his cards from the table. He could barely focus on the present long enough to read them. Nothing but rubbish. "And got control of her late husband's shares of the diamond mines. Then he signs them over to Copeland."

How the hell did Gibson know so much about the business? Oh, right, he'd told him. Colin glared at his cards before collapsing them into a stack and tossing it back on the table. He really shouldn't drink so much at cards. Not that Gibson wasn't trustworthy, of course, but each drink made it a little harder to keep track of whose ears might be nearby. He'd only told them what his sisters already knew, though. No one knew about the contents of the box.

"Another drink sir?"

The damned waiter. Colin jerked his head in an affirmative.

". . . Should get Foyle to confess," Weathersby was saying. "If he mistreated your sister like you say, it should be known."

"He won't be punished," Colin said. "There's no proof he did anything illegal."

"But people would *know*," Weathersby pressed. "Wouldn't that be worth something? To honor your sister's memory?"

Colin glared at him. "My sister's dead," he said. "And memory has less substance than the hallucinations of an opium fiend. If I find Edward Foyle, I'm not going to make him confess. I'm going to make him pay."

"I'll drink to that," Harken said. Weathersby sat back in his chair, clearly uncomfortable. Gibson just shrugged.

"Bets, gentlemen," he said, and the subject was closed. They moved on to other topics, but Colin didn't respond except for the occasional grunt or bet. Tomorrow, he was going to find a way to reach Edward Foyle.

And when he found him, he was going to kill him.

Elinor had never once suffered from insomnia, a pleasant contrast to the men in her family. She was, however, a light sleeper, and used to waking at the tread of her brother's feet in the halls, or the desultory thump of a book cast aside for failing to lull him to sleep. When she woke that night, she thought at first that she was at Birch Hall, and Martin was having another of his restless nights. But, no. She was not at Birch Hall; for that matter, neither was Martin.

She lay still a moment, listening. The thump came again. Her room was at the back of the town house, and she had learned on her first day that when the vent at the floor was left open, she could hear the servants coming and going at the back. But what servant would be up at this hour?

She rose, taking a moment to light a candle and throw a shawl around her shoulders. She supposed she ought to wake a servant, but she had grown increasingly tired of relying on others for her every need and whim. She had spent enough of her life as an invalid; she did not enjoy the fact that wealth demanded a continuation of the same habits.

She made her way lightly to the stairs and crept halfway

down, lifting the candle high to peer into the dark hallway at the bottom.

"Colin?"

The familiar name slipped out unbidden in her surprise. The man in question slumped against the wall, one foot awkwardly uplifted and his body hunched over in an attempt to extract his foot from his boot. He straightened up with a snap and a new thump when he saw her.

"Lady Elinor," he declared in a whisper as loud as a normal voice. "I was trying not to wake anyone."

"I apologize for frustrating your attempts," she said.

"What're you doing here?" he asked, squinting. He was distressingly drunk, she realized. She should fetch a footman to help him to his bed—but the servants were quartered in the basement, and she did not feel she should leave Lord Farleigh alone in this state.

"I heard a noise," Elinor said in answer to his question. "I came to investigate."

"I might've been a burglar. Or a murderer."

"What good fortune that you are neither," Elinor said. "Good night, Lord Farleigh."

"Hrm," he said, apparently an attempt at agreement. He straightened up with limited success, bracing himself against the wall. His clothes were disheveled, and though he kept his wheat-colored hair unfashionably short, it stuck up at odd angles around the crown of his head. Something dark was smeared below his left ear. There was something delightful about seeing the precisely manicured Marquess of Farleigh in such a rumpled state, but her brief delight was replaced with the worrying realization that he was not going to get to his room on his own.

She'd have to fetch a footman after all.

She swept down the stairs, and he startled, nearly pitching over. "Where are you going?" he demanded.

She stepped toward him. The way downstairs to the servants' quarters was past him, and his loose-limbed pose managed to take up an impressive proportion of the hallway. "I am going to fetch someone who can see you to bed."

"I know where my own bed is," he said.

"Even if that is so, and I remain unconvinced, you are in no state to reach it unassisted. If you would move to the side, I can—"

"It's Gibson's fault," Lord Farleigh said. "I didn't even want to drink."

"You are known the world over for your blunt and honest tongue. Your dedication to truthfulness is an admirable quality."

"In that case, I meant to get drunk," Lord Farleigh said. She nodded, not sure whether she was amused, horrified, or annoyed. A little bit of all three. She couldn't remember the last time she'd been in Colin's presence without her brother around to temper his more impulsive side. And the last time they'd been this alone together without any escort, she'd been seven years old. "Didn't mean to get *this* drunk, though. Never do."

"I think that's enough honesty for one evening," she said. "If you would excuse me . . ."

She made to move past him. He grabbed her wrist and, in a startlingly balletic movement, spun her—and then stumbled, lurching toward the wall and bringing her with him. Her shoulder blades brushed the wall without striking it, and then he leaned into her alarmingly, pressing her against the wall. She caught her balance with a startled yelp. "Oops," he said.

"I imagine that was meant to be a great deal more graceful than it proved," Elinor said drily, maintaining her detached tone with difficulty.

"Considerably." His face hovered in front of hers, mere inches away. The scent of brandy on his breath washed over her, and the scent of cigars coiled around them both. She'd braced one hand against his chest, whether in defense or merely for stability, she couldn't say. The other was still trapped, his hand on her wrist. She had never been this close to Lord Farleigh. She hadn't been this close to anyone in years. And she found to her creeping horror that her body, at least, was not entirely immune to Lord Farleigh's charms, judging by the flush of heat washing over her skin.

"Lord Farleigh. Perhaps you should let me go now," she said. She did not sound terribly convincing.

"I'm not certain that would be wise," he said. "I find you a very stabilizing presence, you see."

"I fear I must insist," she said. At least this time she sounded firm.

"Am I hurting you?" he asked.

"No," she said, truthfully. His grip was gentle on her wrist, and his body did not, in fact, touch hers. Not quite. And she could feel every inch of that *not touching*. This was ridiculous. This was *Lord Farleigh*. She needed to get herself under control. And she needed to get *him* into bed.

Oh Lord. *Send* him to bed. She needed to *send* him to bed.

"Lord Farleigh, as relieved as I am that you are neither a murderer nor a robber, I do require the use of my hand," she prompted him, doing her level best to sound stern while her pulse made a game of skipping as fast as it possibly could.

"I might yet be a murderer," he said, voice suddenly soft. "I think I might kill a man."

She set her teeth against her lip. Could he be speaking of Foyle? Did he know that Foyle was back? "But you haven't yet."

"No. Not yet. But I want to." He laid his free hand against her shoulder, his thumb flush against her collarbone and his index finger brushing against the curve of her neck. She tensed, startled by the pleasure of that soft touch. He seemed at once intent and distracted. "I loved her," he said. "My sister. Marie."

"I know," she said. *And so did I.* "Lord Farleigh, we must get you to bed."

"She loved you," he said. He leaned in close, the stubble of his jaw brushing against her cheek as he whispered in her ear. Goosebumps broke out over her arms. She tilted her head back, pressing against the wall to put a little more distance between them. She swallowed. "She loved you like a sister."

"I know," she said again. Fear and excitement scraped the words thin. It was a well-trained fear, one she'd been taught nearly from the cradle. Don't be alone with a man. It wasn't right. It wasn't safe. Rules she had not broken in entirely too long, as that excitement was keen to remind her. Rules she most definitely should not break here, with her brother's best friend, who was clearly in the grips of grief and liquor in sufficient quantity to rob him of his good sense.

"I promised her I'd look after you," Colin said. His hand wandered up, cupping the side of her neck. She could feel his heartbeat now. Nearly as fast as hers. "When she left. She made me promise. And I've tried. But you don't make it easy, Elinor. You don't like being looked after, do you?"

He met her eyes, peering into them as if to find the answer to his question there.

"Lord Farleigh," she said, with every ounce of will she had. "Please let me go."

He stiffened and drew back. Not much. Enough to let her straighten, standing under her own power with an inch between her and the wall, another several inches between her and the man before her. She brushed a lock of hair behind her ear, cheeks flushed and hot. He stared down at her as if she were an insect that had scuttled out from under his shoe.

"Elinor," he said.

"Lady Elinor," she corrected firmly.

"Dear God. I'm sorry—" A stricken look passed over his face.

Dear Lord. Was it really that terrible to discover her pressed against one's body? You'd think she had the pox, the way he gawped at her. "Colin Spenser, if you are going to take such liberties, the least you could do is kiss me," she said crossly, and flushed more deeply.

"Kiss you?"

"I assume we are in agreement that this"—she gestured generally between them—"is scandalous and wholly inappropriate. Generally, scandalous and wholly inappropriate things are a great deal more entertaining than what I have just experienced." She folded her arms. She'd grown used to people treating her like a clever piece of furniture. Oh, Elinor. She's ever so smart. Oh, Elinor, I didn't realize you were there. Oh, Elinor, I would never *dream* of suggesting that *you* might do something so interesting. She was damn well tired of it.

"I should have kissed you?" he said, and now a sly grin made its way from one side of his slender mouth to the other.

"That isn't what I said," Elinor snapped.

"Isn't it?"

"Not exactly," she allowed.

He took a step toward her. "'The least I could do,'" he echoed.

Her shoulders bumped up against the wall again. "A figure of speech," she said. "Lord Farleigh, you're drunk."

"Very," he agreed, and bent his lips to hers.

She had been kissed a number of times before. Dryly, chastely, passionately, warmly, wetly. The first time with the halting, hesitant touch of a boy; the last time with the ardent passion of her fiancé. It had been years since she was kissed at all, but she had enough experience to say with absolute certainty that this was the worst kiss she had ever received.

Lord Farleigh's lips mashed against hers with great force, slightly off-center. The reek of his breath was, if possible, worse with his mouth against hers. He tilted his head to better capture her mouth, leaving a rapidly cooling patch of wet against her lip. His tongue thrust between her lips and swiped at the back of her teeth—a sensation she had always despised—and remained there a moment, swishing to one side and then the other before retracting.

He broke away, that self-assured expression fixed firmly in place. She rolled her lips inward, clearing them of some of the lingering damp. "Well," she said. "I think I'll let you find your own way back to bed, Lord Farleigh." She seized his arm—braced against the wall to cage her in—between two fingers and lifted it aside delicately. She hurried past him to the stairs, trying not to imagine just how red her fair cheeks had gotten.

She paused at the head of the stairs. He looked after her, with his grin giving way to a slightly confused expression. She shook her head and continued on.

Dear God. She'd actually asked him to kiss her. Or at

least, implied heavily that he should do so. What had she been thinking? He was her brother's best friend. She was— well, all right, she was a spinster who should take her kisses where she could get them, but it was still wildly inappropriate to be interlocking with her brother's best friend in the middle of the night.

She sat on the edge of her bed and frowned at the door.

She had definitely expected Lord Farleigh to be a more skillful kisser.

Chapter 5

After an hour of staring at the ceiling, Elinor surrendered to wakefulness. She lit a candle and sat at her writing desk, trying to put her thoughts into order. Things always made so much more sense once she could see them spelled out, but tonight she was having trouble putting words to the thoughts tumbling about in her mind.

Problem:

she wrote at the top, and then paused. She added an *s*, linking the points of the colon.

Problems:

One: Colin Spenser, Marquess of Farleigh, kissed me.
Solution: Avoid him.

There. That was easy. An excellent start. She pursed her lips. If only her other problems would fall into line so simply.

Two: Marie

She stopped. There were too many facets of that problem to distill into a simple sentence. She'd learned so much today. It had been one thing to grieve her friend's death. You could not get vengeance against a disease. But now she knew that Lord Copeland and Edward Foyle had swindled Marie out of her shares of the mine. Foyle had blackmailed her into marrying him, a notion that filled Elinor with horror. That kind of crime could not go unanswered. And anything damaging enough to blackmail Marie with could still be a threat to Marie's family. Elinor had to do something. She owed Marie that much.

A light rap on the door startled her into a jump. She flipped the page she had been writing on over, concealing the damning words there, and rose. Could it be Colin? No. Even drunk, he wouldn't do something so foolish as come to her door in the middle of the night. Besides, he'd made it perfectly clear that he wasn't truly interested in her.

"Elinor? It's me." Phoebe. Elinor crossed to the door and opened it swiftly. Phoebe stood in the doorway, her eyes deeply shadowed and her hands clasped before her. "You're awake," Phoebe said, unnecessarily.

"Is no one in their beds tonight?" Elinor asked. Phoebe's brow furrowed. "Never mind. Come in."

She shut the door behind Phoebe, who crossed to the bed and sat upon it, tucking one foot up under herself. "I'm sorry to disturb you," she said.

"It's all right," Elinor assured her. "I can't sleep a wink. I keep thinking about what you told me."

"Me, too." Phoebe kneaded the palm of one hand with her thumb. "It's so strange to talk about it out loud. It's been so long, and we don't speak of it at all. Saying it out loud makes it feel different, somehow. It was this story that we never told, and now it's—well, real."

"I can imagine," Elinor said. *And how do you imagine I must feel?* she wanted to ask, but instead she took Phoebe's hands in hers. "I am here for you, Phoebe. You know that."

"Of course I do." Phoebe looked down. Her shoulders shook a little, a shudder half-repressed. "I used to think that

I must have been some kind of changeling. Marie and Kitty were always so elegant, and I was always running into things and getting bruises and catching frogs. And it was all well and good for a while, but now . . . Now Kitty hardly speaks to anyone, Mother's given up on me entirely, and Colin . . ."

"What's wrong with Lord Farleigh?" Elinor asked, feigning a mild interest in the subject. What *was* wrong with Lord Farleigh, indeed.

"He's *angry*. He pretends not to be. I think he feels he failed us. He failed Marie, and he failed Kitty, and Foyle has something that could hurt the rest of us and there's nothing he can do."

"He didn't fail Kitty. She's safe," Elinor said.

"And stuck married to a complete *bastard*," Phoebe said, selecting the word with deliberate venom. "I didn't like him, you know. But I thought it was only because he was taking my sister away, and so I was so very, very nice to him to make up for it, and then he turned out to be—to be—"

"Kitty is a strong woman. She will be happy again," Elinor said firmly. "And whatever guilt is to be parceled out, you deserve none of it." She, however, did. She *had* known something was wrong. She hadn't been able to articulate how uneasy Lord Grey made her, not when he charmed everyone, but she'd known to be wary around him. And she'd kept quiet about it.

She splayed a hand against her stomach, taking a bracing breath. Her mind kept returning to two images. Kitty's expressionless face, when they told her that her husband would be leaving for good. And Marie, waving from her carriage the day she left for India, her smile radiant.

She had died alone and afraid, and that could never be forgiven. Nor would Marie ever forgive Elinor, if she knew of a threat against Marie's family and did nothing.

She was not going to stand by again. If Foyle was in possession of something that could harm Marie's family, she had to do something. She had to protect them, as she'd failed to protect Marie and Kitty.

"You say that you cannot touch Foyle because of the

evidence that he has, or had," Elinor said. "If he does still possess it, then we simply need to get it back. Find it and destroy it, if we must, or bring the whole thing to light. And then we can destroy *him*."

"How?"

Elinor let out a choked laugh. "That is an excellent question. A pity that our education has been limited to comportment and sketching, and not the pursuit of retribution."

Phoebe's mouth quirked. "I suppose that murder is out of the question."

"Of course it is," Elinor said sharply.

"Oh, come now. I was joking. I'm not nearly as bloodthirsty as you make me out to be." Phoebe tilted her head, considering. "We might confront him. Force a confession."

"We have nothing to confront him with. You said yourself that Marie was said to be delirious; her letter will carry no weight."

"Maim him, then? Ruin him?"

"Neither of us is in any position to maim the man," Elinor said, considering. "Nor, I hope, would either of us truly act on such an impulse. No. We must focus on the question of the evidence he possesses. Perhaps in retrieving it we will uncover something that incriminates him, without exposing your family to further harm." This was not her area of expertise, and she felt rather like she was building a boat beneath her as she attempted to sail. "If he is the sort of man you claim, surely his actions have not been pure in the intervening years."

It was a thin hope, but thin hope was all she could see. She regarded Phoebe, who had the corner of her lip held between her teeth.

Finally, Phoebe nodded. "Answers," she said. "And the destruction of whatever damaging evidence he has. That's all. No maiming." She paused. "Unless the opportunity presents itself."

"Then the question remains: how do we get to him? And how do we extract information from him once we do?"

"We could use that fellow," Phoebe said. "The burly one. Your brother's pet detective."

"Mr. Hudson? No, I don't think so," Elinor said. "He's too familiar with your brother, not to mention mine."

"You're right. The boys use him for everything these days. He's bound to tell one of them, or they'll spot him and put it together."

Elinor shook her head in amusement at her use of the term *boys*. Colin now had three decades to his name, and Martin had a child of his own on the way. They could hardly be called boys. Which reminded her more forcefully than she preferred that she, too, was well beyond the years of youth. She would be thirty years old in a few scant weeks. She was going to be a spinster all her life.

"*How banaaal*," Marie would have said, mimicking her mother's favorite insult. And then she would have had some joke to make it all seem insignificant.

"Elinor?" Phoebe said.

"Forgive me. I find myself caught up in memories." Elinor sighed. "There is one resource we are forgetting. Joan."

"Of course," Phoebe said, popping upright to attention. "We are ill-used to subterfuge and intrigue, but she was practically born to it, wasn't she? But in her condition—"

"We can't involve her directly," Elinor said. "As much as she'd be eager for the adventure. But she will have the contacts that we need, and the experience to formulate a plan where we have only the vaguest of notions."

"Will you write to her, then?" Phoebe asked.

"Better none of this is in writing," Elinor said. "It's only a day's journey to the new house. We can go in person."

"Excellent. I haven't seen her since Christmas," Phoebe said with a grin. "She never did finish teaching me to pick locks."

"Don't tell your brother about that," Elinor said. "But if you're desperate, I can show you. I was her first pupil, you know."

Phoebe laughed. "I'd forgotten that. It's so unexpected, you two being friends."

"I can occasionally be interesting," Elinor said with a wry smile.

"Definitely," Phoebe said. She leapt to her feet and seized Elinor's hands. "Thank you so much for doing this, Elinor. I couldn't stand the thought of that awful man being out there and nothing happening to him."

She left then, padding down the hallway on bare feet, a slight skip in her step. Elinor sat staring at the door for a long while after she had gone. For Phoebe, this was already victory. Already an adventure. For Elinor, it was like looking up the slope of a mountain, and preparing to climb.

It was strange, how quickly one's understanding of the world could change. Now she knew that her friend had been suffering, and there was a man who had created that suffering. She might be a spinster—might be fit only to play escort for younger acquaintances and wither away in her brother's drawing room—but she had some use in her left. She could make Edward Foyle answer for whatever he had done to her friend.

And she would.

Chapter 6

～

Colin woke in his bed with the distinct impression that his current location was more a matter of fortune than ability on his part. He was face down, fully clothed but for one boot which had somehow made its way to the windowsill. His mouth was dry, his head pounding, and an ache he couldn't quite locate was making its presence known in his midsection.

"Bloody hell," he said, and worked his way upright. Sunlight filtered through the window, and someone had set a tea tray on the table by the wall. So someone had seen him in this state. Lovely. He scraped a hand over his face and tried to remember what had happened the night before. He'd left to meet the boys, and then—

Foyle. He'd learned that Foyle was back in England.

Then—

The evening got hazy at an alarmingly early point in the narrative. He'd clearly made it home. Had Gibson dropped him off? Yes, that was right. They'd been roaring about duels and sticking a sword in Foyle's midsection, and Colin had stumbled out toward the town house. He'd thought to go around the back rather than wake anyone, and he'd gotten as far as the hall when—

"Bloody hell," he said again. Elinor. He'd met Elinor in the hall. He'd kissed Elinor in the hall. He seemed to recall waiting for her to melt into him, eyes dewy and those luscious curves pressed up against him.

He shook his head tentatively, buying clarity at the cost of a rattle of pain. Christ, Martin was going to kill him if he found out about this. Hang on. She'd asked him to kiss her. And then . . . she hadn't liked it, had she? No, it had been a rather awful kiss.

Martin wouldn't have to kill him. Colin was going to fling himself off a bridge first. What the hell had he been thinking?

He shook his head again as punishment for the thought. "That's it," he declared. "I am never drinking again."

"Very good, my lord."

He jumped to his feet and spun, nearly falling over as his single boot threw him off balance. His valet stood in the doorway. "When did you get here?" Colin asked.

"Only a moment ago, my lord. Shall I help you get dressed, my lord? The ladies are preparing to set out."

"Set out?"

"Yes, my lord."

There was something profoundly comforting about the repetition of those two simple words. Not that he needed reassurance about his title or his power—he wasn't so insecure as all of that—but it made it ever so much easier to track the conversation, and know when a sentence had reached a complete stop. "Set out to where?" he asked.

"I believe they intend to visit Mr. and Mrs. Hargrove," the valet said.

"I didn't hear anything about it."

"It is my understanding that the plans were only recently made, my lord," the valet said. Colin pinched the bridge of his nose. What this sudden visit signified, he had no idea. It did not help that his brain was socked in a fog as deep as any London had ever seen.

"My lord," the valet prompted.

"Ah. Yes, I suppose I should get dressed," Colin said. He

took a few steps with caution, and found his stance steady enough. With the valet's help, he was returned to a state of limited civilization in short order, and tea steadied him further. When his jacket was donned and brushed, he hesitated a moment, staring into the mirror. Dark pouches under his eyes gave testament to his rough night, and made it impossible for him to banish what fleeting memories remained.

He'd kissed Elinor. His best friend's sister. Not the woman to whom he was engaged.

And God help him, he could not stop thinking about doing it again. Correcting the terrible impression he must have left, lapping at her mouth like an overeager dog. In the light of day, he would let his hand trail across her hip. He would crook a finger beneath her chin, and tilt it to just the right angle. So many men were too short for her, but he would have the perfect vantage from which to bend his mouth to hers. To begin with, the brush of lips, so light their breath still mingled between them, before capturing her in a deeper kiss. He would make her melt into him.

Elinor. Damn it, he'd fought so hard to put this foolishness aside. Of all the inconvenient—

"My lord."

"Mm." Colin straightened a cravat that had been perfectly set a moment before, earning a pained look from the valet, and exited the room. He adjusted his cuffs as he traversed the hall, smoothed his hair as he descended the stairs, and tugged the hem of his waistcoat as he approached the musical sound of women's voices. Elinor and Phoebe were in the drawing room, dressed for travel.

"Good morning," he greeted them.

Phoebe snorted. "Barely," she said.

"Don't snort," Colin said chidingly.

"Why is it that when mother isn't here, you try so very hard to replace her?" Phoebe asked peevishly. "And why are you so late a-bed, lazy bones?"

"A late night, that's all," Colin said, and could not help a sideways look at Elinor. She trailed a finger down the side of her neck, the corners of her mouth pinched. She didn't appear angry, at least, or frightened. She also did not look as if she were caught up in the memory, shamefully, thrillingly repeating it in her mind. He tore his eyes from her. "I hear that you are departing my superlative company. May I ask why?"

"Mrs. Hargrove is in need of diversion," Elinor said, forcing him to return his gaze to her.

"And I haven't seen her in *ages*," Phoebe said. "And I'm not likely to once she's laden down with a wiggly little infant. Not that I don't like infants. I hope to have a litter of my own someday, but you must admit the little things are quite time consuming."

"It's only that it seems like a sudden change of plans," he said.

"I got bored," Phoebe said. That he could believe. She was much like he had been at her age, and women's pursuits did not do nearly enough to use up her abundant energy. And after the last incident in Hyde Park, their mother had placed strict limits on her riding excursions. Some things were just not safe to do sidesaddle, even if they were within the bounds of propriety. Which they had not been.

"Do you have some objection to the outing?" Elinor asked. He could not read her tone. Was she amused? Scornful? Outraged? She spoke with the serenity she so often projected, and his palms began to sweat.

"None, of course," he said. "So long as . . ."

"Yes?" she prompted.

"Well," he said. "Mrs. Hargrove . . ."

Phoebe blew out a dramatic breath. "Honestly, Colin, what do you think of me? It's not as if a day in her company will have me . . ." She trailed off, as if suddenly remembering the many servants that would overhear.

"I have no fear that you'll turn to a life of larceny," he said. "You're entirely too clumsy. I am sure you will have a delightful time." And perhaps by the time they got back, he would have exorcised the memory of that kiss from his mind. As it was, the tilt of Elinor's head caught his eye, and the recollection of her lips against his got hold of him around the throat.

"We should go," Elinor said. "We don't want to be on the road after dark."

"Of course," Colin said. Phoebe leapt up immediately and swept out past him into the hall, leaving him momentarily alone with Elinor. Well, not quite alone; his sister was only in the hall beyond, and the door was wide open. But his mouth felt stuffed with cotton. He dropped his voice.

"About last night . . ."

"What about it?" Elinor asked. She meant to pretend it had never happened, he realized. Well, she might manage that feat, but there was no way he would be able to.

"I must apologize," he said. "I was very drunk. I never would have kissed you, if I hadn't been."

"Really," she said. He paused. Her voice was alarmingly cold and hard, like iron on a chill day.

"You're like a sister to me," he said. "I've never thought of you that way. I would never make advances on you, you must know that. And you're not the sort of woman men make advances on, so I wouldn't want you thinking that. It was a mistake, and it will not happen again."

"Well, thank goodness," she said drily. "I am so glad to hear I will be spared further exposure to the Questing Tongue of Lord Farleigh." Her voice was so low and soft he was certain that Phoebe could not hear, and yet he flushed with sudden shame and whipped his head around to look in her direction. Elinor made a harrumph in the back of her throat and brushed past him, chin tilted upward and eyes blazing.

Oh, bloody hell. He must still be drunk. Not the sort of woman . . . ? He'd as good as called her ugly. And related to him. He wasn't sure which of the two he wanted to rebut first.

She *should* be like a sister to him. He had tried hard over the past five years to drill himself into a pattern of thought that recognized her as nothing more than that, and nothing less. He had not succeeded particularly well, but he had at least managed to function without constant preoccupation.

Now his mind was making up for the lost time, summoning up scattered memories from the past ten years and more.

The way she laughed. The way the sun struck her hair and lit it with red darts, while in candlelight it shone glossy and dark. The way she always seemed to know exactly what to say to break a foul mood, seemed to know when to tease her brother or cast Colin a smile to lift him from a moment of melancholy.

The way she'd stood in his arms, surprised but unafraid, and all but dared him to kiss her.

"You're engaged to Penelope Layton," he muttered to himself. "And have other things to worry about besides." Like finding Foyle. He straightened up and tugged at his clothing in an attempt to put his mind in some kind of order. Elinor was out of bounds. So far out of them that she might as well not exist.

Oh, he should tell her that, too. *You might as well not exist.* That would certainly endear him to her.

"Idiot," he told himself. Penelope Layton. Edward Foyle. These were the names that mattered right now. He could not afford to be distracted. Suddenly, he realized he'd been standing alone in the doorway of an empty room for quite some time. The girls had already exited from the sound of things. Good. At least he didn't have witnesses.

"My lord," came a voice near his elbow. He jerked around with a huff, only to find his butler, Bolton, an entirely reasonable distance away. Something about the man's voice always seemed closer than reality, and after two years of service Colin still hadn't gotten used to it.

"Yes?" Colin asked, impatient.

"A Mr. Hudson is here to see you."

His brow furrowed. "Mr. Hudson?"

"He says you sent for him. Last night," Bolton explained.

"Really. What foresight on my part," Colin said. Hudson was exactly the man to find Foyle. He was rather impressed with himself for remembering that, given his condition last night. Bolton's nostrils flared slightly in disapproval. "I'm going to try to cut back on the drink," Colin added. "Now. Where is he?"

"I had him wait in the kitchen, sir," the butler said, his disapproval clear in every stiff syllable.

Colin gave a displeased tug of his jacket. "He is my guest. I will see him in the drawing room. No, the study," he amended. The study was more private, and it was assuredly a private business that had called Hudson here. He assumed. Unless he had come up with some other business at some point last night, but that seemed doubtful.

"As you wish, sir," the butler said. "Only . . ."

"His appearance troubles you, does it?" Colin said.

"He does not seem to be of the quality of your usual company, sir," the man said in tones of absolute deference.

"And in another five years, perhaps I shall entertain your opinion on the quality of my company," Colin said. "But I fear we have not yet reached that stage of trust and intimacy. So if you would . . ."

"Of course, sir," Bolton said. He flushed. He'd overstepped and he knew it. If he had been overly familiar on any subject but insulting Colin's guests, Colin might have sympathized with the man.

"Show him up," Colin said firmly, and made for the stairs. He started for the study, but halted. He turned slowly in the direction of his bedroom door.

It had to be done. He couldn't explain this business properly without it.

He strode to his room and opened the wardrobe. The box was where he had left it, in the back, beneath an old discarded blanket. The box was wide and flat, made of battered cherrywood with a brass lock to seal it. He lifted it with care and tucked it under his arm.

He had never shared the contents of this box with anyone. It seemed strange that he should be so calm about it now.

Before he could think better of it, he went quickly to his study and set the box upon the desk. He straightened up while he waited for Hudson, aligning the corners of the papers on his desk and shelving the slender volume of poems he had taken down the morning previous. By the time he had flicked the few specks of dust from the back of his chair, Bolton was back, Hudson in tow. Hudson shouldered past the man, his hat clutched in one thick fist, and stuck out the other hand to Colin.

"Lord Farleigh," he said. Colin took the offered hand.

"Hudson. Delighted to see you again." *Delighted* wasn't quite the term. Their acquaintance was an odd thing, steeped in secrets. Hudson had been one of those involved in the transformation of the thief Joan Price into the respectable Mrs. Hargrove. They'd all had to pledge to keep the secret— Hudson, Colin, Harken, Colin's sisters, Elinor. The keeping of secrets could curdle the air between the keepers, but in this case, the whole cabal seemed closer for it. There was too much of a fairy tale in the secret to be too weighed down. "That will be all, Bolton, thank you."

The man departed, closing the door behind him, and Colin waved at a chair.

"Do sit. Drink?"

"I don't touch the stuff," Hudson said, but accepted the seat. He rested his ankle atop the opposite knee. Hudson was a bulky man, solidly lower class and proud of it. He was also a brilliant investigator.

"Right. Forgot about that. Hope you don't mind if I do," Colin said, already helping himself to a glass of brandy. He sat opposite Hudson, and took a sip before speaking again, ordering his thoughts. "You'll be wondering why I've asked you to come."

"Obviously," Hudson said. "Your message was extremely vague. Not something to do with Mrs. Hargrove, is it?"

"Joan? No," Colin said. "Nothing at all to do with her."

Hudson idly fidgeted with his cuffs. His clothing and his attitude were as rough spun and hard-bitten as the first time Colin had encountered the man, after discovering that Martin Hargrove's beloved was a jewel thief with a stolen identity. You'd never guess that he was now a man of considerable wealth thanks to his share of said stolen jewels.

"A little bit to do with her," Colin amended. "But only

tangentially. Coincidentally? Something like that," he said, and took a generous sip of his drink. "To do with her diamonds, in any case."

"Quite fond of those diamonds, I am," Hudson said, folding his hands over his belly. He grunted.

"I imagine so." Colin had never quite understood the details of the deal Hudson had worked out with Joan, or where the three Copeland diamonds had ended up, but the end result was that the detective, Joan, and Joan's maid were suddenly in possession of a great deal of wealth.

Hudson grunted. "I'm listening."

Colin slid his finger around the rim of his glass before continuing. "I had a sister," he began, and though he had never told the story like this—to someone who didn't know, who had never met Marie—it came easily. Clinically. There were so few details, in the end. A bare summary of facts, and he was done. At least, done with the story as his family knew it.

"That's quite the story," Hudson said.

"It is," Colin said. "And there's more you should know, before you begin."

Hudson had avoided looking at the box so far, but now his eyes went to it. Colin opened the top drawer of the desk and drew out a small brass key to match the lock. It turned with a soft click, and Colin set it gingerly aside before lifting the lid of the box with both hands.

The inside was lined in red. A collection of correspondence topped the contents, but these Colin set aside. They did no more than confirm what he had already told Hudson. Instead he reached for the folio beneath, and held it out, unopened, to Hudson. He took it. Colin settled back. He watched as Hudson unwound the twine that held the folio shut, and drew out the page contained within. He didn't need to look at the page in order to see it perfectly in his mind.

It was a sketch, in charcoal. The artist's hand was assured. Every stroke exuded sensuality, delighting in the interplay of light and shadow across the curves and planes of the chosen subject: a woman, her hair let down, her eyes dark and lively. She was pictured wearing only a shift that had fallen down to bare one shoulder, half-reclined against the back of a chair, one hand lifted to touch the gem hanging at her neck.

Marie. She did not look the way he remembered her, but that did not surprise him. The woman in the portrait was a woman in love. And a woman beloved. This was no stranger's portrait. It had the ache of intimacy, of ecstasy. Whoever had drawn this portrait had been bewitched by that slight smile. And Marie's expression sung of the same bewitchment. She had looked back at the artist, and her eyes had shone with love.

"Is Mr. Foyle an artist?" Hudson asked, tone carefully neutral.

"No. Nor was Lord Hayes," Colin said.

"I see." Hudson put the report back in the folio and closed it. "I don't know if I can find all the information you want, the details about what happened. India's beyond my reach. But I can get you to Foyle. What do you mean to do once I do?"

"I'll worry about that," Colin said, because he didn't think that even Hudson would take the job if he admitted he intended to kill the man.

"You think that he killed your sister," Hudson said.

"It is a possibility," Colin said. He was certain of it.

"I won't be a party to murder," Hudson said.

"All I'm asking for is an invitation."

Hudson considered for a long time before he finally nodded. "Very well, then. The usual fee."

"The usual fee," Colin agreed. "And I don't think I need to tell you that this is a matter which requires great discretion."

"And yet you told me anyhow," Hudson said. He rose. "I'll see myself out, shall I?"

Colin waved his hand in assent. Something had eased within him now that Hudson had agreed to the job. No one could escape the man. Not thieves, not errant earls, not wayward heiresses. He had a positively unworldly ability to locate and procure any thing, person, or piece of information from places as low as the gutter and lofty as the prince regent's dinner table. Securing entry to Beauchene's chateau would not be a challenge for the man.

"You know," Colin said, "you ought to raise your prices."

"Lord Farleigh, do I strike you as a man over-reliant on money?" Hudson asked. Colin chuckled darkly.

"No. I find you to be a man most peculiarly immune to wealth. And thus of more resilient constitution than myself."

"Tell Lady Elinor and your sister I send my regards," Hudson said. "And congratulations."

"For what?" Colin asked.

"Your engagement, of course," Hudson said, and then his hat was back on his head and all of him was out the door. Colin frowned after him.

"How on earth did he know about that?" he asked the air, but received no reply.

Chapter 7

~

Colin had provided one service with his late-night lechery, Elinor concluded as she half-listened to Phoebe's enthusiastic conversation. If she had ever harbored any inappropriate feelings for the man (and, she admitted, there had been periods in her adolescence when her regard for him strayed in that direction), they were now thoroughly extinguished. The kiss had begun the execution, and that encounter in the drawing room had delivered a masterful killing blow.

She would concede that he remained handsome. And she hadn't courted many men she could look through her eyelashes becomingly at. Not that she was courting Colin. It was only that he was tall, and she appreciated tall men.

He was, however, an ass. That much she had known. But now she knew he was a terrible kisser on top of it, which left nothing to recommend him.

By the time they reached their destination—her brother's country house—she had put the incident entirely out of her mind. There was no reason to think about Lord Farleigh at all. She resolved that she would avoid him for a time. Not out of any embarrassment for herself, of course. She had no feelings on the matter. But he was clearly unable to express himself with any eloquence, and she did not wish to damage their friendship any further by allowing him continued blunders.

She was quite firm in this resolve, and determined not to be distracted, when Croft, her brother's butler, appeared at the door with a stricken look.

"Lady Elinor. Lady Phoebe," the butler said. "It is our unexpected pleasure to welcome you. Shall I show you to the drawing room while we prepare rooms for you?"

The evening was gathering, darkness draping over the house and making it look a bit like a hunched gargoyle. The stone caught the light during the day, but had a deathly pallor at night. Elinor had a sudden sense of foreboding. "Is the lady of the house about?" she asked. She had thought to get this task dealt with quickly, and certainly Joan never stood on ceremony, but now she doubted her haste. She ought to have done this properly, sending a letter ahead and making arrangements for a proper visit.

"She is in the study with Mr. Hargrove," Croft said. His voice hitched in hesitation before he spoke again. "I can show you to them," he said.

"With a heavy tread," Elinor said with exaggerated gravity. She had learned the importance of audible footsteps in the weeks following their marriage. Surprising Mr. and Mrs. Hargrove tended to have embarrassing results.

"Very good," Croft said, his cheeks turning red. He'd been their under-butler at Birch Hall, their family estate, and a more loyal man Elinor had never met. He'd entered service so young that family, to him, had always meant *the* family, those he worked for—along with an ever-shifting staff. It was he who had first understood that Elinor desperately needed some small space where not even the maids would tread, a private corner she could be certain belonged to her and her alone. A small room, filled with books, cleaned only when she explicitly requested it, so that she did not have the feeling that a phantom had been about her things.

She was deeply fond of the man, and deeply sympathetic when, despite their conspicuous footsteps and a heavy knock upon the door, they entered the study to find Martin and Joan in a loving embrace, Martin kissing his wife with ardor and, she suspected, far more skill than she herself had recently experienced. She drew back slightly, pulling Phoebe with her. Phoebe was almost incandescent with excitement. She'd been near-shaking the whole ride, and hadn't stopped her constant patter. Elinor was going to have to find a way to keep her calm. The girl was not made for this kind of intrigue.

Croft cleared his throat. There was a rustle and thump; Elinor imagined Martin had disengaged from his wife with alacrity. Croft's posture did not shift an iota. "Sir. Your visitors have arrived," he said.

There was a pause. "Were you expecting anyone?" Martin asked. Another pause, and then, "Who is it?"

Phoebe bounced up on the balls of her feet and back again. Her fingers curled and knotted behind her back. Elinor pressed her arm to still her.

"The Lady Phoebe Spenser and the Lady Elinor Hargrove," Croft said. Elinor drew Phoebe forward, stepping ostentatiously to cover their earlier approach and retreat. Croft stepped aside to allow them to enter. Phoebe was flushed, two points of color high on her cheeks. Elinor did her best to compensate with calm, offering her brother and sister-in-law a warm smile.

"Thank you, Croft, that will be all," she said. He made his exit with the requisite bow. One requirement of Joan's servants was that they know when to exit and never linger past that point. There were too many secrets in this house to permit anything else.

The secret-holder in question was examining them both with unconcealed curiosity. Every angle of the small woman had rounded considerably since they had first met, thanks to abundant nutrition and her current condition, the evidence of which threatened to overwhelm her frame entirely. One of her hands lighted briefly on the curve of her belly before falling to her side. Elinor felt a pang of guilt. She should not be involving Joan in this kind of business, not with the child on the way.

"We need your help," she said nonetheless. It was too late to turn back now.

"Anything, of course," Martin said, sounding startled.

"Not you," Elinor said. She fixed her eyes on Joan, whose lips parted, expression intrigued. "It's a rather delicate matter."

"And possibly illegal," Phoebe added behind her, breathless. Elinor shot her a quelling glance.

"Thank God," Joan declared, and then clapped a hand over her mouth. Elinor arched an eyebrow, but Martin only stifled a sigh. He bent and kissed his wife, earning a gasp from Phoebe, and whispered something in her ear.

"I promise," she said.

His hand lingered a moment on her belly, and then he turned. A grin lit his features. He touched Elinor's shoulder as he passed, and she stared after him, mystified. The joy in that grin was matched only by Joan, who beamed as if their arrival were the best news she'd had all year.

"Thank God," she said again when Martin shut the door behind them. "I am nearly out of my mind with boredom. But I did promise nothing dangerous."

"It shouldn't be," Elinor assured her, and hid a smile of her own. Of course. Joan loved Martin, but she'd grown up breaking into houses and dodging the law. She was always in the mood for trouble, and while her life might be comfortable, it was short on adventure these days. She'd jump at the chance to help. "I should have found you some mischief to get into months ago," Elinor added.

"It would have saved me a bushel of sighs," Joan said. She waved them toward a trio of chairs, claiming a high-backed one for herself. It had come from Martin's study in Birch Hall, and Joan had a peculiar attachment to it. Elinor had asked Martin why, once, and judging by his stammering, she didn't actually want to know the answer.

Phoebe was nearly vibrating with excitement. She perched at the edge of her seat, and Elinor worried for a moment that she'd tremble her way right off it.

"Tell me what this is all about," Joan said. Elinor sketched out the situation in as much detail as she could. When she was finished, Joan considered for a moment. Then she smiled wryly. "I think I have ruined you all," she said. "You were so very proper when I arrived." She scooted forward in her seat, an ungainly motion, and leaned forward—or at least, attempted to. "Have you considered Hudson?" she asked.

Phoebe shook her head. "Not him. He might tell Colin."

"More subtle minds are needed for this task," Elinor said.

"Subtle? I suppose I can still manage subtle," Joan said. "It will take time, though. I will need to locate him. And I assume that direct questioning will not amount to anything."

"Send Elinor," Phoebe said drily. "She's better than a fortune-teller."

That incident was not soon to be forgotten, then. Elinor winced. She ought to have realized that it would be as humiliating for Phoebe as it was for Madame Vesta.

"In any case, leave me to it," Joan said. "If half of what I've heard about this Beauchene's parties is true, it shouldn't be *too* hard to procure an invitation for the right kind of woman."

"What kind of woman is the right kind of woman?" Phoebe asked.

"An intelligent, trustworthy woman," Elinor said.

"Well, you're intelligent and trustworthy," Phoebe said.

"Who sells her company," Joan added blandly. Phoebe blushed furiously.

Elinor raised an eyebrow. "I thought you already knew about the parties."

"Well. I knew that Beauchene has parties and I'm not supposed to know about them." Phoebe bit her lip and plucked at her skirt while Joan stifled a laugh. "I didn't really think through the mechanics of the thing."

"Suffice it to say my reputation would not survive a visit," Elinor said.

"Assuming anyone recognized you," Joan mused. "Wait, no. Pretend I didn't say that. Please. Actually, I have just the person in mind. She owes me a few favors. All we need to do is find out when the party is, then secure an invitation."

Elinor relaxed. There was some burden eased, then. She

wouldn't be alone in this. She wished she could take Joan aside and explain to her exactly what Marie had meant to her, but some part of her rebelled at the notion. Joan belonged to a different life, in so many ways. The life after Marie and Matthew. Inviting her into the past seemed like trespassing on hallowed ground.

"You should find Martin," Joan said. "I don't know how much you intend to tell him, but he'll be worried."

"He does too much of that," Elinor said. "Worrying."

"More and more," Joan agreed. "But he's very talented at it, so it seems a waste for him not to."

"It's only going to get worse, you know," Elinor warned her.

Joan laughed. "I'm hoping that the worry gets spread out among all our children, a bit thinner with each addition. Like jam."

"More like each individual worry is a pair of rabbits, quickly begetting new generations," Elinor said. "I'll speak to him." She rose and turned, and nearly knocked into a new arrival—a red-haired young woman with a soft, sweet face and sharp green eyes that lit up when she spotted Elinor. "Maddy?" Elinor said.

The girl broke into a grin. "Lady Elinor! I didn't realize you'd be home."

"I didn't expect to be," Elinor said.

Maddy was—had been—a maid at Birch Hall. Now she was masquerading as Diana Hargrove's sister, though judging by her accent, she too dropped the fiction entirely when not in public. She was dressed conservatively in gray, the quality of her dress ambiguously serviceable. She'd been seventeen when Elinor last saw her, and since then the gawkiness of her teenage years had abandoned her. But not the enthusiasm. Her eyes sparkled with delight at seeing Elinor.

"You look well," Elinor said. "Where have you been keeping yourself?"

"Here and there, m'lady," Maddy said. "Doing some work for Mrs. Hargrove, mostly."

"She has a remarkable talent for investigation," Joan said. "Actually, Maddy, I may need your help. I'm a bit constrained at the moment, when it comes to mobility. If you don't object, Elinor?"

"No," Elinor said. "Of course not. After all, she already knows our darkest secrets."

"And the shiniest," Maddy said.

"Oh, you're *that* Maddy," Phoebe said. She'd been watching Maddy with a puzzled expression, but now her face lit up. "The maid."

"I used to be," Maddy allowed. "And we've met a few times, actually."

"Yes, but. You were the *maid*," Phoebe said.

"Nothing wrong with being a maid."

"No," Phoebe said. "Only . . . well, I think I can be excused for forgetting what you look like."

Joan caught Elinor's eye and tilted her head, indicating the door and a quick escape. Elinor mouthed a thank-you. Joan enjoyed conflict. Elinor tended to want to sink into a very deep hole to escape it. She sneaked out to the sounds of Phoebe trying very valiantly to justify herself, while Maddy grew increasingly—if politely—irate.

Elinor found Martin outside, looking out over the small garden in the back of the house. He looked up as she approached.

"Did you get things settled with Joan?" Martin asked.

"For now," Elinor said.

"Nothing too exciting, I hope," he said.

"Not yet," Elinor said. "Don't worry, I won't get your wife in any more trouble than she's used to."

He grinned at her. "I've missed you."

"I've only been gone a few weeks."

"Entirely too long," he told her. "Will you walk with me? I'd like to catch some of this sunlight, before we lose it."

He offered her his arm, and she took it. "You are looking remarkably well," Elinor observed of her twin. "I believe it is the woman who is meant to glow, when there is a child on the way."

"We have decided on a division of effort," Martin replied with a smile. "I do the glowing, and she does the groaning."

"You realize that you are consigning yourself to several

decades of chasing after an inevitably mischievous child," Elinor said. "Any child of Joan's—"

"Might well rebel, and decide that being stolid and boring is the best way to infuriate her parents," Martin said. "Though I hope not. I rather enjoy mischief, myself."

Elinor shook her head. She did not know how she had ended up the quiet, retiring member of an otherwise exuberant family.

"You seem to have brought some mischief yourself," Martin went on.

"Not mine," Elinor said. "I'm merely facilitating."

"I hope I won't hear from Farleigh about this," Martin said.

Elinor cut him a sideways look. "It is Phoebe's business." If Martin went running to Farleigh, they'd be in real trouble. "Have you spoken much to Lord Farleigh lately?" she asked.

Martin shrugged. "Not particularly. We've both been busy. Or I have, I suppose; Farleigh's never busy."

"I'm worried about him," Elinor said.

He frowned. "Has something happened to make you concerned?"

"No, only . . ." She couldn't tell him the truth. But she couldn't keep the nighttime encounter entirely to herself, either. Martin had always been her confidante; it seemed strange that in the past few years, she had kept so many things from him. "He returned to the town house extremely drunk the other night, and I went to help him to his bed."

"You helped him to his bed?" Martin repeated, voice devoid of inflection. He had halted completely, and she was brought around to face him by her own momentum and her hand on his arm.

"I mean that I was going to get a footman to help him," she said quickly. "But he was rude, and I left him there. Nothing untoward happened."

He regarded her for a long moment, but seemed to accept her explanation. "Farleigh has always had a fondness for spirits," he said. "I wouldn't worry about it. He's probably broken up with another opera singer, that's all."

"Martin."

"What? You know he's kept mistresses, don't you?"

"I don't keep track," Elinor said archly. She thought *kept mistresses* was a rather dramatic term for Lord Farleigh's habits, personally. It wasn't as if he had them installed in secret apartments, and his arrangements with them rarely lasted more than six months or so.

Not that she had paid attention, but he was so terribly unsubtle about it.

"I should hope not. The last one was dreadful, anyway."

"You met her?" Elinor couldn't help the disapproval in her tone.

"It was before Joan," Martin said. "And it's not as if I was courting her. I don't know who he's been seen with since, come to think of it. But he gets dramatic when it comes to women. I wouldn't read too much into it."

"I won't," she assured him.

"I know you've always had a bit of an infatuation with him," Martin said.

She squawked, pulling away from him. He stared at her. She didn't blame him; the noise had quite startled her as well. "I do not have an infatuation with Colin Spenser," she said. "I have never had an infatuation with Colin Spenser, unless you count the thirteen minutes between our introduction and the first time he directed a comment toward me, which as you may recall was when I was seven years old and thus cannot be blamed for my poor judgment."

He blinked at her. "Wait. I thought you liked Farleigh."

"I do!" She was becoming strident. She was becoming downright shrill. She turned away from her brother, choosing instead to contemplate the grounds. They were not the familiar grounds of Birch Hall, with its green hills and distant trees, its manufactured ruins and neatly tamed gardens. Thornwald Manor was designed for privacy, not to be inviting; the woods clustered up close to the flanks of the great, gray house, gouging deep shadows across the thin expanse of lawn, and the gardens—tucked around the rear of the house—were walled affairs, where one might sit or wander unobserved. Even the approaching lane was shielded from view by the trees on one side and a high wall on the other.

"It's been too quiet, without you," Martin said.

Elinor laughed. "I am not known for making things *less* quiet, Martin."

"More lonely, then. Joan misses you. She hasn't been able to travel with the baby on the way, and you know how she is. She isn't content with a life spent at home. At least when you're here, she has someone to talk to other than her husband."

"You are asking me to stay," Elinor said. "For your sake, or for mine?"

Martin's lips twisted in a half smile. "I don't know why Farleigh has so upset you, but even I, dull-witted as I am, can see that spending time under his roof is not in your best interest. And while I have failed in many things in my life, I have not yet failed at looking after my sister." He touched her arm. She gave a little shiver, and felt a lump rise unexpectedly in her throat. They were twins, born scant minutes apart. They had spent all their lives together, except when he was at school. She had always thought that she needn't worry about marriage, or anything else, because they would always be the two of them, unconquerable.

And then he had found Joan. He had found joy, and Elinor was happy for him. But diminished as well. It was as if she was suddenly not quite family, in the same way that she was not quite family enough to know the truth about Marie.

"Elinor?"

"There are things I need to take care of in London," she said. "I promised Phoebe's mother I would see her through the Season."

"The Season's nearly over."

"But not quite yet," she said. "And who knows? Perhaps we'll find her a husband at the eleventh hour."

He snorted. "Phoebe is not ready for a husband."

"Because she's too opinionated? Adventurous? Wild?"

"Because she hasn't yet learned to adjust her level of adventure to suit the situation," Martin said. "If she were a boy, she'd be the sort to be getting into constant scraps, always sporting a black eye and a bloodied nose. As it is, she can hardly slow down enough to notice that another human being is present."

"Fair enough," Elinor said.

"I don't think there's a force on earth capable of breaking her adventurous spirit, and I wouldn't want to discover it if there were. But I dearly hope there's one that manages to focus it."

"I'll keep my eyes open," Elinor said.

They walked in silence a while longer, and soon found they'd made a circuit, and the house was in sight again.

"Are you sure you won't stay?" Martin asked.

"I'm sure," Elinor told him. She kissed him on the cheek and took her arm from his, turning back toward the house.

"You will always be wanted here," Martin said quietly.

She looked back at him. "I know," she said. "Of course I know that." Of all the places in the world, this might be the one where she was least alone, and it was here that she would spend the many years ahead of her.

It might be enough. It would not be joy, precisely, but it would be enough. And as for Lord Farleigh . . .

Well, she would simply have to avoid him.

Chapter 8

~

THREE WEEKS AND THREE DAYS LATER

Three weeks of dodging Lord Farleigh was nearly enough to drive Elinor mad, but they had finally discovered an equilibrium. He stayed out all night and slept until the afternoon; she rose roughly the same time he stumbled home, and retired early. He had eschewed balls altogether, so the rare evenings when Elinor was not walled away in her room were spent away from the town house. In three weeks, they had spoken precisely fifty-seven words to each other, most of them "good day."

Elinor was in the midst of an early—and solitary—breakfast when a footman appeared to inform her that she had a visitor. A moment later he ushered Maddy in, who eyed the spread of food with great interest.

"Thought you'd be up," she said. "Don't you know ladies are supposed to laze about in the mornings? Eat in bed and stew in their beauty juices."

"You have such a poetic way about you," Elinor said with a laugh. "And I notice you're awake."

"Never shook the habit," Maddy confessed. "I still expect to hear the housekeeper hollering for me to get upstairs and set the fires. I bolt up in bed like I've been pricked with a needle, and then there's no getting back to sleep. But I like to think there's virtue in rising early."

"Unlike certain other ladies of noble birth?" Elinor asked, sipping her tea. Maddy had accompanied them back to London, and though she'd been staying in the Hargrove town house, she joined Elinor most mornings to update her on the progress of their private project. This had the unfortunate side effect of bringing her into repeated contact with Phoebe. The two did not get along. In the place of her usual pointed barb in Phoebe's direction, Maddy offered only a distracted frown.

"Maddy?" Elinor said.

"Yes, well," she said. "I have some news." Then her frown deepened. "Mr. Hudson's here," she said, head cocking to the side.

Elinor strained to hear whatever she had, but could only make out a heavy tread somewhere distant in the house.

"He's got a very distinctive gait," Maddy informed her.

Elinor rose. "We should see why he's here," she said.

They marched out together, Elinor in the lead, and found Hudson in the hall. His gaze brushed right past Elinor and locked onto Maddy.

"What are you doing here?" he rumbled. The butler looked at him askance.

"Visiting a friend," Maddy said archly. "And you?"

"Business," Hudson said. He eyed her suspiciously. "Here to see Lord Farleigh."

"Who is, as I mentioned, asleep," the butler said, obviously desperate to claim some control over the situation. Elinor almost pitied him.

"Then wake him. He said he wanted this the moment I found it, and that doesn't mean six hours from now when he wakes up on his own," Hudson said. "He left me clear instructions. You want to be the one to explain to him why they weren't followed?"

"I'll . . . show you to his study, to wait until he is available," the butler said.

Hudson grunted, apparently satisfied. He gave Elinor a nod, squinted at Maddy, and followed the butler up the stairs.

"What was that about?" Elinor asked.

"Oh, nothing," Maddy said. "Only, a little of Mrs. Hargrove's business overlapped with a little of his, and I might have a little bit gotten one of his clients arrested. Which Mr. Hudson didn't mind, except that then the fellow couldn't pay him. Not that he needs the money. He's very vexing." She frowned.

"You two are oddly suited for each other," Elinor said.

"Agh. You make it sound like we're married," Maddy said, wrinkling her nose.

"Heaven forbid," Elinor said wryly.

"I'm never getting married," Maddy said firmly. "I don't understand the appeal, being stuck living with a man and all."

Given Maddy's habit of deep infatuation with members of her own gender, Elinor did not find this surprising. She looked up the stairs where Hudson had vanished. What was Colin up to? "If you have news, we should wake Phoebe."

"She's already awake," Maddy said. A moment later, Elinor heard footsteps coming down the hall.

"That hearing of yours is practically supernatural," Elinor said.

Maddy grinned. "There's a reason Mrs. Hargrove hasn't fired me yet," she said.

It took a few minutes to get Phoebe herded into the drawing room and to shut the door securely behind them.

"What have you found?" Phoebe asked eagerly, leaning forward.

"Well," Maddy said. "It's more Joan's find than mine. She got a letter and sent it on to me. It's from Madame Lavigne," she said.

"Who?" Elinor asked.

"Her real name is Gertrude Poole, but Joan says don't tell her she told you that," Maddy said with a grin. "She's an old friend of Joan's, from before. She's a courtesan."

Elinor raised an eyebrow. Even after all this time, she

had not gotten used to the fact that her sister-in-law was friends with courtesans. "I take it she's to be our agent?"

"Being as I'm not qualified," Maddy said with an air of tragedy. "Joan says she trusts her, and that she's smart. But the real news is, she got an invitation and all the details."

"What *kind* of details?" Phoebe asked.

"Details that you almost certainly do not need to know about," Elinor said.

"Yes, but we are the ones in charge of this adventure, aren't we? So we really ought to know everything that's going on."

Elinor had to admit she was curious, herself. She'd heard all manner of stories once the wine started flowing at dinner parties and the men had gone off to enjoy their billiards and liquor, but half the tales were too tame to be interesting, the other half too wild to be credited. She did not, for example, believe that Beauchene practiced human sacrifice. Nor that, as one very drunk and very virginal acquaintance had insisted, that the height of excitement was that the men "kissed the ladies on their stomachs."

The other two were looking at her expectantly.

"Oh, fine," Elinor said. "I'm already a corrupting influence, obviously. We may as well have some fun with it."

Maddy grinned. "Then you're going to want to read this for yourselves."

By the time Colin had collapsed into his chair in the study, he was at least awake, though he questioned his sentience at this hour of the morning.

"Taking care of yourself, I see," Hudson said.

"I am a gentleman. Degeneracy and sloth are in the blood," Colin said. He massaged his cheeks, trying to rub some feeling into them. "I take it you've found something?" Three weeks. Three weeks he'd been waiting, and not a word from Hudson. Colin had begun to think that he'd imagined hiring him. "Well?" Colin demanded. "What is it?"

Hudson removed his hat and tossed it onto the desk. He wore a scowl that would send children running for their mothers. "He's been at Beauchene's chateau for months," Hudson said, making the French words sound about as graceful as a pig rolling downhill. "Beauchene's locked the place up. No visitors. And word is Foyle's to go from there to the continent. So you were right that the party's the way to get at him."

"I assume that means that you've secured an invitation," Colin said.

"Trickier than I thought it would be. Not like I knew how to go about getting into a party like that."

"Neither do I," Colin assured him. "Strictly a matter of necessity."

"Strictly," Hudson agreed.

They shuffled their feet a little and didn't look at each other. Colin cleared his throat.

"But surely half those stories are wild fantasy," Colin said.

"Must be," Hudson agreed, though he didn't sound sure.

"And even if they are true, I am only going to see Foyle." And kill him, but he hadn't admitted that to Hudson, and he wasn't going to. The only thing worse than being a murderer was being a fool about it.

"Wasn't cheap, getting that invitation," Hudson said, clearly more comfortable with talk of money than . . . well, decadent displays of wealth, sex, and gluttony. Emphasis on the sex. "Now, if you was a woman, that would be another matter."

"Women aren't invited," Colin said, confused. Then he paused. "Oh. That kind of woman."

"Rather a lot of them invited, matter of fact," Hudson said. "That's the point, isn't it?" He had turned a remarkable shade of red.

"Yes, well. When is it?"

"A week from now," Hudson said. "Sort of a dessert course for the Season, I suppose."

"That doesn't leave us much time."

"It's what I can offer. The party runs for five days. No names. They'll give you a new one when you get there. Dress fancy." Hudson gave Colin a head-to-toe look that suggested that wouldn't be a problem. Colin touched his cravat self-consciously. He did not have the patience to be a dandy, but he did like to think he had a discerning eye for clothing. "There's rules," Hudson said doubtfully.

"I take it you don't want to explain them to me."

"I don't," Hudson said. Red was giving way to purple. "But I'll do my best."

"How elaborate," Elinor said. "Everyone wears masks?" She was still working her way through the dense paragraph of information. She could feel a flush creeping up her neck.

"Only the women," Phoebe corrected, peering over Elinor's shoulder.

"All the men have special names," Maddy said. "Like, Owl or Ferret or something or other. And they get a token, on a ribbon, and if they want to claim a lady—er, woman. Courtesan. Person. He gives it to her to wear. If you—not you, but one of them—isn't—aren't—" She paused. "The men aren't supposed to lech on any of the women who've been claimed by another fellow." She frowned. "I thought the peerage was supposed to be more civilized than the rest of us."

"He's French. It doesn't count," Phoebe said.

"The *guests* aren't French," Maddy pointed out.

"How would you know? Have you been?" Phoebe snapped. Maddy glared at her.

Elinor could not imagine anyone she had met spending five days in the pursuit of that level of debauchery. She considered. Actually, she suspected that there were quite a few men she knew who would leap at the chance. A week of pleasure without consequences? It wasn't just the men who might be interested. "Fascinating," she said.

"Horrifying," Colin said. "Don't they have the good sense to keep such things properly repressed?"

"It's a private party where no one knows your name and all the women wear masks," Hudson said. "Can't get much more repressed than that."

"I can't believe we are discussing this," Colin said.

"Maybe we could stop, then," Hudson suggested, halfway to pleading.

"If this is where Foyle is, I need to know everything about it," Colin said reluctantly. "Keep going."

Hudson sighed. "Well, the wholesome bit's out of the way," he said. "The rest gets a bit racy."

"Dear Lord," Colin said, and Hudson continued.

"It seems like a great deal of effort, given that such diversions are plentiful enough in London. Why go to all the trouble?" Elinor asked.

"I think the trouble's kind of the point," Maddy said.

"Wait," Phoebe said. "What does that bit mean?" She pointed at the letter.

"'Unusual tastes.' I expect that means, you know, ropes, or something," Elinor said with a frown.

"Ropes?" Phoebe asked. "To tie people up? Who gets tied up, the man or the woman?"

"Either one, I guess?" Maddy said. "I'm not sure."

"This is not appropriate conversation," Elinor said. They glanced at her again. "Someone had to say it."

"It all sounds unpleasant to me," Phoebe said. "I mean, the sheer mechanics of the basic act. When a man—you know. It sounds uncomfortable."

"If you do it right, it's quite nice," Elinor said absently. The girls gaped at her.

"How would *you* know?" Phoebe asked.

Elinor blushed. "I *was* engaged," she said. "It's not so very unusual to anticipate the wedding."

"You and Matthew?" Phoebe said. She cocked her head to the side. "Oh. I hadn't realized."

"It isn't precisely something I advertise." She couldn't quite believe she'd admitted it to the two of them. Then again, it was hardly the greatest of the secrets they were bandying about this morning.

"In that case," Phoebe said, shifting in her seat. "I have questions. Starting with what that thing is where . . ."

* * *

". . . Not that I'd know from experience," Hudson finished.

"Of course not," Colin said. "And of course I'm aware that such predilections exist, Hudson. I wouldn't be required to participate in them, would I?" He focused very hard on the man, trying to keep the image of Hudson, and not the possibilities he had just suggested, firmly fixed in his mind. Some of them held no interest, but he would be lying to himself if he pretended that none of the acts Hudson had clinically named held any spark of intrigue.

"It would be odd if you didn't take a woman to bed. It is the point of the exercise," Hudson said. "But you wouldn't be expected to, ah, do anything more than the usual."

"I am not going there to indulge in carnality," Colin said crossly. "I am engaged, after all."

"Right," Hudson said, though he didn't seem to think that had much to do with the question. "It's up to you. Only saying it would be suspicious."

"I believe I have enough information to make a plan," Colin said. He ran a hand over his face. "Very well. I'll attend this godforsaken party. And in the meantime, I have a ball to prepare for." He would be announcing his engagement scant days before he departed for a week to the most notoriously immoral event in England. God help him if Levenbane found out.

Or, heaven forbid, his sisters. May they be spared ever knowing such things even existed.

"Now you're making things up," Phoebe said accusingly.

"No, not at all," Elinor said, deadpan. They'd devolved to sketches now, and all of them were red and gasping with laughter.

"But that doesn't *bend* that way," Phoebe said, pointing. "You'd break something!"

"And there's an extra hand in this one," Maddy said.

Phoebe peered at it. "Yes, that's definitely an extra hand," she agreed.

"Now, now. Who among us has actually experienced the act?" Elinor asked archly.

"*The* act," Phoebe groused. "Not *these* acts." She paled. "Wait, you haven't . . . Oh God! I don't want to think about it!"

Elinor laughed. "Of course not. And I made that one up, but Maddy's is no more likely."

"No, it's real," Maddy insisted. "Joan told me about it."

"Oh, no," Elinor groaned. "Oh, God, now I'm thinking about Joan and Martin."

"No, no!" Phoebe waved her hands frantically. "Think of anyone but that! Think about . . . Harken!"

Elinor snorted. Captain Harken barely reached her shoulder, and had hardly spoken three sentences to her in the space of their acquaintance. He was entirely too distracted by his morose and enduring love for Kitty.

An image flashed through her mind: Lord Farleigh, his exquisitely ordered clothes mussed, his lips closing over hers. She stilled. That was not a pleasant memory, she reminded herself. It had been alarming. Unwanted. Unskillful.

She straightened up. "Well," she said briskly. "That's enough of that, I should think. Back to business?"

The others gaped at her a moment. Then, slowly, they put themselves in order, smoothing their hair and taking steady breaths until the color left their cheeks.

Maddy wiped tears from her eyes. "Madame Lavigne can take it from here, I suppose. Assuming she can hook Foyle—and Joan says she can—she'll have five solid days of wine and conversation to get information from him."

"I'd like to speak to this Madame Lavigne in person," Elinor said. "If we're to entrust such an important matter to her."

"You can't be seen speaking to a courtesan any more than you can be seen at Beauchene's party," Phoebe pointed out.

Elinor sighed. "I suppose you're right. I must be at least forty before I can be *that* daring."

"You have to at least wait until you've found me a husband," Phoebe said sourly. "Speaking of which, the Copeland ball is tomorrow evening. I should probably select a gown."

"You're going to their ball?" Maddy asked. "But aren't they the ones that swindled your sister?"

"I have to," Phoebe said, making a face. "Mother insisted. It's my 'last chance of making a match this whole Season, and you're not getting any younger.'" She let out an anguished moan. "I wish I could just burn the place down instead."

"I've got a better idea," Maddy said slyly. She slid a fingertip beneath the fine gold chain that habitually hung around her neck. It was a long chain, and vanished inside her modest bodice. Whatever pendant hung at its end, Elinor had never seen. She lifted it now, though, and Elinor gasped. A large, perfectly clear diamond winked at its end.

"You kept it," Elinor said with slight awe. It could only be one of the three stolen from Lady Copeland—one of Marie's. "I thought you'd sold them all."

"I bought it back after Joan's investments worked out and had it recut," Maddy said. "There's no way to prove it's the old one, but I thought . . . Well, the Copeland lot wouldn't know, but you would. It might make it bearable."

"It's perfect," Phoebe declared. "Maddy, I should be ever so pleased if I could borrow it for the night."

"Well," Maddy said, and flushed. "It ought to be yours anyway, by rights. Your family's. The least I can do is let you flash it around for one night."

It was good to see them all smiling again, however much of the gallows was in their humor. "I look forward to watching you dazzle the whole of the ballroom, Phoebe," Elinor said. She'd forgotten about the damn thing, but she resigned herself to going. She had promised to play escort and matchmaker for Phoebe, after all.

Besides, it was the one ball in the whole Season that she could be absolutely certain Lord Farleigh would not attend.

Chapter 9

~

The Copeland ball had reigned the past several years as the most popular end-of-season gala, if not the most storied or pedigreed. There were balls yet in the Season, but Lady Copeland somehow always managed to schedule hers for the week before the heat grew too sweltering and the company too repetitive. She bedecked her house in the exotic finery of India; she even had a pet monkey she'd brought back with her, and Colin had once earned a swat from Phoebe for pretending to confuse it with her daughter.

The end result of Lady Copeland's social skill was that Colin's engagement was about to take the fastest possible route from secret to common knowledge, and it was making him feel ill. Or maybe it was the heat of so many bodies in close proximity, or the thick, meaty quality of the air over-stuffed with perfume—which did only feeble battle against the stink of sweat. The whole ballroom was a whirl of fashionable chaos, blobs of clashing colors thrown haphazardly amongst one another.

"Farleigh." Lord Levenbane had found him. Colin clutched his glass of champagne and tried to look busy. Not easy, given that he was standing alone at the edge of the room. "Perhaps you should dance," Levenbane suggested pointedly, and nodded his head in his daughter's direction.

Penelope was radiant. She wore a soft wreath of lilac in her yellow-gold hair, matched in the minute decoration of her frock. She wore lace in abundance without excess, evoking the emergence of spring flowers from a field of crisp, white snow. Her pink cheeks were dimpled with so bright and sweet a smile a charging bull would have paused to let her wreathe his horns with blossoms, and sighed contentedly at her touch.

"My God," Colin muttered. Levenbane grunted approvingly, but Colin hadn't meant it as approval. He was going to destroy this girl, he realized. His bitterness would spoil that smile. He could never make her smile the way she did now, never give her the gentle attention she deserved. And it was far too late to do anything about it.

He left Levenbane and crossed to her, waiting for her to catch notice of him. Her friends, as round-faced and sweet as she, giggled and curtsied out of his way. "May I have this dance?" he asked, voice smooth as the silk glove she slid into his hand. He was practiced in seduction. He knew the proper way to make a debutante blush or a widow smirk, to make a mistress crook her finger in invitation. He could make her love him for a while.

All it would take would be a few whispered words, the soft brush of his lips against her curls—not her ear, not her skin, but close enough to make her wonder what that would feel like. He would tell her she was beautiful; he would ask her a question just as the dance carried them apart. When they came back together, he would prompt her for her answer, scold her for keeping him waiting.

"Lord Farleigh," she said, tentative, and he was not certain if it was a greeting or a question.

"Lady Penelope," he replied, and smiled blandly. They danced; she asked if he enjoyed the ball; he allowed that he did. The music ended. He deposited her back with her friends, his duty done, and kissed her hand. "You look lovely tonight," he told her warmly, sincerely, chastely. She gave him an uncertain smile.

He was practiced in seduction, but he had no idea how to treat his future wife. How to be kind, without risking the illusion of affection. How to tell her by his actions, his glance, his touch—*We will not be blissfully happy, you and I, but we will be content.*

He had known for a long time it was all he could expect. He had not considered until now what a burden it was to lay on her shoulders.

"Your sister is dazzling," Lady Penelope said.

"My what?" He looked dully at her. She inclined her head to indicate a point behind him, and he rotated with a sinking heart.

They were here. Phoebe, exuberant in cream and lace, a positively massive diamond he did not recall owning glittering at the end of a chain around her neck; her official escort, Mrs. Lindon, a subdued gray-blue giving her an appropriately gaolerlike look. And Elinor, in a gown so plain it was nearly a scandal. It didn't matter. She was the most beautiful woman in the room. Any gown would only be a distraction. Hell. He'd somehow managed not to think about the fact that they'd be here. He hadn't even thought to travel with them. And now they'd all be here for the announcement—and he hadn't told them. They were going to kill him.

Elinor started to turn in his direction.

"I beg your pardon," Colin said to his intended. "There's something I must attend to."

He ducked behind the nearest knot of conversationalists, cast around for an exit, and fled.

Elinor had forgotten how much she despised the Copeland ball. She hadn't come since her first Season, before Lord and Lady Copeland left for India, but little had changed. The music was gay, the dancing lively, the food superb—and the crowd so thick she could barely move without knocking into someone. She'd already lost Phoebe and her official escort,

Mrs. Lindon, in the crush. At least Mrs. Lindon would keep a close eye on Phoebe. She took her duties seriously—though she was perfectly happy to leave the matchmaking to Elinor, who, being unmarried, was not qualified for the Phoebe-wrangling role in such rarified environs.

In previous years, she had always had one or two offers of dancing by this point in the evening, but it would appear that she had finally reached expiration. She dodged a flute of champagne, clutched in the fist of a rather sweaty viscount, and pivoted toward the wall, seeking some refuge from the throng.

She came face-to-face with a woman she almost didn't recognize. "Lady Theodosia," Elinor said, more of a startled exclamation than a proper greeting. The woman in question drew back, examining Elinor for a second longer than was necessary for an identification before a smile spread over her features—with the deliberation of spreading butter over toast.

"Lady Elinor. It's such a pleasure to see you. It's been ever so long. Though it's Lady Pelbourne now."

"Of course! My apologies." Elinor flushed. Theodosia had married Lord Pelbourne seven years ago; they'd exchanged a few rote pieces of correspondence in the months following, and Elinor had never made the error in writing. They'd come out in the same year, and for a time they were almost what Elinor would call close.

A mustachioed man with a tidy potbelly drew up, and Theodosia's smile broadened a fraction of an inch. "Darling, you simply must meet Lady Elinor Hargrove. Lady Elinor, may I present my husband, John Ashton, Earl of Pelbourne. Lord Pelbourne, this is Lady Elinor, an old friend."

They exchanged thin-lipped *my pleasure*s, and then Lord Pelbourne lit up.

"Oh, *that* Lady Elinor," he said. Elinor stiffened. "The witty one."

"Quite," Theodosia said. "She was always such a treat. You always seemed to know something about everyone, Elinor, and everything about quite a few somethings. So quiet, but then you'd pop out with some scrumptious bit of commentary."

It was almost complimentary. Perhaps it was meant to be. But something in the way Theodosia was looking at her made Elinor's stomach turn.

"It was such a pity when you got sick," Theodosia went on. "Things were never quite so entertaining when you were gone. And you never did find a match, did you?"

Entertaining. She had been that. It was the only thing she had to catch their attention, those gorgeous girls with their easy conversation. She would be at the edge, trying desperately to grab hold of the thread. They'd hardly even noticed her, until one day she'd said—

She'd said something perfectly innocent about Lady Elise and Mr. Wyle, and all eyes had turned to her. No one else had realized they were infatuated with each other, she'd realized, and it was as if she suddenly held a great deal of power in her hands. She knew so much simply from watching and listening, and soon she knew how to phrase her little treasures of information so that everyone laughed.

That was when they'd become her friends. But they hadn't been friends, had they? She'd been their pet monkey. An *entertainment*. And worse than that, she'd earned her place with common gossip dressed up in wit. No wonder her friends had dropped away so quickly when she'd gotten ill. If she couldn't make them laugh, what good was she?

The press of people lurched forward. Someone bumped into Elinor from behind. The August heat was cloying, the close quarters nearly unbearable. "Please excuse me, I think I need some air," she said, and extricated herself from the unexpected reunion.

She shook her head as she moved away. What a fool she had been. She'd been young, but that was no excuse. She'd savaged other girls to earn laughter. When she thought back to the company she'd earned herself, there was not a single person she cared to remain in contact with.

Thank God she'd gotten ill. All those fluttery half friendships had departed, leaving her with the people who mattered.

Marie and Martin, Kitty and—and Lord Farleigh. He'd always been so kind to her when she was sick, on the rare occasions they saw each other. So much so she'd asked him if he was ill himself, and he'd promised he'd go back to being a beast as soon as she was well.

Perhaps I'll stay sick forever, then, she'd said. He hadn't laughed.

She pushed her way further in the direction the crowd was already carrying her, shouldering past chattering women and nervous men without apology. She cut along the wall and pushed through the first door she came to. The door swung shut behind her, instantly muffling the sounds of the dance, but she kept moving. The hallway was cool and dark, unused. It was still early in the evening, and she was unlikely to come across couples stealing away for a few minutes in private, but she still made plenty of noise before she went through another room. She'd found herself in a library. A large globe stood in the center of the room, and the walls were lined with books that looked too uniform. Probably bought as a set for the aesthetics, she thought, rather than for their contents. What a shame.

Elinor pressed a hand against her stomach, gulping down musty, thick air. Thank goodness for libraries. They were so much more her natural habitat than that swirl and crush. She couldn't believe she'd ever tried to pretend otherwise. "At home in solitude. And isn't that the essence of a spinster? I'm clearly talented."

"Obviously," Lord Farleigh said.

Elinor whirled with such speed that for a moment, Colin feared she would tumble over. He sat forward in the armchair where he had draped himself, setting aside his empty glass.

"I didn't see you there," she said. "I didn't think you'd be here."

"In a library? I do know how to read," he said. She flushed.

"At the ball," she said.

"Ah. Yes. I have . . . business here," he said. Business that seemed very firmly locked on the other side of that closed door. "It's all a bit too much though, isn't it? We had the same idea, finding a quick escape," he said, nodding back toward the door. "Though I had resigned myself to a few minutes of silence, whereas you brought along a charming conversationalist."

"I assure you, I do not normally talk to myself."

"More's the pity. I doubt there are many others who can keep up with you," Colin said. She frowned. He always did seem to say the wrong thing around her, even when he was attempting a compliment. When he was younger he'd enjoyed provoking that frown. Now he couldn't seem to break the habit.

"I made plenty of noise before coming in," she said. "You might have warned me you were here."

He bristled. "Was that what I was meant to do? I thought there was a baby draft horse loose in the hall, given the clatter, and was considering herding it back into the ballroom in the hopes of improving on the night's entertainment." Yes, that would certainly improve matters. Well done, Colin.

"A baby draft horse?" Elinor repeated. He summoned his aristocratic training and managed not to flinch at her wintry tone. "Excellent; I have been overheard wallowing in self-pity, and now been compared to a clumsy foal. This is certainly an evening to remember."

"Self-pity? I imagined it was self-congratulation."

Her mouth shut with a click of teeth. She glared at him. He glared at her.

"Well?" she said.

"Well what?"

"Are you going to apologize? Or leave, at least?"

Colin rose. He came toward her, step by deliberate step, his gaze tracking from the crown of her head to her feet. She would never be as *attractive* as Lady Penelope, because such beauty did not attract. It commanded. No wonder she had never married. No man would dare shackle her to a life of mere contentment, and she had spent her love already.

She imagined she was undesirable. He wished he could prove to her how wrong she was.

"I was here first, I might remind you," Colin said. "As such, I refuse to leave. And what is it you wish me to apologize for?" he asked. "Failing to be deaf?"

"You compared me to a draft horse," she reminded him.

"So I did. I can see now that I was wrong in my comparison," he said. She gave a *hmph* of satisfaction, and God help him, he couldn't let it be. "Still, it must be noted that you have a rather long face." He reached out a finger, touching her chin. She froze, anger beginning to spark in her eyes. He smiled. "Elegantly so, however, an attribute one does not normally associate with gamboling foals. I did once see a rather magnificent stallion whose coat was this same shade of auburn." His hand went to the curl hanging beside her neck, and rubbed it between thumb and forefinger.

In a few minutes, Lord Levenbane would make his cheerful announcement. In a few minutes, Colin would be clapped on the shoulder and offered one congratulation after another, while Lady Penelope blushed and giggled. He had no chance of ever having Elinor. He was not fool enough to believe otherwise. But for the next few minutes, in the darkness and solitude of this room, he could pretend.

"Lord Farleigh, you have embarrassed yourself once where I am concerned. I would remind you that you have expressed deep regret at having implied that you might find me attractive. Your current nonsense is bordering dangerously close to repeating that sin, so for both our sakes, you ought to stop."

He huffed. "Don't be ridiculous, Elinor. You are beautiful. It would take a eunuch not to be attracted to you."

"You've been drinking," Elinor said.

"Yes," he agreed. "It's a marvelous occupation. You should try it."

"When you are sober—"

"When I am sober, I will be wise," he said. "Too wise to see the wisdom in correcting my earlier mistake."

"What mistake?"

"I kissed you," Colin said. She stiffened. He tilted his head, considering the implication. No, that wouldn't do at all. "I kissed you badly. I fear I have left you with the impression that such a kiss is my standard, whereas I assure you it was an aberration."

She licked her lower lip nervously. He tracked the movement, not bothering to hide the direction of his gaze, and her cheeks went red. He expected her to push him away, then. She had always had far more sense than he.

"Well," she said. "It clearly bothers you that you performed so poorly. If it will set your mind at ease, you may make the attempt once more."

He paused, somewhat surprised that his ploy had worked. "My first error, as I recall, was that you declared that you did not want to kiss me. And an unwanted kiss is never good. So: do you want me to kiss you?" He touched her cheek with the very tips of his fingers.

"Very well," she said. Her voice wobbled. "I would not want to deny you the chance to redeem yourself. One kiss, that's all."

He slid his hand around to the back of her neck, drawing her toward him. "One kiss."

One kiss. What harm could there be, in one kiss? Call it a farewell. An exorcism. He harbored no delusion as to its meaning. He did not imagine that her interest was in *him*. She had, after all, been alone for a very long time.

He bent his head toward hers.

"Only one," she reminded him. "And this doesn't mean anything."

"Nothing at all," he promised her.

His other hand found her waist, resting lightly upon it. At first, his lips only brushed against hers, a touch so light it brought a little gasp from her. Then he pressed against her more forcefully, his mouth matching hers. She tasted of champagne and sweetness, her lips soft against his. His lips moved with hers; he employed teeth and tongue nimbly, and she mirrored his explorations, her fingers tightening on his arms until they dug into his sleeves. He pulled her against him, the heat of her body shooting through him.

She broke away from him, lips parted and cheeks flushed. He stared at her, hunger in his gaze. There was nothing of *contentment* in that kiss. There was nothing of contentment *after* that kiss. He reached for her again. She pulled away and smoothed her skirts. "Well," she said. "That was indeed an improvement."

He made a choked sound. "That's all you have to say?" he said.

"Is there more required?"

He forced himself to take a single long breath without speaking. One kiss, he reminded himself. An exorcism. He was done with her now. "No," he said. "I believe our business is concluded. It would have been a great shame, to leave you with such a terrible kiss as the most recent in your memory."

"Because it would be so difficult for me to acquire another?" Elinor asked coldly.

"You aren't attached to anyone, are you?" He smothered the note of panic in his voice. He had no right to jealousy.

"No, and I am unlikely to be, as you well know." She glared at him.

A clock in the corner chimed, and both of them jumped. Colin swore softly. "The announcement," he said.

"What announcement?"

He paused. This was the second-worst way for her to learn of his engagement. Unfortunately, the worst would be when Lord Levenbane made the announcement, and she was guaranteed to hear it.

"I am announcing my engagement," he said.

Chapter 10

❧

Elinor could not speak. Her limbs were cold. She folded her hands together precisely in front of her. "Engagement," she said. Her voice sounded as if it were being forced through a grate. "To whom?" she asked, pitching her voice to express exactly the right degree of interest and detachment. If it was one of her friends, she thought she might retch. But no, it wouldn't be; her friends were all wed and vanished into the management of their households and their husbands.

"Lady Penelope Layton," he said.

"Ah," she said. She thought perhaps a hornet had taken up residence in her ear. There did seem to be a monotonous drone drowning out her voice. "Felicitations."

"Yes. Well. I should go," he said.

"Yes," she said. "You should."

He hesitated a moment longer, then turned, and left her alone in the dark. She dug her nails into the palms of her hands, trying not to think. It was an impossible task.

When he'd offered to kiss her, she'd thought, for one fleeting, fanciful moment, that perhaps she had been wrong about him all this time. He'd called her beautiful. He'd wanted to kiss her. And then the kiss had been incredible. She hadn't been kissed like that since—

She'd never been kissed like that. Matthew was a merely competent kisser. She hadn't minded; she'd assumed she'd have time to train him. Lord Farleigh had clearly looked after his own training. But she'd thought she detected more than skill and practice; she'd thought she tasted true desire in that kiss.

But of course she was wrong. She was an entertainment. A last bit of fun before he married Lady Penelope Layton.

Elinor pressed her hands to her cheeks. She was crying. She was crying over Colin Spenser.

She couldn't stay. She couldn't listen to that announcement.

She slipped out of the library and down a dark hallway until she found an exit, a feeling like panic clawing at her throat. She startled a footman, taking a break around the side of the house. She sniffed back her tears and gave him a charming smile.

"Oh, good. Will you get word to Mrs. Lindon that Lady Elinor has gone home with a headache? Tell her that she is not to let Lady Phoebe out of her sight under any circumstances. Thank you ever so much. Good night." Still smiling brightly, she glided past the blinking footman without another word and hurried for the street. The night was late enough that the near-constant blockade of carriages had thinned as only the truly late arrivals straggled in. Unfortunately, her own carriage would not make the return journey for hours yet. She froze on the street corner, suddenly uncertain where to turn. As she stood, one of the late-to-arrive carriages, having deposited its gowned cargo, started to pull by—and came up short.

"Are you all right, miss?" the driver asked, leaning over to get a good look at her.

"Perfectly fine," Elinor said firmly. As soon as she remembered how to breathe in an orderly fashion.

"Only, you look like someone's made you cry," the driver said. She looked at him in affront, but there was only kindness in his eyes. "Can I take you home, miss? My mistress will be hours yet, and I've got nowhere to be."

Elinor assessed the wisdom of accepting such an offer, and weighed it against the wisdom of striding off through London at night on foot. "Thank you," she said. "I would be very much obliged."

"I'd eat these reins before I left a lady crying on the street," he said, and hopped down to open the carriage door for her. "Just tell me where to."

She gave him the address and climbed into the carriage gratefully. It lurched forward, and for a moment she listened to the cluck of the driver's tongue, his soft, affectionate tones as he spoke to his horses.

She had left without saying a single good-bye. Her absence would not be noted. She would go home, and she would sleep, and in the morning this would seem like a bad dream.

She buried her face in her hands. How had she let this happen? How had she let herself care whether Lord Farleigh kissed her—and whether he meant it? How could she have let herself be so stung when he all but called her a dried-up spinster?

Well damn him. And damn Lady Penelope Layton.

Who was a terrible match for him, anyway. Penelope Layton was twenty years old, plump and pretty, perhaps the sweetest girl Elinor had met in all her life. There was nothing beneath that sweetness, though, no edges to catch against. You'd sink through her like a pudding and plop out the other side, sticky with her goodwill. She would bore Colin, and he would make her miserable. She needed someone who saw the stars when he looked in her face, and delighted in presenting her with sweets and flowers on a whim. Colin would buy sweets and flowers, but they would be calculated gifts, and Penelope was not a stupid girl; she would know it. Still, she was the daughter of an earl and the grandniece of a duke, with enough siblings and aunts and uncles to prove her line was fertile. It was a prudent match. Thoroughly prudent.

"Damnit, *I* am the daughter of an earl," Elinor said, and hated herself for it.

It didn't matter that she was the daughter of an earl. She

was over thirty, she had a reputation for being sickly, and she'd spent five years putting off any interested man that came her way.

She shut her eyes. The sway of the carriage lulled her, soothing her. She was losing everyone. Marie and Matthew, years ago; Martin and Joan to each other; now even Lord Farleigh. They were leaving her behind.

They drew up to the town house in short order, and the driver waited as she climbed the steps and slipped in the front door. The house was all but empty, but the butler greeted her in the foyer with a concerned expression.

"I'm afraid I'm not feeling well," Elinor said. "I'll be going to bed."

"Of course, my lady," the butler said. "There is a letter for you, when you are recovered adequately to read it." He indicated the tray near the door.

Elinor crossed to it, and instantly recognized the elaborate scrolls of the handwriting. She opened it with trepidation, and read.

Lady Elinor—

> *There is a problem. Come to see me as soon as you can.*

—Mme. Lavigne

Elinor crushed the letter in her palm and closed her eyes. "I have to go," she said, and turned back to the carriage.

Colin listened through Levenbane's protracted toast, understanding only every fifth word as Penelope Layton beamed beside him. He was a fool.

No. That night in the hallway, he had been a fool. A drunkard as well. Tonight, he had been cruel. He did not even have the excuse of drink; he'd had only a few sips, wanting to be clear-eyed for the announcement. Now he wished he'd downed an entire bottle. What had he been thinking? He had wanted one last taste of what he was losing before he consigned himself to his engagement. He had wanted one last chance to have Elinor, however briefly.

He had not thought for a moment what it might be like for her. Did she think he had been toying with her? Using her as one last bit of adventure before he settled down? She would not be wrong. If he had hoped that some affection might remain between them after he was married, he had dashed that hope to the ground and stomped it to pieces with his ill-considered ploy.

He had better pray that Martin never found out about this. The man would skewer him through with a saber.

Levenbane concluded, and Colin was swarmed with well-wishers. He accepted their congratulations, clasping one hand after another and somehow remembering the names that went with each face. He spotted Phoebe off to the side, her chaperone standing by at attention. They were looking at him with something akin to reproach. As soon as he was able, he made his way over, steeling himself against Phoebe's reaction.

"Well, well," Phoebe said. "Engaged. Fascinating."

"I forgot to tell you," he said. Or rather, he'd kept putting it off. It wasn't that he was ashamed of the girl or the engagement, individually; it was just that he felt somehow that he was letting his sisters down, marrying in such a businesslike fashion. His mother would be appalled; for all her match-making, her aim was love, not merely satisfaction.

"I want you to imagine, for a moment, what Mrs. Hargrove would say to you under these circumstances," Phoebe said.

Given Joan's vocabulary, he could imagine that quite vividly.

"And now I want you to assume I have said all of those things." She punched him lightly on the arm. "You cad! You ought to have told us. I hadn't even known you were courting her!"

"It was a brief courtship," he admitted.

"Are you madly in love?"

He fell silent. There were too many ears, listening in. "I am extremely pleased," he said, but even that was a lie.

Phoebe looked crestfallen. "Oh," she said. "I see." Mrs. Lindon looked awkward, and as if she wanted to be somewhere else. He felt the same.

"It's all out in the open now," Phoebe said lightly, recovering. "And no harm done. Now. I believe your betrothed is in need of a dancing partner, Lord Farleigh." She sounded cheerful enough, but she only used his title when she was angry with him. He was going to have to bribe her with something later. Or possibly grovel. "You should see to that."

He gave her a bow. No harm done. Was it too much to hope that she was right?

Chapter 11

Elinor's rescuer was far less enthusiastic about depositing her behind Madame Lavigne's town house, but she assured him that she was safe, and he departed reluctantly, unwilling to challenge her. She knocked on the rear door and was greeted by a grim-looking housekeeper who shooed her along the hall, past an eclectic collection of furniture that ranged from roughshod and splintering to polished mahogany.

At last they reached a room illuminated with warm lamplight and lined with paintings of smiling nudes. Filmy white curtains would let in the light during the day without letting out the view, making it the perfect room for a discreet encounter. Elinor paused at the doorway. Reclining on a settee, her rich blue skirts draped becomingly around her, was a woman of astonishing beauty. Raven hair fell in ringlets around her shoulders, and her skin was a light, flawless brown. A dark mole marked her cheek, lending the one mortal flaw that rendered her beauty approachable.

"*Bonjour*," the woman said, curving her cupid's bow mouth into a smile. "You are Elinor, then?"

Elinor regarded her with fascination. If she had not known, thanks to Joan, that Madame Lavigne was in fact a barkeep's daughter, she would have been entirely taken in by the woman's accent. She could better imagine the woman as a gem, even a lesser gem, of the French court of the previous century than scurrying about the streets of London.

"And you are Madame Lavigne," Elinor said. "I apologize. I had not expected . . ."

"You are startled by the shade of my skin. Don't apologize; I rely on that. Do you know how hard it is for a poor London girl to be exotic and unexpected?" Her accent fell away in degrees. "My grandmother came from a sugar plantation on Barbados. My grandfather didn't care enough to free her, but he brought my mother home to England with him. Three generations from slave to this. Not bad, don't you think?"

"That is impressive," Elinor said.

Lavigne shrugged. "Some might say I am as owned by men as my grandmother was."

"You don't think so," Elinor said. Madame Lavigne exuded a confidence few of those at the Copeland ball could hope to claim. She was the furthest thing from *owned*.

The woman inclined her head. "No, I don't. I think that people who say that have never been to Barbados, and stood in my grandmother's place. I think they have not even bothered to imagine standing in mine. But you're not here for my history." She still had not risen. Elinor shifted, wondering if she should take a seat. Was this normal for courtesans?

"You said that there was a problem," she said.

"I'm afraid so," Lavigne said, and drew up her skirts. It was not for stage effect that she had refused to rise. Her leg was bound and splinted, propped up on a silk pillow, the tassels hanging down on either side with an air of wilted apology. "I'm afraid I took a nasty fall yesterday. I've sent Joanie a letter, but apparently word hasn't gotten back to you yet."

"I'm so sorry," Elinor said, cursing inwardly. They could not exactly send Madame Lavigne hobbling her way to Beauchene's party on crutches.

"I can give you a few names," Lavigne said. "If you need someone else."

Elinor considered, then shook her head. "That won't be

necessary," Elinor said. "Joan has faith in you, and I have no doubt those you recommend would serve us well, but we simply cannot take the chance, when it is not only our trust that might be broken." The consequences of indiscretion were too great. She cursed inwardly again. Was it really going to fall apart here, in this room, with no more than a whimper?

First Lord Farleigh and then this. It might not be the most disastrous evening she had experienced, but it was certainly vying for a trophy.

"I thought that would be your answer," the courtesan said, and sighed. "On the other hand, a broken leg is great for sympathy. My Robert was down on his knee this morning. Wants to make an exclusive arrangement."

"Ah," Elinor said, not certain what the etiquette was in this situation. "Will you accept?"

A smile played across Lavigne's lips. "I think I will," she said. "He's the sweetest man. His wife, too. We haven't met, of course, but she knows about me, and I think she's been after him for a while to make things . . . well, not official, but you know."

Elinor choked. "His *wife* wants him to have a mistress?" she asked.

Lavigne laughed. Elinor colored. It was not a laugh of condescension, precisely, but one that prodded at Elinor's naiveté. "She has absolutely no interest in sex, I'm afraid. Which is utterly impossible for me to understand, but then, I enjoy it more than most. She appreciates when I distract the man, so he will leave her to her gardening. It's quite common, dear, though few wives are so pragmatic in their solutions, I admit." She adjusted herself, stuffing a pillow behind her so she could sit up more fully. She settled back with a sigh. "So what's this Foyle done, anyway? Joanie was frightfully vague."

"It's not my place to say," Elinor said.

"All right, that's fair," Lavigne said. "If you do find someone else, they can take my place. My token's over there." She nodded toward a petite table at the side of the room, on which rested a small, carved stone object. Elinor crossed to the table.

The object proved to be a cat, sitting with its tail wrapped over its feet. The token was small enough to fit in the palm of her hand, and while the carving was more suggestive of the form than representative, it had an oddly smug look. It looked, Elinor decided, rather like Lavigne herself.

"A token," Elinor repeated.

"For entry into the party," Lavigne said. "And on the first night, your sign of interest. If you should fancy a man, or should he make advances you wish to accept, you press that into his palm. I am told some men keep them, afterward, and brag of their collections."

Elinor ran a thumb over the rough curves of the cat. If *you* should fancy a man, Lavigne had said, and Elinor could not help but imagine it. A room full of the smells of smoke and alcohol, bodies milling about, her gaze constrained by the holes in a mask. A man across the room. Perhaps she would be struck by the firm set of his shoulders, the tapering of his strong torso, or the sound of his voice. She would steal to his side, and press the little cat into his palm. He would turn, surprised—

She blinked, clearing the image before she saw his face. He was no man in particular, she told herself; there was no face to see. Certainly not Lord Farleigh's. Damn him.

Her heart twisted at that thought, and she felt the fresh sting of tears in her eyes.

"Lady Elinor?" Lavigne asked. She sounded concerned this time. Elinor flushed.

"I'm afraid I am a bit of a disaster this evening," Elinor said.

"Oh, darling. You're far too put together for a disaster. A tribulation, perhaps; that has the proper gravitas." Madame Lavigne gestured to the seat opposite her. "Sit down. I insist. You must have tea, and tell me everything that is wrong."

"I couldn't," Elinor said.

"Of course you can. Most of my job is tea and sympathy, with a few naughty bits thrown in for variety." Her eyes sparkled, and Elinor smiled despite herself. She lowered herself into the seat, still turning the cat over in her hands.

"I kissed someone tonight," Elinor confessed. "My brother's best friend."

"And I am guessing it was less delicious than it sounds."

Elinor chuckled bitterly. "You might say that. I'm afraid I've gone and done something foolish. I've never liked him, you see. I still don't like him."

"But you want him." Madame Lavigne laughed at Elinor's blush. "Are you sure you don't like him?"

"Yes!"

"He annoys you, then."

"Very much."

"Hm. You strike me as a very composed woman," Lavigne said. "Difficult to ruffle. People describe you as aloof, don't they? Cold, even. They're wrong, but it's the impression you give. You guard yourself. You are very difficult to annoy. And he manages it. You are annoyed by him because he can annoy you."

"Circular logic," Elinor said.

"So much of love is," Madame Lavigne said, and Elinor choked. "Does he annoy you intentionally?"

"Yes! No. Maybe? I cannot tell how much of it is that he is an ass, and how much is that he is utterly ignorant of what he's saying," Elinor said. She rose from her seat and began to pace. It was a poor show of manners, but it seemed impossible to sit still while talking about Lord Farleigh. "It's as if the instant he sees me, the most awful thing possible pops out of his mouth."

"If you were one of my friends, I'd say you should sleep with him and get it out of your system," Madame Lavigne said.

Elinor halted, staring at her. "I cannot sleep with Lord Farleigh," she said flatly.

"Lord Farleigh, really?" Madame Lavigne whistled. "You have refined taste."

"You know him?" Elinor tried not to look too interested. Or too relieved when Madame Lavigne answered.

"I've heard of him. Not every woman is as disinclined to gossip as I am, dear. I heard he was perfectly civilized, if a tad blunt. If he's an ass around you, it's probably because he's nervous."

Elinor shook her head. "Lord Farleigh does not get nervous."

"Oh, really."

Elinor sighed, settling back into her seat and letting her face drop to her hands momentarily. "I might have thought he was merely nervous, or that I was more sensitive because of some unacknowledged interest on my part or his. But he was engaged, and he did not tell me, and he kissed me. He told me I was beautiful and I believed him, and then he told me that he was marrying someone else, and I felt as if I had shattered. It has not even been an hour. I am still shattered."

"There's being an ass, and there's being a brute," Madame Lavigne said. "This is most certainly the latter case, and I retract all my previous banter on the subject. There is only one thing to do. Forget him entirely. Ideally, in the arms of a virile young man, but I suppose you wouldn't be interested in such a solution."

"Oh, I have *interest*." What was the point in lying to a woman who made her *living* in the arms of virile young men?

"Unlike wine, virginity does not grow more enjoyable with age," Madame Lavigne observed.

"Virginity is not my problem," Elinor said, and Madame Lavigne gave a delighted smile. She sat up as best she could, leaning forward slightly.

"How refreshing," she said. "The man in question?"

"My fiancé. Late fiancé," Elinor said, meeting Madame Lavigne's gaze. It was a great deal easier admitting that to Madame Lavigne than Phoebe and Maddy. She could be assured of no judgment coming from *this* quarter, at least, and saying it aloud was somehow a relief. "It was very nice," she said.

"Oh, dear. Very nice is a fine start but a terrible finale. You can't possibly leave it there," Madame Lavigne said.

"I'm afraid I'm unlikely to have the opportunity," Elinor said. "I have put entirely too much effort into solidifying my reputation as unmarriageable."

"I didn't say anything about marriage," Madame Lavigne said.

"I remain young enough to suffer scandal," Elinor said with a regretful shrug. "It is an awkward in-between stage, but I am assured it lasts no longer than a decade or two."

"Oh, but there is a way to avoid detection," Madame Lavigne said. "And perhaps it will even get this annoying Lord Farleigh out of your system, as well."

Elinor arched an eyebrow. "Oh?"

"Do you really wish to give up on dealing with this Foyle fellow?"

"No, of course not," Elinor said. "If there were any way . . ." She stopped. "You're joking."

"There would be no risk of being recognized. The masks are quite effective. You would be free to have whatever amount of fun you wish, and gather whatever information you can manage."

Elinor laughed. "Can you imagine that? Me, pretending to be a courtesan?"

"Can you?"

Elinor's laughter died in her throat. She stood, started to pace. "I couldn't."

"You could. You don't have to, but you could."

"I shouldn't."

"Obviously."

Elinor bit her lip. There was no way they would find another trustworthy woman in time to replace Madame Lavigne. Joan was out of the question—even if she were willing to put that kind of strain on her marriage, her pregnancy made it impossible. Phoebe would jump at the chance, up until she thought it through, which would probably be halfway to Beauchene's estate.

It was down to Elinor, or no one at all.

She could not give up now. Not after how far they'd come. And—oh, hell. She *wanted* to. She wanted to have a day, just one day, without consequences, without her reputation hanging around her neck. She wanted to be something other than solid and dependable, quiet and expected.

"I'll do it," she said. She curled her fingers into fists. She owed it to Marie. "But to find Foyle, not to get Lord Farleigh 'out of my system.'" That would merely be a useful side effect.

"You are delightful," Madame Lavigne said. "I find myself greatly pleased to have the opportunity to interfere with your life. Now. You're going to need lessons. No one will believe you are a courtesan."

"You have only a week to transform me," Elinor said. Her mouth was dry. In a week, surely she would have thought better of her decision.

"Oh, I don't need nearly that long," Madame Lavigne said with a wicked grin.

"I'm only going for the information," Elinor said. "I don't need the *other* sort of lessons." She paused. "Though I find myself curious about the subject, in an academic sense."

Lavigne smiled. "I like you. I was worried that Joanie was stuck with people who would look down on her, but you don't, do you? You don't even look down on me."

Elinor laughed softly. "I think I was worried that *you* would look down on *me*," Elinor said. "I'm always so in awe of Joan, and the life she led."

"No one is ever half so interesting as they appear from a distance," she said. "Your first task is always to convince them that they are."

Elinor sat back down. The tea arrived, and Madame Lavigne went on, until light brushed against the horizon. Elinor departed in a hired hack, certain that as soon as she got some sleep, she would come to her senses. This was a ridiculous scheme, more ridiculous than anything Phoebe could have come up with.

And somehow she suspected that she was fool enough to see it through.

Chapter 12

❧

Elinor was missing. The staff could only tell Colin that she had returned briefly before setting out again, and no one seemed to know where she had gone. It was now morning, albeit not an hour of the morning the nobility generally familiarized themselves with, and there was still no sign of her. Colin paced in the drawing room. He had no idea where she would go. He had no idea what he should do. Send the Bow Street Runners out after her? Hire bloodhounds?

The front door opened, and footsteps sounded in the foyer. Elinor's footsteps.

Colin lunged for the door. He stuttered to a stop in the hallway as he clapped his eyes on her. She was whole and well, dressed in the same plain frock she had worn to the ball. She eyed him with distaste as she pulled off her gloves.

"You are up at an unprecedented hour, Lord Farleigh," she noted. "Or is it that you failed to find your bed at all last night? I am given to understand that has been a problem for you in the past."

"You're all right," he said.

"Of course."

"When you weren't at home—"

"I had business to attend to," she said. "Forgive me if I

fail to specify. You did not specify about your own business last night, after all, and in that case it was highly relevant to the conversation."

Ah. Yes. The "business" of his engagement, which he certainly should have disclosed to her before that kiss. But if he had, she would not have kissed him.

And she would not be looking at him with such wounded fury.

"I assign you no blame for the outcome of that conversation," he said. "I am well aware that it would have been different if you had known the particulars."

She lifted both eyebrows in weary skepticism. "Lord Farleigh, in all your years of fine schooling, did no one ever teach you how to apologize?"

She turned away from him. He lurched forward a step. He couldn't let things remain like this. He had to push past this muddle. Forward momentum. "Lady Elinor—"

She pivoted on her heel and speared him in place with a narrow-eyed glare. "Lord Farleigh. You have made it perfectly clear by your actions how highly you esteem me. There is no need for further exploration of the subject. I think it is best if we leave the matter be from now on. In fact, I think it best if we leave each other be entirely. I will be returning to Thornwald this afternoon, which should make the task easy even for you. I wish you great happiness in your life with Lady Penelope."

"Lady Elinor—"

"Good day," she finished, and marched up the stairs.

Oh, hell. He'd cocked this one up, hadn't he? She was never going to forgive him. He needed to make her listen. He needed her to understand that they could get past this, be something new to each other.

No. He needed to forget her, as she was determined to forget him. He'd done himself a favor, he decided. He didn't have the strength to keep his heart and his thoughts away from her. But she would enforce the separation for him. He could enter his marriage knowing that Elinor Hargrove no longer haunted him, however much he wished she would.

He owed Lady Penelope that much, at the very least. A husband who, if he did not love her, was not mooning after another woman.

He owed her, too, the clearing of his debts before they became hers. She was such a bright and joyous creature. He could not burden her with his darkness.

He needed to deal with Foyle. Immediately.

Elinor had made the decision to replace Madame Lavigne on Beauchene's guest list, but one evening of conversation was not adequate preparation for the task. She needed proper tutelage, and with the scant time they had, Madame Lavigne had insisted that Elinor come to stay with her for a few days.

Not precisely something she could explain to Phoebe, much less Lord Farleigh. Both seemed mollified by her claim that she was returning to Thornwald. She only had to hope they didn't think to check on her story.

She bade Phoebe farewell, took the carriage to the city limits, and paid the driver well for his silence when she disembarked. Martin and Joan expected her to remain with the Spensers for two weeks more, the Spensers expected her to return home, and she was free to make her way back to Madame Lavigne.

The woman greeted her with a grin. "I wasn't sure you'd be back," she said.

"Neither was I," Elinor admitted. "But I owe it to a friend."

"You owe it to yourself," Madame Lavigne corrected. "Every woman ought to have an adventure of her own, however brief, so that she might always be reminded that she is capable of it."

"I am not the adventurous sort," Elinor said.

"That's why you need only have the one," Madame Lavigne said. "I myself adore adventures. I have them whenever I can. But you would be miserable with endless adventure."

"Most people don't understand that," Elinor said. "You don't know how often I've been told I don't know what I'm missing. That I don't know how to live until I—oh, go

galloping across the fields, or get groped in a disused study."
Or a library.

"Most people are imbeciles. Never forget that," Madame
Lavigne said. "Now. We need to make you considerably less
respectable if you have any hope of getting through this. Ann!"

A middle-aged woman trotted in with lengths of fabric
draped over her arms. She looked Elinor up and down and
harrumphed. "This won't do at all," she declared, and bran-
dished a measuring tape like a whip.

For three days, Elinor submitted to instruction. Nothing
about her was suitable. Not her hair or her dress, her voice
or her walk. Madame Lavigne instructed her on elocution,
bribed and badgered her into swearing, drilled her on how
to hold her head and tilt her hips. Elinor danced with Ann
across the room—too stiff! Too proper!—and stood and sat
a hundred times before she could curve her body at the correct angle. Her smile was wrong, too disinterested.

"Everything must be an invitation," Madame Lavigne
said. "But he must never doubt you are willing to rescind it
at the slightest provocation."

"She will be the provocation," Ann declared, holding
fabric to Elinor's cheek and tutting, and then it was back to
walking endlessly across the floor.

By the third day she ached. Her cheeks ached from smiling; her feet ached from dancing; her back ached from draping herself just so. Then Ann appeared, gown draped over
her arms, and declared it ready for inspection.

It took a great deal of time to get into it. She suspected
it would take far less time to get out of it. She glanced down.

"Oh," she said, peering at her bosom. "I didn't know they
did that."

"She'll do," Ann said.

"She'll do," Madame Lavigne agreed. "But as ever, only
if she wants to."

Elinor examined herself in the mirror. Her cheeks were
rouged, her eyes lined with black, her lips stained a berry
red. Her mother would die to see her like this. Her brother
would fling himself off a bridge. And Lord Farleigh . . .

Well. She rather enjoyed thinking about what Lord Farleigh's reaction would be. She'd fix him with her gaze. That *invitation*. And then she would turn her back on him, and walk away.

The woman in the mirror was no sickly spinster. She was not Elinor Hargrove at all. But she was exactly the sort of woman who could whisper into a man's ear and learn all his secrets. She was the sort of woman who could do what needed to be done.

"I'm ready," she said. "I'll do it. For Marie."

And for me.

Chapter 13

～

They'll spot you out in a moment, Colin thought as his carriage made its ponderous trek up to the chateau. He was grateful he had thought to bring a flask. He tipped it, and found only drops. Drat.

He lurched out of the carriage before it had fully stopped. A woman swept up the steps in front of him, clad in a green dress that bared her bosom to the very limits of decency. She cast him a look over her shoulder. She already wore a mask, a white porcelain thing with painted lips and eyebrows fixed in a skeptical expression. He heard her giggle behind the mask and then she was gone, pausing only to show the doorman something she had in her reticule.

He fumbled in his coat pocket and came up with the folded invitation Hudson had supplied. The doorman inspected it and nodded, then handed over a black cloth pouch. "We will bring your belongings to your room, sir. It will be the egret, sir, as will you."

"What's that?" he asked, upending the pouch and spilling its contents onto his palm. It contained a key and a black ribbon, at the center of which hung a silver charm shaped like a wading bird.

"Your name, while you are here, is Mr. Egret," the

doorman patiently explained. "In addition to appearing on your token, the animal is engraved on the door of your private rooms."

"I couldn't have gotten something a little fiercer?" Colin asked. "Lion was taken, I suppose?"

"The egret is a thoroughly fashionable creature," the doorman pointed out. "Much prized for its feathers, to decorate hats."

"Not the highest honor one could claim," Colin said. "Very well, Egret it is. And the rest of the gentlemen have such appellations, I suppose?"

"Indeed they do, sir. And should you recognize someone, you may not speak their name under any circumstances, nor allude to the encounter once you have left." He paused. "The rules ought to have been explained to you before you came, but if you need to be reminded, I can arrange for someone to—"

"No, no, it's all coming back to me," Colin said. Hudson had supplied him with a written list. He just hadn't gotten around to reading it. He was only going to be here long enough to get Foyle alone, call him out, and settle this matter.

He stepped past the doorman, tucking both key and token into his waistcoat pocket. He had expected dim, dank chambers, but he found himself in a hall spangled with light. A crystal chandelier hung overhead, dripping wax on the floor and decking every surface with glimmering specks of light. Twin staircases swept upward at the back of the entryway, flanking a wide hallway. More open doors led off to the left and the right, and each doorway was wreathed with a different sort of garland—poppy, lily, bluebells. He wondered if they had some meaning. It occurred to him that they might be some kind of *menu*.

The woman in green was retreating down the main hallway. Loath to be alone in this place, he decided to follow.

He had gone a dozen steps when the woman vanished. For a moment he thought his eyes were deceiving him; then he made out the stark black curtain. He parted it. Darkness lay beyond.

Darkness, and a woman in green. She held her hand out to him. "This way," she said, voice low and smoky.

"Are you to be my psychopomp, then? To guide me into hell?"

She laughed. "Not into hell," she said. "Only to the buffet."

He took her hand. She tugged him along, picking up speed. They passed through three more curtains before they burst out into a wide open room. Candles flickered on every surface, leaving shadows dancing on the wood-paneled walls. The crowd was thin, but there were already three men gathered around the buffet, helping themselves to wine and food and eying the knot of women that was forming at the far end of the room, where a cluster of sofas and chairs made a lopsided circle.

Colin started to turn toward his guide, then stopped.

The buffet was a woman.

She was pale-skinned, nude, and strategically covered with fruits, cheeses, and petite pastries. A bunch of grapes concealed the v between her thighs. Slices of melon and wedges of apple formed a sort of bodice, and a line of berry-filled pastries trailed down her already sparsely covered torso. Every tidbit claimed would reveal a little more of her. She took slow, steady breaths, and did not move an inch.

His guide stood on tiptoes to whisper in his ear. "She's supposed to be some countess," she said. "They come sometimes, to feel scandalous. If you ask me, it's half the reason we're made to wear the masks."

"Surely not," he said.

She shrugged, as if she didn't care that he believed her. "You're new," she said. "Do you want a tour?" She paused. "Or a bite to eat?" she suggested, mischievous.

"Is there a woman at the bottom of the wine as well, or is that safe to drain?" he asked.

"Perfectly safe," she assured him.

"Then wine, and a tour," he said. "Though—I'm sorry, I don't mean to make any claims, if this is . . ."

She waved away his concern. "This early in the evening,

no one is making promises. Least of all me. But I wouldn't mind the excuse to look around."

"I would appreciate it," he said. He'd thought he could muddle along on his own. He could see now that he'd been wrong. He was in a labyrinth—and while he would much rather turn a corner to find a beautiful, naked woman than a minotaur, he was no less lost for it.

She got them each a glass of wine, and led him through the adjoining rooms. Some seemed to have themes—one boasted sculptures of satyrs and a woman in Grecian robes, while another was styled with Oriental rugs and smelled thickly of incense—but most could have belonged at any house party, if that house party required its women to go masked.

"The gentlemen all have their own rooms," she said. "But if you don't feel like going that far, there's always a few empty rooms. Or just a dark corner to duck into. Definitely be cautious about stumbling into dark corners if you don't feel like interrupting someone."

"That much isn't so different than a standard summer party," Colin said, which drew a fresh giggle from her. "I had a friend who forgot to label the rooms with the guests' names one year. People kept popping into the wrong room in the middle of the night. One man accidentally slept with his own wife."

"How terrible," she said gravely.

"He was entirely traumatized," Colin said. Gibson had been the host of that particular summer's festivities. There was a reason he had never allowed his sisters to attend.

Unlike at Gibson's, there were dozens more rules here, he learned. Some of the staff could be approached to arrange various types of encounters; there was a rather alarming amount of equipment squirreled away in wardrobes and closets; and various sections of the house had much different standards of dress.

"But honestly, most people just like to know that it all *could* happen," his guide said, as they finished their rounds. "Nine out of ten of 'em just grab a pretty girl and stick to the usual." She planted a hand on her hip. "How about you? Anything in particular bring you?"

"I'm looking for a man," he said idly.

"Oh, we don't do that," she said apologetically.

He choked out a laugh. "No! I mean, I hoped to meet up with an old friend. I'd heard he was here. His name—"

She tsked, and he stopped.

"Right. I suppose I'll have to look myself," he said.

"Sorry," she replied.

"I don't suppose I could have your name, at least?" he asked.

She put a finger to her porcelain lips. "Where's the fun in that?" she asked, and danced away.

Colin watched her go. He had always considered himself something of a libertine. He had a reputation as a rake. But this was all too much for him.

He drained his wine. Just as well he wasn't here for the women.

There is only one thing you must remember, Madame Lavigne's voice said in Elinor's mind. *You belong there. If you act without doubt, there will be no doubt.*

It was easier said than done. Elinor sat in a hired carriage, watching the chateau draw closer. It sat at the top of a hill, and though the evening had barely begun to dim, it was already festooned with lanterns. Every window blazed. Carriages trundled along the lane before and behind Elinor's own, joining a ragged line making their way up to the open double doors. She spotted small figures, women in rich silks and men in gaudier colors still, ascending the steps.

Soon they would be close enough to see her.

She retreated into the shadows of the carriage and tried to steady her nerves. No one knew that she was here. And once she donned the mask, no one need find out.

As long as she retained her mask, which covered her entire face, she would be safe from recognition. Madame Lavigne had been clear: Beauchene's rules were sacrosanct. The men must charm their way into women's favor, not force it. Such charm was not difficult to come by, when the women were paid to be there and often given additional gifts by their paramours, but should a woman refuse a suitor, he must accept her judgment. Elinor need not surrender her virtue for this bit of madness.

Unless she wanted to.

She had to admit she was halfway tempted to do it. One night with a stranger might finally banish the memory of Lord Farleigh's kiss. And all that came after. And if she was to go to her grave a spinster, why not have an evening or two of entertainment?

She sighed. Except that she most certainly would not go to bed with Foyle, and if tonight went as planned she would be spending the entire evening with him. God willing, she could accomplish her task in that much time and slip out before dawn. No time, then, to tug an anonymous young man into a back room.

You're becoming scandalous in your old age, she chided herself, and could not deny it as she slipped on her mask and secured the ribbons behind her head.

The world instantly contracted. She would have to turn her head to see side to side, and the mask made her breath loud. But the sure knowledge that no one could see her face lifted the tension from her shoulders.

You belong here, she told herself, and by the time she stepped down from the carriage she believed it.

She was ushered with restrained deference through the front doors after only a cursory glance at the little token she still carried. She had expected a separate entrance for the women, but there were several men—she would not presume to call them gentlemen—coming up the steps behind her as she entered. She moved quickly to get out of their way, ducking down a side hallway through a garland of forget-me-nots before she had a chance to do more than glance at the opulent foyer.

She found herself in a long drawing room, done in a surprisingly spare style. The only other occupant was a nervous-looking woman with her hands fitted tightly to her waist, pacing and muttering to herself. She halted abruptly when she saw Elinor.

"Am I not supposed to be here?" she asked.

"I was going to ask the same thing," Elinor confided. "I only just arrived, and I'm really not certain how I'm meant to go on."

"There's rooms upstairs," the girl said. "For us, I mean. That's where your things will be taken, and you can sleep there if you're not sleeping somewhere else." She made an odd quarter turn toward the window and then bobbed back. "Do I look all right?"

"You look lovely," Elinor assured her. The girl looked wrung out, and her neck was a furious red. "Are you feeling all right?"

"Just nervous," she said with a tittering laugh, then clapped her hands over the mouth of her mask. "I'm not supposed to do that. Oh, hell. I can't believe I'm here. I'm not good enough for this, and they'll throw me out when they realize it. I do hope they don't. I've heard there are fireworks on the last night. I'd love to see fireworks. But I'll never last that long."

Elinor caught the girl's frantically gesturing hands. "You belong here," she told her firmly. "If you believe it, they'll believe it." She'd managed to convince herself that the whole house would be full of Madame Lavignes, women who owned themselves and their circumstances proudly. She couldn't decide if it was comforting or horrifying to find that it wasn't true.

"Can I stay with you for a little while?" the girl asked.

"How about we explore?" Elinor suggested. "You'll be more at ease if you know how to make your way around."

"I've already explored a bit," the girl answered. "I can show you. I'm Daisy, by the way."

"You can call me . . . Theodosia," Elinor said, and clasped the younger woman's arm.

∽

Chapter 14

Elinor drifted, having deposited young Daisy with a similarly lost-looking young man who looked about as rakish as a bedraggled spaniel.

She wanted to see everything, and she thought it would take her a week just to do that much. It was intoxicating to be behind the mask. Men saw her; men *stared* at her in a way they never would have at home. But they couldn't see her the way she could see them. She even recognized many of them. Men with wives, men in politics, men who acted with utmost restraint and respectability.

I know your secrets, she wanted to whisper. *And you will never know mine.*

She had studied a portrait of Edward Foyle. She knew what he looked like, and she knew the moment she spotted him. It was getting late in the evening, and she had begun to worry. But there he was, in the Grecian room, leaning against a statue of a satyr. He was speaking to a man, and their expressions invited no interruption, so she drew against the wall beside a painting of a dryad and examined him.

He was a rangy man. His face was full of hard angles, like iron beaten into form, and with all the warmth of iron, too. He spoke with short jerks of his hands to punctuate his words, and his lips curled around each sentence as if he did not like the taste of them. His hair was shot through with gray, mingling with straight, thin strands the color of mud. He wore a ring on one finger, she saw; a diamond glinted from it.

Was that part of your price? she wondered.

"Would you like a drink?" a voice asked her.

She managed not to start. She turned slowly, appraising the man who had approached. He had dark skin that liked the candlelight, picking up its glow, and rich black hair cropped short. His accent and features were unmistakably Indian, though he was not dressed in the style she expected from illustrations; he wore the same suit and cravat as any other man present (apart from the few in the western side of the house who had already dispensed with their clothing entirely).

"It is only that I seem to have two, and you seem to have none," he said, indicated the two flutes of champagne he carried. "A pair of problems with one obvious solution."

"Thank you," she said, and took the drink he offered. She was not certain how she was meant to drink it, and glanced around the room. Some of the women had tilted up their masks just enough for the glass, while still keeping their faces in shadow. She followed suit, careful that the angle did not reveal her features. If she recognized some of the patrons, they would surely recognize her.

The champagne was light and sweet, and easy to drink.

"Not too quickly," the man warned. "It is best to keep one's head in such places, yes?"

She lowered her mask, leaving the champagne flute half-full. "I would expect so," she said.

"Then you have not been here before?"

She flushed, and was grateful he could not see. "I have not," she said. She'd given away too much. She was bad at this already.

"Neither have I," he confessed, though it seemed to her to be the opposite of a confession, given their environs. "To be honest, I would prefer not to be here. My employer, though, requested my attendance, and so here I am."

"Your employer?" she asked.

"Mr. Lamb," he said. Of course. No names. "The gentleman you were so carefully examining a few moments ago."

She stiffened. "I was not—" she began, but he silenced her with a shake of his head.

"Everyone here is doing the same. Staring. Wondering. Telling themselves stories about who these people really are. I am not immune. For example, I find myself wondering who you might be, when you step out of the dream and back into the waking world. Do you entertain many lovers? Or is there one man who has your keeping? Did you fall to your position, or rise to it? A great many questions, all too impolite to ask."

"Very impolite," Elinor agreed.

"When I woo a woman, I prefer to be able to ask questions. And to answer them. Such as the simplest question of all: what is your name?"

Elinor was silent.

"Of course you will not answer. Neither will I, though all these men have me at a disadvantage. There are not nearly so many of us in England as there are of them, hm? It would not be so difficult to find me when they wake. And so I think I will keep to the walls."

"I am not here to keep to the walls," Elinor said.

"Of course not. But you should keep away from him," he said, inclining his head toward Foyle. "Let some other woman make that mistake."

"And why are you so certain it would be a mistake?" she asked. "Do you think so poorly of your employer?"

"He is not a kind man," he said. "And not a gentle one. And not a clever one, or a strong one. He is remarkable largely by his failings."

"Then why work for him?"

"I owe him," he said, and did not elaborate. "It is your choice, of course. All things are your choice, in this place. But I would find a different man to dream with. And if you should find yourself in need of company along the walls, I suspect I will be very lonely, these next few days." He bent over her hand and kissed it.

"And who should I ask for?"

"Mr. Tiger," he said, his eyes glittering. "Your men are not so imaginative, I think."

"No," she said. "Apparently not." She might have picked another creature for him. The tiger was too obvious, too brutish. Some kind of cat, though, a slender, understated one with pricked ears and bright eyes.

"It seems you are not the only one interested in Mr. Lamb," the man said, and inclined his head. Elinor turned— and nearly fell over. Lord Farleigh stood on the other side of the room, a glass clutched in his hand and murder in his eyes.

"Mr. Tiger," she said. "We have not long been acquainted, but I must ask you for a favor."

He raised an eyebrow. "What favor would that be?" he asked.

"Get your employer out of this room as quickly as possible," she said, and hurried across the floor.

Colin had no idea which rooms best suited Foyle's proclivities, so he visited them all. Most seemed tame; the occupants of a few seemed to be trying very hard to be otherwise, to the point of creating an air of earnestness that quite spoiled the attempt. He had recognized many faces. They had undoubtedly recognized him. But the benefit of a party like M. Beauchene's was that no one could point a finger without implicating himself. Besides, there were plenty of circles in which his standing would rise if it was known that he had achieved such an exclusive invitation.

He guessed there were about thirty men in attendance, though the winding corridors and self-contained rooms made it seem like more as they moved to and fro. There were at least twice as many women, and a sizable staff. He hoped women and staff alike were being paid well. He had been reminded on three occasions—without provocation—that any woman without a mask who wore a white band around her arm was staff, and not to be touched or spoken to for anything but the most mundane request.

For a man of notoriously depraved appetites, M. Beauchene was certainly concerned with the well-being of the women in his employ.

Next to women, the thing in the greatest abundance was alcohol. Colin imbibed generously. It gave him something to do with his hands, which increasingly felt necessary, lest those hands appear available for a less wholesome occupation. In the spirit of variety, he endeavored not to repeat himself. It was not a difficult task. Brandy, whiskey, wine (red and white), champagne, port, Madeira, a cloyingly sweet cordial, and something that was served in tiny sip-sized cups and scorched all the way down.

He was sampling the port when he entered a room adorned in Grecian excess and spotted Foyle. He had only ever seen a picture of the man, and Foyle had his back to him, but Colin recognized him instantly. The rest of the room vanished. There was only Foyle. He had the look of a rat, and the same twitching mannerisms. Colin could not imagine those long-fingered hands anywhere near Marie. Not by her consent. He could not imagine her looking at this man with anything but contempt.

Or fear.

Suddenly, answers did not matter. The law did not matter. All that mattered was getting his hands around that man's throat. His vision swam, but he shook his head to clear it. Dratted wine.

He started forward.

A hand caught his. He jerked around, lips peeled back from his teeth. A woman stood beside him, her masked face tilted up toward his. He stilled.

She looked like Elinor. Or perhaps it was only that he had hardly been able to think of anyone but Elinor, the past few days. This woman had the same auburn hair, pitched nearly black in the dim light, hints of fire in every strand where the candlelight caught it. Pale skin, a long neck. His eye followed the swoop of her clavicle, dove to the low cut of her collar.

He wetted his lips, and realized that she had pressed something into his palm. He looked down. It was a token. A small cat, its tail tucked over its paws in an almost coquettish pose.

She was offering herself to him. This woman who, beneath a mask, was indistinguishable from the woman he had dreamed of for five years.

He tore his gaze away from her. Foyle. That was why he was here.

But the man was gone.

Two doorways led out of the room; he might have gone through either. Colin lurched toward the nearest. The woman's hand closed around his wrist, fetching him up short.

"I have to . . ." he said, but she put the tips of her fingers to his lips and shook her head. She tugged on his arm. When he didn't move, she stood up on the tips of her toes. Cool porcelain brushed his ear.

"He can wait until tomorrow," she whispered, her voice oddly hoarse. "I will not."

Oh, hell. He was drunk. Entirely too drunk to hold his own in a fight. And God, the woman was beautiful. Her hands were around his neck, now, her touch light, sending prickles down his spine. She ran her fingertips over his shoulder and down his chest, then spun. She cast an inviting look over her shoulder and crooked a finger.

Tomorrow. Tomorrow he would be sober. He would be ready to face Foyle.

She'd done him a favor, he decided, thoughts muzzy. He couldn't kill the man in front of—what were they called? *Witnesses.*

He dashed back the rest of the port and handed the glass to the nearest satyr, resting it on the creature's upturned palm, and followed the woman. She led him through the rooms with practiced ease, and around to a staircase.

"Which room?" she asked, still in that hoarse whisper.

"Erm." He patted his pockets, looking for his token. "Bird. White one. Hats."

She let out a short huff and seized hold of his hand. She all but dragged him up the stairs.

"Egret!" he remembered as they crested the top, but she was already moving for the marked door. She held out her hand. Lovely hand, it was. Elinor had lovely hands, too. Graceful.

"Key," she said.

She didn't sound quite so inviting as she had downstairs. He frowned, but fumbled around until he found the key and handed it over. She had the door open in a moment and herded him in. Herded him. It lacked the elegance of a proper seduction, but he was suddenly beyond caring. There was the bed, the linens crisp and overlaid with burgundy and silver silk coverings, and there was the girl, standing with her back to it.

He moved to her. Some part of him insisted that he stop, that he was being foolish, but it was easy to ignore. He put his mouth to her neck, his hands pulling at her collar, trying to slip her dress down over her shoulders.

She pushed him away with one hand and reached for her mask. He caught its edge, held it in place. "No," he said. "Please, leave it."

The moment she removed it, the illusion would shatter. He would be looking at some other woman.

He knew he would regret this. He knew it wasn't her.

It didn't matter. He wanted her. And for tonight, he could pretend she wanted him.

Chapter 15

❧

Elinor had only seconds to react. She'd had to hope that Mr. Tiger would follow her directive; she didn't have time to convince him. She all but sprinted across the room. The cat was in her hand before she had quite realized what she was doing, and then she was pressing it into Lord Farleigh's palm. She was twining her hands around his neck, she was whispering to him.

She wasn't altogether certain where it had all come from. She had never attempted to seduce someone, much less in such a compact timeframe. The most shocking thing was that it *worked*. The Indian gentleman whisked Foyle away, and Lord Farleigh fixed his attention on her.

It helped, she reflected, that he appeared to have drunk half his weight in spirits. He could barely stay upright; she doubted he would remember Foyle had been there once the man was out of sight. And once his attention was fixed on her, it was simple to guide him up to his room.

There, her plan faltered. He fell on her like—well, like a man who had just been led up to his room by a courtesan. His lips were on her neck and his hands on her shoulders, making their way to her breasts with determination. She shoved him away. She hadn't wanted to reveal herself, only to get him away from Foyle, but she needed some kind of shock to shake him out of his single-minded fixation. She reached to untie the ribbons that secured the mask.

"No," he said. He held the mask in place. "Please, leave it."

She froze. The raw desire in his voice sparked an answering heat in her core.

Then, "Elinor," he whispered, as if to himself. Her hands shook, and she bit back a sharp gasp. He knew. "You look like her," he said, and then she understood.

He'd kissed her twice. He'd wanted her. Her body, if nothing else. He wanted her now. And God help her, she wanted him. One night. Behind the mask. It would mean nothing in the morning. She wouldn't remain; she would vanish. He need never know the truth, but she would have this for herself.

And so she drew him toward her. He pushed her back, onto the bed, and she pulled him with her. His fingers were more sure now, finding the buttons that secured her dress. He fumbled with them a moment, his hands under her, then yanked her up and tore. The buttons flew off, scattering over the bedspread. Together they worked her arms and torso free of the dress, leaving the fabric bunched at her waist. She wore a thin corset beneath, and he made a sound of frustration halfway to a growl. She almost laughed.

"A moment," she said, remembering to roughen her voice so he would not recognize it. She sat up, reaching back to loosen the laces. He rolled to the side to give her room, one hand on her hip, playing at the lower edge of the corset.

The laces snagged. She muttered a curse and bent her neck, trying to get a look. Finally they came loose, and she tugged at the corset to get it loose enough to slip over her head. "Sorry," she muttered. Lord Farleigh did not reply.

She looked over at him. He lay on his back, one finger still propped on her hip. His eyes were closed, his mouth half-opened. And as she watched, he began to snore.

"You must be joking," she said to herself. She touched his shoulder. "Mr. Egret." No response. She gave him a little shake. "Lord Farleigh. *Colin.*" But there was no reply. She let out a groan. "You are *insufferable.*"

He did not reply. The drink had caught up with him, apparently, and dragged him well and thoroughly under. Elinor scowled at him. She smacked his shoulder, then gave him a hard shake. He shifted a little, and the snoring stopped. He didn't wake.

"Drat," she said. There was no waking him up from that. She rose. Her skin was still hot, the core of her filled with a warm pressure that demanded what had been promised.

A ewer of water and a basin rested in the corner of the room. She poured cool water over her hands and splashed it on her neck and chest. Cold droplets ran between her breasts, only serving to elicit a little shiver from her. She shut her eyes.

"That's quite enough of that, Elinor," she told herself, and braced her hands against her sides. She inspected herself in the mirror on the wall. Her hair stood around her mask in frayed wisps. The top of her dress hung about her waist, shapeless and smushed. Her skin was flushed, and her pulse was coming entirely too fast.

She removed the mask. It was her, then, in that mirror. Not a fearless courtesan.

But it was not fear or shame she felt, staring at that reflection. She suspected it was simple disappointment. She had to admit she had not been *entirely* put out at the sudden redirection of her evening's efforts. She had to admit that she had wondered rather extensively just how deserved Lord Farleigh's reputation was, where women were concerned.

"Not very, judging by this evidence," she muttered peevishly, and straightened her shoulders. She'd handled the problem. Not the way she wished to, granted, but Lord Farleigh was not currently engaged in murdering Edward Foyle, so she could only count this as a success.

Now it was time to get back to the business at hand.

She got her arms back into her sleeves. The buttons were done for, and it gaped open at the back, but she was at least covered. She left the mask cocked up, letting her see and breathe freely, and went back to Lord Farleigh.

His legs hung over the side of the bed. He was going to

have a hell of a headache in the morning, she thought with some satisfaction.

She bent and unlaced his boots, then pried them from his feet. He hardly twitched.

He'd managed to get the buttons of his breeches undone, and after a moment's consideration she tugged those off, too, leaving his drawers in place. With more effort, she divested him of jacket, waistcoat, and peripheral items, and folded everything on a chair near the bed. At least he would have something to wear in the morning; she couldn't abide the thought of such lovely clothes being slept on.

She stood with arms akimbo and watched him sleep. There was nothing more to be done for him. He certainly posed no danger to Foyle in his condition.

And it was not even eleven o'clock. She had time yet.

She slipped back out of the room, remembering to secure her mask, just as another masked woman trotted down the hallway, adjusting her bodice.

"That was quick, *cherie*," she said, pausing. "Did I not just see you go in there?"

"He passed out," Elinor said.

The woman chuckled. "He is not the first tonight, and he won't be the last. Oh no, your dress! Quick, let's get you a new one." She waved at Elinor to follow. Elinor fell gratefully into her wake. There were other women about, some masked and some now with bare faces and flushed cheeks. They called greetings to one another, but all seemed to have somewhere to be. Elinor's savior brought them through to a room where rack upon rack of dresses hung. None terribly well-made, but they'd pass for beautiful in candlelight, Elinor supposed.

"Here, try this one," the woman said. "It'll look lovely with your hair." She'd selected a deep red gown with a low waist and a collar that would cut just above the crest of Elinor's bosom. "Need help?"

Elinor accepted the assistance gratefully, and the woman helped her step out of the ruined dress. Then she was tutting over Elinor's hair, buttoning up the new gown, and patting her on the cheek—or rather, the mask's cheek.

"There you are. Pretty as can be. Are you holding up? No problems?"

It took Elinor a moment to catch up with herself. The woman seemed to be running at twice the speed of a normal human being. "Fine," she said.

"Well, if you have any trouble, we want to know about it."

"We?"

"Monsieur Beauchene and I," she said kindly, and for the first time Elinor detected the hint of a Parisian accent. "This is not some Hellfire club. We have *standards*," she said. Elinor realized with a start who this woman must be.

"Madame Beauchene?" she said, voice fluttering with the hint of nerves.

"Not tonight," the woman said, and winked. "Now. Go back out there, and do try to enjoy yourself."

She patted Elinor's cheek again, clasped her hands, and then turned her around by her shoulders. Elinor stumbled away, reeling. She'd assumed Monsieur Beauchene was a bachelor. Or at the very least, that his wife would be very far away and very ignorant.

She took the woman's advice, though, and hurried back down the stairs. There might still be time to find Foyle. She went to the satyr room first, but found no sign of either Foyle or his employee. She wandered, then, passing through each room slowly. Twice a man caught her arm and whispered a suggestion in her ear. Each time she shook her head and slipped by.

She found Mr. Tiger in a room made to look something like the inside of a circus tent. A woman in an acrobat's outfit sat suspended from a hoop, hanging a few feet off the ground, her mask painted in an expression of eternal laughter.

"Looking for Mr. Lamb again?" the Tiger asked her when she approached. "What happened to your other friend?"

"He is asleep," she said delicately. "Thank you for helping me."

"A blind man could have seen he had violence on his mind," he said. "Lucky for my employer that you provided a more engaging subject for his thoughts. Why are you interested in Mr. Lamb?"

She swallowed. "I have questions for him," she admitted. She did not know that trusting this man was wise, but she was not trained in subterfuge.

"Did he do something to you?" he asked. "Have you one of his little children hidden away, and you are looking for a few coins for the child's education? If so, I am happy to handle the matter. I have done so before."

She tasted something sour in her throat. "No," she said. "I have no children."

"Hmm." He looked out over the room and took a sip of his wine.

"How did you come to work for him?" she asked. "You said you owed him, and that is why you don't leave. But did he hire you in India? That's where you're from, isn't it?"

"It is," he said. "And yes, that is where I was hired. I worked for a cousin of his."

Lady Copeland. It had to be. Perhaps she would not need to speak with Foyle at all.

"I believe I know which cousin you mean," she said. "Tell me. Did you know a woman named Marie Hayes?"

He stilled then. He did not look at her, but tension stole across him like the slow closing of a fist. "Do not ask these questions," he said. "Do not speak to Mr. Lamb. And keep your friend away from him. No good will come of it."

"I need—"

"Mr. Lamb has already retired for the evening, and you should be grateful it is with someone else," he snapped. Anger entered his voice for the first time. "Go back to your friend. And if you have any sense, leave tomorrow."

"Mr. Tiger—"

But the false name only made him flinch. "Good night, memsahib," he said with exaggerated courtesy, and was gone before she could speak another word.

The woman on the hoop gave a nervous giggle. Elinor glared at her.

"Sorry," the woman said. They were the only two in the room now. "You might try the atrium. The poets like to drape themselves among the foliage. At least you'd get to hear every possible word for the color of your hair."

"And the shape of my bosom, I suppose," Elinor said. "Thank you for the advice. Do you get to get down at any point?"

"Not for another hour," she said. "But there's always at least one chap waiting when I do." She winked. Or at least, Elinor thought she did; it was hard to tell through the blasted mask.

"Good luck, then," she said.

She trudged back up the stairs. She hadn't ever located her room; she hadn't thought she'd need it. She hadn't thought she'd need more than one dress, either.

After a moment's hesitation, she slipped back into the Egret room. Lord Farleigh had dragged himself further up on the bed, and sprawled out across most of it. She eyed the chair in the corner. It looked terribly uncomfortable, and she was suddenly exhausted.

She stripped down to her chemise and considered the bed. She'd very nearly let Lord Farleigh ravish her. She was dressed as a courtesan in a house full of courtesans. It was not the time to fret about propriety.

She wriggled beneath the covers, shoving Lord Farleigh off to the side enough for her to slot herself against the edge of the bed. She set her mask on the table beside her and, after one last glance at the sleeping man, blew out the candle.

Chapter 16

Light pressed against Colin's eyelids, bringing with it searing pain. No, *searing* wasn't the right word. Stabbing? Better. He groaned and covered his eyes with his hand. *Brilliant, Farleigh. Exactly what you should do when you set out to kill a man: get so stinking drunk you can't stand up straight.*

He hadn't killed Foyle. He remembered that much. Most of the evening was excessively hazy, but he remembered the interruption. And what an interruption.

He rolled over and squinted. He had a companion in the bed. Her hair was still up, baring those lovely shoulders. Over the curve of her cheek he could see the mask she'd worn the night before, resting on the table beside the bed. He supposed in a moment he'd see her properly, and any resemblance to Elinor would flee.

Just as well. Such sinful fantasies did not deserve to survive in daylight. The way he'd fallen on her—he would never have treated Elinor like that, not even if she would have him. He'd acted like a beast. And he'd . . .

He frowned. Damn the drink. He remembered her smooth skin, remembered tearing off her dress, but everything went dark after that. Just punishment, he decided. He should not have indulged his base desires so. Let the memory of pleasure be denied him, then, and leave only the shame.

The woman stirred in her sleep. He supposed he should apologize to her. Or perhaps it was better to slip out now, and pretend it had never happened.

She turned, brushing the back of her hand against her face as her eyes began to open.

His heart stopped.

She looked up at him through dark lashes. Her face was sleep-creased and her eyes bleary, but there was no mistaking that face.

"Elinor?" he said, voice a strangled croak.

She yawned and sat up, tucking strands of hair behind her ears. "Oh good, you're alive. I thought you might have drowned yourself," she said.

Her chemise clung to her curves. He could see the dark outline of her nipples beneath the thin fabric. There was a tear at the sleeve. He'd done that. He'd . . .

"You can't be here," he said. "You can't be you. She was . . . she wasn't . . ."

"Relax, Lord Farleigh," she said, in a tone that banished all hope that this might be some lingering effect of alcohol. He thrashed his way out of the bed and stood, the room tilting around him.

"No," he said. "God. Martin will kill me. Kitty will kill me. Joan will kill me twice."

"Sit back down before you fall," Elinor snapped.

"I'm a dead man," he said. If he had any decency at all, he'd off himself and spare them the trouble. He'd ravished Elinor Hargrove. "I am so, so sorry," he said. She raised an eyebrow. "I am the worst of men. I had no idea . . . you were wearing the mask, and . . ."

"I didn't tell you not to," she said reasonably.

"But it wasn't *you*," he said desperately. "You realize what this means? I'll have to break the engagement, of course. I'll apply for a special license. We can take care of it before we even speak to Martin; that will be best. He's less likely to gut me if we're already married."

"We don't have to get married," Elinor said impatiently.

He paused. "Of course we do. I . . . you could be with child." A not insignificant part of him was rather thrilled at the idea. But he didn't want her that way. Didn't want a marriage of necessity or regret, even if it would mean he had *her*.

She seemed on the verge of saying something. Then she shut her mouth with a soft click of teeth and narrowed her eyes. "You were going to kill Edward Foyle, weren't you?"

"How . . . how do you know about that? Hang on. What are you doing here?" Reality seemed to catch up to him all at once. He looked around, as if an explanation were hiding in a corner somewhere. The light from the window lanced across his eyes again, and he shut them with a wince. "You were a courtesan. Last night. Why?"

"Because this is where Edward Foyle could be found, and being a courtesan is how I could get in," Elinor said, as if it were the most reasonable thing in the world. "Your sister—"

"Dear God, is Phoebe here?"

She laughed at that. "Heavens, no. It's only me, Lord Farleigh. But she wanted information from Foyle, and I volunteered to get it for her. She doesn't know I'm here; she thinks I sent a courtesan. A real one, I mean. I intended to get Foyle alone, and find out from him what he has on your family."

He stared at her. "That's not a bad plan," he said. "*Apart from the fact that you had to pretend to be a courtesan. What were you thinking?*"

"That I was bored, I suppose," Elinor said. "And that it was worth trying. It is a good thing I was here, too, or you would be dead or brought up on charges by now. What on earth were *you* thinking, going after him like that?"

"I wanted revenge," he said darkly.

"For what?"

"For—what happened."

"Which is?"

"I don't know the details. But I know enough."

"Then you still intend to kill him."

"Of course I do."

She sat back, examining him with the intense scrutiny she

so often employed. He felt dissected under her gaze. "What if there were a chance to find out exactly what had happened? To make sure that the right men pay for what happened, and that your family is protected? And to do it without resorting to murder?"

"I know who is responsible. Foyle is the only one I can reach. It will be enough."

"As you have mentioned, you are engaged. Do you intend to leave your fiancée so stained? No. And have you thought of what damage Foyle could do? He surely has arrangements in the case of his demise, regarding whatever materials he has on Marie. You are a smarter man than that, when you are not drunk." She stood. The chemise shifted over her skin. The light pierced through the fabric with the same insistence as his muddled mind, lighting every curve of her body. His own body responded despite him.

"I should take you home," he said.

"You will do no such thing. I had a conversation with an associate of Foyle's last night that has left me no doubt that there is far more to the story of Marie's death than your sisters know. More than you know, as well. It is obvious that you will not be content until some form of justice is delivered. Your approach is unacceptable. Therefore, I insist on mine."

"Why do you care? She wasn't your sister."

"She was family," she said. "And so are you, as a consequence. It's obvious that this is killing you. Marie would be heartbroken to see it. And so I won't allow it."

He came around the bed. She stood her ground, glaring up at him. There was such fire in her eyes. He had never seen her like that.

"I could throw you into a carriage," he said. "I could tie you up, if I had to. God knows there are enough ropes in this place." She gave a shiver. He clenched a hand, desire spiking through him. *Degenerate*, he berated himself. "I will not allow you to stay here."

Her eyes hardened. "What do you supposed would happen if I told my brother that you bedded me?" she said. "I could tell your future father-in-law."

"It would ruin you."

"I would bear it," she said. "I have no prospects to damage, and God knows my family would not throw me out."

"Then we'd marry," he said, trying to sound nonchalant.

She turned up her chin. "I would refuse you."

That stopped him in his tracks. For it to be known, and for her to turn him away—it would be the end of his friendship with Martin. His sisters would never forgive him. And neither would Levenbane. It was one thing to take a mistress quietly, after the wedding. Another to humiliate his bride-to-be.

"What do you want from me?" he asked.

"I am in need of assistance and protection," Elinor said. "And you cannot get close to Foyle. We can help each other. Claim me."

Oh, God. He watched her lips form the words, and found himself compelled forward another step.

"If you claim me, the other men here will leave me be," she said. "I can focus on Foyle."

"Not if you are claimed."

"I can if you are the sort who enjoys seeing his woman with other men," she pointed out.

"I am not," he ground out. He did not want to picture her with another man. Any other man. To picture her with Foyle was an abomination.

"And I am not a prostitute," she said. "We play our parts. And at the end of it, perhaps we will know enough to offer some peace to your sister's memory."

She was right. At least, if she had been anyone else she would have been right. But he couldn't let her do this. Martin—

"Don't think about my brother," she said sharply.

"Has anyone ever accused you of witchcraft?" he asked.

"It does not take a witch to guess where your mind is going. Especially as I imagine it is operating quite slowly this morning," she said. "That's another thing. You will stop drinking."

"You are setting terms now?"

"I'm blackmailing you," she said plainly. "For your own good, mind you."

"And what about my terms?"

"I was not aware that you had any."

He had to talk her out of this idiotic notion. The only thing worse than leaving and accepting the ensuing scandal would be to stay and have Elinor discovered. The loss of her virginity might not destroy her, but word of this surely would.

"Elinor," he began.

She raised an eyebrow. "Lord Farleigh, I would like you to contemplate history for a moment. When have you ever won an argument with me?"

"I'm usually smart enough not to start one," Colin said.

"I have made the decision to stay. You can either help me, or leave me on my own in this place. That is the decision before you. Make it wisely."

He had the sudden urge to shake her, as if the foolish notion would rattle right out of her skull and onto the floor. He ground his teeth together. His fist clenched at his side. "I cannot allow you to ruin yourself further."

"I wasn't the one who did the ruining," she shot back.

He blanched. He was definitely going to hell. And Martin was going to send him there. Well. Perhaps there was still a way to dissuade her from this madness.

"Fine," he said. "I agree. On one condition."

"And what, precisely, is that condition?" Elinor asked.

Elinor was impressed with how level her voice remained. One might imagine, observing her without the advantage of hearing her thoughts, that she was calm and composed. In truth, she could barely believe half of what she was saying.

Sometime last night she had decided quite definitively that come the morning, she would leave the chateau, taking Lord Farleigh with her. The plan had begun to fracture when she witnessed the level of horror in Lord Farleigh's eyes at discovering her in his bed. The truth was, she was still rather irritated with him for interfering with what had been a perfectly serviceable scheme.

Not to mention for his failure to make that interference a pleasurable diversion.

She ought to have simply told him that he had passed out, leaving her virtue—such as it was—intact. Failing to tell him was unconscionable. Except that she was absolutely certain that the moment she did tell him, he would make good on his threat to toss her in a carriage headed back toward London. And then he would kill Foyle, because he was the most idiotically stubborn man she knew.

"Your condition," Elinor prompted him.

"It's a very simple one," Lord Farleigh said. "But I'm afraid that it is not negotiable." He walked to the chair where she had folded his clothes and began to rummage through them.

"And what is it?" she asked. She supposed she ought to afford him *some* concession. He was looking thoroughly browbeaten. She was only protecting him from himself, of course. He could not be allowed to take irrevocable action against Foyle.

Lord Farleigh straightened, turning back to her. "You are asking me to shield you. To *claim* you. And you offer nothing in return. I am not a weapon to be wielded, *Lady* Elinor. I am not your tool. And when I claim a woman, I do it thoroughly." His gaze pierced her. Her mouth felt dry; she wetted her lips. He paced forward, and suddenly she was aware of just how little she was wearing.

"What exactly do you mean?" she asked. Her voice bordered on hoarse. She knew exactly what he meant, and it made her skin flush with the unfulfilled promise of the night before. He could not be saying what she knew he was—and yet she wanted him to say it.

"If I claim you, you are mine," he said. "For as long as we are here. For as long as you wear that mask." Another step, and he was nearly to her. He opened his hand, letting the silver egret drop, dangling from its black ribbon. "Mine to do with as I wish, as long as we are inside this room. Out there, I will obey your rules. Here the rules are mine to set."

"I will not risk getting with child," Elinor said, practicality leaping to the fore. She blinked. She was not genuinely considering this, was she?

"Any more than you already have, you mean?" Lord Farleigh asked. "Don't worry. There is plenty of pleasure to be found without risking that. Especially in this house."

A blush was creeping up her neck. She had seen enough last night to considerably expand her imagination on that front. It should have sent her running.

But no one knew that she was here. Lord Farleigh could never tell anyone. Would never tell, even if he could. And God help her, she wanted him. Wanted this, however fleeting an illusion it was, for the space of an hour or a day or a week. She could see the long path of her life laid out before her, growing old in her brother's household, and she wasn't ready for it.

He was waiting for her to flinch. He was waiting for her to break that stare, to agree to go home to that life of loneliness. And that, more than anything, made her decision for her.

She closed the last of the distance to him, and tilted her chin so that their lips nearly met.

"I accept."

They were the two most exquisitely painful words that had ever graced a woman's lips, Colin decided. And he could not quite believe she had spoken them.

"You accept," he repeated.

She rocked back on her heels, drawing away from him. "It is what you wanted, isn't it?" she asked. Now she was waiting for *him* to flinch, was she? Then she'd be disappointed. The Marquess of Farleigh did not back down. "The worst is already done, isn't it?"

"The worst." Not how he liked his lovers to describe their private interludes.

"I wouldn't worry," she said, hinting at a smile. "Your second attempts do seem to go much smoother than the first."

He wanted more than anything to have her, in that moment. To crush her to him, and feel her body against his. To prove to her that he was indeed more than capable of making a lasting second impression.

If he had possessed a shred of honor, he would have quashed that instinct. He would have backed away from her. He would have made arrangements for them both to leave, and accepted whatever consequences he must.

Instead, he set the ribbon around her neck, tying it loosely into place, and then traced the edge of it, letting his fingertips come to rest at her clavicle just below the silver bird.

"We have a deal, then," he said.

She nodded tightly. "Right. A deal."

He wanted to kiss her then, but she looked as if she expected him to pounce on her that moment—and it was not desire in her eyes so much as trepidation. He was a brute. She didn't know what she was promising him. One night—which he dearly hoped had not been so terrible as she intimated—would not rob her of her innocence completely.

He dropped his hand and cleared his throat, batting back the desire still thudding away at him, body and mind. "To begin with, we will need a plan," he said.

She relaxed a fraction, and stepped back briskly. "That does seem necessary," she said. "Though I suspect you need some food and a great quantity of water before any serious thinking occurs." She spoke rapidly, covering her nervousness badly.

He couldn't have her, he realized. He must retain some shred of honor, because he couldn't bring himself to bed a woman who didn't truly want him, however willing she insisted that she was. He half-smiled, rueful. He had never more wished to be a man without morals than in this moment.

"What?" she said. "Why are you smiling?"

"Food sounds excellent," he said. "And water, yes. A great deal of it. Someone appears to have siphoned all of mine out of me in the night."

"I should go find some, then," Elinor said uncertainly.

"Definitely," Colin said, and he watched the last of the

nervousness bleed out of her. He crossed to the bedside table and held out her mask to her. "Don't forget this," he said.

She took it from him, her movements hesitant. She held it in front of her for a long moment. He thought that she might say something, but finally she turned from him. She secured the mask and slipped into her gown, and was gone without speaking another word.

Colin sank onto the bed.

Maybe by the time they had eaten, one of them would have found out where they'd misplaced their sanity.

Chapter 17

❧

Elinor did better than simply bring food. She brought a mountain of it, along with a veritable ocean of strong tea. She set it all out on the bed and they sat across from one another, silent while they ate their fill. Colin watched her as they ate. She had borrowed another dress, this one suitable for daytime wear. It was white with petite bundles of red flowers, and sat a bit tight around her bosom. He did not mind the effect, though she kept tugging at it. He didn't really mind that, either.

"We should make sure that we are operating from the same set of information," Elinor said after she had finished off her tea. "What Phoebe was able to glean is incomplete at best."

"I thought I had put her off this particular line of inquiry years ago."

"Apparently not thoroughly enough."

"I cannot abide dull-witted women, but I admit they would be easier to manage," he said.

"Do you prefer dull-witted men, then?" she asked sweetly. "I believe that is a different party entirely."

He choked. "You shouldn't know about that sort of thing."

"I am not an innocent," Elinor said. Not in mind nor in

body, and he was reminded that the latter was his fault. "In any case, Marie. You believe that she was tricked into marrying Foyle, and swindled of her rights to the mines. Do you know what he used to blackmail her?"

He considered whether he should tell her about the sketch. He'd brought it with him, thinking perhaps to confront Foyle with it. But he wasn't ready to tarnish her memory in Elinor's eyes. Not yet. "I'm not certain," he said.

"We need to know."

"We don't," he said. "What we need is to see Foyle punished."

"And how do you intend to do that, exactly, unless we know what we are punishing him for?" she asked.

He let out a snarl and stood. "This was meant to be simple. It was meant to be clean."

"There is nothing clean in murder," Elinor said. "And it is worth a little effort to refrain from the deed. Now sit down."

He spun and pounced on her, pinning her wrists to the bed beside her legs. She leaned back, away from him, but kept her torso stiff, refusing to fall back. "May I remind you," he said, "that while we are inside this room, I make the rules?"

"Then do you wish to change the topic?" she asked. She arched her back, lifting her breasts. His gaze darted down without prompting, but he wrenched it back up again. She met his eyes with a look of challenge. "You need only tell me what to do, and I will do it."

Oh, how he wanted to oblige. But he released her wrists, straightening up. He bit the inside of his cheek to break that particular train of thought. "No," he said. He turned away and began to pace. She let out a breath. She almost sounded disappointed.

"Which is more important to you, Lord Farleigh?" Elinor asked after a moment. "To see Foyle punished, or see that your family is safe?"

He paused in his pacing. "I want both," he said.

"You may have to choose," Elinor said. "Certainly if you had killed him last night, your family would be anything but safe. You must realize that."

Damn her. Of course he did. A thing like this ought to have been simple. "Then I won't kill him outright. I'll challenge him to a duel. They never convict for that."

"Oh, yes. Your sisters' reputations will be ever so improved. I'm sure Lady Penelope will be thrilled to wed a not-actually-convicted murderer," Elinor said. "The moment you challenge that man, he'll use whatever leverage he has to get out of it. Unless you think he has some well of courage I am not aware of."

"I will not let him escape without punishment."

She sighed. "Then at least let us deal with the matter of the blackmail before it's down to pistols," she said.

"That much I see the wisdom of," Colin said. "That was my intention in the first place, you know. But then he was there, and—"

"I understand," she said. "I cannot say I have never contemplated strangling the man myself."

He sat beside her on the bed heavily. "Which returns us to where to begin," he said.

"We get him to speak to us." She paused. "Foyle has an employee with him. Mr. Tiger, or so he is to be called here. He has a poor opinion of Foyle. He said that he owes him, but then he warned me away from him. He knows more than he has said, but I don't think he'll tell us anything. And he knows we're both interested."

"Then we will have to get Foyle alone, away from him," Colin said, considering. "I think I saw him last night. Mr. Tiger, I mean."

"Are you sure you didn't see two or three of him?" Elinor asked, teasing.

"It probably *is* best that I don't drink." He'd resented her for that one, but she was right. And God knew he wasn't going to keep sober on his own.

"I have an idea to keep Mr. Tiger"—here she paused and made a face—"away from us for the evening. Then you and I should approach Foyle together. He doesn't know you, does he?"

Colin shook his head. "We've never met."

"Good. Then we can simply be friendly and interested. Get him drunk, and get him talking about India. We'll see what comes up. We don't have enough to push in any particular direction, so we'll have to hope he feels like talking."

"Scoundrels like that always do, sooner or later," Colin said.

"And you have so much experience with scoundrels."

"More than you," he said. She gave him a look that suggested she could argue the point.

"You should meet some of the guests at Thornwald," she said. "Joan keeps interesting company."

"Apparently, she's quite fond of courtesans and blackmailers," he said.

The corner of her mouth quirked. "You're looking for the singular on the second count, unless there are other blackmailers I haven't met," she said.

"But multiple courtesans?"

"One that might claim the title. The others are, I think, less lofty in their practice of the occupation. Have you heard of Madame Lavigne?"

"Heard of her? I know men who would give a significant portion of their teeth for a glance from the woman," he said. "They say she's the illegitimate daughter of a French courtier, and that a hundred men wrote letters begging her not to leave the continent. You've *met* her?"

"Mm," Elinor said, clearly enjoying his shock. "She taught me a great many things."

He had stopped pacing. She watched him with half-lidded eyes. *No, don't follow that thread*, he told himself. *Whatever you do, don't go there, or we will not get anything done.* He cleared his throat emphatically. "Fascinating," he managed, and Elinor looked away to hide a smile.

"What is our first step, then?" she asked.

"We should begin by observing from afar," he decided. "Then we will be able to determine the most appropriate method of attack. I wish you'd seen who caught his eye last night."

"I know it wasn't the acrobat, but that's it," Elinor said

with an apologetic shrug. "We shall have to hope he isn't particular."

Colin frowned. "Just to be clear," he said, "we're only to talk to him."

"That is the plan."

"He won't touch you," he continued.

"I think jealousy is frowned upon here," Elinor said.

"It isn't jealousy. It's that it's *him*. After what he has done to my family . . . If he lays a hand on you, I am not certain I will be able to let him keep it."

As with any social occasion worth its salt, the day's activities did not properly begin until the midafternoon. Elinor spent the intervening time securing herself a wardrobe that would function for the remaining days. The house had the dense quiet of a rest after overexertion, and she made a circuit of the rooms in daylight. The curtains had been drawn back, the glasses cleared away, the spills sopped up. The decorations remained eccentric, but the mystery was gone out of the place. With different props, it might be a cheerful summer home. She supposed it very well might be, for all but this one week.

One by one, the partygoers emerged, flocking out to the lawns with picnic baskets and outdoor diversions. The ladies dressed in fresh frocks, light and simple compared to the fare of the evening before. If it were not for the masks, it might have passed as any other summer party.

Elinor took Lord Farleigh's arm as they exited the house, forcing herself to remain relaxed. She could not reconcile her nervousness at his touch with her eagerness, her fear with her longing. It was not as easy as she'd hoped to shed her real life, and embrace this fantasy.

"It seems so normal," she commented.

"You know, I've met most of these men," Farleigh said. "I knew we were a debauched bunch as a rule, but honestly. You know that man over there is a magistrate? Lewis, as I recall. Very fair-minded. Sterling reputation."

The man in question was currently being fed grapes by a buxom redhead.

"You're not going to face censure for being here, are you?" Elinor asked.

"God, no. It can only improve my reputation," Lord Farleigh said.

"Being a man must be very strange," Elinor replied, then nodded down the lawn. She'd spotted Foyle, reclining on a blanket with two women in attendance. The Indian gentleman leaned against the lip of a fountain some distance away, watching but not joining in. He noted her presence and gave her a nod. As much a warning as a greeting, she thought, and steered Farleigh to a point she hoped would not seem too close for the Tiger's comfort. The wind lifted Foyle's voice, carrying it clearly to her, and she stopped. There was a bench only a few feet away; by silent agreement, she and Farleigh took their seats.

One of the girls was giggling. Neither, Elinor noted, wore a token—lamb or otherwise. "And have you ridden an elephant?" the laughing girl asked.

"I've ridden a dozen elephants," Foyle said, with the air of a boastful man trying to sound casual.

"I should be ever so frightened," the girl said. She played with his sleeve, gazing up at him adoringly. "It would be such a long way to fall. And those things they have—the trunks. They're frightful!"

"Oh, I don't think you'd be afraid of a thick trunk," Foyle said, and the three of them laughed.

"So far," Farleigh said, bending his head to her ear, "he seems more crass than evil."

"Did you expect him to start every conversation with a good cackle?" Elinor asked. Foyle glanced briefly in their direction. "We should probably come up with some way to appear occupied."

"I could lay my head in your lap and let you stroke my hair," Farleigh suggested wryly.

"You most certainly could not."

"You will have to relax, if you wish to play your role," he said.

"I am relaxed." A blatant lie. She was coiled tight as a cobra. He placed a hand lightly on her back.

"No one will hurt you when I'm here. Least of all me."

She looked at him sharply, and found only sincerity in his expression. She willed her limbs to relax. His thumb made a soft circle against her shoulder blade.

"Better," he said. He gave her a teasing smile. "Now are you sure you don't want me to put my head in your lap? I thought that you might enjoy it. I do have excellent hair."

"I'm sure the opera singers rhapsodize about your golden locks," Elinor said with a roll of her eyes. He was trying to goad her out of her nervousness, and it was working, damn him.

Farleigh cleared his throat. "You know about them? It's been two years since I had a mistress, you know."

"It doesn't matter to me."

"And they were all short-term arrangements. Purely for mutual entertainment, you understand. I like to think we both got what we were looking for."

"Then you were looking for dramatic fights in the middle of the street? Because those are the stories I've heard," Elinor said. Truthfully, she was envious of her male peers' ability to casually take lovers, to taste the fruits of womanhood before they bought the whole tree. But she did enjoy watching him squirm.

"They were not that dramatic," he protested.

"I believe one woman threw a shoe at your head." Elinor said.

"Oh. She was *not* my mistress," Farleigh said with a theatrical wince. "And rather upset about the fact."

"The lovely thing about that story is that it *seems* like you are being self-deprecating, but the moral is that you drive women mad with desire," Elinor said.

"Huh. Must be why I like it so much," Farleigh said. "Hush."

She started to berate him, but he put a finger to her lips and nodded toward Foyle. She quieted, listening.

"I could never go back," Foyle was saying.

"Why not? It sounds exciting," said the bolder of the women.

"India holds too many painful memories," he went on with a sigh. "You see, I lost my wife there."

"Your poor thing," said the giggler, smoothing her hand against his forearm. "That's terrible."

"She died in my arms," he said, voice growing distant. "I watched the light go out of her eyes. She breathed her last, and then . . . then she was still. I carry her with me in my heart, always. And so I cannot bear to return to the place that she loved." He heaved a long, sorrowful sigh. The girls cooed and plastered themselves to his sides, stroking at him with comforting motions.

"Bastard," Farleigh muttered. "He's using her to impress *whores*."

"Mr. Egret, I would mind my language," Elinor said. Whatever their profession, she did not like hearing these women referred to with such contempt. Not after more than one of them had been so very helpful to her. "Besides, you've missed the most important part of all of that."

"I have?" he said. His teeth were set. Even sober, he wanted to kill the man. She couldn't blame him, not entirely. If it had been her sister, she might have tried to thrash him herself.

"He's bored," she said. "He finds them dull. They are trying to please him, and he doesn't want to be pleased. He wants to win."

"You can tell all of that from an overheard conversation?"

She shrugged. She was used to learning a great deal from very little. It was what had kept her useful to her old, shallow friends for so long, and kept her occupied through years of her illness. She used to get herself close to the dance floor and make a game of guessing the content of a conversation by the few words she could overhear as a couple spun by.

With Foyle, it was mostly his tone, and the way his eyes roved. It was also the set of his arms, where he had them around the women. His hands were idle about their waists, and when his thumb grazed the underside of one girl's breast, and she leapt and laughed with delight, he recoiled. He was searching for more challenging conquests.

Perhaps if Elinor could make herself seem to be one, she could entice him to share more interesting tales of India than riding an elephant.

"Before we can hope to approach him, we shall have to deal with the bodyguard," Colin said, tipping his head toward the watchful Mr. Tiger.

Elinor patted his arm. "That much is simple," she said. "Leave it to me."

Chapter 18

❧

Elinor parted ways with Lord Farleigh as the afternoon wore on, and began an exploration of her own. Her mask provided her with a certain degree of protection, but she almost didn't need it; men's eyes slid first to her throat and, spotting the egret charm, slid just as quickly away. She doubted they would have registered her face if she'd thrown the mask into the bushes and paraded across the lawn. That she belonged to another man was a stronger deterrent than any expression of disinterest, which rankled her even as she recognized its use. She had always had the unspoken protection of her male relatives, her wealth, her position in society; she had never had cause to fear that her refusal would be disregarded. Now she was not Lady Elinor Hargrove; she was only a harlot like all the others, and as carefully as Beauchene constructed his rules, most of the men here would assume that her answer was yes without bothering to ask.

Except that she was owned.

By the time she located Madame Beauchene, the realization had nursed itself into a low-simmering resentment against Lord Farleigh. It was hardly his fault—except that he had placed terms and conditions on her ability to pursue

her own ends, and that it *was* his fault that her plan had been
interrupted the first night.

Madame Beauchene was entertaining a trio of men in a
room of red brocade and endless mirrors, her mask dangling
idly from one hand. Elinor supposed she could afford to
ignore the rules. Gold accents gilded every frame and piece
of furniture. The room had a kingly look the men could not
match. Nor could Madame Beauchene, though her audience
did not seem to care. She was a plain woman, no beauty to
look upon, but she entranced the eye nonetheless. Elinor
drew close, hesitating at the palpable edge of the woman's
sphere of attention, and was rewarded only with the flick of
Madame Beauchene's eyes to acknowledge her.

The older woman finished the anecdote she was sharing,
something about a muddy horseback ride and a stray sheep,
and then pardoned herself. She rose, smiling, and glided over
to Elinor. Every one of her fingers sported at least one ring,
and on them glittered gaudy gems. She was not a woman of
subtlety; she couldn't afford to be, Elinor decided, with looks
like that. She found another way to bowl men over.

"The girl with the torn buttons," Madame Beauchene
said. "I see you recovered your stride."

"I had a lovely night," Elinor said, not certain if that was
the right way to describe it.

"I wondered," Madame Beauchene said, "who you were.
You haven't been here before, and I didn't remember interviewing you."

"Interviewing?" Elinor said, mouth suddenly dry.

Madame Beauchene's tone was light, but with a chill
edge. "Nor did my husband. We try to speak to every one
of our girls before they arrive."

"Madame Lavigne referred me," Elinor said quickly.
"She said nothing of an interview."

"Ah, Madame Lavigne," the woman said, as if that settled
the matter. "That explains it. I was surprised when she asked
to come, and more surprised when she did not arrive."

Elinor saw a way toward an explanation, and smiled
warmly. "She had a fall, and injured her leg, but she did not

want to miss out. She asked me to go in her place, and tell her all about it on my return."

"As long as the telling omits certain details," the woman reminded her. "The privacy of our guests must be sacrosanct."

"Of course," Elinor agreed with a dip of her head.

"But there is a reason you've sought me out. Don't let me chatter on! What do you need?" She was the warm woman from the night before again, a shift so sudden that Elinor had the lurching feeling that it was an orchestrated performance.

"There is a man," Elinor said, refusing to lose her stride. "He became very interested in me last night, and today I find I am having a hard time avoiding him."

The woman's eyes lit. "If you feel threatened, we can speak with him."

"No," Elinor said quickly. She wanted the man out of the way, not confronted directly. "I do not think he means ill, but I'm not interested in his sort." The words curdled in her mouth as she said them. She sounded beastly.

"His sort?"

"His name is Mr. Tiger," she allowed, and the older woman's mouth pressed into a thin line.

"I did not think Mr. Tiger was much interested in the young ladies here."

Elinor gave a half shrug, as if helpless to explain it herself. "We spoke at some length last night," she said. "He gave me a drink. I did not think that obligated me to anything."

"It doesn't," Madame Beauchene said with a sigh. "It may seem odd, the rules we have in place. But it saves everyone trouble in the long run. It keeps us elevated above common entertainment, and attracts a finer class of guest. It is not against the rules to converse, or to linger longingly. If he laid hands on you against your wishes . . ."

"He hasn't," Elinor said.

"Then perhaps it would be better simply to distract him," Madame Beauchene said with a speculative look in her eye. "I think I can manage that, at least." She patted Elinor on the shoulder. "Now go enjoy yourself. You are too tightly

tensed! This is meant to be enjoyable for both of you. It is
Mr. Egret you are attached to, yes?"

"For now," Elinor said dismissively.

"Mm. Perhaps you should remain attached to him. I
would very much like to hear how our newest guest is enjoying himself. And perhaps if you learn something interesting
about how he has enjoyed his stay, we could have a conversation. And perhaps you could be invited back, next year. We
have certain allowances for our regular girls, beyond the
normal payment." She smiled broadly, and Elinor felt a chill
creep up her spine.

"Perhaps," she echoed. Madame Beauchene was curious
about Lord Farleigh, then. And of course she would be. It
did not sound like it was the first time she had made such an
offer, and Elinor wondered how many of the courtesans took
up the Beauchenes on the offer of extra pay in exchange for
a few overheard secrets.

Madame Beauchene was done with her. It was obvious,
like a candle blown out; she turned away, returning to her
attentive flock, and Elinor was left adrift in the middle of
the room. She gathered herself and departed, still mulling
over the meaning of the offer.

She found Lord Farleigh on a sofa in a sunlit room, alone.
She stood a moment in the doorway. He had not seen her yet;
his eyes were fixed on a far distant point, and his face turned
half away from her. The sun made his skin glow, and inattention
had settled his features into a more restful calm than his usual
default frown. He was not so striking that way, she thought; it
made it obvious that he was not a handsome man, by normal
standards. Without the scowl, he seemed . . . normal.

He seemed like the sort of man you could simply sit
beside. The sort whose silence would not needle, but would
lay across your shoulders like a stole, half-forgotten yet still
comforting.

Then she shifted; her foot made a sound upon the floor,
and he turned. The downward tug of his lips was quickly followed by a hardening of every line in his face, and in the space
of a blink he was stern again. Handsome again. She drew

forward. She supposed the sudden change in expression was her fault. She had not given him much reason to like her today.

"It's done," she said.

"Good."

She sat beside him, leaving a foot between them. They stared in the same direction, unspeaking. The silence was not comforting. They wounded each other when they spoke, and when they did not. They were ill-suited for one another, she thought, and wondered if she had ever thought differently.

"I have been thinking," she said softly. "When this is over, I do not want to go back to the way we have been."

"And what way have we been?" he asked.

"Cruel," she said. "Argumentative."

"You are an argumentative person," he said. "I cannot be faulted for responding in kind."

"I am not," she said, and looked at him crossly when he snorted. "It's only that you say such ridiculous things. Things that I would despise any other man for saying."

"Ah, then I am glad you don't despise me," he said.

"I didn't say that." She folded her hands in her lap. She was not going to allow him to draw her into an argument.

"There is a reason I say the things I do," he said.

"An excellent one, I'm sure," she said primly.

"You make it difficult for me to think clearly," he said. "I am always so caught up in wondering how you will analyze each little thing that my words quite get away from me."

"So it's my fault that you insult me."

"Yes. You're so in control," he said, a hint of frustration in his tone.

It was her turn to let out an unladylike snort. "Not around you," she said. "Around you, I feel anything but."

He looked at her, a long and steady look that made the back of her neck prickle.

"What?" she said.

"Nothing," he said. "It's only that I am sometimes surprised that I've known you so long, and so little." He rose, hand extended. "We have Foyle to find," he reminded her.

She took his hand, and stood. He'd meant to say something else; she was sure of it. But Farleigh of all men she could not understand. It should have been easy. He spoke his mind; he was honest and blunt. Everyone knew what he thought, what he felt. And yet she did not trust it.

And she had not quite decided whether she could trust *him*.

Too much depended on things they couldn't control. They did not know if Foyle had recognized Lord Farleigh, or if Foyle had seen him and Elinor together the night before; they did not know if the enigmatic Mr. Tiger had said anything to warn him off of them. They wouldn't know how to play the scene until they actually spoke to the man. Elinor did not understand how Lord Farleigh suddenly appeared so unconcerned.

Elinor fussed. She was a woman who liked knowing the angles, and she was not, by her nature, a performer. It made it all the more impressive that she had managed this long, she thought, but surely that was at an end. By the time they located Foyle she was tense as a rabbit scenting a fox.

They had come around to the red-and-gold room, no longer host to Madame Beauchene. Foyle was still with one of his companions from earlier, the fair-haired girl. She was chattering on about something, and he nodded and murmured every so often. He was indeed a discontented man.

Colin caught Elinor's arm as she passed into the room and leaned in close. "Relax," he whispered into her ear, which had the opposite of the intended effect. She stiffened and pulled away from him, but he held her close. "This will be easy," he said. "Only be yourself, and he will be intrigued."

"I am not so intriguing," she said. "Or I would not spend so many dances alone."

"It is because you are alone at so many dances that men find you intriguing," he said. He brushed his fingers across her neck. To maintain their illusion, she told herself. "They wonder what secrets you're keeping."

"I don't keep secrets," she said. "Not my own, at least."

"All women keep secrets," he said.

She arched an eyebrow at him before realizing that the gesture was concealed behind the mask. She settled for jutting out her chin instead. "I have found that when a man makes a claim about the whole of the female species, he is more often describing some corresponding feature in his own character," she said.

His jaw tensed. "You're right. I should strive for specificity. You keep secrets, Elinor; it's only that you do a fine job of keeping yourself ignorant of them as well."

If he could see her scowl, it would have withered him. It was a clever thing to say, more full of wit than meaning, and it was exactly the sort of thing he seemed to reserve only for her. "I presume, then, that you can tell me these secrets? That you can better elucidate the contents of my mind and heart than I can myself?"

He kept his mouth shut, blessedly. He'd lasted mere minutes since the promise to treat each other more kindly. Perhaps that was proof that they were never meant to be in proximity to each other.

"Don't hover over there," Foyle called, and they both jerked around. Elinor had momentarily forgotten the man was there. "If you mean to come in, come in. Or go out; it's all the same to me, only that indecisive lingering gives me a headache."

He clutched a cup of wine in one hand, and Elinor suspected that it was not their presence that was giving the man a headache. Better him than Lord Farleigh.

"Apologies," Lord Farleigh called cheerfully, and steered Elinor toward the trio. There was a cushioned bench perpendicular to the sofa where the three lounged, making an L-shape suited for conversation. Foyle sat up a little when the two of them took seats upon it, Elinor taking the nearer position. "Mr. Lamb, isn't it?" Lord Farleigh asked. Elinor tried to remember her lessons, arranging her spine in a curve Madame Lavigne would be proud of.

"Is it? I suppose," Foyle said with a shrug. "Silly business, all these false names. Most of us know one another anyway. Though I don't think you and I have met before."

"I don't think so," Colin agreed. "Mr. Egret."

Foyle smirked. "And you, dove? Oh, that does nicely, actually. Dove. Don't you think?"

Elinor inclined her head, repositioning herself subtly to appear demure, a touch pleased. It was amazing how expressive she could be with her entire face concealed. "That would do," she agreed softly. Shyly.

Shy was not a word one applied much to the women Beauchene employed. Some aped it, of course, but Elinor wasn't pretending; she channeled her natural impulse to withdraw, and she saw Foyle's eyes flicker with faint interest. The girl on his arm noticed it, too. She narrowed her eyes at him. "Have you been here before, Mr. Egret?" he asked, though his gaze remained fixed on Elinor. Lord Farleigh shifted. Elinor wished she could kick him. Foyle's attention was the whole point of this ridiculous exercise. Lord Farleigh couldn't let any misguided jealousy get in the way.

"No," Lord Farleigh said. "It's my first visit."

"Mine as well," Foyle said. "I admit I was terribly curious, but the pageantry is rather wearing after a while. These markers, for example." He stretched out an idle hand. The very tip of his finger brushed the silver egret. "An odd way to claim a woman. If she's truly yours, she shouldn't need claiming."

Elinor's breath hitched. She didn't like him so close to her. Neither did his companion; she nestled herself against him, trying to redirect his attention.

Foyle's lips thinned. "Don't tell the man I said so, though," he said, and nodded at the doorway. The man who had entered was thin and oddly colorless. His cravat, a mint green, stood out in startling contrast. It ought to have livened the look, but instead struck a note like an ill-timed joke.

"I have ears like a hawk," the man said in a heavy French accent, drawing close. The little smile he gave made the phrase seem like an old jest, an intentionally misspoken phrase. "I miss nothing. One would think you were perfectly suited for theatrics, Mr. Lamb. You do lead a dramatic life."

"I lead a boring life, with dramatic interludes thrust upon me," Foyle said. "My friends, M. Beauchene, our host."

"I hope you do not mind if I prevail upon you," Beauchene said.

Lord Farleigh gestured expansively. "Of course. An honor, sir."

Beauchene waved away the greeting and selected a seat, inserting himself between Elinor and the edge of the bench. It was a tight fit, and she was forced to adjust herself—to either angle her body away from Beauchene, and thus Foyle, or to let her knees touch against his so that she could keep her focus. She chose the latter. Lord Farleigh slipped a hand around her waist. She was still too tense. He pulled her against him, and she leaned against his chest. The picture of a relaxed couple. Having him there, whatever the friction between them, made her feel safe. It might be an illusion, but she clung to it.

"You're acquainted, I take it," Lord Farleigh said.

"Mr. Lamb and I are old friends," Beauchene said. "Old friends indeed. It is a pity it has taken him so long to take me up on my offer of hospitality."

"I've been away from England," Foyle said.

"In India," said the fair-haired girl, seemingly pleased to have the chance to interject.

"India," Elinor said. "How interesting. Did you not find it to your liking?"

"I haven't been there in years," Foyle said, dismissive. "Hot and damp and full of Indians. I've been on the continent, mostly. Saw some fighting, did my part."

"A soldier," Elinor said.

"Does that frighten you?" he asked.

"Why should I be frightened? You are one of *our* soldiers, are you not? I assume you did not fight for France, however fond you are of Monsieur Beauchene." Bold words, but she kept her voice quiet. As if the words she spoke were only a whisper, meant to reach only one man's ears. A private thing, and so no need to be shy at all. Lord Farleigh's hand tightened at her waist.

"My country of birth is not so fond of me," Beauchene said with a chuckle. "Nor is yours, alas, as hard as I have worked to correct the situation. A few years more, and the rancor will settle down, hm?"

"We have too much of a taste for your imports to do otherwise," Foyle said with a chuckle. "Though our domestic goods have their charms as well." He looked at Elinor as he spoke.

"You always did want what you cannot have," Beauchene said with a tsk of his tongue. "Tell me, Mr. Egret. Are you a possessive man? Do you mind that we are admiring the blossom you have selected from my bouquet?"

"Not at all," Lord Farleigh said stiffly. "I consider myself a generous man."

Beauchene took Elinor's hand, playing his thumb across her palm. She shivered. His was a skilled touch, but clinical. Testing. At her shiver, she felt the lowest rumble in Lord Farleigh's chest. She laid her hand against his leg and squeezed, a subtle gesture that might have been missed through casual observation. *I can bear this*, she said with her touch. *Don't do anything stupid.*

That last part might not have come across, but she was confident he could fill it in himself.

"I collect sketches," Beauchene said. His thumb kept up its winding path. "Nothing elaborate; simply images of beautiful women. I wonder if you might let me add you to my collection."

Elinor realized that this was not a competition between Lord Farleigh and Foyle, or Lord Farleigh and Beauchene. The two men seemed to have forgotten her companion entirely.

"And such a large collection it is," Foyle said lightly. "Such beauty deserves more than to be simply one page among many."

"Are you an artist, then?" Elinor said.

"He cannot draw a straight line," Foyle said.

Beauchene shrugged. "I may not have skill in that area. But I make it a point to keep track of those who have skills I lack, and employ them when I have need."

"Is that why your wife spends so much time with other men?" Foyle asked.

Elinor tensed, expected violence, or at the least some show of anger. But Beauchene only laughed.

"I, too, am not a jealous man. My wife has her pleasures, and I have mine. Occasionally, they intersect. In my experience, insisting that one derives all pleasure from one's spouse results in less enjoyment for both."

"Unless you are lucky enough to find someone with whom all your pleasures intersect," Elinor said, doing her best impression of Madame Lavigne's amused drawl. "And what about you?" she asked Foyle. "Do you think you could ever find enough pleasure in a single woman?"

"Oh, I did," he said. "I found all my pleasure in her, and she found none in me." He said it as if it were meant to be a joke, but bitterness stained it. Elinor kept herself from sitting forward by sheer force of will. Surely he meant Marie.

The fair-haired girl saw her chance for relevance once again and leaned forward, cooing and stroking at Foyle's hair. He brushed her away, and she flopped back, looking suddenly bored. "I am going to find something to eat," she declared.

"Fine, then," Foyle said.

With a pout, she rose. She cast Elinor a look over her shoulder that seemed to translate to something like *better you than me* and stalked out.

"You should treat your women better," Beauchene said in a scolding tone.

"Women should be more interesting," Foyle countered. "Didn't we have something to discuss, Beauchene?"

"We did, indeed," Beauchene said. "We must depart, with reluctance. And you must let me acquire your likeness, young woman."

"You haven't seen my face," she said. "How can you be sure you want it for your collection?"

He laughed softly and kissed her palm. "I don't need to see your face to know it will intrigue me," he said. "Will you come to my study tomorrow afternoon, then?"

"I'm not certain," Lord Farleigh said.

"Then it is a good thing that it isn't your opinion I

solicited," Beauchene said. There was a challenge in his words, and a test, and suddenly Elinor understood. She almost laughed. Beauchene's rules were not about keeping the courtesans safe and happy. They were about making sure his guests were the ones controlled, not the ones in control. His guests played their little pleasure games, but his game began with their arrival and did not pause until they had left. And if he broke his own rules, it wasn't as if anyone would speak out against him.

"I would enjoy it," Elinor said, with the feeling of fitting a key into a lock and turning it. This was how to hook them. "And perhaps I will see you again, Mr. Lamb."

"Perhaps," he said.

She kept her languid pose, her weight against Lord Farleigh, until the both of them had left. Then she straightened up, brushing at her sides. His hand fell away from her waist. "That was interesting," she said. And oddly invigorating. "Though not quite as extensive as I had hoped."

"We'll have a chance to try again," he said darkly. "You certainly played your role admirably."

"Don't say it like that. You know I didn't enjoy that."

"Didn't you?"

She paused. "A bit," she said. He stared at her. "I liked knowing I was fooling them," she said. "I liked feeling like I was winning."

"I didn't enjoy watching that man touch you," he growled.

"But did you enjoy watching me win?" she said, a laugh behind the words.

"You haven't won yet," he said. "But when you do, I think I will enjoy watching it very much."

She rested a hand on her chest and splayed her fingers, looking there so that she would not have to meet his eyes. Her heart was still beating a little too fast, and with the thrill of nerves came an entirely different sort of thrill.

"We made a deal," she reminded him. "And I have not upheld my end of it." Perhaps she was a fool. But she wanted him to look at her with the hunger she'd seen in his eyes the night he'd kissed her. Even if it was only lust, even if he felt nothing but dutiful friendship toward her, the *wanting* and the *being wanted* were more intoxicating than drink.

"Foyle—"

"We must give him an hour or two before we attempt contact again. We can't risk him becoming suspicious," Elinor said. She bit her lip.

"I won't hold you to that deal," Lord Farleigh said. "I couldn't possibly."

"But I want you to," Elinor said. She flicked her eyes up to meet his.

"I've already done too much. Last night I was drunk. And I didn't know who you were. Now I don't have that excuse," Lord Farleigh said.

She ought to have told him the truth then, she knew. But she also knew that if she did, this would all be over. "You don't need an excuse. I'm asking you directly," Elinor said. She felt as though she might shake apart, but she pressed on. "Please."

He took her hand, lacing his fingers through hers. "Well. I certainly wouldn't want to leave you with last night as the sum of your experience. It does not sound as if I impressed."

She pressed her tongue to the roof of her mouth. The guilt in his voice was unbearable. She might at least ease his mind and tell him he had not taken her virginity, even if she allowed him to think he had bedded her. But she thought again of the look in his eye when he spotted Foyle. She'd tell him when this was over, and she was certain he could do no harm to himself.

"Elinor?"

Instead of speaking, she rose, his hand and hers still linked, and led him toward the stairs.

Chapter 19

❧

Colin had thought he wouldn't have to face this until night had fallen. He'd thought he would have time to think of the right way to maintain what little there was left of his honor without offering insult. Because he could not follow through on his degenerate suggestion—he couldn't. It would be selfish of him, satisfying his desires—and oh, they burned. He yearned for her. But when she felt no such yearning for him, it was deception at best. And he did not know if he could bear it, to have her—if only for a moment, if only in body—and to lose her.

That night five years ago at Birch Hall had wrecked him. He had pieced himself back together, and now, with a single touch, he might fall to desolation once more.

And yet he followed her. Even sober as clear day he could not stop himself. She led him to the room without once looking back, and when he closed the door behind them she stood in the center of the room, her arms wrapped around herself, her back to him. She was shivering, ever so slightly.

Now that would not do.

He rested his hands on her shoulders, and her shivering slowly stopped. Still she didn't look at him; her head was bowed. She reached up, and undid her mask's ties. "Don't be afraid," he said. "I won't make you do anything you don't want to."

She turned slowly. "Our deal—"

"Oh, yes. I have claimed you. You are mine to command. Remember, in this house any courtesan may refuse any man. We don't have to do this."

"But I know that men—"

"What is it you understand?" he asked, voice low and dangerous. "What do you know about men? That we cannot control ourselves? That once you excite us, we're little more than slavering dogs?"

She shrugged, let out a strangled laugh. "More or less."

"If you tell me to stop, I will stop," he said. "That's the only way we can do this. If I know that you will tell me if something is amiss, if you have changed your mind. I couldn't stand to hurt you, Elinor."

"You didn't stop before," she said. "The night you kissed me. I told you to let me go, and you didn't."

He released her hands then. "Ah," he said. "I had thought . . . You were enjoying it."

She tilted up her chin. "Yes," she said. "And I still wanted you to release me."

"Because you were worried about your reputation? No one could see us."

"I am so glad you know my mind better than I do," she said, and now anger was rising in her voice. "It shall make it all the easier to enjoy myself, knowing I need have no input on the proceedings."

He made a sound like a growl in the back of his throat. How could he not have realized? He'd treated her like she had no mind of her own. He'd accepted her desire, and rejected her misgivings as inconvenient, and justified it all to himself in the moment because she *enjoyed* it. And she had. But now, she did not trust him. And that, he could not bear.

"The rule is that I get to dictate what happens in this room," he said.

"But—"

"And I dictate that you tell me exactly what you want,

and exactly what you don't want," he said. "I was a drunk fool that night. It won't happen again."

"You may have to swear off drink eternally to promise that," she said.

"Then I will." He said it so easily, so quickly, that they were both briefly startled into silence.

"Very well," she said at last. "Then what . . . what do you wish me to do?"

"Tell me what you want," he said.

"I think I already have."

"You have certainly hinted," he said, with the ghost of a teasing smile on his lips. "But we have established that I am exceedingly dull-witted when it comes to sorting your desires from mine. You shall have to be explicit."

"I'm not certain that I can," Elinor said.

He reached down and took the mask from her. "Perhaps you can't," he said. "But tonight, you do not need to be Lady Elinor Hargrove." He gestured for her to turn, and when she had he helped her secure the mask in place. He stepped back. He could almost see it: the layers she was shedding, the persona she was wrapping around herself. Her posture changed. She touched her mask once, as if to remind herself that it was there.

He touched the base of her neck, brushing at the few stray hairs that lay there. It was easier for her to hide behind the mask. And easier for him as well. He could lie to himself. He could tell himself he did not love this woman, that he did not dream of touching her, and that the thought of losing her when this was done did not tear at him.

"You know," he whispered. "You look very much like a woman I know."

"Is she beautiful?" Elinor asked.

"She is radiant," Colin said. "And so are you."

She faced him. He let his fingers trail up the side of her throat and nip at the edge of the mask.

"Tell me what you want," Colin said.

"I want to be touched," she said. "I want to be brought

to pleasure, and to bring a man to pleasure. Is that explicit enough for you to understand?"

Every word seemed to arrow through him. Heat coiled at his core, desire a quick pulse through his body. It was all a dream, this place, and when they woke he would no longer have her. But he was not a strong enough man to free himself, to deny himself the illusion's pleasures, even knowing it would make the waking world that much dimmer.

"I understand."

"Tell me what to do," Elinor whispered. She spoke in the low, honeyed tone Madame Lavigne had taught her, but her own practical voice was nattering away at her as well. That was the voice that added *Please, since I have very little idea what to do myself.*

Then Lord Farleigh's hands ghosted over her arms, and both voices went silent at the pleasurable hum the touch sent through her. He bent and kissed her neck, and she gasped, tilting her face upward. She wanted to kiss him—but she was safe behind her mask. She was someone else.

"Take off your dress," he whispered against her neck, and drew away again.

He stayed an arm's length from her as she unhooked the buttons one by one. She watched him watch her, studied the languid desire in his eyes that he made no effort to hide.

When the buttons gaped, she slid the sleeves from her arms, and let the gown pool about her feet. She wore a single petticoat beneath. It came off more quickly, her motions hurried now, that twining feeling in her gut beating with a heartbeat all its own.

She stood only in her chemise, its flimsy fabric falling only to her thighs. She reached for the hem.

"No," he said. "Keep that on." He reached out and grabbed the front of the chemise, tugging her toward him. She stumbled against his chest. His hand stayed between them, pulling the fabric tight across her back and hips, his fist against her stomach. The touch of the taut cloth sent prickles across her skin. So did the light trail he drew down her neck with his nails, a touch as light as a breeze. She wanted his lips there again, wanted his breath against her skin.

"You want me to kiss you," he said. He spoke it like truth, but it still demanded an answer. A confession.

"Yes," she said.

"Mm," he said. "Not yet."

He turned her, keeping his grip on the chemise, and backed her up until the bed was against her legs. She was forced to sit, and then to lie back as he bent over her, his lips still inches from the sensitive skin of her throat.

"You said that you would do what I wanted," she reminded him. The only part of him that touched her was that hand. She wanted to raise her hips against him, to press him between her legs where that unbearable pressure lay.

"No," he said. "I promised I wouldn't do anything you *didn't* want. There is a difference."

"Then I *don't want* you to *not kiss me*," she said, frustration sparking. She wanted him to catch her lips with his, to press down on her, to taste her as he had before.

"Now you're playing games," he said. "I will kiss you, though."

He bent his head. His lips found the corner of her jaw. She gasped at the touch, but he was dipping further down. He held her in place, his kisses wandering to her sternum, to the crest of her breast, and then—

His touch was rough through the cloth of her chemise as his mouth closed around her nipple. She bit her lip and arched her back, and he laughed softly, the breath and sound making a vibration against her skin that only intensified the pleasure.

He rose, eye-to-eye with her again. The wet place where his mouth had been cooled. "Did you like that?" he asked.

"You couldn't tell?" she asked.

He tapped a finger against her jaw. "Who's in charge in this room, again? I asked if you liked that." His eyes were sparkling. He was enjoying himself entirely too much.

And God, so was she.

"Yes," she said.

"And would you like me to do it again?"

"Yes."

He grinned slyly. "I thought this was a high-class establishment. Where are your manners?"

"Yes, please," she amended, a hoarse whisper, and he obliged. His mouth closed around the same spot, and his hand cupped her other breast, fingers teasing at the nipple as his lips and tongue and teeth explored the other. She shut her eyes, tipping her head back. The movement of his hand rucked her chemise up, its filmy edge brushing against her sex, but still he held himself braced above her. She crooked her knees up, bracing her feet against the edge of the bed so that she could lift herself.

His hand returned to her stomach, catching a fistful of cloth. He tugged, pulling up and back, and she followed the motion, climbing up further into the bed. He followed, and propped himself over her with one knee between her legs. He looked down into her eyes. "You truly want this," he said, as if still trying to convince himself.

"I do," she said crossly. And added, sweetly, "Please."

"What is it that you want me to do?" he asked. "Exactly."

"I want . . ." she trailed off. A blush crept up from her neck to her cheeks.

"Be specific," he instructed her, playing with a strand of her hair. "I'm frightfully dense."

"I want you to touch me."

"Where?" he asked, his lips nearly against her throat.

I am anyone I want to be. She caught his hand, and pressed it between her legs. "Here," she said. "Please touch me there."

He pressed his palm against her sex. She let out a soft moan of pleasure as the pressure within her met the pressure of his hand. He moved it in slow rhythm, his lips against her neck, and she moved with him. The pressure moved upward, tightening in her belly and then clenching back to a single point of intense pleasure. His rhythm increased. His fingers were slick with her wetness. They slid over her nub, first in quick, fluttering strokes and then a quick, hard pulse that made her back arch. A shudder ran through her, from her thighs to the crown of her head—and then suddenly it was too much, pleasure tipping into so much sensation it was almost pain.

"Wait," she said, gasping. "Stop."

He pulled his hand away at once, trailing his fingers over her hip instead. And finally he kissed her, at the curve where her shoulder met her neck, a soft reassurance. He shifted his weight over her, and she felt his erection pressing against her sex—weight only, no movement, letting the pain recede back to steady warmth. Her brief flutters of nervousness settling back into excitement.

And with it, impatience. "You are still wearing all your clothes," she pointed out.

"How shortsighted of me," he answered, and drew away suddenly. She yelped, every inch of her protesting the sudden deprivation of touch. But he stilled her with a hand against her shoulder and stood. He disrobed with remarkable efficiency, leaving scattered pieces of clothing around him, rather like an oak dropping its leaves for winter. When he stood only in his drawers he turned back to her. Pale hair lay in whorls across his chest, then arrowed down until it vanished beneath the fabric. His desire was obvious, and she examined it with interest.

He knelt on the bed beside her, then maneuvered himself between her legs. He ran his hands along the outside of her thighs and spread his knees, drawing her legs up onto his.

"We can't risk . . ."

"I know," he said. He shifted, bending forward, moving both of them so that his whole body lay atop hers. He kissed her lightly on the shoulder. "You needn't fear."

He moved against her, and her concerns vanished. He was firm and hot against her, his member taking the place of his hand as he reclaimed the rhythm of before. She clutched his shoulder as he moved, slowly at first and then with increasing urgency, responding to every moan and sigh with more pressure, less, with a thumb flicking over her nipple or a touch of his teeth against her neck.

She was practiced at bringing herself to pleasure alone, and now she lifted her hips to strike the familiar places. And then it was a game of reading every minute movement, guessing and adjusting and murmuring in frustration when they shifted wrong—and then *there*, a touch that cracked her open like an eggshell, and she drew in short, quick breaths, body moving swiftly against his as her climax found her.

It broke, and she pulled him against her, her movements stilling slowly.

"Was that . . . ?" he asked. "Did you . . .?"

"Yes," she said, and coyly added, "Thank you."

"You were quiet," he said. "I wasn't sure."

"I come from a family of light sleepers," she whispered. "I am accustomed, when I pursue such pleasure alone, to staying silent."

"And do you do that often?" he asked, overly casual. His member still pressed against her, insistent.

She lifted herself to whisper in his ear. "Every night," she said.

He surged against her. The peak of her pleasure was passed, but she rode the remnants of sensation as he stroked against her. He gave a final, groaning thrust and heat spilled against her thigh, wet through the fabric of his drawers.

She settled back, the pulse of pleasure fading, satisfaction sweeping through her like the touch of sunlight on her skin. She wanted to hold him there, his warmth against her, for as long as she could.

But he pulled away. He walked to the corner and stripped off his drawers, using them to clean himself efficiently. He kept his back to her, and even as she admired the firm curve of his backside, she frowned.

"Is something wrong?" she asked.

He glanced back. "No. Nothing," he said. He was lying.

"Did I do something wrong?" She slipped off her mask, the better to see him. He looked swiftly away. Ah. That was it, then. The illusion was broken with his pleasure.

He crossed to the wardrobe without looking at her and seized a clean set of drawers. She slid from the bed.

"Lord Farleigh?" she touched his shoulder. He spun, caught her wrist.

"I should not have done that," he said. Guilt made his voice thick.

"You have nothing to regret or apologize for," she assured him.

He let out a long sigh. "Elinor, I am not always a good man. But I have never violated a woman that could suffer from it the way you could." She glared at him. A moment ago she'd been muzzy and happy with the afterglow of their activities; now she felt the cool air on her thighs, and a cramp in her side.

"You didn't *violate* me," Elinor snapped. Really, were all men like this after the deed? Matthew had done his fair share of groaning—during and after, it must be said—but that hadn't stopped him showing up for a repeat performance the next night.

"I have risked your reputation and your future for my own desires."

"They were my desires, too," she said.

"I don't expect you to understand."

"I thought we were done arguing about this," she said. It was certainly too late for it to change anything.

"So did I," he said. He released her and stalked around her, pulling on his clothes rapidly. She crossed her arms. He dressed in a remarkably short time, though she had never seen Colin Spenser look quite so disheveled. He glanced at her. "You should get dressed," he said. "We have work to do."

"Not for some time yet," Elinor said. "Colin—"

"Elinor, I'm sorry. I just need—something. I need to collect myself."

"Then do it somewhere else," Elinor told him. She sat on the bed and crossed her arms.

Colin looked as if he might say something more. An apology, perhaps. It had been alarming when he ignored her protests in favor of her desire, but it was at the very least *irritating* to have him dismiss her desire so thoroughly. She had *asked*, after all, and now he was acting as if she didn't know what she was doing.

Finally, Colin walked to the door. She looked away. The door shut behind him. She resisted the urge to scream.

Lord Farleigh was an idiot. He was occasionally—and largely accidentally—cruel, but he was not a complete blackguard. In fact, she was quite certain that his reason for abandoning her in a dampened chemise, her hair disheveled and her shoulder bearing the red mark of an enthusiastic nip, was an overblown sense of chivalry.

She thought she had made it quite clear to him that she understood this to be purely physical. A matter of enjoyment, that was all. He could not have detected her errant surges of stronger emotion with her face concealed beneath the mask. She had not hinted at the pleasure she felt not just at his touch, but at the thought of belonging to him—with him—for a few stolen moments.

She shut her eyes. She was not quite sure when it had happened. He was infuriating. He was unsettling. And yet.

She sighed. She had feelings for him. The precise dimensions of them she was afraid to explore, as if knowing them would make them impossible to ignore. And ignore them was exactly what she intended to do. Ignore them and conceal them. They would amount to nothing. He was engaged—and had on numerous occasions made it clear that he harbored no such feelings for her.

The point was, she was quite certain that she had successfully concealed her feelings from him. Yet he had somehow decided she harbored them. It was the only explanation for his sudden departure. He felt guilty, because he thought he was leading her on, playing on feelings for him that he could never return—and did not wish to. The fact that he was *right* did not make it any less galling. He once again refused to take her at her word when she stated her desires. Or lack of them.

She glared at the door. It was just like a man to assume that a woman could not help but be all tangled up in emotion.

Idiot, she thought, and this time she wasn't sure which of them she meant.

Colin strode down the hall, halted. Went two steps back, halted again. He shouldn't have left like that. He should have stayed, should have held her. Should have let them both revel in the exquisite pleasure of their encounter. But the moment he had finished, he'd been flooded with shame.

He was not being honest with her. As long as it was purely physical, purely pleasure given and taken, she welcomed him. But if she knew the depths of his feelings for her, she wouldn't touch him. She'd be so *kind*, not wanting to torment him. She'd be so *concerned* about his engagement.

And so, like an idiot, he'd left. Because certainly it was far better for her to be angry with him than to be *kind*. And wasn't that why he had been brusque with her, that night that Matthew proposed? Along with so many occasions since. He could bear not having her, but he could not bear her pity.

He'd thought he could bear not having her.

He'd thought it would be better not to have her at all than to have only part of her. And then his want had overwhelmed his will, and he would give anything to go back.

Or would he?

He slammed the side of his fist against the wall. "For God's sake, every other man in England is quite capable of putting his cock ahead of good sense without a crisis of conscience, why the hell can't you?"

He'd failed at the honorable course when it came to his fiancée, his duties to his best friend, to Elinor herself—and now he was making a mess of being dishonorable. It was almost funny.

He needed a drink.

He was at the head of the stairs before he remembered that he'd promised to avoid alcohol. The need gripped him as firmly as his desire for Elinor had earlier. He could imagine the first sip, subtle and startling at once. He could picture the light through the liquid, the way it moved when he swirled his glass. There was something erotic about a good glass of liquor. But it wasn't the pleasure he sought right now. It was the oblivion.

He halted three steps down. He needed to keep a clear head. *One drink, then*, he thought. But he had never in his life stopped at one drink. He didn't understand how anyone could. It was impossible. Like willing your own heart to stop beating.

He gripped the bannister. What harm could it do?

What harm, indeed. Drunk, he'd ignored Elinor's protests. He'd kissed her when she didn't want him to. He'd bedded her. *I didn't tell you not to*, she'd said, but he wasn't certain that he'd have listened if she had. He didn't remember what had happened. Who could say what might have happened, when he was so far outside himself?

He'd given his word that he would remain sober while he was here.

That finally broke through his longing. He seized hold of it. He'd given his word, and what good was a man if he could not keep such a simple thing?

He would refrain, then. Until this journey was over, and Elinor was safely home.

He sighed. The decision was made, but now he was faced with a new conundrum. What did one *do* with oneself when one didn't drink?

Chapter 20

❦

Elinor had been glaring at the wall for less than a minute when a knock sounded at the door. She lurched upright. It must be Lord Farleigh, slinking back to make some mumbling apology. She threw open the door before remembering that she was still wearing only her chemise, and found herself staring at Edward Foyle.

A look of delight passed across his features. She strangled the urge to cross her arms over her chest, instead keeping one hand on the door and every inch of her barely concealed body on display. A courtesan would not flinch, she thought, and in any case she did not want to give him the pleasure. She'd seen enough bare bosoms the past twenty-four hours to realize that it was quite silly to worry about hiding hers, even if it made the back of her neck hot.

"Yes?" she said.

"Is Mr. Egret not here, then?" Mr. Foyle asked, but by his tone she guessed he was well aware of the answer, and had been before knuckle met wood.

"He's out," she said.

She was not wearing her mask.

She stiffened, then forced herself to relax. They had never

met. Her face was not well-known—nor was her name. There was no reason to fear him.

"Perhaps I can keep you company," he said. "Would you care to share a walk with me?"

"I—" She paused. She couldn't very well put him off. Not when speaking with him was the entire point of this exercise. "I must get my mask," she said.

"That isn't necessary," he said smoothly. Forestalling her next complaint, he added, "Nor is your dress, I think." He flourished a neat stack of guineas. He took her hand, turning it palm-up, and dropped the coins one by one so that they clinked. "Consider it a bonus," he said. "Mr. Egret has no need to know."

"Five guineas for a walk?" Elinor asked lightly.

"You have been claimed. I can ask for no more. I can only hope that you will reconsider which man you have allowed to claim you," he said.

You can refuse him, she reminded herself. "Let me put these away," she said, and pulled away from him before he could protest. She slipped the coins among her dresses and reached for the mask. He tsked.

Maybe no one would recognize her. She'd only been back for the Season twice since Matthew's death; she led an isolated life by design. And who would expect to see Lady Elinor Hargrove in a place like this? Who would admit to having seen her, if they did?

Her reasoning was not sufficient to calm the icy dread that gripped her as she returned, smiling, to Edward Foyle's side.

"Where shall we walk?" she asked. If Lord Farleigh spotted them, perhaps he could intervene. But should he? This would likely be her best chance to get information from Foyle. And one that Lord Farleigh would certainly not allow her.

"Let me worry about that," Foyle said. He guided her down the stairs. The carpet was soft against her bare feet, and the air warm enough that she did not miss a pelisse or proper clothing for physical comfort's sake, but it took every ounce of her will not to wrap her arms around herself to conceal her body. Her hair was disheveled, and the state of her chemise left little doubt as to what sort of activity the afternoon had witnessed.

She imagined her mask. Cold and pale, only the slightest hint of a smile to give it an expression. Serene, knowing, amused that you might even *think* of passing judgment. She was not Elinor Hargrove; she was not even a mortal being. She was a creature of imagination and promise, one that no one could touch.

She held onto that, and perhaps it showed. The men they passed in the hall looked at her not with judgment but with a distant kind of desire. One that knew it could not have her.

They exited the house at the rear doors, out onto the sun-drenched lawn that sloped down toward sparse trees. Foyle steered her westward, toward a large greenhouse. "I hope you might indulge me, Dove," Foyle said. "I find that I have been thinking about you since we spoke. You asked me about India. I told you I didn't care for it."

"And was that a lie, Mr. Lamb?" Elinor asked.

"Oh, I despised the place," Mr. Foyle said. "But not all of it. Here." They had reached the greenhouse, and he opened the door to usher her in. She slipped inside. The summer heat was still more intense within, but the light more diffuse. The glass panes were somewhat clouded with condensation and the faint green of plant matter. Inside were row upon row of wooden tables, bursting with every manner and color of plant. Blooms rose exuberantly toward the ceiling, or trailed toward the ground. Plants with thick, meaty stalks or stems fine as thread.

"This is beautiful," Elinor said. It was beautiful chaos, and it took a moment to begin to pick out the individual blooms in the madness.

"I want to show you one in particular," Foyle said. He took her hand and slotted it into the crook of his arm again. She swallowed against her revulsion and let him lead her toward the back of the greenhouse. "Here," he said, and pointed.

A large clay pot hosted a plant that reached past shoulder-height, supported by narrow stakes. Its leaves curled away from a half-dozen central stalks. At its peak were the most striking flowers Elinor had ever seen. They had wide-spaced petals of the brightest yellow at their bases, lightening to rich scarlet at their tips. The edges of each petal were rippled, so that they looked like tongues of flame, curling inward.

"There is beauty in India," Foyle said. "Though it was sometimes easy to miss."

"What is it called?" Elinor asked. She reached to touch one of the blossoms. Foyle caught her wrist.

"It can be quite irritating to the skin," he warned her. "I first heard it called senganthal," Foyle said. "In English we call it the glory lily or the flame lily. You can see why."

"Did you bring this from India, then?" Elinor asked.

"No. I had it brought, on Monsieur Beauchene's request. He collects beautiful things other than women, on occasion," he said with a wry smile. "It has medicinal properties as well. But like most things that you wish to heal you, it has its deadly side. I knew of a woman once who killed herself by consuming it."

"Accidentally?" Elinor asked.

He was staring at the flower. He hadn't removed his hand from her wrist, hadn't moved. "Her husband had died," he said. "And her children, too. Seven of them. Some illness. She alone was spared. I suppose it was too much for her, to be left alone."

"That's terrible," Elinor said.

"Yes, it is. Isn't that just like the world, though? To create something beautiful and then to contort it into something foul." He dropped her hand at last. She rubbed her wrist surreptitiously, as if she could rid herself of the lingering sensation of his touch.

"You sound as if you were hurt there," Elinor said. She made her voice a different sort of invitation now. Not an invitation to pleasure, but to unburdening. "Who did you lose, Mr. Lamb? Who broke your heart so?" Biting back distaste, she brushed the hair lightly from his brow.

"She was my wife," he said. She stayed silent. He had been waiting for someone to ask, she realized. Hoping for someone to pry. Was he truly wounded, and in need of comfort? Or did he merely enjoy the sort of attention such revelations of heartbreak might bring? "Her name was Marie. I loved her more than the sky loves the stars. And I lost her."

"She died," Elinor said softly. "You poor thing."

"Yes, she died. But for weeks before that, months, it was as if—" He paused. "She was hardly alive. Hardly sane. She seemed to fold in on herself. She seemed to see things that no one else could, things that terrified her." He sounded genuinely distraught. Could he be telling the truth? Could he have loved her? She'd written that he blackmailed her, but what he was describing was a kind of madness. Perhaps she'd been wrong. Perhaps she'd been delusional after all.

They couldn't have been wrong about Foyle—could they?

Foyle sighed. "She was troubled before the child was born, but after it was like she had shattered."

Elinor froze. She struggled to keep her expression relaxed. In as casual a tone as she could muster, she said, "You have a child?"

"What? No. It wasn't mine. We weren't married yet when she— She was a widow," he said briskly. "And the child was stillborn. Tragic, of course. But she was hardly the only woman whom such a fate befell." He frowned at the lily. His performance had fractured. There was more anger in his voice than sorrow, now, and Elinor's suspicions of his sincerity faltered. "I could have helped her, you know. If she'd let me. But she didn't. And then she was dead. Cholera." He looked at Elinor, eyes narrowing. "Why are we speaking about my dead wife? You don't care."

"Of course I do," Elinor said, smiling sweetly. "If it concerns you, it concerns me."

He planted his hands on her hips. His thumbs dug in by her hip bones, almost painfully, and the fabric of her chemise bunched beneath his palms. "No, you don't," he said.

"You're just a silly whore, playing at sympathy in the hope that I'll give you a few extra coins after I fuck you."

She slapped him.

It was instinct. Her whole life, no one would have dreamed of saying anything half so horrible to her. A dozen men would have offered to duel him on her behalf if he'd said it at the parties she *usually* attended. But she wasn't at one of those parties. She stared at him in horror as he put a hand to his reddened cheek. A chuckle rumbled through his chest.

"The dove has talons," he said. "Careful that she doesn't scratch you, Beauchene."

Elinor turned stiffly. Beauchene, still in his lurid green cravat, lounged near the entrance of the greenhouse.

"Monsieur," she said with exaggerated civility, and curtsied. A mockery of the form, given what she was wearing, but she refused to be cowed.

"I apologize for the interruption," Beauchene said. "I can come back another time, if you wish." He directed this not to Elinor, but Foyle, who only grunted and shrugged. Beauchene beamed. "Excellent. Now, my dear. Perhaps you'll come with me."

"I should be getting back to Mr. Egret," she said.

"That can wait. I have asked a more talented artist than myself to complete our little project," he said. His eyes trailed up and down her form.

She eyed the doorway. She might be able to slip past him. But the hard glint in Beauchene's eye told her that would be pointless. Beauchene might have rules for other men, but this was his house. And she—she was no one. A prize to be handed from one man to another.

She walked to him. His fingers closed around her wrist, dry and cool, and pulled her forward. Back out toward the sunlight. She looked back at Foyle. He watched her go with an expression she could not quite read. Disappointment?

Whatever it was, she was glad to leave it behind. As glad as she was afraid of what lay ahead.

* * *

Colin thought that fresh air would clear his head, but a circuit of the grounds had only left him scowling at every entwined couple—or trio, or quartet—he came across. He had coaxed himself from a dark mood into a black one by the time he reached the sculpture garden, and he slung himself down on a bench in the shade, thinking maybe he'd have a good brood. Brooding required solitude, however, and he was not to get any today. A woman had spotted him, and came across the grass at a light if purposeful gait, settling herself on the bench beside him.

"I'm not looking for company," Colin said.

"When a man comes to our house and shuns company, it is a sign that something has gone quite wrong," the woman said. She had the trace of a French accent. Madame Beauchene, then. He looked at her with new interest. "Is the entertainment not to your liking?"

"It's a personal matter," Colin said.

"My favorite kind," she said with a little laugh. She had a commanding presence. More than that, it was as if the whole world had shrunk down to the two of them as soon as she began to speak. A remarkable gift, and one that Colin distrusted instinctively. "Tell me your troubles, Mr. Egret."

"I didn't realize we'd been introduced," he said.

"I know everyone here," she replied with a dismissive toss of her head. "I am entirely familiar with you." She slid her arm through his, a friendly gesture shaded toward possessive. He restrained himself from pulling away. "Did you know that your brother-in-law is here as well?" she asked.

"Which one?" he asked. "The dead one, or the one who's traipsing around Spain?"

"Edward Foyle," Madame Beauchene said. "You spoke to him earlier. I wasn't certain you recognized him."

"I've never met the man," Colin said. Damn and double damn. If she was telling him this, he could hardly pretend not to know who Foyle was. Had she told Foyle as well?

What the hell sort of game was she playing? "Nor do I care to."

"A pity. You would have so much to talk about," Madame Beauchene said.

"I doubt it."

"I think that you would be surprised," Madame Beauchene said. "Or perhaps you wouldn't. You were the last name added to our list, did you know that? A regular guest dropped out quite at the last moment, and insisted that we forward his invitation to you. It seems that he developed gout. I suspect it has more to do with the sudden divestment of his mistresses, and the precarious nature of his wife's good graces."

"Are you suggesting that I blackmailed him?" Colin asked. For all he knew, Hudson had. That put a sour taste in his mouth. Blackmail was what had drawn him into this mess in the first place.

"You wouldn't, would you? Interesting," she said, delighted on some level Colin couldn't begin to fathom. "Don't imagine that you are any less welcome, of course. We thrive on new blood. However, it is also essential to maintain a level of congeniality among our guests. You understand. There are reputations that might grow tarnished, should another guest speak out of turn. And disagreement leads to temptation."

"You don't have to worry about that from me," Colin said. "I'd have to admit that I was here in the first place, wouldn't I?"

"So you would," Madame Beauchene acknowledged.

"I'm impressed," Colin said. "I've been here not even two full days and you already know my particulars."

"Information is essential," Madame Beauchene said. She patted his arm. "Do let us know if there is anything you require, Mr. Egret. A change of rooms. A change of companionship."

"My companionship is entirely satisfactory," he assured her.

"Everyone needs some variety," she countered, but she

rose without pressing the point. What was her angle, he wondered? Perhaps to pair him with someone to root out his secrets, as he sought to root out Foyle's. "Good evening, then," she said, and left him once more alone.

He remained a few more minutes, thinking through the conversation word by word. What did this change? Nothing, and everything. He still needed to find the material Foyle had used to blackmail Marie. But he could hardly pretend at ignorance of the man's identity now. Someone would expose him.

He needed to tell Elinor.

He hurried back to the room. He was not looking forward to seeing her after stalking out like that. He ought to have stayed. Talked things through with her. Explained.

Not that she would listen.

An argument was already rising on his tongue when he opened the door to the room. And found her gone.

She must have gone to get something to eat.

But, no. There was her dress, still on the ground. And on the bed, amid the rumpled covers, her mask.

His mouth went dry. She was out there alone. And she was exposed.

Beauchene drew Elinor in next to him, his arm around her waist, as they walked. "You are a very interesting woman," he said. A man passed them in the hall. His eyes caught on her, curiosity and idle lust in them, and then he slid away. She wouldn't find help here, not unless Lord Farleigh was near. And she suspected Beauchene knew exactly where he was.

"Not particularly," she said. "I'm sure you know plenty of women like me."

"What is your name?" he asked. "I meant to ask about you, with Madame Lavigne, but I realized I do not know your name."

"I thought there weren't any names here," she said. He'd turned her toward a staircase, leading upward to the third level. The third level was out-of-bounds to guests. Any hope of bumping into Lord Farleigh evaporated.

"Not for the guests, no. But for me, the rules are different."

"I am beginning to understand that," she said drily, and he laughed.

"Your name, my dear?" he prompted.

"Theodosia," she said, remembering her earlier lie. She wished she'd pretended to be someone a bit more useful. Theodosia would probably have resorted to having the vapors by now. A useful technique for avoiding unwanted conflict in civilized company, but Elinor doubted that courtesans ever had the vapors.

"Such an ungainly name for such a lovely woman," he said. They'd reached the top of the stairs. The hallway above was dark. Curtains shrouded the window panes, letting only slender blades of light through. They turned to the right. The carpet *shush*ed beneath their feet. "Here we are." He pulled her around sharply and released her arm long enough to push open a door.

Beyond was an oak-paneled study. The furniture was thick-legged and dour, the bookshelves stuffed with ponderous tomes. A low, red-cushioned chaise longue was set in the middle of the room, as if awaiting her; the curtains had been drawn from a single window, casting a brutish beam of sunlight onto it.

"Sit," Beauchene ordered, and gave her a light push. She walked with as much dignity as she could muster to the chaise longue and settled near the arm. Her chemise was a mess. The shoulder was torn slightly, the hem damp, spots of dirt apparent where she'd brushed against the tables in the greenhouse. She propped her elbow on the arm of the chaise longue and arched an eyebrow at Beauchene.

"So where is this artist?" she asked.

Beauchene's eyes went to the corner of the room. She twisted. Mr. Tiger stood in the shadowed corner, stiff and scowling. She froze.

"Mr. Bhandari, your subject. I look forward to the finished product." With that, Beauchene turned and left, closing the door behind him. Elinor's lips parted, not sure where to look—at the closed door, or at the man glowering from the other side of the room. Now she did cross her arms and cross her ankles, drawing herself together and near the back of the chaise longue, using it to conceal her from Mr. Bhandari's gaze. But he was not looking at her; rather, his eyes were fixed on a point above her head.

"Bhandari," she said. "That's your real name, is it?"

"It is," he said.

"It suits you better than Mr. Tiger," she said.

"If you say so." His accent was more pronounced now than it had been when last they spoke, anger clipping the words. Anger at her? Or at Beauchene?

"I thought he'd stay," she said. "I assumed that was the point. To watch."

"It is a better display of power if he leaves and may simply assume that we will do as he has instructed," Mr. Bhandari said. He still hadn't looked at her. His mouth was downturned, his hands clasped stiffly behind his back.

"We could leave," she said.

"That would be unwise. M. Beauchene is an expert in punishing those who disobey him," Mr. Bhandari said.

"He doesn't even know who I am," Elinor replied. She drew her knees up to her chest. "But you would get in trouble, wouldn't you?" She shook her head. "I don't understand why you work for them. Beauchene and Foyle. You don't seem like them."

"I'm not like them," Mr. Bhandari said. "You did not tell me you knew him."

"Who?"

"My employer."

She winced. She'd used his name. "I know who he is, that's all," she said. "Are you going to tell him?"

"No," he said, after a moment's consideration. "I don't believe I will. I have no idea why you are so interested in him. If you have any sense, you will avoid him. But I won't get you in any more trouble than you already are."

"Am I? In trouble?"

"It's hard to tell with Beauchene. You've caught his attention. That is trouble enough." He sighed. "We should begin." He strode forward, making for the side of the chaise longue. Elinor stiffened.

"Don't," she said. She drew herself into the corner. "Please."

He paused. "You weren't modest with him," he said. "Do I frighten you that much?" There was a note of old pain in that, a weary pain. It was true that she had found his dark skin startling for a moment, in that first encounter, and intriguing since. But his race was not the source of her discomfort, and she shook her head.

"It's not that," she assured him. "It's . . . I don't care if he sees me. I think he would have enjoyed it if I tried to hide myself, and . . . I don't care what he thinks of me."

"And you care what I think?" He sounded surprised.

"I might," she said. "I haven't decided yet."

"And you think I would think less of you, if I saw you undressed."

"I think that modesty is respect, for those who value modesty," Elinor said.

"Circular logic."

"All humanity is circles," Elinor said. "We're turned around in confusion everywhere we go. This place makes you uncomfortable, I can tell. You value modesty, don't you?" He inclined his head. "Then in your presence, I do as well."

"And what about in your own habitat?" Mr. Bhandari asked. "Left alone, with no one else to turn in circles with you, do you value it?"

"I do," Elinor said. "But I refuse to be shamed by that man's gaze."

Mr. Bhandari chuckled. "You would walk naked down city streets to spite a man like that, I think. I admire you. I am glad that you are not my wife or my sister, I admit, but I admire you. Here." He slipped out of his jacket and tossed it over the back of the chaise longue. "Put that on," he instructed her. "And sit like so." He gestured with his hands.

She obeyed, tugging on the jacket—it barely closed over her bosom, but it fell past her buttocks, and when she sat

sideways as he had instructed, with one foot tucked beneath
her and the other stretched in front of her, it gave her some
semblance of modesty. Only her legs, long and pale, showed.

"Will that do?" he asked. She nodded. "We will do this
quickly," he said. "And you can go back to your Mr. Egret
before he can become concerned."

"I hope you're right," she said.

Colin strode through every room of the ground floor. Twice
he thought he caught the lilt of Elinor's voice, or spied a
flash of auburn hair—but they belonged to other women.
He could taste something bitter in the back of his mouth.

He should have taken her home as soon as he'd realized
who she was. He should have had the courage to face the
consequences. Never mind that those consequences would
fall on her as well—he could have found a way.

He threw himself around a corner and bowled right into
a petite girl and her companion, nearly knocking both of
them off their feet. He muttered quick apologies, hauling
them upright by the elbows and startling a laugh from the
girl. Her mask had come askew, revealing a cherubic face
and bright pink cheeks.

"Are you looking for Theodosia?" she asked. He looked
at her blankly. "Your companion?" she prompted. "I saw
her with the sour-faced gentleman. Mr. Lamb? They were
out in the greenhouse." She gave him a winning smile as
dread pooled in his belly like ice water. "She didn't seem
too pleased with him, but I'd hurry just the same."

Her companion was tugging at her arm, clearly intent on
maneuvering her upstairs. She swatted at his hand impatiently.

"Thank you," Colin managed, and pushed between them.

"How rude," said the young man, but Colin was past
caring. He hit the lawn at a run and thundered down the hill
to the greenhouse. The door hung open. He fetched up at
the threshold, his eyes adjusting to the dimmer light. Foyle
stood at the back, leaned against a table and smoking. Colin

crossed to him in a few long strides and seized hold of his shirt, hauling him upright.

"Where is she?" Colin demanded.

Foyle let out a low, hollow laugh. "Lost track of her, have you? And what would I know about it? Why come running to me?"

"I know who you are," Colin said.

Foyle twitched. Tension quivered at the corners of his eyes and mouth. "And who am I?"

"Edward Foyle."

"Beauchene has strict rules about the use of names," Foyle said, but gave a little shrug. "It doesn't change the fact that I don't know where your woman is, so get your hands off of me."

Colin released him. For now. He stepped back, barely restraining his hands from closing into fists, as Foyle straightened out his jacket and dumped his pipe ash on the ground with an overly casual gesture. "So who are you, then? Do I owe you money? Did I insult your wife?"

"You married my sister."

Finally Foyle stiffened. He straightened up slowly. "You're Lord Farleigh."

"Names," Colin reminded him coldly. "We wouldn't want your dear friend upset with you."

Foyle spat. "Beauchene is not the sort of friend you want, believe me. Then this is about Marie. I wondered when I'd hear from you lot."

"You went to a great deal of trouble to avoid us."

"I went to a great deal of trouble to avoid everyone," Foyle said. "I loved her. She died."

"You loved her," Colin said. Disdain and doubt dripped from every word. Foyle looked away. "Why the hell did she marry you? Her husband not two months in the ground? And the mines—"

"The mines. The damned mines. That's what all of this is about, isn't it? It's always the diamonds."

"This isn't about the diamonds. It's about where my— *companion* is. It's about what *exactly* you think I won't do to the man who took my sister from me, if he doesn't tell me where my *companion* has gone."

Foyle laughed. It was a harsh, hollow sound, like the last giving-way of a dead tree. "Your sister was a whore," he said.

Colin moved before he could think. His fist flew out, met Foyle's jaw with a crack. The man fell back, struck the table, and landed in a heap at Colin's feet. He looked up at Colin with a bloodied smile, red in the gutters between his teeth.

"She spread her legs for whoever came her way, and her husband was a blind idiot."

"Do not speak of her that way." *Get up*, Colin willed the man. *Stand up so I can beat you down again.* But Foyle only propped himself on one elbow, wiping blood from his lip with the side of his thumb.

"It took a mine's worth of diamonds to buy her reputation's safety, and she died before she could enjoy it," Foyle said. "You've been waiting all these years to hear the truth, have you? Well the truth is that we saved her, Lord Copeland and I. It would have been ugly for her. You wondered why you couldn't find answers? It's because Lord Copeland kept his bargain with your sister. Silence was what she paid for, and silence was what she got."

"You're lying." His teeth ground together until he thought they'd crack. The edge of his vision blurred; there was only Foyle, a sneer distorting that rattish face. "My sister was not—"

"A whore? No, I suppose she never did get paid. Unlike that sweet dove of yours. You've quite the affection for whores, don't you? Though I suppose she isn't yours anymore."

"What the *fuck* are you talking about?" Colin demanded. His hands were tight fists at his sides. He thought if he moved, even a centimeter, he would kill this man. And so he kept himself still, perfectly still, not even allowing his breath to stir his chest beyond the barest degree.

"Beauchene asked for her," Foyle said. "And who am I to deny an old friend? If you're lucky, he'll give her back. Though you should be careful. The man has a taste for secrets. I hope you haven't told her too many of yours."

Colin moved then. He seized Foyle by his shirt, hauling

him upright and slamming him back against the table again. He pushed the man back, spine contorting, his skull half an inch from a trembling orchid. "Where is she?" he demanded.

"Why do you care? Do you think she cares who sticks his cock in her, so long as she gets what she wants? Lord Hayes learned that lesson, and so did I. Let me spare you the trouble. A woman like that isn't worth a single thought. Not Marie. Not your dove."

"If you do not tell me where they are, I will dig out your eyeballs with my thumbs," Colin said tonelessly.

A strange sort of calculus seemed to go through Foyle's mind. It took Colin a moment to realize what it was. Foyle was deciding whether he cared if he lived or died. And Colin could see the exact moment he decided that a few more miserable moments were better than whatever pain Colin could inflict. "She'll be in his study," he said. "The floor above the guest rooms."

Colin released him. Foyle slumped before catching himself against the lip of the table. Colin didn't wait around to watch him compose himself. He strode away, a sound like the beat of a drum echoing in his skull.

"I loved her," Foyle said. Colin halted, half-turned. Foyle still clung to the edge of the table, but as Colin watched he straightened. "I loved her. I was kind to her. I *protected* her. And she threw it in my face."

"If my sister had such lax standards as you say," Colin said, voice chill as a winter storm, "she must have found something exceptionally disappointing about you to deny you so." He turned away. He would listen to no more of the bastard's lies.

Elinor was with Beauchene, and unmasked. Which meant she was in danger. The dead could wait. Elinor needed him now.

Chapter 21

∽

Mr. Bhandari worked in silence; the one time Elinor tried to engage him in conversation, he only answered with a soft humming sound and a shake of his head. So she remained still, posed in her cage of light, and listened to the rasp of charcoal across paper.

Just as she was growing unbearably stiff, the door opened. Beauchene entered. When he caught sight of her, his lips twitched in a frown. Then he chuckled. "An interesting choice of costume," he said. "Are you finished?"

Mr. Bhandari made one final mark upon the paper and nodded. Beauchene crossed to him and looked down at the image, eyes sharp with appraisal. "Good," he said. "Very good."

Elinor craned her neck to catch a glimpse, undeniably curious. Beauchene laughed again, an unkind edge bringing the sound to the border of mockery, and took the drawing and the board it rested on from Bhandari's hands. He turned it around with a flourish, holding it up for Elinor to see.

It was as true a likeness as any mirror could offer, and somehow more. He had drawn her face and shoulders with exacting, detailed lines, quick hash-marks bringing to life the texture of the jacket, soft wispy strokes delineating each wayward strand of hair. Details softened as they grew more distant from her face, leaving her bare legs only the impression of grace and sunlit flesh. There was nothing tawdry about the drawing, nothing frantic or debauched about the disarray of her clothing and hair. She looked, she thought, like a wild creature who had allowed herself to be captured, if only for a moment—to draw about herself the trappings of civilization, without belonging to them.

She was not that wild creature, but she wished she were. Somehow, looking at the image, she felt an echo of that woman inside of her. Unafraid of this place, of this man. Certain that as soon as she wished, she could be unfettered once again.

Beauchene snapped the drawing back around and removed it from the bands that secured it to the board. "Excellent," he said. "Not what I expected, but your work never is, Mr. Bhandari." He crossed to his desk. He drew a key from the inside pocket of his waistcoat and opened the center drawer, setting the drawing within it. Elinor watched with interest. Mme. Beauchene collected secrets. M. Beauchene collected the obedience of men, and she had no doubt that those secrets helped him do it. A blackmailer, perhaps. A blackmailer with Foyle's obedience, which meant that somewhere, Beauchene possessed a catalog of Foyle's sins.

She almost felt sorry for the man. How many people were holding his leash?

The door crashed open. Elinor jumped up with a yelp. Mr. Bhandari rose, taking a step to interpose himself between Elinor and the intruder—between Elinor and Lord Farleigh. She relaxed. She shouldn't have. Lord Farleigh strode forward, shoving Bhandari out of the way. He halted before her, as if unsure what to do next.

"Mr. Egret," Beauchene said. "You've decided to join us. How delightful."

Lord Farleigh's head whipped around. There was violence in his eyes. His knuckles were bloodied. She grabbed at his hand before he could move. "We're done here," she said, a chirrup of cheerfulness more false than any lie she'd even spoken. "Shall we go back to the room?" Her hand tightened around his. When she stood, the jacket gaped open, baring her thin chemise to Beauchene's view once again. The safety she had briefly felt evaporated, and she wanted only for Colin to get her away from here. Away from this man.

His jaw was tight. She squeezed his hand again.

"Please, let's go," she whispered. "Please."

Colin did not know what to think when he burst into the room. Nor did he quite know what to think as he guided Elinor out, an arm protectively encircling her shoulders. Beauchene watched with dry amusement, while the Indian man withdrew against the window, his eyes on the floor and his posture stiff. Every instinct in Colin insisted that some ill must be corrected, some violence done to right the obvious wrong of the situation, but Elinor's hand in his stilled his rage. She didn't need his rage. She needed his help.

And so he left those men untouched. He left Beauchene with his smug grin, as he'd left Foyle. He felt as if he had released all his purpose, all his direction, felt it slide through his fingers like the reins of a charging carriage team. And yet it did not matter. Elinor needed him; that was purpose enough.

By the time they reached the room she was shaking. They did not speak. He took the jacket from her shoulders and wrapped a coverlet around her instead, and when she would not release his hand, he sat beside her on the bed and drew her against him. She rested her head on his shoulders and drew in breath after breath, each on the edge of tears he knew she would never allow herself to shed.

"Did he hurt you?" he asked.

"If I said yes, would you hurt him?" Elinor asked idly, tracing the edge of his lapel with her finger. There was something alarmingly distant in her voice. "Would you charge back up the stairs to defend my honor?"

"No," he said.

"No?"

"I wouldn't leave you alone again," he said.

She pulled away from him, but only to turn, to press her lips against his. The touch began lightly, then deepened, her hands ghosting up to lace at the back of his neck. She broke the kiss and pressed her brow against his, eyes downcast.

"Elinor," he said, and she kissed him again, a beat longer this time, her hands darting down to tug at his shirt. "We don't need to—" he began.

"Oh, Colin," she said. "When will you learn to shut up and take yes for an answer?" she asked.

Now, he decided.

There was no question of playful banter and carefully granted permissions; there was no need. She guided his hands where she wanted them, stripped his clothing from him with only scattered moments of hesitation. She left him in his breeches, but cast off the chemise. It was the first time he had seen her stripped of all her clothing. He ran a hand over her hip, marveling at the softness of her skin, the slight curve of her stomach, the perfection of her breasts. She straddled his lap at the edge of the bed, clearly not interested in giving him time to soak in the view. His disappointment was fleeting in the face of the gentle rocking of her hips. He was already engorged. Even through layers of fabric the friction was intense. She rode him, pressing herself against his cock, head tipped back as he tasted whatever part of her he could reach.

Her rhythm was fast, her peak quickly found. She cried out and the sound jolted through him. He caught her around the waist, pulling her down against him as he ground upward in one thrust, two, and then the last, liquid heat spilling. He groaned in wordless pleasure. She gathered him against her, his head resting at her bosom, and they rested a moment, perfectly still as their heartbeats fell back into a steady pace.

"What was that?" Colin asked, a little stunned.

She kissed his cheek. "Proof," she said. "Proof that insidious weasel of a man took nothing from me."

He frowned. Had she thought he needed it? Then he realized—she meant proof for herself. "He didn't touch you, did he?" he asked. Two murders would have him hanged no more than one, he thought. Foyle and Beauchene both would be a worthy pair.

"Not like that," Elinor said. "He wanted to humiliate me." She stroked Colin's temples, brushing back his hair. The evidence of their activities was becoming uncomfortable, but he didn't dare move. Then she might look away, and he would lose that half-drowsy look in her eyes, that soft satisfaction. It might not matter that it was his body she had borrowed to reclaim her own and not some other convenient man's—but he didn't care.

"Then he's a fool," Colin said. "He could not have chosen a more formidable opponent."

She kissed him—on the nose this time. "You are sweet," she said. Not what he wanted to hear. "When you aren't being an ass." Definitely not what he wanted to hear.

She swung off of him and stretched, showing off the whole, curved length of her body. If he were a younger man, that sight alone might have brought him immediately back to attention.

"That can't be comfortable," she said, without indicating the intimate area she clearly meant. "You should get cleaned up, and we should talk. I've found out a few things."

"I—have as well," Colin said.

She crossed to the wardrobe where she had hung her gowns, and he forced himself to stand. He walked gingerly to the wash basin and cleaned himself. He was glad for once that he overpacked for every outing. He was going through drawers and breeches at an alarming pace. By the time he was clothed again, at least to the waist, Elinor had clad herself in a sky-blue gown that did not quite suit her coloring. She sat on the far side of the bed, one knee bent and her body turned to face him. She had regained her composure and secured the knowing, calm expression that was her default.

"What did you find out?" she asked.

He cleared his throat. "It's not so much that I found something out," he admitted. "I heard quite a bit, but I don't believe any of it." He couldn't believe any of it.

"And?"

He adjusted his collar. He did not care to admit how bull-headed and hasty he'd been, but there was no way around it. "I told Foyle who I am."

She gaped at him. "You *what*? What did he do?"

Colin scrubbed his face. "He ranted. He said . . ." He couldn't repeat what Foyle had said. "He claimed that Marie had ruined her own reputation, and that Lord Copeland and he protected her, in exchange for her stake in the mines."

"Ruined her reputation in what way?" Elinor asked.

"I don't wish to speak of the subject."

Elinor pursed her lips. "Colin."

When had she started calling him that? He hadn't noticed the moment of the shift, but he liked it. There were so many barriers between them; the simple name invited her in past all of them, until it was only the two of them, unfettered by past or promises. "He said she had lovers. Many of them," he said sourly, and sat on the bed with his back to her. A moment later she was behind him, her arms crossed over his shoulders and her chin resting on her forearm, so her cheek was beside his. The casual proximity startled him. It was almost as if they were lovers—true lovers, not this odd arrangement of inconvenience—and she was unthinkingly seeking the simple pleasure of his touch.

"I don't believe that's true," she said.

"Nor do I," Colin said, more harshly than he meant. "But there are things I can't ignore."

"What sort of things?" Elinor said.

"There is . . ." He paused. He had brought the portrait. Perhaps he'd thought to confront Foyle with it. He went to his bags now, and found the wide, flat box where it lay. He set it on the bed gingerly while Elinor watched in expectant silence, holding still, as if he would startle if she moved too quickly.

He slid the portrait from its envelope and laid it on the bedspread. Elinor pressed a hand to her lips. He found himself looking at it again, at the strokes that did not so much suggest beauty as command the viewer to acknowledge it.

"Lord Hayes was no artist," he said. "My sister had at least one lover."

Elinor touched the edge of the portrait. "He loved her," she said.

"Perhaps."

"Look at this," she said. "Truly look at it. He made her a goddess. And the way she looks at him . . ." Her fingertips hovered over the page, above Marie's staring eyes, and then she drew away. "It's the same hand. Mr. Bhandari drew this."

"Mr. Banderwho?"

"Bhandari. The Indian gentleman," Elinor said. "Foyle's employee. He drew me, and I guarantee that the portraits were done by the same hand. It's unmistakable."

He furrowed his brow, staring at her. "An Indian?"

"She *was* in India," Elinor said. She drew her legs in beside her, propping herself up on one arm. The pose accentuated the length of her torso, drawing the eye inexorably to the swell of her breasts. Colin wished she did not look so much like she *belonged*—in his company, not in this place. "And Mr. Bhandari is a handsome man."

"Is he?" He frowned. He had not appraised the man's looks, other than to note his race. That was so defining a feature that he hadn't bothered to notice much else, and now he found he had only a hazy recollection of the man's appearance. The realization made him feel odd, almost guilty. That guilt mingled with curiosity, with confusion, with unnamable emotions that swirled at the thought of Marie with the man— with any man. "You said that the man who drew that portrait loved her," he said.

"He did," she said firmly. "And I believe that she loved him."

"Then why marry Foyle?"

She hesitated.

"What do you know?" Colin asked.

"There was a babe," she said. "Stillborn."

"But . . . If Marie was with child, she would have told us. She would have written," Colin said. "Even if it ended in tragedy."

"Unless she was not certain that the child was Hayes's,"

Elinor said softly. "If she was not certain that she could pass the child as his, if it was not."

Colin closed his eyes. This was not how he wanted to remember his sister. Unfaithful to her vows. Keeping secrets from her own family. "She wouldn't have needed a dozen lovers, if he was the one she'd chosen. A relationship with that man—"

"Mr. Bhandari," Elinor said, a bit crisp.

"—would have been dangerous for them both, even without the proof of a child. With the child . . . if Foyle knew of its parentage somehow, had proof, he might have asked anything of her, and she would have had to give it. Or risk exposure." A child. His niece or nephew. It didn't matter, suddenly, whether the child had been Hayes's or Bhandari's or the Second Coming—he'd almost been an uncle, and he'd never known it. The loss, however far removed, seized in his chest.

"If that is what he used against her, I don't see how we can protect against the scandal of its revelation. It might not be the talk of the town, this many years after the fact, but it would do harm nonetheless," Elinor said.

"Then there is nothing to do," Colin said dully. "Nothing to do but leave, and hope that Foyle never chooses to deploy the weapon that he has. We should leave now, before Foyle or Beauchene can act against us."

"Act against us? What are they going to do, exactly? Beauchene is far too interested in you to let you go, or scare you away. He'll want to find a way to get at you, first, at the very least."

"He already has. Which makes you entirely too vulnerable," Colin said. Elinor blinked at him.

"As far as he knows, I'm just a courtesan," she said.

"Who I am obviously in love with," Colin snapped, and then shut his mouth with a click of teeth.

Elinor rolled her eyes. "I will admit you displayed a remarkable protective streak, and I am grateful for that. But there's a world of difference between possessiveness and love—and I don't think Beauchene is the type to read the latter where it is lacking."

He adjusted the buttons at his sleeve. "No," he said. "I suppose he isn't."

"Still, you're right. We should leave. But in the morning. There's a chance—a slim chance, but a chance—that I might know how to shut Foyle up for good."

"Don't leave me in the dark," he said. Leaving was the first sensible suggestion she'd had. And yet a part of him rebelled at the notion. When they left, he would take the sorrow with him, and leave behind their time together. However illusory that togetherness was.

"Beauchene collects information," Elinor said. "I think Foyle is hardly the only blackmailer in this house. If Beauchene has something on Foyle, and I would bet anything that he does, we can use it just as well as he can."

"Blackmail the blackmailer?" Colin asked.

"You may have noticed I have something of a talent for the process myself," Elinor said with a faint smile.

He kissed her, swiftly, before he could think better of it. It felt like a good-bye. She blinked at him, surprised, when he was done. "One last night," he told her. "Then I take you home."

Chapter 22

∽

Lord Farleigh objected to Elinor's plan at first, once she'd actually laid it out in detail; she'd known he would. But she wore him down. They stayed secluded in their room through the evening, both of them tense with unspent energy, until the night wore on and the house settled into silence. Not everyone was asleep, but nearly everyone was abed. It was the time for mice to scurry and thieves to skulk, and tonight the two of them were thieves.

Elinor led the way down the halls, her feet slippered and silent. Lord Farleigh stalked behind her, still taut as a bowstring. They stole up the stairs together, and down the corridor to Beauchene's study. Elinor paused, checking the gap beneath the door for telltale light, then felt for the doorknob in the pale moonlight. Locked. She'd expected that, and pulled two heavy pins from her hair.

One of the advantages of having a thief for a sister-in-law was learning a number of unladylike tricks. Picking locks had been the first thing Elinor had insisted Joan teach her, and she'd proven talented. She probed carefully at the lock, smiling with satisfaction when she felt the resistance that told her she'd found the right spot. *You have to charm it open*, Joan had said. *Most people will go on about how it's like a woman, but that's too obvious. Think of it like a conversation.* Elinor met point with counterpoint, and like a smooth change of the subject eased the lock open. She pushed the door, letting it swing on well-oiled hinges, and gave Lord Farleigh a triumphant look.

"Going to take up jewel theft next?" Colin asked. He sounded as if he was struggling to appear disapproving instead of impressed.

"Not tonight," Elinor replied, and slipped in.

Here, they could not do without light. Colin had brought along a candle and tinder box, and in a few moments he had the candle lit.

"The desk first," Elinor declared. Colin followed dutifully, keeping the light above and behind her, so that it could shed light without dripping wax down her back. She tried the main drawer first, and found that it slid open without resistance. The drawing lay on top of a slender ledger. Colin made a soft sound behind her, a grunt somewhere between approval and anger. A rather confused sound, she had to say. "Hm," she said. She lifted the drawing free. "I rather like it. Don't you?"

"I'm not sure I should answer that," Colin said. Elinor smiled to herself and set it on top of the desk. She picked up the ledger and paged through it, but it seemed to be simple household accounts, obviously tied to the expenses of the party. Unless *60 bottles Madeira* was a very clever code for something, it wasn't of use. She put it back where she'd found it and moved on to the other drawers. Two slid open readily, but she found only odds and ends—quills and inks, a ball of twine. The next contained personal correspondence of a very intimate nature between the Beauchenes. Her French was good enough to have her blushing by the second paragraph, though as she skimmed through them she noted a few particular promises and recollections that intrigued her. Perhaps before this was over, she and Colin could—

No. She and Lord Farleigh would leave directly, once they were done here. They had risked quite enough already. And they would have no more time for the more enjoyable side of their little deal.

She stifled a pang of regret. She was honest enough to admit she'd fallen rather foolishly into an infatuation with Lord Farleigh. She was also smart enough to realize that it had to end. When they left, she would simply train herself out of the feelings. Surely by the fall and Lord Farleigh's wedding, logic would prevail against the vagaries of sentiment. Though perhaps she should contrive to be ill that day; certainly the thought of sitting through the ceremony made her queasy.

She'd gotten one of the locked drawers open. It was empty. She frowned. "Why lock an empty drawer?" she asked.

"Oh, I know this," Colin said. "It has a false bottom."

She eyed it dubiously, and placed a hand at the top and bottom of the base. "There's only a narrow bit of wood," she said. Then she reached back. The back of her hand brushed something. "Ah!" she said, and felt upward. A thick file was secured to the wood above the drawer. She worked it free and laid it atop the table.

It was not one file, she realized, but many—packets of paper, bound with string and marked with cards bearing initials. The first—*A.W.*—contained financial records of some sort. She could not see anything obviously amiss in them, but her eye was untrained. The next included a rather more obvious sin: letters, *signed* letters, between the wife of a prominent member of parliament and a member of the opposing party.

"Hm," Colin said, reading over her shoulder as she paged through them. "That makes me worry for the breadth of the man's imagination. How many times can it be thrilling to read that your lover intends to—"

"Hush," Elinor said, before he could utter the phrase in question. It was as straightforward a description of the procreative act as she could imagine, and it appeared at least twice in each letter. The woman's responses, carefully interspersed between the man's letters, were far more varied in their requests. And increasingly frustrated, as apparently he had no more imagination—or openness to suggestion—in bed than in his missives. The correspondence ended with a demand to *discover a better use for that tongue than droning on about taxation or do not bother showing up again.*

"Probably not relevant," Colin whispered, with a throaty chuckle. She bit her lip with a smile.

"But very entertaining," she pointed out. She skipped past the next few—gambling debts, something about a parcel of land, another unwise (though less descriptive) affair. The next card read *E.F.*, and she halted. It was a thick packet, contained in a long, folded sheet of blank foolscap. She opened it with trepidation, and began to page through.

"Oh, hell," Colin said.

Elinor's throat constricted. The pages added up quickly, telling a story worse than any she had concocted herself. There were letters from Foyle to Marie, professing his love. A single letter from Marie, insisting he leave her alone. Letters from solicitors regarding the refusal of Lord Hayes to abide by some informal verbal agreement and share his interests in the mine with Lord Copeland. The record of Hayes's death—not mysterious, it seemed; the man had a weak heart, and it had caught up to him. Forms and correspondence regarding the sale of the mines by Edward Foyle, after his marriage to Marie, to Lord Copeland for a paltry sum.

And then the worst of it. Records of Marie's death. Of an investigation begun—and promptly halted.

"God," Colin said. "She didn't die of cholera."

She'd drowned. Or at least, been pulled from the river. "This says . . ." Elinor trailed off.

"Mr. Bhandari was the suspect," Colin said dully. "He was arrested. And then he was released, because suddenly she wasn't murdered. She died of cholera. And no one gets arrested because his lover died of cholera."

She flipped the last page, her limbs numb. Mr. Bhandari couldn't have killed Marie. Could he?

But she could imagine it. A lover, forced to hide and conceal his feelings, not only because of her marriage but because of the cast of his features, the color of his skin, the language he spoke. When Lord Hayes died, perhaps he had entertained some hope that at least he would not have to watch her with another man. And then she'd married Foyle.

"Bhandari said that he owed Foyle," she remembered. "Foyle

must have had a hand in hiding the manner of Marie's death—in clearing Bhandari's name." Whether or not he was guilty, Bhandari's life would have been destroyed by the accusation.

"I should have killed Foyle when I had the chance," Colin ground out.

"Don't be ridiculous. Then we wouldn't have found any of this," Elinor said. She peered at the remaining items. There was a brief note, instructing an unnamed agent to ensure that the 'usual payment' to one Mrs. Fincher was doubled, to make up for a missed payment the previous month, and then three letters from Foyle to a 'Mister O—,' which seemed largely to concern the birds he'd seen on his travels and the state of the weather. Dull fare, but she lingered a moment over Mrs. Fincher. The name sounded vaguely familiar, but she could not recall where she had heard it before. In any case, this was nothing terribly interesting, so why was it included in such a meaty collection of misdeeds?

A footstep sounded in the hall outside. Too near. If the night-time wanderer meant to come in here, there was nowhere to go. No time to hide the evidence of what they'd done. On instinct, Elinor grabbed a few of the pages and rolled them swiftly into a tight tube, then shoved them down the front of her dress. Thankfully, her bosom and the ill fit of the gown concealed the odd shape. She scattered the remaining pages, praying it would be difficult to tell at first that anything was gone.

Colin seized her, drawing her down below the desk even as he blew out the candle.

The door opened. Elinor froze in Colin's encircling arms, trying not to move or breathe. Light spilled over the floor, the warm glow of a lantern. A laugh sounded from the doorway.

"Stand up. Let us be adult about this," came Madame Beauchene's voice. Elinor looked at Colin, who nodded tightly. There was little point in staying crouched there when it was obvious someone was present, the evidence of their spying still spread across the desk. The two of them rose in unison. Elinor opened her mouth to speak, but was rendered mute by the sight of a pistol in Madame Beauchene's hand. "Well," she said. "What a fascinating turn of events."

Chapter 23

❦

Colin's mouth went dry at the sight of the gun. He grabbed for Elinor.

"Madame Beauchene, I can explain," Elinor said, stepping around the desk.

Madame Beauchene lifted the pistol. "I do not require an explanation," she said. "It is quite clear to me what is happening here. I don't blame you, girl. You are not the first woman to be caught up in a man's schemes." She lifted a shoulder in an uncaring shrug. "So I do not wish you to think this is personal. Now come here."

Elinor stayed where she was. Colin circled to join her, placing himself slightly before her, so that he could interpose himself if he needed to. He gauged the distance to the other woman. Could he cross that space without her putting a bullet into one of them? "You can't shoot us here," he said. "What would people say? You won't pull that trigger."

"Won't I? They will say many things, Lord Farleigh. They will perhaps say that a marquess became obsessed with a courtesan, and when she was disloyal to him, he killed her and then himself. So tragic. Awful, it happening in our house, but what could we do? Or perhaps they will say that the jealous courtesan killed her noble lover, hmm? And who is to say differently? Her? She is a whore."

Colin raised a staying hand. "She's not a courtesan," he said. "She's the sister of the Earl of Fenbrook."

The woman laughed. "The Earl of Fenbrook's sister is a spinster," she said. "A virginal monument to virtue, without a trace of sensuality. Besides, you are a man of honor. You would never allow such a woman to remain in place like this."

Damn. Damn and double damn. "What do you want?" he asked.

"I want her to walk over here," Madame Beauchene said. "Slowly. And then I want her to turn around."

"No," Colin said, but Elinor squeezed his arm.

"It will be all right," she said, in a voice he had heard a hundred times. A thousand. She was the reassuring voice, the voice of calm, in every piece of chaos he and Martin had ever found themselves in. When they were young, he had found it irritating. Superior. Now he marveled at the strength it must take when he felt as though he would shatter from the force of the blood pounding through him.

"No," he said.

"We don't have a choice," she pointed out. *Unless you think you can get that gun from her,* her expression seemed to say, a sort of dim hope that vanished with a little shake of her head. He would only get them killed.

So she walked away from him as he curled his hands ineffectually into fists. She turned, head held high, and Madame Beauchene pressed the muzzle of the pistol against her ribs. "Hold this," the Frenchwoman said, and handed Elinor the lantern. "Now," she said. "We are going to exit the room, and step to the side. You are going to walk in front of us, Lord Farleigh, and if you take one step in the wrong direction, I will kill your little pet."

The gun dug hard against Elinor's ribs, and she flinched. He flinched with her, and raised his hands, placating. He kept them up as Madame Beauchene and Elinor backed out of the room, and as he followed. He gave the woman a wide berth in the hallway, calculating distances and velocities. Imagining the damage a bullet could do, fired at that range through Elinor's ribs.

Madame Beauchene directed him down the hallway to a new set of stairs. Her husband was waiting there, looking harried.

"Really?" he asked his wife in French. "Is this necessary?"

"It is," she insisted.

Beauchene looked Colin up and down and gave a helpless shrug, as if to absolve himself of guilt. "Apologies," he said. "But you understand, we must place the privacy of our guests above all other concerns."

"Privacy from everyone but you," Colin said, which only drew a laugh from the Frenchman.

"My father died in France," he said. "Along with my sisters, my brother, my friends. I would have been killed. I fled here, and do you think I found sympathy? No. Suspicion and contempt were my gifts. It became obvious that I could not survive here unless I had friends, and no one was willing to befriend me. I have done what I must to protect myself and my wife, no more."

"It seemed like a bit more," Elinor said drily.

"It is good to have contingencies. And to punish wicked men," Beauchene said. "And to live comfortably. I don't want to kill either of you."

"Then let us go," Colin said. "We'll leave. You'll never hear from us again."

Beauchene looked as if he was considering it. Considering it seriously. Colin believed him—the man was slime, but he was not a murderer.

"We cannot risk it," Madame Beauchene said with a hiss.

Beauchene looked regretful then, and Colin's heart sank. He opened his mouth to speak.

A bang sounded in the hall. Colin let out a cry, reaching for Elinor—but she was fine. Madame Beauchene turned toward the window with a gasp, the unspent pistol in her hand.

"The fireworks!" she cried, as red light glittered through the windows. "Someone has set off the fireworks!"

As she turned, the pistol went with her. Colin lunged—a second behind the swing of Elinor's arm as she flung the lantern against Mme. Beauchene's arm. The glass shattered. Oil spilled over Madame Beauchene's sleeve; she screamed, beating at the flames that followed. Beauchene dove for her, whipping his jacket off, and Colin grabbed Elinor's arm.

They ran. Down the stairs, as pops and crackles and the flare of multicolored lights marked the explosions in the sky outside. As they reached the lower floor, half-clothed bodies emerged from their rooms, cooing and gasping in confused excitement. Colin pushed through them, Elinor's hand in his. He spotted a man he knew, careened past him—the man halted, staring at Elinor, but Colin could only pray that he would put down the sight of her to lack of sleep and a trick of the shadows.

Then they had reached the next flight of stairs. A figure loomed, halfway up, and Colin prepared to shove him aside.

"Come with me," the man said. Mr. Bhandari. He smelled faintly of gunpowder and smoke.

"That was you?" Colin asked.

Mr. Bhandari's teeth gleamed in the darkness. "I thought you might appreciate a distraction. I have horses ready."

Colin looked back at Elinor. Could they trust the man? She nodded once, expression tight. "He didn't do it," she said. Marie, she meant. He didn't kill Marie. Colin didn't know if he believed that. But between Bhandari and Beauchene, he would take Bhandari. "Let's go," he said.

Bhandari let them around to the servant's entrance at a near run. A scullery maid stood outside, holding the reins of three horses. Bhandari tossed her a coin, and she vanished inside.

"Can you ride astride?" Bhandari asked Elinor.

"Of course," she said. "Though not with dignity." She had already begun hiking her skirts up. Colin and Bhandari helped her into the saddle of a bay mare, then took to their

own horses. The animals sidled and champed, disquieted
by the fireworks still crackling overhead. Bhandari spurred
his mount with a cluck, and the others followed with little
prompting, nerves giving them speed. Colin glanced back.
There was no sign of Beauchene, only the guests spilling
out onto the lawn to watch the final explosions as the fuses
burnt to their ends.

They rode at a canter, not wanting to tire the horses too
quickly—or go so fast one of the mounts lost its footing in
the dark. Bhandari seemed to know where he was going.
Elinor was glad. It was all she could do to keep a grip on the
horse's mane and stay seated. Her breath came in short, sharp
gasps as she struggled against a tightening chest, like a corset
cinched too tight. *Not again*, she thought, and tried to draw
in a single, long breath. To resist, more than anything, the
urge to panic. These spells always got worse once she pan-
icked, once she started to fight for as much air as quickly as
she could. And the headache was beginning—a throb behind
her eyes that she knew would spread until she could not bear
even the pale flicker of a candle's light against her lids.

It had not been this bad for years. Not since she was a
teenager, whirling around on the dance floor when suddenly
all the air was stolen from her lungs. Not since that last,
humiliating collapse, her dance partner reaching out for her
too late. After that, she'd been an object of pity. She hadn't
cared; she'd been too frightened to care. It had felt as if she
was dying. It felt that way now.

Only hold on, she told herself. *Let the horse do the work.
Only breathe.*

But it was an impossible dictate. Her throat was closing
up. Pain arced around her ribs, and spots began to dance in
front of her vision. She coughed, hunching over the saddle.

"Elinor?" Colin said, drawing up short as her horse sidled
to a stop. She coughed again, pressing a hand to her throat.

"Was she hurt?" Bhandari asked. She shook her head.
She only needed one good breath. Just one, but she could

barely draw a small swallow of air, and it felt as if there was nothing under her at all—no solid horse, no ground, only a plummeting fall. She tilted in the saddle.

"Elinor!" Colin said, but his voice came as though from a great distance. She pulled herself forward with effort, falling across the horse's neck, not wanting to know what would happen if she struck her head against the ground. She heard the shift and clatter of hooves, the low murmur of anxious voices, and then strong hands were hauling her from her seat, settling her sideways in front of Colin. His arms bracketed her in, holding her stable while she labored with breath after breath. He was saying something. She really should pay attention. "What do I do?" he was asking. "Elinor, tell me how to help."

"Rest," she said. She had to stop, take another breath. "Steam."

"There's a house up ahead," Bhandari said. "We can find help there."

Elinor sagged against Colin, gripping the front of his shirt. The movement of the horse jarred her, interrupting what little rhythm she could inflict on her ragged breathing. She tried to focus on something, anything else.

When she was young and these episodes came upon her, Martin or Marie would sit by her side. They would read to her, or simply talk, for hours or for days. And Colin—Colin had sent books, she remembered, with jokes written inside the covers for her. He'd always treated her like such a nuisance, but never when she was ill. Never when she couldn't match him, barb for barb. Now each breath brought his scent, his taste to her. All mixed up with leather and horse and the summer night, but unmistakably *him*. She'd been memorizing him, these past few days. Memorizing the parts of him that could never belong to her.

It didn't ease her breathing, but it made the ride bearable. And then they were halting, Colin shouting to rouse the occupants of whatever house they had arrived at. She shut her eyes and wrapped her arms around his neck, pressing her face against his shoulder. One breath, two, three. All she had to think about was the next bit of air, because he was there; he would keep the rest of the world at bay.

She was hardly aware of being handed down, then lifted again into Colin's arms. It was only a long while later, seated in a rough wooden chair, when hot, steaming tea was pressed into her hands, that she roused herself enough to open her eyes. She took a scalding sip and held the mug beneath her lips, breathing in the steam as the hot water slid down her throat. Colin was rubbing her back, murmuring to her. A man she didn't recognize—the occupant of the house, no doubt—hovered anxiously across the small kitchen. There was no sign of Bhandari.

She sipped again. The episodes didn't fade quickly, but as long as she was still, as long as she had the steam coiling around her face, she could begin to relax. To believe that it would pass.

And pray that her delay had not cost them.

Chapter 24

~

Elinor woke in a strange bed, fully clothed. She had been awake most of the night, her breath slowly easing back to a normal rhythm. It was the worst attack she'd had in a decade. They had always been the most difficult of her maladies, these spells of breathlessness. The headaches she could handle, though they were agonizing. The various illnesses, weaknesses, dizzy spells—well, half of those she was certain were more the products of the cures she was offered than any innate flaw in her own biology.

The spells of breathlessness were the only ill she feared might kill her. And it very nearly had, last night. If they had not chanced upon the house, if they had not been able to stop, to rest—she shuddered.

Today, her chest was sore, but her breathing even. The lingering pangs of a headache ghosted at the back of her skull, but they were fading as well. Beyond that, the worst discomfort she suffered was that of sleeping in a corset—one stuffed with a roll of paper, at that.

She extracted the documents with a slight frown. She'd forgotten she had stowed them there. They were crumpled and creased now, but largely undamaged.

Perhaps this had not been an entirely wasted venture.

She rose and oriented herself. The room she was in had not a door but a curtain drawn around the bed for privacy. Once she drew it aside, she saw a narrow staircase leading down, and caught the low mutter of men's voices. Bhandari and Colin, she thought. She made her way down the stairs, sighing when the voices abruptly cut off. She knew the expressions that would greet her. This was always the moment she turned from a blood-and-flesh woman to a fragile porcelain doll. And sure enough, both men wore looks of stricken worry when she entered the main room. They were seated around a rickety table, the occupant of the house nowhere in evidence. Colin rose and strode toward her.

"Are you all right to be up?" he asked, voice nearly slurring under the weight of his worry.

Elinor waved a hand. "I'll survive," she said, trying not to sound as if she'd ever doubted it. "You know this sort of thing happens to me now and again."

"I thought it had stopped," he said.

"Very nearly." The worst of it had ended with the treatments; a restful, idle life had kept the remaining episodes from becoming too difficult to endure. Or conceal. Even Martin wasn't aware of the extent to which they lingered. "Are we safe here?"

Bhandari shifted. "For now," he said. "But we should not stay. I have arranged for a carriage to collect the two of you."

"How did you know to help us?" Elinor asked. "And—why? Forgive me for asking, but you do work for Foyle."

"Ah. That does require some explanation," Bhandari said. "Mr. Foyle told me who you were, Lord Farleigh. Lady Marie's brother. He feared that you would kill him. He began to speak of killing you first, before you could act. It was then that I had the horses prepared, and went to find you. As for the why—I owe Marie that much, at least. Far more, in fact."

"You prepared three horses," Elinor said. "You intended to come with us, then."

"It was clear to me that I would be unable to remain," Bhandari said. "And I wished the chance to speak with Lord Farleigh, in any case. To tell him things that ought to have been spoken of many years ago." He could not meet Colin's eyes, or speak to him directly, Elinor realized. "I found that you were not in your room, and I sighted Madame Beauchene traversing the halls with pistol in hand. I took the chance that a distraction would be in order."

"It very much was," Elinor said. "Thank you for your help. It was . . . unexpected."

Bhandari inclined his head. "You are welcome."

"Do you think Beauchene will come after us?"

"He will not expect us to have stopped so soon," Bhandari said. He gave a half smile that contained little amusement. "It's almost clever, ending our flight so quickly."

Elinor walked to the chair opposite him and sat, not yet steady on her feet. She set the rolled papers on the tabletop. "Did you know about these?"

He reached across the table and spread the pages, frowning. "Ah," he said. "No, though I suspected Beauchene possessed something like them. There was little other reason for my employer to be so interested in friendship with the man."

"That's why you work for him, isn't it?" Elinor asked. "You were suspected of Marie's death."

He looked sharply at her, then away.

"Did you kill her?" Colin asked. He sounded too calm. Elinor didn't trust it.

"No," Bhandari said, though there was an odd note in it—doubt? "I loved her."

"She was married."

Bhandari gave a choked laugh. "I knew that. I tried . . . Do you think I wanted to fall in love with an Englishwoman? I had a marriage arranged, a girl I knew in childhood. We would have had a happy life together. But Marie . . ." He shook his head. "I did not kill her. But I might have been able to save her, and I did not."

"What do you mean?" Elinor asked. "It seems like there was a great deal of chaos after Lord Hayes died."

"Chaos is one word for it," Bhandari said.

"Was he murdered?" Colin asked. "It said his heart failed, but obviously records are not trustworthy."

"No, no," Bhandari said, with a quick shake of his head. "He and Lord Copeland had reached an arrangement about the mines. Neither of them was happy, precisely, but it would have saved both a great deal of hassle in the courts. Mr. Foyle, though, offended Lord Hayes, before the papers could be signed."

"Offended him how?"

Bhandari spread his hands. "I am not certain. It likely had something to do with Marie. Mr. Foyle was . . . entranced. I cannot blame him for that, but he would not allow her refusal to dissuade him from his affections. It became very awkward for all of us. I suspect that Lord Hayes believed Marie was unfaithful to him, and this is what angered him."

"He was right," Colin said darkly.

Bhandari rested his hand flat on the table. "You must not think of your sister in that way," he said. His accent made the precision of his tone all the more cutting, like each word was carved carefully from stone. "She was a good woman, whatever her transgressions. A moral woman, whatever her failures. She is not alive to atone for them. She can only be forgiven."

Elinor looked to Colin. He was holding himself very still, but whatever anger was in those eyes was not for Mr. Bhandari. She rose and walked to him, tucking her body against his and taking his hand. She met his eyes for a long beat. He had to know the truth. He might not enjoy hearing about his older sister as a flawed being. He had spent so much time worshiping her. But he had to listen.

He did not have to listen alone. His hand tightened around hers.

"What happened then?" he asked. "After the deal fell apart."

Bhandari waited a long time before replying. "Marie had stopped speaking to me, perhaps because of the falling-out. She would not see me—or anyone. She remained in her rooms, in her home, for months. And then Lord Hayes died. Lord Copeland went to Marie, asking her to honor the agreement in her husband's place. Marie despised Copeland; she would not sign the proper paperwork. And then . . . then she married Foyle. He owed debts—a great many of them. Copeland made them vanish in exchange for the mines, and Foyle was all too happy to comply. But I never understood how he convinced Marie to marry him. She despised him, but then . . ."

He didn't know. Elinor shut her eyes briefly. "She had a child," Elinor said. Bhandari's eyes widened. "Those months she hid away, she was with child. It was stillborn," she said. "Foyle told me as much."

"He has never spoken of it to me," Bhandari said, confusion and sorrow written in his features.

"Because it was yours," Colin said in a rumble. Bhandari stared at him. "Your bastard child. That's what Foyle used to make Marie marry him. Threat of exposure, because she'd borne *your* child."

Bhandari turned his face away, as if to hide any emotions there. Elinor did him the courtesy of looking away as well, but Colin fixed his gaze on him, as if to discover the quality of the man's character by witnessing his pain. Perhaps it worked. In any case, Bhandari looked back at last, and spoke in a steady tone.

"I never meant to hurt her," he said. "I loved her."

"That, I believe," Colin said. "And in a better world, perhaps that would have been enough to protect her."

"After all of that, how could you work for Foyle?" Elinor asked.

He gave a hollow laugh. "Because I had no choice. It was the price he demanded, for saving my life. He protected me, when they came to arrest me. He told them that I could not have killed Marie, that he knew where I had been. It was a lie, of course, and I do not understand why he did it. Or why his price was my service." Elinor could guess. Foyle was a jealous man. What better way to nurse that jealousy than to lord power over the man Marie had truly loved? "I agreed. I was eager for a way to leave the country. I thought he was a devil I understood." He shrugged. "And he was, for the most part. As long as I did not complain at his endless parade of minor sins, there was little that was onerous about serving him. And it felt like a penance."

"Do you believe that Foyle killed her?" Colin asked.

"No," Bhandari said. "I do not. I have come to know him very well. He is a coward. He is not a murderer."

"You said that you could have saved her," Colin said. "I don't see how."

"If I had insisted on seeing her. If I had somehow stopped her from marrying that man—"

Colin shook his head with a violent jerk. "Do not lift the burden of blame from others' shoulders by putting it on your own. It diminishes her. It diminishes their guilt. Don't."

Bhandari stared at Colin for a long moment, then bowed his head. "I understand," he said. "I wish that I could give you more answers. I wish that I could have spared you the last few days."

Elinor bit her lip lightly. For all that had happened, she was glad that she knew even what little Mr. Bhandari was able to provide. And she could not say she regretted this adventure. She would be glad when the danger was over, when she was home and safe—but she did not want to think about what else that entailed. The end of her arrangement with Colin. The end of a simple touch like they shared now.

As if echoing her thought, he pulled away from her. "We will go to my estate," he said. "Will you come with us?"

Bhandari shook his head. "I must return."

"You don't know what sort of welcome you will receive," Elinor pointed out, not letting her alarm show in her face.

"Nor what retaliation my employer will take if I do not return," Bhandari said.

Colin snorted. "Let him try. You've given me more of the truth than anyone else in this mess, and you likely saved our lives last night. You'll have my help, if you need it. God knows any debt to Foyle is long since discharged, simply by having put up with him this long."

Bhandari looked stubborn. Elinor sighed. "You will not bring her back by suffering without cause," she said. "You'll come with us. And then you will go wherever you like. Do you have a profession?"

Bhandari seemed taken aback. "I was a teacher," he said. "A tutor. That was a very long time ago."

"And I imagine a great deal more enjoyable than following Foyle around," she said. "Promise me you will come with us. After all you've done."

"How can I refuse?" he said. He rose. "I will see that things are prepared. And I must ask . . . who are you, memsahib?"

Elinor gave a startled laugh. She had never introduced herself properly.

Colin spared her. He stepped forward, face schooled into perfect formality. "May I present Lady Elinor Hargrove, sister to the Earl of Fenbrook," he said. "Who has most certainly not been in our company, nor anywhere near the residence of one Mr. Beauchene."

"Of course not," Mr. Bhandari said, sounding a bit strangled. "My Lady."

"I promise I'm not normally this scandalous," Elinor said. She didn't feel scandalous. She felt assaulted, and in need of comfort. If she had been a braver woman, perhaps she would have asked Colin for such comfort. Braver, or more foolish. It could only make things worse to rely on him, when she would not be able to again.

❧

Chapter 25

Elinor had the carriage to herself, as Mr. Bhandari had chosen to drive and Colin to ride alongside. They stopped one night at an inn, where enough money exchanged hands to quell any awkward questions. Elinor slept lightly, half-expecting Colin to steal into her chamber, but she did not see him again until the morning. It was late the next day when they reached the Farleigh estate. Colin rode up beside the window of the carriage as they approached.

"This will be difficult to explain," he said, brow furrowed.

"You should ask Joan for references," Elinor said. "Discreet staff are ever so useful."

"I don't normally find a need for excessive discretion," Colin said ruefully.

"The best explanation is no explanation," Elinor said. "They won't question you. Don't give them a story to pick apart; just stride in as if you own the place. As, in fact, you do."

"I do at that," Colin said. He rubbed the back of his neck. "I dearly hope Martin never hears about this."

"If he does, I am going to claim everything was your fault," she told him with a sly smile. He chuckled and urged his mount forward. Her smile fell away as soon as he had turned from her. It was so difficult to reconcile the emotions churning within her. There was the horror at the thought of Marie's death and the vile circumstances surrounding it at the fore. But there was also that persistent desire, that longing, every time she glanced at Colin. And twinned with it, her sorrow at the sure knowledge that he was slipping further from her with each step toward home.

A rather confused footman handed her down from the carriage a few minutes later, eyes going to her ragged dress and his mouth pressing into a thin line with the effort of avoiding comment. She held her head high and swept in, then claimed the first maid she saw and asked for a hot bath and a change of clothes. The clothes appeared while she was soaking, and by the time she was scrubbed pink, reclothed, and her hair put back into a semblance of its proper order, she felt nearly human again. The dress was one of Kitty's, which meant it was too short at the hem and too tight at the shoulders, but it would do. She hesitated before stowing the egret charm in a borrowed reticule. She felt somehow reluctant to put it away.

"Do you know where Lord Farleigh is?" she asked the maid who had helped with her hair.

The girl gave a quick, cautious smile. "In the billiard room, I believe," she said. "My Lady."

"Good. I'll go see him," Elinor said brightly, not inviting contradiction. Her heart was beating a little fast. It was one thing to ignore propriety when she was masked and among those least likely to care, but here, under the eyes of men and women she'd met, who knew who she was, and who— God forbid—might get word to her brother, she felt rather sick. Still, she steeled herself against the feeling. They were not done with their caper yet. They had yet to determine how, exactly, she was to return home without being noticed.

She expected to find Colin and Bhandari together, but Colin was alone, practicing shots. She paused a moment in the doorway, admiring his figure as he bent over the table, eying the trajectory of the ball he was about to strike. It emphasized his length, the lean muscle that gave him that almost harsh look. He paused, straightened up. "There you are," he said.

She stepped in. "Here I am," she said.

"You look almost like yourself."

"Didn't I, before?" she asked. She drew forward another step.

"Another version of yourself, maybe," he said.

"And what did you think of her?"

He gave an odd smile and a tilt of his head. "I enjoyed meeting her," he said. "But I don't think I would like to enjoy her company at the expense of yours."

"I think I agree," she said. "That was an . . . interesting interlude. I don't think I care to repeat it." It might be more frightening, in a way, to be without that mask. But she felt better without it.

"The interlude isn't over yet," he said. His grip on the cue was like a stranglehold. He would drown himself in his brooding at this rate. She felt as if she were drowning herself. Perhaps they could keep each other afloat, for a time. She closed her fingers around his.

"It can be," she said. "We don't need to chase any more answers. We can leave things as they are, and forget."

"You don't believe that."

"No, I don't," she admitted. "Perhaps before Mr. Bhandari told us what he knew, but now?"

"Now we must know who killed her," Colin said. "However impossible a task that seems."

She let her hands run up to his wrists, running lightly over his skin, and felt him shiver. "Do something for me," she said.

"Anything."

"Pretend, for a few minutes. Pretend that we can forget."

He set the cue aside, half-turning away from her. "I don't know if I can do that. Even for a second."

She touched his shoulder, drawing close to him. "Please," she said.

He turned with such suddenness she stumbled back, but

he caught her wrist and drew her up short. His grip was tight, almost painful. Almost. "Ask again," he said, his eyes locked on hers.

"Please," she said. "Forget. Help me forget. For a little while."

He tugged, pulling her arm to maneuver her against the side of the billiard table, using his body to trap her there without touching her. "You will have to be more specific," he said, voice perfectly calm and cold.

She met his eyes boldly. "Kiss me," she said.

"If you want me to do something, you will have to ask properly," he reminded her, and gave her wrist a light squeeze.

"Please kiss me," she amended, and leaned toward him, eager. She wanted him, and in this moment it didn't matter that he didn't want *her*. That he wanted her body was enough; that he wanted only her body made her thrill in a way that she could not explain.

He kissed her. It was a sharp, precise kiss, calculated. She pressed herself against him, eager, deepening the kiss, urging him silently to do the same. But he broke away. Trailed a finger down her cheek. "You like that," he said.

"Yes," she breathed.

"What do you like?"

"I like it when you kiss me," she said.

"What else?"

She flushed. She still couldn't say it, couldn't spell it out. "We are not in the room anymore," she reminded him. "You don't make the rules."

"This is my house," he said. "I am always the one who makes the rules, here. Which means that this is all my responsibility. My desires. You can ask for anything, because I am the one in charge. Do you understand?"

She paused, unsure. She had been trained for so long not to think of such things, not to desire them or admit her desires. Not to ask. But they were his rules, and she was only being obedient. It made it easier. It made it exciting. She could be bold, because it was obedience.

"What do you want?" he asked her again, softly.

"I want you to touch me," she said. She hesitated. "I want you to take me, Colin."

It was his turn to still, his hand against her neck, his face an inch away from hers. "Are you certain?" he said. "The risk—"

"Can be diminished," she said. And laughed. "And if I am to bear a child, we certainly have the resources and cleverness to arrange for its well-being without admitting to the circumstances of its conception." The thought of having a child was a joyous one, whatever the circumstances. The thought of having his child—

It was better not to chase that thought.

"We must be clear on one point," Colin said. "If you bear my child, I will marry you. There is time before the wedding to be certain. But if you are with child, I will not allow it to be a bastard. Do you understand?"

She rested both her hands on his chest. Her body craved his touch, but she could not let her desire make this decision. He had a right to such a demand. And she could have him, without the risk, could enjoy him as they had already enjoyed each other. Was it worth the cost, after all? Could she survive, married to a man she loved who did not love her in turn, in exchange for this pleasure?

She couldn't focus on the question. She could only think of how he felt against her, of the heat of his hand where it scorched her neck. "I want you," she said. "Whatever the cost."

"Cost," he echoed, and smiled wryly. "Well. I shall do my best to see that you do not have to pay it."

She wasn't certain what prompted the bitter edge to his words, and she didn't have time to contemplate it. He spun, moving away from her, and shut and locked the door.

Oh, good Lord. It hadn't been closed before, had it?

He chuckled when he turned back to her. "Don't worry. No one's been by. That I noticed. Now. Where were we?"

The front of his breeches would have been an obvious reminder if she had somehow forgotten in those few seconds. She slid her hands down his torso, but he caught her before she could run them over his erection.

"You said you wanted me to touch you," he said. "You said nothing of touching me in turn."

"But—"

"I insist," he said, and spun her. She fetched up against the side of the billiard table, catching herself with both hands. A delicious feeling coiled in her core. "Don't move," he instructed her, and pressed his hands over hers once, briefly, to emphasize the point. She turned her head. He clucked his tongue. "Don't move, I said," he reminded her, and she tensed, forcing herself to stare straight ahead, anticipation making her skin come alive with phantom sensation. She could not see him, but she could feel him, hear him moving behind her. He did not touch her for an agonizing moment, and then his fingertips grazed the back of her neck. She sucked in a breath, but his touch roved upward, and then came a tug at her hair. He dropped a pin onto the lip of the table, beside her hand. Then another.

"There are a great deal of pins in my hair," she warned him. She didn't know if she could survive long enough for him to remove all of them.

"You are more pins than patience, I think," he said, his lips against the back of her neck. She arched back against him, but he only laughed and drew away.

The next pin, he trailed down her neck. Then two ghosted across her bare arms, and then one nipped along the collar of her dress. The cold metal made her skin turn to goose bumps; the touch made her heart beat quickly, made her long for more.

"Please," she said, remembering. He kissed the place where her neck met her shoulder, bit down. She cried out, pushing back against him, just as he pulled the last pins free, her hair now hanging loose and wild around her shoulders. "Please," she said again, as his teeth found her earlobe.

"You are still distressingly clothed," he reminded her.

"I don't care," she said. "I want you." She was burning with it, ached with it. His hand darted around her body, skimming her hip, and slid between her legs, pressing hard through her dress. The heel of his hand ground against her sex, and she moaned, moving against it.

He gave a harsh yank at the collar of her dress, forcing it and her thin corset down, baring her breasts. His erection pressed against her back, and she grinned—his breath was no less uncontrolled than hers, his desire no less potent. "You want me," he echoed, his voice hoarse. "You want me to take you, do you?"

"You don't need to take me," she whispered, shutting her eyes. "I'm yours already."

He gave a sound like a growl and pushed her forward, guiding her to brace her hands against the table. Then he was rucking up her skirts around her hips, and his hand was between her legs again, fingers sliding through the wetness at her cleft. His touch sent a jolt through her, and she bit her lip to keep from crying out too loudly.

"I do still have servants," he reminded her, desire and humor setting his voice at an odd pitch. "Try not to startle them."

He slid two fingers inside her with the final word, and she clamped her lips together to keep the sound from escaping them. He moved in and out of her, and her hips moved with him. She could feel her climax building, and her fingernails dug into the fabric of the table.

Then he withdrew. She let out small sound of protest, but the rustle of cloth promised that her pleasure was not to be long delayed.

The head of his cock pressed against her, and his hand followed the curve of her spine. "I will have you, this once," he said, and thrust forward.

He slid into her slowly, tenderly, and even that motion was nearly enough to push her over the edge. She moaned, and he echoed the sound, beginning to move slowly within her. She did not want him to be tender or slow. She moved with him, urging him to move faster, to thrust hard against her. His fingers found her nub again, and matched his rhythm as he complied. She shut her eyes, letting everything but the exquisite sensation of his movements within her disappear.

Her climax broke over her suddenly, and she rocked back against him, sucking in a sharp breath. He held her there, his fingers pressing against her most sensitive spot, letting her ride it with slowing movements. She came down from her peak gasping, grinning, and he drew sweat-dampened hair back from her neck. His cock gave a faint twitch within her, and she shifted her hips, enjoying the subtler feeling.

"We can be done, if you like," he said, his voice stretched with such reluctance she almost laughed.

"Let me face you," she said.

He drew out of her, and she turned, hitching herself up onto the table as she did so. She parted her legs and tossed back her head.

"Come here," she said.

"I thought I made the rules," he said.

"Please come here," she said, teasing. "And let me watch you."

He was against her again in an instant, sliding inside her without hesitation. His thrusts were quick now, insistent, and she wrapped her legs around him. Pleasure coiled low in her belly, and she gasped against his neck as a second crest found her. The sound seemed to undo him. He grunted, and withdrew abruptly, thrusting once more against her thigh before he came.

He gripped the lip of the table in both hands, to either side of her, and rested his brow against her shoulder, catching his breath. She had to catch her breath herself; that second peak had not been as intense as the first, but it still left her panting.

"You amaze me," he said softly.

"It was good, wasn't it?" she asked playfully, brushing his hair behind his ear. "Better than I expected."

"I gave you little cause for optimism, last time," he said. He handed her a handkerchief and winced. "God. I did at least withdraw last time, didn't I?"

Elinor froze. She hadn't thought—it hadn't occurred to her— "I'd forgotten," she said. "Oh, God. I forgot that you thought . . ."

"What did I think?" he asked, puzzlement creasing his brow.

"That you'd bedded me," Elinor said, shame creeping through her and banishing every remnant of pleasure. "That first night at Beauchene's. You passed out; nothing happened between us. I only told you otherwise because I feared you would get yourself killed if I left you to your own devices."

Slow horror crept over Colin's face. He pulled away from her and turned, rearranging his clothing as he did. Elinor wiped her thigh with the handkerchief and pulled and tugged her dress back into a semblance of order, not daring to look at him. "Colin—"

He turned, his expression tortured. "You let me believe—everything we've done since—"

"We wanted to do," Elinor said. "I wanted to. I know you did."

"I would never have done what we just did if I had known you were still a virgin," he said.

"I wasn't," Elinor said.

He blinked. "You—what? You weren't?"

"No. I never said I was."

Colin stared at her as if she had revealed she had a second head. "You have had sex before," Colin repeated. "You. Elinor Hargrove."

"Yes. Twice," Elinor said, and jutted out her chin defiantly.

"Oh, well. Twice!" The sarcasm dripping from his words stung, but she knew she deserved it.

"I should have told you. About that first night, I mean, not—I'm sorry. I didn't even think of it," Elinor said. "I only wanted you." She looked away. She had deceived him. Did it matter that it was for his own good? "I should know soon enough if I am with child. I doubt it. You can forget this ever happened. It need have no significance."

"Significance," he said flatly.

"You know. It need not be personal," Elinor said. "You can marry Penelope Layton and I'll . . ." She waved a hand. "I'll go be scandalous and take lovers, or lock myself in a tower and read myself to death. I'm a rich spinster; I'm practically required to become eccentric." She was talking too much. On the edge of babbling. She couldn't stand to look at him, didn't dare glance and see the anger that must be glinting in those eyes. "I should think you'd be relieved," she finished airily, her mouth sour.

He was silent for a long moment. Then his expression stilled, and he slowly, purposefully, arched a single eyebrow. "Relieved. Yes. I had feared I'd have to make an ass of myself, breaking my engagement," he said. "What a fool I'd look, marrying Elinor Hargrove."

Anger sparked, chasing away the shame for a heartbeat's time. "For only a fool would marry me?" she asked acidly.

He shrugged. "I've known you for over twenty years, Elinor. I'd have to be a fool not to have asked you to marry me before now, if I had any desire to do so."

"And Lord Farleigh is many things, but never a fool," she said. Always precise. Always not a stitch out of place. Well, she'd seen him knocked askew now, and she wasn't taken in any longer. "One thing I can guarantee," she said. "You will always be a fool to me, Lord Farleigh." Her cheeks hot, she strode past him, tugging her skirts into order.

Had he only been sober for two full days? It felt like a great deal longer. Long enough, in any case.

Colin barricaded himself inside his study on the strength of a few well-placed scowls in the direction of the staff and poured himself a healthful quantity of brandy.

She'd lied to him. She'd let him believe for two long days that he had committed the worst of transgressions against her. And on the strength of that belief, he had—he had given into his desires, and risked everything. His friendship with her, with her brother; his engagement; his future. There was no other barrier of honor, propriety, and reputation that he had not breached.

And it was all her fault.

The brandy struck the bottom of his glass with enough force to splash over the rim and onto the back of his hand.

He touched his tongue to the wet spot, and the heat of the liquor stung his mouth. That was what he needed. That was exactly what he needed.

What had these few days accomplished? He had failed to kill Foyle. Failed also to find evidence of his criminality, or a definitive answer regarding Marie's death. He had, perhaps, aided Mr. Bhandari in an escape from Foyle's onerous employment, but that was little consolation. And he had tortured himself with intimate proximity to the woman he loved and could not have. And just now, of course, he had said unpardonable things. But for once, they had been on purpose. They had been born of his anger, his hurt. And he had spoken them with vicious pleasure. Pleasure that refused to return now, instead leaving a sick, curdling feeling that entirely ruined the taste of the brandy.

She'd deserved every ounce of it, he told himself. She'd tricked him. Tricked him into doing exactly what he wanted, mind you, but she'd tricked him all the same.

Tomorrow he'd see her returned home. And see her as little as possible from that moment on.

Tonight, though, he was going to drink. Extensively.

Chapter 26

❧

Elinor did not weep, as a rule. She found it to be an undignified affair. She was not one of those women who could shed tears becomingly; she always wound up red-nosed and snotty. She did not weep now. She would not allow it. She had only herself to blame for all of this. She had quite rightfully ignored Colin as any kind of romantic possibility since she grew out of her childhood infatuation with the boy. She had thought herself capable of separating such an emotional entanglement from the enjoyment of their mutual pursuits, these last few days. To be proved wrong so spectacularly was humiliating.

She did not know how she would ever be able to apologize to him. Especially as she could not imagine seeing him ever again, just at this moment.

She was stalking the halls, getting turned about. She'd spent time here now and again, but it was always Birch Hall their flock of friends flew to when it came time to gather. She wasn't as familiar with these corridors. And so she was not entirely surprised to find herself in the salon when she meant to find refuge in the library. She was far more surprised to find Mr. Bhandari there, and Lady Farleigh, the dowager marchioness and Colin's mother. Elinor froze in the doorway.

Lady Farleigh adjusted the gold-rimmed spectacles on her nose, the better to peer over them. She and Bhandari were seated to either side of a round table, the papers Elinor had liberated from the Beauchenes spread between them.

"Lady Elinor," the older woman said. "There you are at last."

Elinor remembered her manners belatedly and managed a rushed curtsy. "Lady Farleigh. I had no idea you were at home. I apologize for not greeting you."

She waved a hand. "I only just arrived. I would have made my presence known, but I was given to understand that you and my son were indisposed." Her lips pursed. Elinor cleared her throat, frantically searching her mind for an explanation and finding none. "Mr. Bhandi has been keeping me company in the meantime," she said.

"It's Bhandari," Elinor corrected.

Lady Farleigh's eyebrows shot up, and she looked at Mr. Bhandari. "Is it really? How dreadful of me. You ought to have told me."

"I did not wish to offend," Mr. Bhandari said meekly. It was a tone Elinor well recognized. Lady Farleigh tended to have that effect on men, whatever their station; she gave the impression of a hawk stooping before a strike, and gentlemen instinctively recognized themselves as her preferred prey. It probably did not help that Mr. Bhandari was likely imagining what would happen if the woman found out about his relationship with her eldest daughter.

"Elinor, sit down," Lady Farleigh said. "Looking up at you is wearying. Whatever possessed you to grow so tall?"

"I can't imagine," Elinor said. She sank into the chair between the two of them and looked down at the scattered papers. "Have you found anything out?" Her mouth was dry. Lady Farleigh shouldn't see these documents. The story they told was too brutal.

"I have found a great deal out," Lady Farleigh said. Her dry tone didn't waver, but she paused before speaking again, and sorrow filled in the silence. "Mr. Bhandari has been explaining to me what he knows about Marie's time in India."

Elinor looked to the man in question. His lips were pressed into a thin line, and he did not quite meet her eyes. Lady Farleigh must have employed quite a bit of persuasion to get him to explain all of that to her. "I am very sorry," Elinor said. "It must be difficult to hear."

"Lord Farleigh thinks he hid his suspicions from me completely," Lady Farleigh said with a sniff that indicated it was definitely not true. "When I learned Mr. Foyle was returned to England, I was rather concerned that Lord Farleigh would take things into his own hands. It seems I was right. And it further seems that I owe you some thanks, for dissuading him from rash action."

"I'm not certain we entirely avoided rash action," Elinor said.

"Obviously," Lady Farleigh drawled. "My son remains engaged to Lady Penelope Layton, does he not?"

"He does," Elinor acknowledged, her back teeth clenching.

"And is that a failure on your part, or by design?"

Elinor stared at the woman. "I don't see how—"

"It is any of my business?" Lady Farleigh finished for her. She sighed. "I have one daughter dead. One married to a waste of good breeding. And one who seems utterly immune to my attempts to arrange a suitable match. Which leaves my son. I would very much like to be able to count one successful marriage among my children. And Colin has not made the best start of his. I was madly in love with his father, you see; I think Colin rather rejected the notion that he might be able to replicate the phenomenon, and I fear it may have led him to ignore the match he most desires. You would make him a most suitable bride, Lady Elinor."

"I would not," Elinor said stiffly. "For he is certainly not madly in love with me, or in love with me to any degree. He made that quite clear. I believe he said that he had absolutely no desire to marry me, to be precise."

"Pity," Lady Farleigh said. "Lady Penelope is such a . . . confection."

"We are against confections?" Elinor asked, feigning detachment.

"Entirely, I'm afraid," Lady Farleigh replied. "Well, if you and my son will have nothing of each other, you will have nothing of each other. Understood?"

"That won't be a problem," Elinor assured her.

"Less of one if we manage to get you spirited back to where you belong," Lady Farleigh said. "It won't do to have you found here. I will escort you back to London. That will minimize the chance of your brother determining your origin. And Mr. Bhandi—Bhandari—will accompany us, of course," she added.

"I will?" Mr. Bhandari asked, adding a belated *My Lady* at the end in a gulp.

"You will. It is the most likely place to begin finding you a position."

"That is not necessary, Lady Farleigh," Mr. Bhandari assured her.

"Of course it is. My goodness. You begin to grow gray and everyone assumes that your brain has dribbled out your ears," Lady Farleigh said. "You were very fond of my daughter, were you not? And she was fond of you. It would take an idiot not to realize as much when you speak of her. I cannot say I approve, of course, but I have had precious few opportunities to honor my daughter's memory. And I dare say I see the appeal." Elinor gaped as Lady Farleigh gave Mr. Bhandari an appraising—and lingering—look. "Let me do this small favor for my daughter, Mr. Bhandari. Do not take it from me." Her eyes shone with rare intensity. He bowed his head in acknowledgment.

"Now, I am going to go speak to my son," Lady Farleigh said. "And you, Lady Elinor, should take another look at these letters, and tell me what you see." She pushed the ledger page toward Elinor. Elinor frowned.

"I've seen them," she said. "They seem remarkable only for their dullness."

"You had only a brief moment to look them over. Look closer," Lady Farleigh prompted.

Elinor scanned the page. All she could see were the names of birds, coupled with descriptions of the weather.

Then she frowned. "Hang on. Why is there 'a scattering of snow' in the midst of June?"

"Much less a lesser kestrel midwinter," Lady Farleigh said.

"It's a code," Elinor said, realization dawning, and read through again. "Number of birds . . . nest locations . . . weather. These were written during the war. Foyle was a spy."

"The question is, for whom?" Lady Farleigh said.

"If Beauchene thought these were worth keeping, I would guess it was not for England," Elinor said. "Have you ever seen these, Mr. Bhandari?"

"I may have seen him writing them, but the contents are unfamiliar," Mr. Bhandari said. "And Mr. Foyle most definitely did not have an interest in birds."

"What about soldiers?"

"He was very fond of buying officers drinks," Mr. Bhandari said darkly.

"Well. I am certain you clever young folk can figure all of this out," Lady Farleigh said. Elinor and Mr. Bhandari rose with her, but she waved them back to their seats. "Bend your heads together and see what you can make of it," she said. "And then be ready to leave. I do not intend to tarry."

She swept out in a rustle of skirts. Bhandari cast Elinor a bemused glance. "Are they all like that?" he asked.

"All of who?"

"The ladies of this house," he said.

"No," Elinor assured him. "At least, Kitty isn't. Phoebe's getting there. And don't worry, she intimidates everyone. Except possibly Colin."

"I suspect that you are incorrect on that account," Mr. Bhandari said. "With respect, only a madman would fail to be intimidated by that woman."

Colin glared at his glass. It was half full with the most delicious-looking shade of brandy. He could smell its heady aroma from here. It had been taunting him thus for some time now, promising that as soon as he slugged it down, he would obliterate every one of the memories dancing through his skull. Elinor's laugh. The delight in her eyes when she had burst out of that room, Matthew's hand in hers. The taste of her lips. The venom in her voice. Every cruel thing he'd said to her, intentional or not, in the past twenty years.

"A marquess should never feel sorry for himself," his mother said, and he sat bolt upright in the armchair he had been slouched in. She entered the room with hands folded before her and a stern look on her face. He staggered upright, surprise making him as clumsy as drink.

"Mother," he said, with a trace of a gasp about the word. "What on earth are you doing here?"

"It is my primary residence," she said. "As you may recall. Unless you care to relocate me."

"No, of course not," he said. "I was given to understand you were remaining with Kitty the whole summer."

"I was. I returned when my mission was successfully completed."

"Your mission?"

"I took charge of your sister's household, ordered her servants around, drew up menus of her least favorite foods, and finally had to begin redecorating the entire house before she grew irate enough to form an opinion. I think it's the first one she's held since that rat of a husband abandoned her. I left her undoing all my hard work and threatening to burn the curtains I'd so thoughtfully acquired. I consider it a triumph."

Colin gave a startled laugh. "Is that what you were doing?"

"Someone had to. The girl was moldering. In any case, I do not intend to stay long. I depart for London in the morning," she said. "Lady Elinor will require an escort."

Colin paled. She knew Elinor was here? What must she think? "I can explain everything," he said.

"Good Lord. Please don't. What I know is bad enough already," she said. "I have no desire to hear the particulars of whatever misadventure you and Lady Elinor have undertaken. I understand that it has been entirely inappropriate and somewhat fruitful, and that is enough detail for me. Now. There are a few questions you must answer. Sit."

He obeyed automatically. He might be the marquess, but his mother had never lost her ability to command him.

"First. Are you in love with Lady Elinor?"

He looked up swiftly in alarm. "No," he lied.

"I see. And why haven't you told her this?"

"Told her that I'm not in love with her?"

"Darling, you have never been able to lie to me. Please stop trying. Why have you not told Lady Elinor that you are in love with her?"

"Because she won't have me," he snapped.

"Is that so?"

"Yes."

"You are absolutely certain."

"*Yes.*"

She sighed. "Then I suppose you'll have to marry the Layton girl after all. A shame. No wonder you're drinking."

"I'm not," he said. He waved at the glass. "I've been staring at that glass for an hour now."

"You have rarely needed an excuse to drink. Now you have the perfect one, and you abstain? What has gotten into you?"

"If I start, I won't stop," he said darkly. "I knew it as soon as I tasted a drop of the stuff."

She nodded. "Your father had the same problem."

He jerked his gaze toward her, startled. "He did? He never said anything."

"He was no more fond of confessing his weaknesses than the rest of the world," she said stiffly. "In any case, I applaud your restraint. I have full faith in your ability to do what needs to be done. In the meanwhile, here is what must happen. Elinor and I are traveling to London tomorrow. You will put yourself in some semblance of order and follow. By the time you reach the city, I expect you to have decided what to do with yourself. Because you cannot continue to pursue this vendetta against Edward Foyle if you wish to be

married. It has too much of a potential for scandal and
worse. Decide what you want, and take it. I have no patience
for this brooding."

He gritted his teeth. He was too old to be lectured by his
mother. And much too old to need it. "Thank you for your
advice, Mother," he said. "I shall take it under consideration."

"Do," she said, and sighed. "I am terribly weary. I believe
I will retire. Do try to cease wallowing in your sorrows long
enough to see me off in the morning, will you?"

He scowled and nodded. She patted his cheek with another
little sigh, and then wafted out the way she had come. Colin
turned his glass in his hand, frowning at the amber liquid. At
least when he was drunk, he had an excuse for the horrible
things that came out of his mouth.

He set the glass down on the table beside him. Enough.
His mother was right. He was wallowing, and it was beneath
him. It was time to let go of what he could not have, and look
toward the future. That future was one with Penelope Layton
and no thoughts of vengeance. No thoughts, either, of Elinor
Hargrove.

But he wouldn't end things like this. He needed to speak
to her. He started for the door, and stopped. No. If he went
to speak to her now, their wounds still fresh, he would only
make things worse.

Tomorrow. Tomorrow he would speak to Elinor. And
hope that it would bring him some imitation of peace.

Chapter 27

Lady Farleigh had never had much patience for the late start of the typical society member's day. When she stated that she meant to leave first thing in the morning, she meant it; a maid was sent round to Elinor's door as the first rays of light filtered their way over the horizon. Elinor was already awake, having seemingly acquired her family's vulnerability to insomnia at last. She dressed swiftly in another ill-fitting gown, unbecoming but suited for travel, and made her way to the front hall. She had no bags to pack, and yet she felt as if she were carrying a great weight. The bundle of letters was tucked into her reticule, tugging at her attention however thoroughly she tried to put it out of her mind.

It was not proof. Not yet. But it might lead to proof, and by extension, Mr. Foyle's downfall. If she could bring it to the right person's attention, she could begin the process of bringing the man to his knees. And she could imagine walking up to Colin, telling him that she had news. That she had accomplished at last what they had set out to do. It could be a wedding present, she thought fiercely, and he would look at her as he realized what a poor choice of brides he had made. And she would walk away, triumphant, and even as he rejoiced he would regret letting her go.

Oh, it was a foolish fantasy, and beneath her. But she nursed it nonetheless, feeling a hot spike of pleasure and spite in her core.

Lady Farleigh was waiting. She had more than made up for Elinor's lack of luggage judging by the state of the carriage beyond the open double doors. She cast an eye over Elinor's garb and heaved a little sigh.

"You are so very tall," she said with regret. "I suppose you will be reunited with your own clothes in a few days, but it's such a shame."

Elinor murmured something vaguely resembling words. Mr. Bhandari was already outside, speaking with the driver, who was examining him with unconcealed interest. It must be a strange life, she thought, to be in turns invisible and an object of utmost curiosity.

"Mother. Lady Elinor."

Elinor flinched at Colin's voice and turned slowly, doing her best to keep her expression cool. Years of practice made it achievable, if barely.

"Colin, darling. How good of you to see us off," Lady Farleigh cooed. She swept up to her son and planted a kiss on his cheek. "I really must go check on the luggage now." She did an abrupt about-face and hurried out and down the steps before either one of them could speak a word of protest. Colin smiled after her ruefully and turned to Elinor, raising a shoulder in a helpless shrug.

"I suppose she wishes us to make up," Elinor said. She had no intention of doing so.

"It's more that she expects me to apologize, which I do," he said. Elinor stilled. He had not often apologized to her in all the years they'd known each other, and here was the second such instance in recent days. It was beginning to resemble a habit. "What I said to you yesterday was designed to cut, and I fear it did its job. I insulted you."

"I deceived you," Elinor pointed out.

"Yes." He paused. "I do not require an apology from you, Elinor. I understand why you did it, even if I do not agree that it was the right course of action. The truth is that I needed you, these past few days. I needed to not be alone. And that was the mechanism by which our partnership was possible. So as much as I might hate that you employed it, I do not regret the result. I do not hate you, and I regret deeply my reaction to the news."

Elinor listened to it all with her eyes fixed on a point over his shoulder. "I don't have any right to be angry with you," she said. "And the deception was not entirely for your benefit," she reminded him. "I might have wanted to prevent you from making a grave error, in attacking Foyle, but I also wanted . . . Oh, I don't know."

"The dream of being someone else," he said. "Of living a different life than the one so clearly laid out before you. It was a dream I enjoyed as well, Elinor. You should not feel ashamed of dreams, nor bear any lingering obligation after waking. Can this be a dream, then? Can we go on as if we were only sleeping?"

"Go back to the way things were?" Elinor asked. She shook her head. "I don't know. I don't believe so. Too much has happened."

"Better not to think of each other," Colin said. "Not to see each other."

"Yes," Elinor agreed. She did not think she could stand to see him with Penelope Layton. She had turned into one of the swooning girls she always scorned, unable to control her own emotions and infatuations. It was not his fault he didn't love her. And yet she was punishing him for it. "There is something you should see," she said. She reached into her reticule and withdrew the letters, a faint tremor in her hand fluttering the paper. She held it out.

"I've seen these," he said.

"Examine them more closely. I went over them with Mr. Bhandari. We believe that they contain a code, meant to communicate British troop movements during the war. According to Mr. Bhandari, Foyle made a habit of socializing with English officers. It is not conclusive, but someone may be able to find evidence to confirm it."

He took the letters and swept his gaze down the top one,

frowning. "My God," he said. "This would be the end of him."

"And such a stain might even inconvenience Lord Copeland, if only temporarily," Elinor said. "At the least, it may give you leverage to learn what truly happened to your sister."

"Why didn't you show me this last night?" Colin asked. She tensed, but he sounded more curious than angry.

"I thought to chase it down myself," she said, with a little laugh. "I suppose I was not quite done playing the adventuress."

"Better to give it to Hudson, I think," Colin said. "I think we've both had enough of skulking through dark corridors and dealing with dangerous men."

Elinor smiled faintly. "I want to know the end of the tale," she said. "But I don't think I care to have any more pistols pointed at me, to be sure."

"If I learn anything, you'll know," Colin pledged. "Thank you for giving this to me." He shuffled the letters and paused, frowning. "Hm," he said.

"Oh, Yes. Mrs. Fincher. I left that one in," Elinor said. "Something about it bothers me. Why the regular payment?"

"A favorite whore?" Colin mused aloud, and cast a chagrined look in his mother's direction.

"One generally pays them per appointment," Elinor said. "An informant, perhaps? But even then . . . And the name feels familiar somehow. I feel certain that I've heard it before." She shook her head. "I have no idea where. But it's worth investigating."

"Another task for Hudson," Colin said. He cleared his throat and tucked the page into an inner pocket of his jacket. "You should go, Elinor. Lady Elinor. I've kept you here long enough."

She hesitated. He wasn't angry any longer. Perhaps— perhaps if she only admitted to him what she felt, they might . . .

Might what? He was engaged. If nothing else, she could not do that to another woman. Certainly not one as sweet as Penelope Layton, who had never wronged another living soul. Elinor gave Colin a smooth, formal curtsy. "Lord

Farleigh," she said. "It has been a pleasure, as always. I expect I will see you at your wedding this fall."

"I expect so," he said, and matched her formality in a shallow bow. "Safe travels, Lady Elinor."

"Good-bye," Elinor said, startled by the finality of the word. How could such intensity come to such a leaden close? But she turned away. It was better this way. She would survive this, and when she was old and gray, she would remember the few days she spent dreaming of a different life.

Elinor had quite forgotten how much she enjoyed Lady Farleigh's company under normal circumstances. Which was not to say that these circumstances were normal—but they had nothing to do with the ongoing quest to pair Phoebe with a suitable husband, which had consumed Lady Farleigh's attention for nearly half a decade. It seemed that a Season away from the task had reminded Lady Farleigh that she had more interesting topics to apply her considerable mind to, and Elinor was entertained to learn that she had taken up reading a rather overwrought series of novels about a perpetually virginal and winsome heroine, whose sterling qualities were matched for improbability only by the nefariousness of the villains she encountered. Lady Farleigh was dissecting the plot of the latest of the installments when they at last reached the Hargrove town house.

"—who of course proves to be her uncle, disguised with a false mustache. I must say, I would think I would recognize my own uncle, however bushy his facial hair," Lady Farleigh said as the carriage rolled to a stop.

"You'd be surprised the mistakes one can make in poor lighting and unfamiliar circumstances," Elinor said.

"Oh?" Lady Farleigh asked, perhaps sensing a personal anecdote. Which there was, but Elinor was not about to regale the dowager marchioness with that debacle of an encounter. "Oh, we're here. You have been excellent company, dear."

"And you are too kind to have accompanied me," Elinor told her. She could feel the faint pressure around her temples

that presaged a headache, and she sent up a silent prayer of
thanks that her own bed was near at hand. She felt as if she
could sleep for a week. "I would invite you inside, but . . ."

"It is probably best if we part without comment," Lady
Farleigh said.

They said their quick good-byes. Mr. Bhandari gave her
a wave and a nod when she exited the carriage, and then it
was trundling off again. Elinor stood outside the town house
a moment, her hands clasped before her. Home. She supposed she ought to be disappointed, but in truth she was
relieved. Martin always accused her of being more fond of
excitement after the fact, when she could turn it into a story
and not have to suffer the disruption of routine. She was
willing to admit he was at least partially right. She was glad
she had gone on this adventure—or misadventure—but she
was quite finished with the experience.

She walked up the steps and rang the bell, hoping that
the house was not entirely abandoned; with Joan conducting
so much business in London, they usually left at least a servant or two to keep the place open, but she would not be
shocked to find it shuttered. In that case, she'd have to find
someplace to spend the night, and then head to Thornwald
in the morning, for she certainly was not ready for any further travel today.

To her relief, the door opened. To her surprise, it was
Croft who stood in the doorway. When he saw her, his
expression shifted swiftly between one of shock to one of
relief, before settling into his professional blank-faced gaze.
"Lady Elinor," he said. "Please, come inside. We have been
quite concerned for you."

"Concerned for me?" Elinor asked, stepping through.
Now she could make out voices, raised and angry—Joan
and Martin. Since when did Joan and Martin argue like that?
She hurried toward the sound. They were in the drawing
room, and Martin was pacing swiftly back and forth.

"—irresponsible to the most extreme degree!" he was
shouting. "If I had suspected even a fraction of the trouble
you were seducing her into—"

"Seducing?" Joan asked, voice strained but a great deal more level. She had her hands folded over her bulging belly, and she, unlike Martin, had already spotted Elinor's arrival. Which largely meant that her glare was fixed on her, and not on Martin. "I did not seduce her into anything, and I certainly did not advise her to vanish off the face of God's earth without a word of warning."

"I'm sorry," Elinor said. Martin spun. He stared at her for a long, tense moment, fury burning in his eyes. And then he strode across the room in three quick steps and wrapped her up in a bone-crunching hug.

Elinor yelped. "Martin! Put me down."

He obliged, but grabbed hold of her shoulders. "Where have you *been*?" he asked.

"I . . ." Elinor glanced at Joan. "I left word with . . . our mutual friend," she said.

"Yes, well. I told him that I knew where you were, I just rather thought he'd be better off not knowing the particulars," Joan said. "By the time we learned that you weren't with Phoebe, it was too late to send anyone after you. So."

"Where were you?" Martin demanded again. "Did something happen to you?"

"No," Elinor said. She paused. "Well, a great deal, but nothing you need to be concerned about now. I'm home and well, and that's all you need know. Joan is quite correct. You do not want to hear the particulars."

He looked at her for a long moment, jaw tense. "Whatever I can imagine is worse than what you could tell me," he said.

"It's really not," Elinor assured him, which had the opposite of its intended effect. Which she might have predicted, if her brain did not feel a bit like warm pudding. She sighed. "I was at an exclusive party," she said. "I suffered no harm to myself or my reputation, and none of this is Joan's fault. She had a perfectly sensible plan in place that did not involve my attendance, but it ran into a snag and I was forced to improvise."

"This is about whatever Phoebe dragged you into," Martin said.

"Mm," Elinor said noncommittally. She took hold of his hands and drew them downward, so she clasped them between hers in front of them. "I know you hate to be left out of the matter, but it truly is better for all of us if you avoid the details. Now, I must rest. I am extremely weary."

He looked into her eyes. They were twins, he the elder by only a quarter hour; of all the people in the world, he was one of the few who could usually read her as easily as she did everyone else. "Elinor," he said softly. "Are you certain you're all right?"

She opened her mouth to assure him. Instead, to her horror, she burst into tears.

Chapter 28

"And then Mr. Bhandari set off the fireworks meant for the last night," Colin said, flipping a letter opener around in his hand nervously. Across the desk from him, Mr. Hudson watched with an unreadable expression.

"Uh-huh," he said, which was the most he had contributed to the narrative thus far.

"We fled," Colin concluded awkwardly. "Ah, and the rest is rather boring."

"And Lady Elinor's home safe," Hudson said, with a tone that suggested an answer in anything but the affirmative would be suicidal.

"She is. God, I can't believe I told you she was there," Colin said. "Only there's no one else I can tell, you see. Plenty who could keep a secret, but I couldn't stand to have anyone thinking about her that way."

"Whereas you do not care what I think," Hudson said.

Colin shut his mouth. "You know," he said, "I have quite the reputation for blunt honesty. I think I shall now cultivate a reputation for contemplative silence. I have always let my mouth run ahead of my mind. I am not certain when I started to care."

"I suspect the lady might have something to do with it," Hudson said. "You're a blasted fool for letting her get away."

"She wanted to leave."

"Uh-huh," was the answer, and then Hudson rose. "I'll look into the letters," he said.

"Good," Colin said. He was reluctant to see the man go. He was reluctant to be alone. Well, not alone. In the company of a great many people he could not speak with freely. Phoebe was at the house, along with Mr. Bhandari and Colin's mother. Also, inexplicably, that red-headed maid. Of all of them, only Mr. Bhandari could come close to knowing the full story of what had transpired at Beauchene's house, and Colin still did not feel entirely comfortable speaking with the man. He thought well of him; the worst that could be said of the man was that he had allowed himself to become a martyr to Marie's memory, and remain in proximity to evil for too long as a result. But it was that connection to Marie that Colin found so discomfiting. It made him uneasy to be in the presence of someone who had known Marie in India. Had known her, perhaps, better than Colin ever had.

What he really needed was distraction. Thorough distraction.

What evening was it? Saturday. Could it really only be Saturday? He frowned. The boys would be at the club. Cards, drink—well, water and inevitable teasing—and conversation would do him well.

He hopped up with sudden enthusiasm. Nothing would drive the last few days' inventive debauchery from his mind like a good dose of the old, staid debauchery. He was nearly skipping when he headed down the stairs, calling for a hack to be brought 'round. He'd left his walking stick in the drawing room, he recalled, and strode to the door. He pushed it open, a whistle verging on a tune on his lips, and froze.

Phoebe and Maddy sat on the sofa together. Phoebe's hands were tangled in Maddy's coppery locks, and Maddy was leaning into the kiss, her eyes shut in perfect bliss. It lasted half a second. Then both girls let out yelps—Phoebe's was, in truth, more of a shriek—and leapt to their feet, springing apart with speed that a detached part of Colin's mind found downright comical. He cleared his throat and walked deliberately across the room to where his walking stick rested against the wall near the fireplace. He turned slowly, twirling it idly in one hand.

Well. This was interesting.

"Colin . . ." Phoebe began, but fell silent. Maddy was white with terror, edging toward the door.

"I suppose this is why you are so impossible when it comes to marriage," Colin said. He felt like there were two versions of himself. One, stupefied, was muddling through a soup of thoughts and feelings that did not have the decency to solidify into any one impulse he could name. The other stood in a positively casual stance and spoke with remarkable calm.

It was of course at that moment that his mother made her arrival. "What on earth is happening in here?" she demanded. "Has someone been murdered? For I cannot imagine another reason for such a shriek, Phoebe."

Phoebe turned to her, wide-eyed. "I saw a mouse," she said.

Colin suppressed a groan. Phoebe had never in her life been afraid of mice. She was chasing after them like a kitten when she was two, and found special delight in planting them on his person while he was distracted. His mother was unlikely to be fooled. And sure enough, her eyes narrowed. She pushed her spectacles up her nose and advanced a step, scrutinizing her daughter—and then Maddy. Maddy's hair was disarranged, strands of it jetting out in wild tendrils where they had escaped the pins. Maddy's lips were pressed so tightly together they had nearly vanished, and she drew backward one flinching step after another.

"I see," Lady Farleigh said. "Colin, you should go."

"I will not," Colin said. "Not before I have an explanation from you, Phoebe."

"Does it really need explaining?" Phoebe snapped.

He glared at her. She glared at him. His sister. Engaged in what anyone would tell you was a perversion.

As opposed to your conduct and environs, of late, the calm half of him remarked.

This was different. This was his sister, and she had been entwined with—

He looked over at Maddy, and his thoughts drew up sharply to a halt. She was shaking, her eyes wide and her shoulders pinched together as if to defend herself against a blow. She was terrified. Of him. Of his mother. Whatever her sin, he could not bear to be the source of such naked fear. He forced his grip to ease on his walking stick, forced his face into a gentle expression, even as confusion and anger welled inside of him. "It will be all right," he said. He couldn't imagine how just this moment, but he could not bear knowing that the girl expected him to harm her.

She did not look less frightened, but when he held her gaze she nodded once, hardly a dip of her chin.

"We must discuss this," Lady Farleigh said. "Colin, you should go."

He took a protective step forward. In all the swamp of uncertainty inside of him, one thing was clear and unassailable. Phoebe was his sister, and he would protect her. Even from his mother. "I think I should remain," he said. He couldn't think too hard about what he'd witnessed. It made his stomach clench and lurch, gave rise to a revulsion that was unacceptable paired with his sister. And so he caged it. What mattered, he decided, was her protection—and nothing else.

"You most certainly should not," Lady Farleigh said. "Dear Lord, Colin. I am not about to sprout extra heads and devour them. We are merely going to discuss the future in a calm and rational fashion. We take care of one another in this family, and it has just become more challenging to do so. It requires a frank conversation on a number of topics you are unlikely to be able to listen to without an excess of emotion."

"What sort of discussion?" Colin asked.

"A detailed one," Lady Farleigh said. "Now. Go. No male presence is required."

Phoebe snorted. Colin shot her a quelling look. Now was not the time for humor. "Do you want me to go?" Colin asked her seriously.

She glanced at Maddy, then at her mother. "It's probably best," she said. She paused. "Are you angry?"

He sighed. "I don't know," he said. "I don't understand this."

"Don't be angry," she said. "Please, don't be angry with me, I couldn't stand it."

He put his hands on her shoulders and bent, kissing her brow. "It will be all right," he said again, and then he had to leave. His mother was right. He was holding onto his calm demeanor by the narrowest thread, and standing still was making it fray all the faster.

He left, closing the door behind him, and prayed that his mother could put the whole situation into some order that made the world make sense again.

Martin and Joan sat to either side of Elinor as she wept, neither demanding answers. Joan held her hand; Martin's arm encircled her shoulders protectively. When at last she thought she could speak again, she gave a weak laugh. "I'm so sorry," she said. "I am quite the mess, aren't I?"

"Don't apologize," Joan said. "You should see me these days. I cry if I drop a spoon."

"To be fair, it's largely since it is an impossible operation to pick it back up," Martin said, and his wife shot him a playful glare. Elinor laughed more genuinely this time, though it hiccuped into a little sob.

"This is ridiculous," she said. She'd thought she had better control of her emotions than this.

"What's wrong?" Martin asked. "I promise, I'll do whatever it takes to put it right."

Elinor shook her head. "There's nothing you can do," she said. "I'm afraid I'm in *love*."

There was a moment of stunned silence. Then Joan edged away enough to get a good look at her, tilting her head to the side. "In love? And this is a problem?"

"A gigantic problem," Elinor assured her. She had somehow ended up with Martin's handkerchief in her hand, and was wringing it between her fingers so firmly it had begun to cut off her circulation. She forced her hands to relax.

"Is he married?" Joan asked.

"No," Elinor said.

"A servant?" she guessed. "A groom? A farmer? A criminal? French?"

A series of quick shakes of the head.

"Then what is the problem?" Martin asked.

"He's *Colin*," Elinor said, and buried her face in her hands. She could not believe she had told them that. They would think her such an idiot. Martin's arm slid away from her shoulders.

"I always thought you two only pretended to get along, to keep things peaceful for the rest of us," Joan said thoughtfully. "Hang on, isn't he engaged?"

"To Penelope Layton," Elinor said. "She's *sweet*. They'll hate each other within a year."

"Oh, dear. No, Lord Farleigh can't marry anyone sweet," Joan agreed. Martin still hadn't said anything. Elinor was too afraid to look at him. "Farleigh's been missing as well," Joan said slowly. "You were together, weren't you?"

Elinor felt Martin stiffen. She put a hand on his arm to still him. "We were coincidentally at the same party," she said. "And socialized. There is no need to become overprotective." Her voice sounded ridiculous to her own ears, with her nose stuffed and snotty from the crying.

"He has somehow reduced you to sobbing," Martin said. "Usually this is the point where some violence is called for."

"He's your best friend," Elinor reminded him.

"All the more reason," Martin said. He needed to unclench his jaw before he cracked a tooth.

"Don't. It's not his fault. He doesn't love me," Elinor said. "That's all. I'm foolishly infatuated when I swore I never would be. I've only myself to blame."

"I will kill him for you, if you want," Martin said. "Or

perhaps just disfigure him. I could dump a bucket of water over his head, at least."

Elinor felt the hint of a smile steal across her lips. "I will take that under consideration," she said. "But I think the best course of action is to avoid him. Eventually I'll stop feeling this way, won't I?"

They exchanged a glance. "Well," Joan said slowly, "we did manage a year apart."

"And you were both absolutely miserable the whole time," Elinor said. "And got married at the end of it. But that's different. You were in love with each other. Colin is perfectly indifferent to me."

"Are you sure?" Martin asked. "Are you absolutely certain?"

Elinor snorted. "You don't think I could tell if someone was in love with me?"

"As I recall, you had no idea with Matthew until he proposed," Martin pointed out. "An hour before, you were telling me that he was perfectly insufferable, and that his only redeeming quality was the symmetry of his features."

"I did say that, didn't I?" Elinor said. "But this is different. Colin told me he didn't wish to marry me."

"That seems definitive," Martin agreed. "And he is engaged. I don't suppose you're willing to tell me the context of this conversation."

"No," Elinor said firmly. "It is a private matter."

"What do you want to do?" Joan asked. "How can we help you?"

Elinor let out a strangled breath. "I don't want to feel this way anymore," she said. "How on earth did you two survive this?"

They exchanged another look. "Italy," Joan said.

"Drinking," Martin said.

"Perhaps you could try drinking in Italy, but as neither of the attempts succeeded particularly well, we may want to try a different approach," Joan said.

"I think I'll start with a nap," Elinor said. She wanted her mind to cease its spinning. She wanted darkness and silence and the solace of dreams. "Thank you," she said. "Both of you. And don't blame Colin. This isn't his fault."

Her brother and sister-in-law shifted. She could read every tilt of an eyebrow, every angle of their limbs. They were going to continue this discussion without her, whatever she said. She supposed she ought to be irritated, but instead she found it comforting. She hadn't lost Martin when he'd married; she'd gained another ally, one she desperately needed right now.

She would survive this. She had to. Even if she had to travel to Italy and drink all the wine in the nation.

Colin arrived at the club in no better a mood than when he'd set out. The usual crowd was there—Harken, Weathersby, and Gibson. It should have been a pleasant diversion. It instead proved to be utter torture. Weathersby was in a foul mood for some reason none of them could determine, and Gibson could only do so much to keep the conversation flowing. And Colin suddenly found that without the application of liquor, Gibson wasn't particularly interesting. They were all grateful when an early night was declared and they parted ways.

By the time Colin returned home, the house was silent, but he could see a light in the drawing room. He poked his head in, more cautiously this time, and found Phoebe curled on the sofa with her feet under her and a book on her lap. She looked up at him as he entered. "Oh," she said. "I was waiting for you."

He took a seat on the opposite side of the sofa and slung an arm over the back. "I thought you might have been," he said. "Mother didn't say anything dreadful, did she?"

"No," Phoebe said. She bit her lip. "Colin, are you certain that you aren't angry with me?"

"I'm still not entirely sure what I should be angry about," Colin said. He cleared his throat. "You were . . ."

"Kissing," Phoebe supplied. "We're in love, Colin, and

we want to be together, and I know you'll say it's not right, but at least promise you won't do anything to hurt her." Her eyes shone with unspent tears.

Colin leaned forward, bracing his elbows on his knees. "That I can promise," he said. In love. That was the worst version of it. The version that did not allow for easy dissuasion. "She's a woman," he said.

"Obviously. Or did you think I merely needed to put my spectacles on?"

"So are you," he said, as if she hadn't noticed, and then shook his head. "How can you be in love with another woman?"

"I don't know," Phoebe said. "I just am. Haven't you ever been in love?"

He laughed. She gave a startled jump and looked at him in suspicion. "Completely and miserably," he confirmed. A piece seemed to click into place. It didn't need to be more complicated than that, did it? His sister was in love with someone she shouldn't be. Was feeling, perhaps, some version of what he was. And he would do anything to turn that pain into happiness. "You will have to be very, very careful," he said.

"You don't disapprove?"

"I absolutely disapprove," Colin said. "I also know that I have never been able to dissuade you of anything, *especially* through disapproval. I know you, and I know Maddy a bit. I know Joan and Martin trust her. I want you both safe and well, and the rest comes second. What did Mother say?"

"A lot of things," Phoebe said. She looked down at her book and traced a finger idly along the edge of the pages. "She said that she had an aunt who . . . It's not important. She said that it would be easier if we were only friends. She asked if we could manage it."

"And what did you say?"

"I couldn't," Phoebe said. "Thinking about it makes me feel like I'm buried under a cartload of rocks, and my chest is caving in."

Colin knew that feeling well. It was the one he felt now.

"We talked for a long time," Phoebe said. "And I've agreed to marry."

"What?" Colin said. "Phoebe, you just said—"

"Lord Philip Mayhew," Phoebe said. Colin's objection cut off short. Lord Philip Mayhew was the third son of the Marquess of Galcombe. He and Phoebe had always gotten along grandly, but they had dismissed him as a prospect because—well, because he very obviously had no interest in the female sex. "Assuming he's amenable to the arrangement, that is, which I think he will be. We've always been good friends, and I think we would run a household together well, and we could both have our own lives as well. We'd only need to produce an heir or two, and I could manage that. If it meant I could have Maddy, too." She swallowed.

"Trust Mother to be practical," Colin said. "It's a good idea, Phoebe. You'll be protected as long as you're married. And he's a good bloke."

"And I do want children," Phoebe said earnestly. "It wouldn't be so bad, as long as we liked each other, would it?"

"We do what we must," Colin said. He covered her hand with his and gave it a squeeze. "I will never be angry, as long as you are loved."

She gave a choked cry and threw herself at him, wrapping her arms around his neck. He returned the embrace, holding her thin body against his and remembering when she would throw herself at him as a child, when he came home from school. He'd sweep her up and spin her around, and she wouldn't stop asking questions long enough for him to answer a single one. He could not claim that the disgust and the discomfort had bled out of him entirely, but one thing was obvious. He could not lose another sister, and if he fought this, he would lose her.

"You'll see," she was saying. "You'll love her, too, you'll see."

He broke away from her. "Be especially careful the next few months," he said. "It's probably best for the two of you to return to the country. Once you and I are both married, there will be a great deal less risk."

"Oh! Your engagement," Phoebe said. "I hadn't even thought— Colin, I'm so sorry. I promise we didn't let anyone catch on. Oh Lord. Can you imagine what would happen if Lord Levenbane found out?"

"I would really rather not," Colin said. "And I really should speak to him soon," he added belatedly.

"And Penelope," Phoebe reminded him. "She *is* going to be your wife. You should probably have more than a single conversation with her."

He sighed. "I truly wish Spenser women weren't so smart," he said, and was gratified when she punched him in the arm. Some things should never change.

Chapter 29

❧

Colin arranged to take Penelope Layton on a walk through Hyde Park the next day. The day dawned bright and beautiful, if a bit overly warm, and despite the thinning London crowd the park was well-supplied with overdressed men and women. Lady Penelope's escort trailed a respectable distance behind, just out of earshot. She would have been all but unnoticeable except for the impressive feat she was performing: neatly avoiding every obstacle in her path while her nose was planted firmly in a book. Colin found her sidestepping and page-turning somewhat entrancing. Much more interesting than the subject of his and Penelope's conversation, which had turned to bees.

"Yes, bees," he said dutifully. "Very useful creatures, what with the honey."

"Have you ever tried your hand at beekeeping?" Penelope asked.

"Can't say I have," he said. She seemed crestfallen. "Perhaps when you live with me, we could arrange for you to look after a hive," he said quickly, and she brightened. "If you would enjoy that sort of thing."

"Oh, I would," she said.

"You're not afraid of being stung?"

"Not in the least," she said. "It's only a bit of pain. And besides, it's quite easy to avoid, if you're kind and cautious. Bees don't mind company, as long as it's polite." She smiled, her cheeks dimpling.

"I will try to make you happy," he said.

Her smile faltered. "Lord Farleigh?"

"I know I haven't done this properly. But I want to assure you, I'll provide you with whatever you desire. I won't be an onerous husband."

"I'm certain," she said, still bright, but with a hint of doubt in her voice. He shook his head. He was making a hash of things. "Is something wrong?" she asked.

"No," he said. "No, nothing's wrong." Everything was wrong. He glanced back at the escort. And frowned. A figure was approaching at a rapid gait—a figure he recognized. Weathersby. He had never seen the man move with such speed or purpose, nor seen such a scowl on his face. "What on earth . . . ?"

Lady Penelope turned to follow his gaze and gave a startled gasp. "Cecil!" she declared as Weathersby approached. "What's wrong? You look in a state!"

Weathersby drew up, momentarily knocking the escort from her path. She frowned at his back and snapped her book shut, clearly ready to intervene at the first sign of misconduct. Weathersby was sweating, his blond locks plastered to his scalp, and his breath came in little heaving gasps. How far had he hustled to reach them?

"Sit down before you fall over, Weathersby," Colin advised.

"I will not," Weathersby declared. "I've let this go on long enough, and I'll never live with myself if I don't do something."

"Let what go on?" Colin asked. "What the hell are you talking about?" Penelope gasped at the invective.

"You can't marry him," he said to Penelope, and then wrenched his attention back around to Colin. "You can't marry her. I can't believe you would do this."

"Do what? Get engaged? I can still play cards once I'm

married, Weathersby," Colin pointed out. He was growing more confused by the second.

"When you knew how I felt," Weathersby all but squeaked.

Colin stifled a string of further curses. The universe was laughing at him. "I had no idea you even knew each other," he said. Lady Penelope had both hands clasped over her mouth. The escort had let her book dangle from one hand and was watching the events unfold with a blatantly curious expression, mouth opened in a little O.

"I talk about her all the time!" Weathersby said.

"Do you?" Colin squinted. He seemed to remember Weathersby was interested in some young lady, but he was always so very drunk at those card games. "I honestly didn't realize, chap." He turned to Lady Penelope. "Lady Penelope, I hope you will forgive me. I did not realize that I was inter-fering with any prior attachments."

She said something completely muffled by her hands. At his blank stare, she dropped them and tried again. "There are no prior attachments," she said. "Cecil, I had no idea."

"All those hours we spent together," Weathersby said. "All those long conversations. You didn't realize?"

"You didn't *tell* me," she said in a tortured wail. They were drawing quite the crowd. Colin's ears were ringing—though whether from the pitch of Penelope's distressed voice or from his sudden sense of vertigo, he wasn't certain. "Why didn't you *tell* me?" she demanded.

"I thought it was obvious," Weathersby said.

"And I thought that when you said I was *such* a *good pal*, it meant you weren't interested!" She threw up her hands. "Cecil, do you have any *idea* how much time I've spent mooning after you! And you didn't! Say! Anything!"

"Neither did you!" he countered.

"That's not fair," Lady Penelope snapped. "When a *man* is in love with someone who doesn't want him, it's poetic and tragic and wonderful. When a *women* does the same thing, it's pathetic."

"It's really quite pathetic when we do it as well," Colin said. "Trust me." He took his fiancée's hand. "Lady Penelope.

I must at this juncture beg you to release me from our engagement. I fear I am most horrifically in love with someone, and it has just occurred to me that I've never actually said as much. If there is any hope of forgiveness for such pathetic men as Weathersby and I, perhaps you would be kind enough to grant my request, and consider his?"

Lady Penelope stared at him, wide-eyed. "Are you sure?" she asked. "What if she says no?"

He winced. "Then I suppose I'll have no choice but to turn to poetry. Do you want to marry Weathersby?"

She bit her lip and cast a look over his shoulder to where Weathersby waited, shifting nervously from foot to foot. "Rather desperately," she confided in a low voice.

"Would your father approve the match?" he asked. He couldn't abandon her if it would only lead to tears.

"An earl's not quite as good as a marquess, but I can convince him," she said. "Especially if I cry a bit. He does so hate it when I cry at him."

He peered back at Weathersby. "Weathersby. You're an earl?"

"Earl's first son," Weathersby said glumly. "Father's quite old. I have told you. A few times."

"Huh," Colin managed. He really did have to stop drinking. "Well, then. May I suggest you two go see the man? Feel free to tell him that I'm a terrible cad who's broken your heart. The only possible remedy is a swift marriage to show you aren't affected in the slightest."

She was smiling now, and somehow it was brighter and more lovely than any she offered him before. It was not merely a smile of polite agreeableness. She was radiantly happy.

Colin bent and kissed her hand. Then he turned and grabbed Weathersby's hand, shaking it firmly. "Thank you," he said, "for showing me how much of an idiot I am."

"By being one myself," Weathersby said, but the same radiance beamed from his face. "Good luck," he added, as Colin strode away. He caught one last glimpse of them, resuming the walk as if they had always been together.

"Damn it, man. You never *told* her," he muttered to himself, and picked up his pace.

Elinor's headache had receded by the time she rose from her rest, and she was relieved to find that Joan's recently acquired habit of a midafternoon nap continued unabated, sparing her a full debriefing. Hearing Martin's distant tread, she swiftly decided to take a walk. She needed open skies and clear air, and no more interrogations, however well-meaning.

The ride to the park was stifling, but once she exited the hack she was glad of her decision. The day was beautiful, and the mere sight of so many people who had no idea where she'd been or what she'd been up to raised her spirits considerably. She strolled idly, waving and nodding in greeting to those she recognized, but never pausing for more than a moment. Yet something remained like a gray wash over her vision, tarnishing the beauty of the day. She enjoyed her walks in isolation, with the quiet of her mind and the company of her thoughts, and today she wished very much to be alone. The trouble was she found herself wishing she had some company in her solitude.

It was a ridiculous thought. She could not be alone if someone else were about, but there was an emptiness more solid than mere absence today. She found herself wishing that someone was waiting for her to return. Relaxing on a bench, perhaps, while she made her turn about the park. Or even at home, absorbed in his own work. And she knew exactly who she wished that person to be.

And he was standing not fifty yards away. She froze. It took her a painful moment to take in the scene before her—Colin, Lady Penelope, some round-faced man she didn't recognize—and a second more to stir herself from horrified stupor into action. She turned at once, wrenching her eyes from the tableau—were they arguing?—and strode back the way she had come. She hissed between her teeth. Could she not even have a moment without the man creeping into her mind and her presence?

And he'd been with Penelope. Somehow she'd managed to relegate the girl to an abstract, so long as she didn't have to see them together. Now she couldn't think of anything else. He would kiss that woman. Touch her. Make love to her the way the two of them never could.

Footsteps grew close behind her, keeping a quicker pace than hers to close the distance between them. She stiffened. He'd seen her. Followed her. For what purpose? Didn't he see that anything he said would only deepen her humiliation?

She spun. And Edward Foyle closed the gap between them.

"Lady Elinor Hargrove," he said, voice warm with vicious pleasure. "I believe that you and I should have a word."

Colin covered the distance between Hyde Park and the Hargrove town house in an interval of time that he was certain would set records, if anyone bothered to write such things down. It was such a brief interval that he had managed to stay at least a few paces ahead of his good sense, which was a damn good thing, considering what he was about to do. He bounded up the steps, chancing a glimpse behind him in case said good senses or Lord Levenbane were on his heels, and then rang the bell. He endured a few seconds of anxious weight-shifting before it was answered, and then he bulled his way inside, nearly upending the footman who'd answered.

"What the—" Joan began, emerging from the drawing room, and stopped herself short of what Colin was certain would be a most entertaining blasphemy. She was very good at her ruse in public, but tended to let it slip behind closed doors. "Lord Farleigh. What an unexpected surprise." The sour set of her mouth suggested it was not a pleasant one.

"Mrs. Hargrove," Colin said with what he hoped was a winning grin. "You are looking absolutely fetching and delightfully round. Is Lady Elinor at home?"

"No," Joan said, lips pursing further, as if she'd bitten a lemon. "And she wouldn't want to see you if she was, I expect."

He flinched. She was still upset, then. But he could not

allow himself to be dissuaded. "I need to speak to her, urgently," he said.

"Does this regard her recent excursion?" Joan asked. "If so, I can handle the matter." She folded her hands over her protruding belly and gave him the most staunchly unamused look he had ever seen on someone who wasn't guarding the royal family.

"It's not," he said. "Not directly. It is a related matter."

"Oh?"

She was not going to be moved. Martin appeared, descending the stairs with an expression of deep suspicion. Damn. What had Elinor told them, exactly? "Martin," Colin said brightly. "You look well."

"Farleigh. Something I can help you with?"

"He's looking for Elinor," Joan said.

"Is he." Martin's suspicion only deepened. "I think it's best if you don't, Farleigh."

"I only need to speak to her for a moment." He only needed a yes or a no. Though, he might need some time to lay out his case. His apology, rather. His explanation. His baring of his soul. No, don't get maudlin. He would simply detail the explanation, and await her judgment.

"Well, you can't," Martin said. "She has expressed in no uncertain terms that she does not wish to see you, and I agree that it's for the best. I don't know exactly what went on between the two of you. I would like to assume the best of you. You are my oldest friend, save one. Unfortunately for you, Elinor is my oldest friend save *none* and it is with her that my loyalty must lie. So. I wish you a good day, Lord Farleigh, but I must ask you to leave."

Colin scowled. "For God's sake, Martin. One conversation won't kill her."

Colin was spared the consequences of his outburst by another ring of the doorbell. The footman obligingly opened the door to reveal a grubby child, blinking at them with a narrow-eyed look older than his years. "I've got a message," he said before the footman could shoo him away. He held out his hand, brandishing a crumpled note. The footman looked a question at Martin, who nodded. He reached for the note. The child held fast. "I was supposed to get some more," he said.

"More?" the footman asked, but Joan had already sighed and trundled forward. She pressed a coin into the boy's hand, extracting the note, and turned back as she unfolded it. Immediately her eyebrows creased in consternation.

"Martin," she said urgently, and held it out to him. His expression darkened as he read.

"What is it?" Colin asked.

"A summons," Martin said. He looked up. His eyes blazed with anger, and Colin felt cold dread spread through his core. "I expect there is one waiting for you at your home as well. It says that a Mr. Foyle is expecting my company, and yours, at a tea shop. It's written in Elinor's hand."

"Oh, hell," Colin said. He felt the blood drain from his face. A tea shop. That was good. It was a public place; he couldn't have hurt her, then. Unless she wasn't there. What if he had her held elsewhere? How had he even found her?

"I think you have some explaining to do," Martin said.

"On the way," Colin said. "If he has Elinor—"

"That is what's happening, then. This is someone dangerous." Martin's voice had gone from fire to ice.

"Yes," Colin said. "Very. We shouldn't delay."

"Have the carriage brought around," Joan ordered the footman.

"You're not coming," Martin said immediately.

"I have explaining to do as well, and I don't mean to miss Lord Farleigh's part of it," Joan said. "I'll stay in the carriage, don't worry."

"You realize that is a physical impossibility," Martin replied.

"Which? You not worrying, or me remaining where I promise to?"

"Both," Martin said, but he didn't protest when Joan heaved herself after them down the steps.

Chapter 30

~

"I've never been here before," Elinor said. "It's quite nice." She sipped her tea and peered around her. The tea shop made an unlikely location for blackmail, extortion, and kidnapping. Every surface was bedecked in extravagant lace; she had the feeling that someone's elderly female relative was being indulged. The other patrons were clean folk, well-dressed, and the woman who had served them tea had precisely the manner Elinor preferred from her waitstaff: polite, efficient, and not overcurious. It was the only aspect of the establishment that lent itself to the current situation.

Edward Foyle sat across from her, drumming his fingers on the table and scowling out the front window. He had not touched his tea; it was doubtless growing cold. A great pity, considering the quality.

"I'm certain they'll be here soon," Elinor said. He turned his glare on her, and her gut clenched in instinctive fear. She sipped again to cover her fear. He had not harmed her. He had intimated that he had a weapon on his person, but by the time they had reached the tea shop she had begun to suspect it was a ruse. He had the advantage of information, though. Information that could be used to harm her and her family. And that was enough to keep her here, waiting for her brother's arrival and trying desperately to keep her hands from trembling. She would not show him her fear. "It might save us a great deal of time if you simply explained to me what you wish to discuss," she said.

"Your curiosity will be satisfied soon enough," he growled. His harsh tone was enough to draw several curious looks, but they quickly dissipated. Elinor traced the brim of her teacup and counted her heartbeats. Too fast. She needed to remain calm. He wasn't going to hurt her in such a public place, even if he was in possession of a weapon. The harm he intended to cause was more insidious, and he would not be calling Colin and Martin here if there were not a way to circumvent it. He'd want something. Money, probably. A guarantee of their silence.

Well, she'd find out soon enough. There were Martin and Colin, striding around the corner with murder in their eyes while Joan struggled gamely to keep up. Elinor sat back, feeling satisfaction curl catlike within her. It was almost amusing, the way they burst into the tea shop as if into a den of thieves. She rather hoped *they* weren't armed; they all looked in the mood to enact some violence on her "host." To forestall them, she stood, smiling blandly. Joan, a little out of breath, fetched up behind the boys.

"Lord Farleigh. Mrs. Hargrove. Dearest brother. Please sit down; the tea here is excellent. I hope you're well; I am in good health, I assure you."

It was doubly amusing that the men's expressions were such perfect twins of each other. She could tell that both had the overwhelming need to throttle Mr. Foyle, and she watched reason war with instinct across their expressions in a give and take to match the most dramatic martial clash. Each settled into seething anger over outright violence within a few moments, and took his seat reluctantly. Joan plopped into hers with a grunt of relief and immediately reached for a biscuit.

"What the devil do you think you're doing, Foyle?" Colin asked.

"Having a civilized conversation," Foyle said. He leaned

his forearms on the table. "How much do you know about what your sister has been up to, Mr. Hargrove?"

The set of Martin's jaw suggested he knew too much. Elinor felt as if the floor had given out under her. How much had Colin told him? Dear God, he couldn't have told him *everything*, could he?

"I know enough," Martin said.

"Then you know it would be very unfortunate for all of you if her activities were widely known," Foyle said.

"What do you want, Foyle?" Colin asked. "Just spit it out already."

"You took something from Beauchene. I want it destroyed," Foyle said.

"What we have is proof that you are a spy," Elinor said. "That hardly balances against anything you might say of me."

"Perhaps," Foyle said. "But I can also offer you something that no hidden record or forgotten letter will reveal. I can tell you how Marie died." At their stony silence, he looked between the four of them. "It's simple enough. Your family's reputation, Mr. Hargrove, will be preserved. And you, Lord Farleigh, will have your answers. All I ask in return is those letters. And a modest sum."

"Money?" Joan said. "Really, how dull."

He shrugged. "Funds will make my exit from your proximity all the faster. I will return here in one hour. You will bring five hundred pounds and the letters here."

"I will discover what happened to my sister," Colin said. "And I will do it without supplying you with the means to so much as buy a drink."

"Farleigh. You have to consider Elinor," Martin said levelly.

"I'll be fine. This is Colin's decision," Elinor said.

"Yes, it is. And so I know he will do the right thing," Martin said, and Colin glared at him. Elinor found that she had no doubt as to his answer. Of course he would accept Foyle's agreement. It was the only way to be certain of protecting her.

The realization was a curious thing. Her infatuation,

alternately heady and heartbreaking, solidified suddenly into an absolute calm. A certainty. Whatever they were or weren't to each other, they had that. They would protect each other to the last.

If she could not have him, she had that.

"I agree to your terms," Colin said rigidly.

Foyle looked at Martin. "Mr. Hargrove, you understand that if Lord Farleigh reneges on this agreement—"

"My family's privacy is forfeit," Martin snapped. "I understand. I will hold Lord Farleigh to whatever deal is struck here. Take your money, tell your tale, and let us be done with this."

Elinor touched his wrist. He looked at her, and for a horrified moment she saw nothing but contempt in his eyes. But his expression soothed. Contempt for Foyle, she realized, not her. Never her. He covered her hand briefly, and gave her a nod that meant *we will speak later*, and she knew that things would be all right between them, whatever came. She chanced a look at Colin, too, and was surprised to see guilt and fear contorting his features. He looked away from her the moment her eyes met his, and fixed his gaze on Foyle.

"One hour," he said. "And we will return."

The sum Foyle named would not be difficult to put together; all things considered, it was quite conservative. That did nothing to ease Colin's anger as the four of them trooped out of the tea shop and back to the waiting carriage.

"To the bank?" Martin asked. "Or your home, first?"

"I have the damn letters with me," Colin said. They were folded in his coat pocket; he'd given Hudson copies for his investigation.

Martin declined to comment on the invective as they took their seats in the carriage. Elinor sat across from Colin, her eyes half-lidded. He wondered at her calm. He supposed it had not been a proper kidnapping, but he expected more relief from her.

"He didn't hurt you, did he?" Colin asked.

"I told you I was well," Elinor said. "I meant it. He wasn't even particularly menacing, once I realized he did not have a weapon."

"Not the kind to leave a physical wound, at least," Martin muttered. "We'll go to the town house first, to drop off you ladies. I'll come back with you to make the exchange, Farleigh."

"Nonsense," Elinor said. "You can come if you like, but I insist on being there."

Colin nodded. Of course she would be there. She'd been with him the whole way; he could not imagine hearing what Foyle had to say without Elinor beside him. He could not imagine anything about his life from this moment forward without her beside him.

He still hadn't told her. He'd been so worried about her that he'd nearly forgotten, and now here they were with their knees nearly knocking, but he still couldn't say the words he longed to. It wasn't the right time. But it would be soon.

One hour.

"Oh, hell. There's no way I'm going to win this argument, is there?" Martin said.

"Were we having an argument?" Elinor asked sweetly.

"No, but I was doing a good job of scripting it out in my mind," Martin said. He scowled at them each in turn—friend, sister, wife. "I need to find some more respectable acquaintances."

"It's so sweet that you think you're still respectable," Joan said.

"I suppose you'll insist on going, too," Martin said.

"No, I don't think that would be wise," Joan said. "I appear to be otherwise engaged." She winced and pressed a hand over her belly. Colin blanched. Martin went white as a sheet, and Elinor let out a little *oh, my* that Colin thought rather understated the situation.

"We have to get you to a doctor," Martin said. "Driver!"

"Home," Joan insisted. "You can make the doctor come to us, remember? And I think there's still plenty of time." She prodded a finger into her belly thoughtfully.

"Could you not . . . *poke* our child?" Martin said. "You might damage something."

"You were supposed to wait until we were back at Thornwald," Joan told her belly, and prodded it again. "I don't want to be stuck in London for weeks. Do you know how hard it is lugging you around in this heat?"

"It will be all right," Martin said, taking her hand, and something in the tone of his voice made Colin realize that he was afraid.

"We'll be quick," Elinor promised. "And then I'll be with you, the whole time. Or I could stay . . ."

"No," Joan said. "No, go, both of you. See this through. And Lord Farleigh? If she is not back in one piece in a reasonable time frame, they will never find your body."

Chapter 31

~~

Foyle was already waiting inside when Elinor and Colin met again outside the tea shop. Colin inspected the man through the window. He was too plain to be a villain. He ought to have had a brutish brow or greasy locks; instead, he looked so ordinary as to be nearly invisible.

"Are you ready for this?" Elinor asked.

"No," he confessed. "But I don't think I would be, had I all the time in the world."

"Nor I." She folded her hands in front of her and took in a long breath. "I have discovered so much about Marie these past weeks. I feel as if I have discovered that she was a stranger to me all along. No. That isn't quite right. I feel as if . . ."

"As if by asking the questions, you have made her into a stranger yourself," Colin said. "That you have created this reality by wondering."

"Let's be done with this," Elinor said. Her hand touched his briefly, and then she moved past him, leading the way into the shop. Foyle watched them approach, his jaw tense and eyes narrowed.

"Almost thought you'd back out," he said.

"Your money," Colin replied, setting the case in which the funds were hidden on the ground between them and taking his seat. "And your crimes." He withdrew the bundle of letters from his jacket and slid it across the table. They still had the copy, he told himself.

Foyle took the bundle and considered it. "French bastard," he said at last. "He's guilty of worse than I ever was, you know. He played every side he could during the war. How do you think he got these?" He grunted. "But it wasn't enough. No, he kept on digging. Traced me back all the way to India. I think he was hoping for something on Copeland, but of course *he's* too polished for mud to stick to him."

Foyle slipped the bundle into his pocket. Then he sighed, rubbing the back of his neck with his hand. "I can't believe it came to this," he said. "It was supposed to fix everything, marrying your sister. It was supposed to make us happy."

Colin contemplated the exact distance between them, calculating the effect of the intervening table on his ability to launch himself at the other man. Elinor's foot bumped up against his, and she gave him a pleading look. *Keep yourself together another few minutes, Farleigh*, he admonished himself.

"I was in love with her. Pitifully so," Foyle said. "She didn't want anything to do with me. Then Hayes died. Lord Copeland wanted those mines. He threatened her. I protected her from him. Gave her a way out, but she never once showed a bit of gratitude."

"And what did she have to be grateful for?" Colin asked, voice flat.

"They used me. Lord Copeland. Marie. Everyone. She knew that I had the kind of connections to—to cover up what she'd done. She came to me while she was still pregnant. She wasn't sure if Lord Hayes was the father. Though it would be damn obvious once the whelp was born. She wanted help getting rid of it, if it came out wrong."

Colin listened with gritted teeth. *Get rid of it*. The Marie he'd known would not have spoken that way. Would not have thought that way. She would have been afraid, yes. But she would not have been so callous.

"I didn't have to marry her. Copeland knew about the child, about the affair. I could have let him ruin her, but I told her I'd look after her. That I'd sort things out with him, if she'd marry me, and she did. And then you know what she told me, while we were walking away from the altar? She leaned over and said, 'I'll never love you.'" He gave a hollow laugh. "After everything I did for her."

"And your debts had nothing to do with it, then," Elinor said flatly.

Foyle shrugged. "And what if they did? It still saved her. The least she could do was show some hint of gratitude."

Colin could hear his blood in his veins, the oppressive cadence of his own pulse. "What happened to her?" he asked through gritted teeth.

"She killed herself," Foyle said. Colin's skin went cold. Elinor gave a jolt. "She wasn't the same after the child. I was there. I hired a local woman, paid her to be quiet, so no one else would know. And after it came—well. She wouldn't let go, would she? Kept singing to it. Saying it would be all right, everything would be all right, when anyone could see that it wouldn't."

"Anyway, after that she was strange. Those words at the wedding were the only ones she spoke to me, almost. She hardly ate. Slept most of the day. Then one night, she left. Hadn't left the house in weeks, but she walked out into the street without so much as pair of slippers. Just in her nightgown. I went looking for her, but she was gone. Didn't realize what she'd done until they pulled her out of the river."

Colin turned his face away. He could not listen to this. "My sister did not kill herself," he said. He tasted bile. "She wouldn't," he said.

"No, she wouldn't," Foyle said. "Except it wasn't her. She was broken somehow. Sick and broken. If I was a superstitious man I'd say she was possessed." He gave a hollow laugh.

"You didn't actually see—"

"She left a note. Said it'd be easier for everyone this way. I think she believed it, too. She had no idea the trouble she'd cause Bhandari. Or me."

"How selfish of her," Colin said, and perhaps Foyle had some sense of how close to death he was treading, for he shut up at last.

The bell over the door jangled. Foyle straightened up. "I suppose that's everything then," he said. He started to stand. Colin began to rise, but Elinor's hand found his thigh, and her nails dug in. "I should be going."

"I'm afraid you won't be," Elinor said. She looked behind her, and Colin turned to see what she was looking at. Three men had entered the tea shop, and seemed to be waiting for some signal. "This is him," Elinor said, raising her voice slightly, and they started forward.

Foyle bared his teeth. "What's the meaning of this?" he said. "We had a deal."

"Oh. I'm sorry, I rather broke it," Elinor said, wide-eyed. "*This* is a magistrate and two very muscular constables. *This* is you being in possession of letters that clearly indicate your treasonous activities in wartime. *This* is me not being afraid of whatever lunatic lies you try to spin about me. Honestly, gentlemen. Can you believe this man thought that he could blackmail me by claiming that I was some sort of covert courtesan?"

"Preposterous, Lady Elinor," the magistrate said. "Terrible business, this. Lord Farleigh. May we take the villain off your hands? You're welcome to retrieve your money, of course. Blackmail and espionage. Not a good day for you, Foyle."

Foyle had gone extremely pale. He looked nervously between the two burly constables, who were closing in on him from each side.

He bolted, lunging past the bigger one. The man grabbed for the back of his coat, but Foyle was past him in an instant, worming between the tables and toward the door. He struck the magistrate in the side, sending the man toppling.

Colin leapt out of his chair. Foyle was three steps away from the door. Colin grabbed at him. His hand closed around the back of Foyle's arm. He swung the man around with all the force he could muster, anger and grief raking through him like the teeth of a wild creature.

Foyle flew out of Colin's grasp, shoulder-first into the window at the front of the shop. Glass shattered. Foyle rebounded and slumped to the floor, a thin shard of glass impaled in his shoulder. He clutched at it with a howl. Colin advanced.

Elinor caught his hand. He wheeled on her, his heart pounding in his ears, but she only shook her head.

"Enough," she whispered. "It has to be enough."

Slowly, he nodded. His heartbeat slowed. The constables moved past him with muttered thanks and collected Foyle. Colin didn't look. He stared at Elinor instead, watched her watching them, traced the lines of her face with his gaze.

"They're gone," she said after a time. "You're shaking."

So he was. Foyle was gone. He'd hang, no doubt. But not for what he'd done to Marie. Even through all his rage, Colin wasn't certain he deserved to hang—and yet it seemed not enough. He was being punished for the wrong crime.

The patrons and workers were all staring at him. At them. He stepped neatly around the table and picked up the case in which rested his five hundred pounds. He weighed it in his hand. That was the price he'd been willing to pay to know the truth. And now the money was his again.

He walked to the counter, where the owner stood, glowering.

"My apologies for your trouble," Colin said. He set the case on the counter between them. "This should cover the damage to the window. Good day."

With that he turned, and walked out onto the street.

Elinor did not care about propriety. When Colin hailed a cab, she climbed in after him, and sat on the bench across from him. He hardly seemed to notice her. She could not blame him. She could read the grief in every line of his face, and it echoed her own.

Marie had killed herself.

There remained the possibility that Foyle was lying, but she didn't believe so. Those final letters, the letters that spoke of being afraid, had a quality to them akin to madness. She'd been afraid and alone and desperate. She'd had a child who could destroy her, and she'd been surrounded by enemies who claimed to love her.

Elinor knew her friend, and knew that it would have

destroyed her. There was no villain to blame. No hand but her own. Other men may have owned her misery, but she had taken the final step. Lord Copeland surely shared some blame, but however much Foyle tried to shunt responsibility onto him, it did not sound as if he had taken any direct action against Marie. Foyle himself would face punishment for the role he'd played, though she suspected that in his own mind, he was telling the truth when he said he'd loved her. That he'd meant to protect her. And Bhandari—Bhandari was to be blamed least of all, for of all of them he had loved her the most, and would have saved her if he could.

They stopped in front of Colin's town house. He got out without a word, and strode for the door. Elinor hesitated. He was in worse pain than she had ever seen him, and she was absolutely certain that he was heading inside for the nearest bottle of liquor. And she was not certain he would stop drinking once he had started. There was too much surcease of pain to be found in oblivion, too much torture in cogent thought. Drink had not been the vice of her grief, but she knew the temptation of self-destruction.

"Miss? Where can I take you?" the driver asked.

She stood. "Nowhere. I'm staying here," she said.

She exited the carriage with her shoulders squared and her hands nervously smoothing her skirts. It took her thirteen steps to reach the front stoop. Seventeen seconds to work up the nerve to ring the bell. Thirty-two words in all to learn that Colin had headed for the library and to express that she was quite all right, thank you, she would show herself in. She hoped the halls would be clear, but Phoebe was in the hallway, looking puzzled.

"Elinor?" she said. "What on earth is going on? Colin just barreled past me, and now he's in the library with mother and that Indian fellow, and they locked the door."

Of course. They needed to be told. "It's to do with Marie," she said.

Phoebe's eyes widened. "What about her?"

"They should tell you," Elinor said. "It's not my place. But I'll wait with you, if you like."

She nodded, apprehensive, and the two of them stood together in silence for several minutes. When the door opened, Mr. Bhandari came out first. He strode away without so much as a word of greeting, and then Lady Farleigh emerged, looking older than her years.

"Mother, what's going on?" Phoebe asked immediately.

Lady Farleigh sighed. "I suppose it can't be put off, then. Come with me." She looked at Elinor. "I assume you're going in there to see him."

Elinor steeled herself before that withering gaze. "Yes," she said.

Lady Farleigh waved a hand. "Well, have at it, then. It will be the least improper thing that has happened in this house all day." She took Phoebe's hand in the crook of her arm and headed down the hallway.

Elinor didn't knock. Colin had been Lord Farleigh long enough to forget that there were people who did not respect the sovereignty of a closed door; he hadn't locked it behind him. She darted in quickly and shut it behind her, and she *did* throw the lock. She had no wish to be interrupted.

Colin had already poured himself a glass of brandy. Filled it nearly to the brim. He looked up at her with a bleak, empty expression. "What are you doing here, Elinor?" he asked, voice hoarse.

"I'm worried about you," she said.

"Don't worry," he said. "I'm not going to kill myself. I should think one suicide is enough in the family, don't you?"

"Colin." Elinor stepped forward tentatively. She didn't know what to say. There were no scripts for a thing like this. No sequence of words that would make this right. "I know you are hurting."

He gave a choked laugh. "Your insight never ceases to amaze."

"Don't be cruel," she said softly. "Please, Colin. I can bear it when you blunder into cruelty, but not when you embrace it."

"You shouldn't," he said. "You should not bear cruelty by any means, from anyone. Least of all me." He set down his glass and turned his back on her. "I want to be alone, Elinor."

"I know," she said. "And I'll leave you alone, in a moment. But today I found myself wishing very much that I could be alone, and very disappointed that I was alone without you waiting for me. And I wanted you to know that I am waiting for you, when you are done being alone."

He turned slowly. "Waiting?" he said.

A tremor went through her. She knew, she *knew* she could not have him, but she could not stand beneath the weight of this feeling any longer without saying something. "I love you," she said. "I am quite ridiculously in love with you, against all my best judgment and reason. I know that you do not feel the same way, and it needn't obligate you to anything. I need only be your friend. But I need you to know that you are only as alone as you wish to be, because I am waiting if you need me."

"Because you love me," he said. His voice was dull. She wet her lips.

"As I said, I have no expectations," she said. "You're engaged, and—"

"I'm not," he said.

"Not what?"

"Engaged. At least, I don't believe I am."

"I see." She paused. This was not an eventuality she had planned for.

"I've had an idea, though," he said.

"What sort of idea?" she asked.

He took her hand, and reached into his pocket. He withdrew something small, something concealed in his palm, and pressed it into hers.

It was a small, carved cat, its tail tucked over its paws. Her token. She curled her fingers over it.

"I thought maybe I could get engaged again. To you," he said. "You see, I've been rather inconveniently in love with you for five years."

"What?" She stared at him. "But you never *told* me," she said, shock making her tone accusatory.

To her further surprise, Colin threw back his head and laughed.

Chapter 32

Once Colin began to laugh, he found it quite difficult to stop. He knew he should. He knew he shouldn't be laughing in the first place. There was so very little to amuse him, today. Even as he laughed, Foyle's words kept playing through his head.

His sister had killed herself, and he was happy. Was *laughing*. He choked on the convulsive sound, and wrenched himself into silence. "You must think me insane," he said.

"Not really." Elinor hadn't moved. "I'm a bit too much in shock to think much of anything."

"I was at your house to tell you," he said. "To explain how much I love you. To ask you to marry me. It was supposed to be happy. It would have been."

She smiled, shook her head. "I think we are too old for such simple happiness," she said. "Life has grown too complicated while we were distracted."

"You could never be described as a simple woman," Colin said. He shut his eyes. It was too much all at once. But his grief did not own his happiness. "Tell me again," he said.

She did not have to ask him what he meant. He heard her draw forward, felt the very tips of her fingers against his cheek. "I love you," she said.

He caught her hand and kissed the palm. "And I love you. I have loved you for so long the constant pain of it made me numb, but somehow you have opened up my wounds anew."

"I wound you?" she said. "Colin. Your eloquence is sometimes lacking."

"I swear, I am only ever so foolish around you," he said, and kissed the smile that was beginning to form at the corner of her mouth. She turned her head and met his lips. It was only a kiss, soft and gentle and sweet, and yet it was the most intimate act they had shared. It felt as if there were no space between them, nothing around them. Only the beating of their two hearts, and all the complexities of their lives twined together. "I should have told you long ago," he said.

"Oh, no," she said. Their fingers were laced together, their bodies nearly touching. "If you had told me long ago, I would not have listened. We had to wait, you see. For the people we have become."

"Are we different than we were? I confess I hadn't noticed. I still say the most foolish things. Sometimes I even mean them. You really shouldn't love a man like that," he said. He was waiting for her to realize her mistake. To take it all back. For it must be a mistake. She could not be saying what he had dreamed for so long.

"I told you. I don't mind it when you don't mean it," she said.

"And I told you that you should." He kissed her again, quick and light. "I am sorry for all the foolish things I've said without meaning them." He kissed her again, lingering for a long moment. "And I am deeply, deeply sorry for all the things I said intentionally. You did not deserve them."

"I owe you apologies, as well," Elinor said.

"You have only ever been cruel in answer to my anger," he said. "And let us not begin this way. With recrimination and apology. Anything you have done, I forgive, though I do not accept the premise that there is anything *to* forgive. Except the matter of that small deception on your part. And I have a very simple proposal for making that up to me."

"Oh?" she asked, but she was smiling, a knowing glint

in her eye. "I suppose we could arrange for such an act of contrition. Once we are properly married."

"Must we wait?" he asked wistfully.

"Yes," she said firmly.

He looked at her askance. "Why? I mean, I understand the normal reasons, but given our prior activities . . ."

"I want to wait," she said. "Perhaps *because* of what we did. Call it ridiculous if you will, but after the way we began . . . I want something of sacredness in my love for you, Colin. And what we have done has been enjoyable, but it has been the furthest thing from sacred. I don't mean in the eyes of the Church, I mean between us. I want there to be more than pleasure."

"There is," he said. "And I will prove it." He released her hands, and made for the door.

"Where are you going?"

"To get a special license," he said.

"Now?"

He turned, his hand on the knob. "I have waited long enough for this," he said. "And I have spent long enough on matters of the past. I want the future to arrive, for it is bright and what has come before is anything but. And also—" He released the knob and returned to her, leaning close so that his mouth brushed her cheek. "I want you," he whispered, and she shivered against him. "In every way I can have you. The sacred and the profane."

"I think we've made plenty of progress on the latter," Elinor said. Then, "Oh, hell. Martin."

"What about him?" Colin asked. Martin was the last person he wanted to think about, right this moment.

"He would never forgive either one of us if we didn't speak to him first," she said.

He groaned. "Can it wait until tomorrow? We'll talk to him between the special license and the wedding."

"No. Before," she said firmly. She planted a hand on her hip and looked at him sternly.

"I don't suppose I could persuade you by mentioning that

I've recently had some very bad news, and getting a special license would cheer me immensely," he said. He smiled, but the smile was forced. The truth was, he had shoved the revelation of Marie's suicide aside for a few seconds, but now it was encroaching on him again, like a great beast prowling at the edge of a campfire's light. And Elinor, of course, saw it.

"I don't want to be a distraction," she said. "Or you will only be disappointed when the whirl of motion ends, and we are at rest together. We must speak to Martin. But it needn't be today. Or tomorrow. It will be when you are ready."

"But I am ready to be with you now," he said.

She shook her head. "And I'm *not*, Colin. I need the marriage. Not the wedding, but the marriage. I don't expect you to understand."

He kissed her brow. Of course he understood. "You don't want it to be part of the dream," he shared. "Part of the game, the charade, whatever you want to call it. You want it to be part of your real life, your life here, and in that life, you would wait."

She laced her hands behind his neck. "You know, I have spent so much time being irritated with you in my life, I have too often forgotten how smart you are."

"Is that a compliment? It sounds almost like a compliment, yet it has the sting of an insult."

"Your favorite kind, as I recall," she said.

"You are beautiful, and brilliant, and I adore you," he said, because he had never said it before, and because it made her laugh, made her kiss him. Made the sorrow at his heels fall back.

"Mrs. Fincher," Elinor said, her lips against his.

He pulled away from her. "What?"

"Mrs. Fincher. The odd name on the odd letter. I've realized where I've seen it before," Elinor said.

"What of it? Foyle's finished regardless."

"You have to come with me," Elinor said.

"Can we perhaps slot this in after Martin, the special

license, and the marriage? And the profaning?" Colin asked
lightly, covering for his confusion.

"No. This comes first. I'm probably wrong. Surely I'm
wrong." Elinor frowned. "I don't think I'm wrong."

"You rarely are," he reminded her.

"Get Mr. Bhandari," she said. "And have the carriage
brought 'round."

Colin's mouth went dry when he saw where Elinor had taken
them. Mrs. Fincher's School for Girls was an austere, inhos-
pitable building. Its entrance was gated with black iron bars,
its windows shuttered and dark. When Elinor rang the bell,
a plump woman answered, looking as drab and gray as the
building itself.

"Can I help you?" she asked, peering at the four people
on the stoop—for whatever impropriety she had tolerated
so far, Lady Farleigh had insisted on coming along as escort.

"I hope so," Elinor said. "My name is Lady Elinor Hargrove. This is Lord Farleigh and Lady Farleigh, and Mr.
Bhandari." With each honorific the woman's eyes widened
a touch, and she seemed to take in the quality of their clothes
and the fine carriage behind them for the first time. "We're
looking for a girl. She'd be about six years old."

"We've got a few of those," the woman said, but her eyes
slid to Mr. Bhandari, standing at the rear. "But I think I can
guess which one you mean. Come in."

She stepped aside, and they filed in one at a time. The
interior was far more welcoming, lit as best as it could be with
warm lamplight, the floors polished and the walls papered
with cheerful prints of daisies. Colin found that he was having
a rather hard time thinking. Or doing much of anything. He
looked at Elinor, entreating her to tell him that he was right
in his guess of why they were there, that *she* was right, but
she looked as nervous as he did. Mr. Bhandari and Lady
Farleigh simply looked mystified.

"Wait here, then," the woman said, and vanished down
a side passage.

"What on earth is going on, Elinor?" Lady Farleigh asked. "Why have you brought us here?"

"I could be wrong," Elinor said, sounding desperate.

"You aren't," Colin said with certainty that he could not explain. And then the woman came back around the corner, leading a little girl by the hand.

She was small. So small, with wide brown eyes and dark brown hair that was almost black, bound up with a single red ribbon. She had a sharp, elfin face, a perfect echo of her mother's.

"Do you know her, then?" the woman asked. "We've gotten money for her upkeep every month and strict instructions, but no one's ever come to claim her. Is it you, then? Were you sending all that money?"

Colin couldn't breathe. Neither, it seemed, could Mr. Bhandari.

"No," Elinor said. "We weren't sending the money, that was someone else." She walked forward and crouched in front of the girl while the rest of them stood frozen. "What's your name, sweetheart?"

The girl looked up at her guardian, and the woman gave an encouraging nod. She looked back at Elinor. "Marie," she said softly. "My name is Marie."

"Well, Marie. This is going to sound very strange and startling," Elinor said, and her voice fluttered with the hint of tears. "But your mother was a friend of mine. A very good friend."

"You know my mama?" the girl asked. She grew quiet. "Is she dead, like Lettie says?"

"Your mother is gone, sweetheart," Elinor said, touching her arm. "But your family is not. May I?" She looked at the woman, who gave a quick nod, her own eyes a bit starry with tears. Elinor took the girl's hand and led her back toward the others. Colin watched her come with a feeling in his chest like an avalanche. He was going to smother under it. He could not tell if he was overjoyed or choked with sorrow, and he never wanted it to end.

"Mr. Bhandari, may I present your daughter," Elinor said.

Mr. Bhandari did not move. He stared at the little girl, his lips parted in shock. Lady Farleigh gripped his arm. "She's yours, can't you see?" she said. "She's yours."

Mr. Bhandari bent to one knee with exquisite slowness, and touched Marie's cheek with the very tips of his fingers. There was no mistaking that face.

"You are my father?" the girl asked. She looked around at all of them, plainly confused, and just as plainly overcome with hope, with the promise of a fairy tale told by every orphan coming true at last. "But why did you leave me here? Why didn't you come for me before?"

"I did not know," he said. His voice was thick. "I didn't know that you were here, my little angel. I did not know that you were mine."

Lady Farleigh clutched Colin's arm in both hands. She seemed to be having trouble staying upright, and Colin wasn't certain he could offer much more stability. And then the little girl threw herself into her father's arms, her face shining with trust that her fairy tale ending had come. Mr. Bhandari swept her into the air, crushing her against his chest, a sound in his throat like a sob.

The woman—Mrs. Fincher, Colin presumed—looked at the rest of them in pleased befuddlement. "Is that true? He's her father?" she asked.

"It would appear so," Colin managed. "She was never claimed?"

"No. Dropped off by a man hired to do it, and all she had was a note pinned to her. Said her mother drowned, and we were to look after her."

"Why?" Lady Farleigh asked. "Why would Foyle lie to you, Colin? Why say she was dead?"

Colin's pressed his lips together in a grim line. "Never give up leverage," he said. "If he thought he could take her out of his pocket when the need arose, why give her to us? And if he'd said she was alive, we wouldn't have let him leave without knowing where."

"There's no question, then," Elinor said. "It's not just me. She's Marie's daughter."

"There is no question whatsoever," Lady Farleigh said firmly.

"Then . . . who are the rest of you, anyhow?" Mrs. Fincher said. "Meaning no disrespect."

"We're her family," Colin said firmly. "We are all her family, and we should very much like to take her home."

～

Chapter 33

The next few hours were chaos. It took ten minutes to gather young Marie's belongings, but two hours to sort out the legality of bringing her home with them, and to allow her to say a temporary farewell to her friends (with many promises to allow visits). Elinor became rather concerned as a flock of pint-sized females swarmed Lord Farleigh with tearful exhortations to look after their friend that he would adopt the whole brood. Luckily, it seemed the majority were spoken for, their parents being in good working order.

Mrs. Fincher finally agreed to allow Lady Farleigh temporary guardianship until they could arrange for Mr. Bhandari to take custody of the young girl. Young Marie was installed in the town house and showered with so much attention and so many hastily acquired gifts that Elinor worried the girl would be suffocated. Luckily, she took more after her mother than Elinor, and clearly thrived on the attention.

Which left Elinor to return, belatedly, to the Hargrove town house, where she discovered Joan in the process of packing.

"False labor," Joan said. "Doesn't *feel* false, I'll tell you that. But at least I have the chance to escape back to Thornwald. Are you married yet?"

Elinor blinked. "Married?"

"You and Farleigh. I'm joking, mostly. I assume you've sorted yourselves out. You look significantly less morose. I think you might be on the edge of effervescent, actually." Joan grinned.

"There's rather a lot going on," Elinor said. "I imagine it will be some time before everything gets sorted out enough to even talk about marriage."

There was a knock on the door, and Martin peered in. "Elinor, Farleigh's at the door. He says he's on his way to get a special license if I say yes, and wants to know if tomorrow will do for the wedding. Am I saying yes?"

"What? Oh. Yes," Elinor said. "Joan, can you hold out another day?"

"If this child is anything approaching as stubborn as his parents, we have weeks," Joan said.

"*Her* parents," Martin corrected, apparently an automatic reflex. "Tomorrow's fine, then?"

"Tomorrow's excellent," Elinor confirmed.

"And you're sure you wouldn't rather I dump a bucket of ice water over his head and never speak to him again?" Martin said.

"Yes, I'm sure!" Elinor declared, throwing up her hands. "For God's sake, Martin!"

"Just checking," he said with a grin, and disappeared.

"I have no idea how you put up with him for so long," Joan said with a sigh.

"You're the one that married him."

"And look where that got me," Joan said, but she was grinning, too.

It was not one more day, but three. Three days, long enough for the rest of their siblings to arrive, long enough for little Marie to put the whole household under her spell, long enough for sorrow and joy to rise and fall again and again in a constant dance.

It was strange, grieving a thing that had happened so long

ago, and rejoicing in discoveries freshly made. It felt almost like madness, Colin thought. And then he stood at the altar in the chapel, and looked in Elinor's eyes, and looked at their families gathered in the pews, and the two sensations— that plummeting low, that exultant height—twined together into something that did not seem contradictory at all.

Kitty was holding little Marie's hand. Kitty was smiling, the first time he'd seen her do so in months. Mr. Bhandari stood to the girl's other side, and could not seem to help glancing down at her every few seconds, as if to assure himself that she was there. Lady Farleigh herself, she who had glared down the minister when he objected to Mr. Bhandari's placement, was surreptitiously dabbing at her eyes. And Phoebe, brilliant Phoebe, had finally put her spectacles on in public because, as she had declared, she wouldn't believe it if she didn't see it clearly. She was sneaking her own glances, flashing secret smiles at Maddy, who sat with the Hargroves.

There was so much love in this room. It didn't make anything easy. It didn't fix things. Phoebe still had so much to navigate. Little Marie would never have an easy time of things.

But it bore them up. And when Colin kissed his bride, if there was something of sorrow in the kiss, it only made it sweeter.

Epilogue

◠

"Well," Colin said, closing the door behind him. "That was a rather smashing success, don't you think? I admit I don't have much experience getting married, but I seem to have a natural aptitude."

"Lord Farleigh, you appear to be in my bedroom," Elinor said, arching an eyebrow. She was dressed in the most exquisite cream dress; it clung to all the right parts of her and floated airily over the rest, and looked extremely easy to remove. Colin intended to test this theory momentarily.

"I am your husband, now," he pointed out.

"Indeed. And my husband's quarters are to the other side of that door," Elinor said, pointing toward the adjoining room.

"There is a slight problem with my room," Colin said delicately.

"Oh?"

"It lacks a bed," he admitted. The raised eyebrow shot up further. He advanced a step, spreading his hands helplessly. "I've had my eye on this town house for years, but the sudden acceleration of the timetable required certain compromises to be made."

"We could have *rented* a room. Or just stayed at your *old* town house," Elinor pointed out.

"Yes, but my old town house was full of my female relatives. And this was rather exhilarating. I had no idea one could acquire real estate so quickly."

"So long as you don't mind compromising on the number of beds," Elinor observed. She turned her back on him and patted the bedspread. "Ah, well. I *suppose* I could be convinced to share my bed with you. But you will have to be very, *very* convincing."

He moved up behind her, setting his hands to either side of her perfectly curved waist. She looked back toward him, her lips ever so slightly parted, and he leaned in to whisper in her ear. "Please," he said.

The dress was, indeed, very easy to remove.

Keep reading for a preview of
Kathleen Kimmel's Birch Hall Romance

A Lady's Guide
to Ruin

Available now from Berkley Sensation!

Elinor's arrow struck a scant few inches off center with a satisfying *thunk*, and she gave a tight nod, pleased. "I haven't entirely lost my skill," she said. "Though I would once have called that shameful."

They stood on the lawn before the great house, several hounds lolling behind them—along with Mrs. Wynn, who was perched on a stool brought out for her comfort—and three targets arrayed at a respectable distance. Elinor had insisted on the first shot and on stringing her own light bow. Joan, clad in her favorite of the gowns Maddy had tailored for her— a dove-gray with sleeves that clung without restraining and a frothy petticoat just showing beneath—hung back.

Martin stood near her, though not *too* near, a distance that felt carefully calculated. Despite the bright day, the only clouds being some wispy things off in the middle distance, his patch of lawn seemed overcast. The man was withdrawn. More than that, *brooding*. Yesterday had been entirely without incident. She could not imagine what left him scowling so. It was not a good look for him. Or at least, not one she preferred. He was handsome even in such a dark state, and she knew plenty of girls who would swoon all the more for it, but unhappiness had never allured her.

"It is your turn, cousin," Elinor said. Joan hefted her own bow, smaller and lighter than Elinor's. It was no more than a length of wood in her hand. She might have more luck walloping the targets directly.

"Perhaps we should move the dogs," she said, a little desperately.

"You won't shoot backward," Elinor pointed out.

"If it can be done, I'll manage it," Joan said, and for once Joan and Daphne spoke as one. "Someone will have to show me. Else I will not be responsible for the mayhem." She widened her eyes a bit at Elinor—the safer instructor of the two. Elinor started forward.

"Here," Martin said, striding forward before his sister could reach her. "It's easy enough to get it going in the right direction, at least. And once you have that, we'll work on your aim." He offered her a smile—a strangely delicate smile, like one might offer a small child one didn't know. He stood beside her. She cast an apologetic glance at Elinor, who only shrugged. Nothing for it.

"Hold the bow in your right hand. Yes, like so. Now, do not draw yet but make the motion." He demonstrated, drawing his hand back toward his ear. "You will be able to sight down the arrow, to see that it is straight. There, yes. No, your elbow is too low, lift it up." His hand twitched, like he'd been about to correct her with a touch, but it stilled. He walked her through the steps of drawing and releasing once, twice, three times, all without moving closer than five steps from her.

Which was a good thing, she reminded herself for the hundredth time, but still she could not help a little sigh when he handed an arrow to her from as far away as their arms' length allowed. *There must be some middle ground between broken hearts and pure standoffishness*, she thought peevishly. She fitted the arrow to the bow. It slipped from the string when she tried to set it. When she got the end fitted rightly, the head drooped off the bow like a nodding tulip. She caught herself just before she uttered a very un-Daphne-like curse.

Martin's curse was quiet but her ears were sharp. She

looked at him with an eyebrow raised in mimicry of his habit. He did not seem to catch the reference but closed the distance between them. "May I show you?" he asked, voice clipped.

"I think you'll have to," she said.

One hand closed around her right, adjusting her fingers. His touch was firm, his skin warm against hers. He took her left hand next and guided her to nock the arrow to the bow. His breath was against her ear when he spoke. "There," he said. "Can you see?"

Not really. This was a terrible idea. Standoffishness was preferable. His chest was against her back, so close she could feel the heat of him. His fingers, gentle as their touch was, were like brands against her skin. And the scent of him—*cloves,* she thought, *and honey, and saddle leather.* She wanted to turn her face against his neck and drink him in. "I see," she whispered.

His hand moved near her hip, but he did not touch her. But she could feel the touch, where his hand would have rested, how his fingers might have splayed, pressing flat the fabric of her skirts. "Widen your stance," he said. "You need stability. Drop your shoulders. Your strength is in your chest as well as your arms. Now draw."

She drew, and he moved with her, guiding her hands, sliding his fingertips out to her elbow to mark the straight line of her arm. She sighted down the arrow. It meant nothing. His touch meant nothing. Not to her, not to him. It could not mean anything.

"It helps if you think of someone you despise," Elinor called.

"And breathe out before you let go," Martin told her, voice a growl in her ear.

Moses. She almost whispered the name as she loosed. The string sang. She heard an intake of breath from behind her. The arrow struck. Dead center. She stared. Then Elinor whooped and clapped, and Joan grinned. Even Martin laughed, and turned her around with his hands on her shoulders.

"Quite the Diana we have," he said. She darted a glance at his hands. One thumb rested on the neckline of her dress, a millimeter's grace from bare skin. He followed her gaze and flinched, dropping his hands.

"Forgive me," he said.

"For what?" she asked, mystified. He only shook his head.

"Try again," Elinor urged. "Let's see how far your talents will take you."

Martin stepped back, hands folded behind him, and inclined his head. She scowled as she drew the next arrow. *Hugh,* she thought, aiming at the rightmost target.

Thunk. Center.

Another arrow. Another draw, another release. *Joan Price,* she thought, and the arrow struck the left target at its heart. *If only I were Daphne.*

Elinor was cheering. Martin had a dumbstruck look on his face, and then he grinned, storm cloud banished.

"Diana indeed," he said. "Our goddess of the hunt! You've played us, certainly. You've shot before."

She shook her head. Slings and rocks, a brick or two, clots of mud, a post heaved like a spear, once. But never a bow. "It is only that I am standing so close," she said. "And I got lucky." *And had excellent targets.*

"Not to mention the finest of instructors," Martin added.

"Well, then, we'll have to see how long your luck holds," Elinor said. "Martin, won't you take your turn?"

"I don't think my pride can withstand it, matched against the two of you," he said. "I am content to watch." He gave a formal bow and retreated again to a safe distance. Joan took up another arrow. Imagined his hand on her waist, setting her stance, then on her shoulders, her elbow. Running down her back. Imagined him behind her, a solid wall. Not taking the shot for her, but steadying her.

This time, the arrow went wide. It struck the target, but barely, wobbling at the edge. She sucked in a breath through her teeth. "D—rat," she said, catching herself short of worse blasphemy.

Elinor chuckled. "Oh, good. I had worried you would never miss and I should have to hang up my bow for good. You let yourself think too much, but that's all right. You'll have it in your limbs if you keep practicing, and the limbs are slower to forget than the mind."

Joan nodded and set her teeth. She wouldn't let a round of straw and burlap conquer her. *Moses*, she thought. *Hugh.* She and Elinor stood aligned and the arrows sailed one after the other. And all the while she felt Martin's eyes on her.

He had feared he would harm her by his touch. That she would flinch or shrink from him. But she did not, any more than she had on that excruciating ride. Now, as then, it was all he could do not to lean close, feel her hair against his cheek. Let his hands wander to her back, her waist. Creep higher. Hell. He might as well think of tearing her gown from her in full view of Mrs. Wynn, the dogs, and the damned gardener.

He paced in his study. It was long past the hour he should have retired but he could not abide even the thought of lying down, of trying to sleep. She had not flinched from him. Shouldn't she, if she had been ill-treated at some other man's hands?

He did not know that she had been, he reminded himself. He had written to Mr. Hudson, instructing him to quietly investigate the matter, but news on that front would be some time in coming. He could pace all the night and into the morning and it would not speed the information to him. He should rest. He should behave like a sane man, but he did not feel like one.

Daphne clearly did not wish to be handled like a piece of porcelain. Nor did she want him; that was clear enough. Every time he thought she might, whatever Elinor said, she fluttered her lashes and vanished behind her role. If only he could make himself stop thinking of her.

A floorboard creaked in the next room; a scrape of metal sounded. He stiffened. No one should be about at this hour. Next door was the Blue Room, though the color that lent it its name had long since been replaced with the dull cream his father had preferred. It was where the ladies took their tea. A thump, rustling. Someone was definitely in there. He seized his walking stick where he'd leaned it against the wall and moved with all the stealth he could muster. The door was open a sliver. Warm light spilled from it into the hall. He pushed open the door, wincing at its deep groan.

Daphne knelt by the hearth, stoking a small fire to life. She jerked to her feet when he entered, pale-faced as a thief caught with hands on the silver. She wore a pelisse over her nightgown, the sleeves billowing around her wrists. Her hands were dark with streaks of ash from the grate.

"Daphne," he said, loosening his grip on the walking stick. "I see you are still having trouble sleeping."

She cast her eyes downward. "I'm sorry I disturbed you. I had forgotten."

"Don't apologize. I had hoped that you might find sleep more easily at Birch Hall. Do you . . . is it nightmares, that keep you awake?"

"Sometimes," Daphne said. "But more often only the racing of my mind. And what keeps the Earl of Fenbrook awake?" she asked lightly. Deflecting his attentions. If he were a kinder man, he would allow it. He had a vague answer balanced on his tongue, and a farewell ready to follow it. But instead he stared straight at her.

"You," he said. It had the desired effect: the mask beginning to settle around her features dropped and she stared at him with no one's eyes but her own.

She ought to laugh. Or tilt her head quizzically, like a bird examining an insect. But instead she said, "And why would I keep you awake?"

"I worry about you."

"I'm well," she said, managing caution, at least, if she could not quite claim wisdom.

He fell silent, and his fingers worked at the handle of his walking stick. "Who hurt you?" he asked after a long pause.

She parted her lips, confused. "I told you I did not know

them," she said. Did he doubt her story? He had seemed sold enough on it in London.

He shook his head once, fiercely. "Not them. Before. The marks on your body are older. Who hurt you? Elinor would not tell me."

Her breath caught in her throat. There was no answer she could give him. The men who had chained her, held her in the water, cut off her hair—those men did not even have names or faces in her mind. They did not matter. They did not have her, and she did not fear them. It was Hugh and Moses she feared, and to tell him that was to tell him everything.

"I must know," he said. "Tell me."

She shook her head. "I can't."

"I can protect you," he said. "Daphne."

She looked away. Yes, Daphne. He wanted to protect his cousin. If he knew the truth, he would not be so forgiving as Elinor. That anger in his voice would be for her, not on her behalf. "I cannot tell you," she said. "Please don't ask again. It's over. They will not harm me again."

"No, they won't," he said. He'd drawn closer. Too close. Close enough to touch. The firelight glowed against his skin, marking the tense lines on his neck and temple. She locked her gaze on the mantle. "Daphne." He touched her chin. Turned it toward him. She let out a sound she did not recognize, a short hum that turned into a sigh. "You must tell me."

"I can't," she said again. His hand had not left her. His thumb stroked her jaw. Made a soft circle. It brushed the corner of her mouth. "You told me I would be safe here," she said. "I am." If he did not move his hand, all the promises in the world would not stop her from kissing him. "Martin," she said. She meant it as rebuke. But he gave a huff as if in frustration and bent, moving his hand to cup her head, turn her face toward his—but she had already tilted her mouth upward to meet his. Their lips brushed once, softly.

Then hesitation was gone. He pressed his lips to hers and her body against him, his hand at once firm and impossibly light on her back. She nipped his lower lip, sending a shiver through him she felt to her core. His hands ran into her hair, down her shoulders, as to map her by touch, settling at last at her neck and the small of her back, gentle pressure holding her in place. He parted her lips with his. His tongue slipped into her mouth. She returned the gesture playfully, and then hungrily. The hand at her back crept to her ribs. His fingers chanced against the underside of her breast. Then—

He drew away abruptly. They stared at each other.

Elinor. Her promise. She cursed herself and looked away from him, trying to ignore the hammering beat of her heart.

"I'm sorry," he said.

"You apologize too much," she chided him.

"Then I shouldn't be sorry?" His voice was low. It sent a shiver up her spine. She swayed into him, reached up. Tangled her fingers at last in that dark hair, gave a tug. He let out a sharp hiss of pleasure. She rocked her hips against him, lifted herself onto her toes, and kissed him. Slow and sweet, this time, once more and for the last time.

She fell back on her heels. He leaned in toward her. She stopped him, her hand to his chest. "You should not be sorry," she said. "But we cannot do that again."

He folded his hand over hers and lifted it to his lips. They touched each finger in turn. She bit her lip, held her breath. *Let me go*, she thought, and hoped he wouldn't.

"I would never let anyone hurt you," he said. "Never let anyone touch you."

"I cannot be what you want me to be," she said.

"What is it you think I want?"

"I—" She didn't know. She had thought he wanted only to look after his cousin, but that kiss left all such thoughts in ruin. He was not a man to lie with his kiss. She tasted enough such lies to know the difference; told them, too, with moans and sighs and false caresses. She had not lied, either. She wished to write essays worth of truth on that skin. She tilted up her head, squared her shoulders. "You will say you want to wed me, but that is only because you are a man of honor confronted with dishonorable desire."

"I do desire you," he said.

"But not a wife."

He did not answer. She'd hit her mark, square in the center, and they both knew it. It didn't matter that she had no desire to *be* a wife; he would never ruin his cousin by making her his lover, and she would not betray Elinor that way. Nor him.

"I think I shall try to sleep after all," she said. When she moved past him, he made no attempt to stop her, or to follow. She kept a steady, forced pace until she reached her room and the door was shut behind her. Then she leaned her head against the wood and pressed her hand between her breasts.

"You fool," she whispered. "Oh, Joan, you fool."

The darkness gave no comfort or reply.

Martin watched her go and said nothing. He wished her accusation were unjust. He wished that he could fall to his knee then and there and pledge that it was her hand he wanted, above all else. And he did want *her*—not only her body, but her company, her trust. But not marriage. Not yet, at least.

He could not propose to Daphne without telling her about the search for Charles—ensuring that she understood that his title was a tenuous thing. And he could not tell her that without telling Elinor, and he could not tell Elinor yet. Not until he was certain, one way or another, what had happened to Charles. He couldn't bear to raise her hopes only to see them dashed.

Maybe he could go ahead with it. Propose, explain later. He would still have his money if Charles was found, and he liked to think that kiss had nothing to do with the *lord* before his name. But that would mean proposing under false pretenses.

He knuckled at his brow at the point between his eyes. What if he called Hudson back? What if he let Charles stay dead, and stayed Lord Fenbrook? But, no. He could not abandon hope of seeing Charles again, of making peace with him.

He struck the mantle with the side of his fist. Perhaps he

should go back to London, so that he did not have to see her each day. It was a kind of madness, this preoccupation. Watching the mask slide on and off, straining to catch those moments when she laid it intentionally aside. She wanted him. He wanted her. Why could it not be as simple as that?

But there was Daphne, and Daphne's role. There was Martin, and the title. The inconvenient half could not be tossed aside, however much they ached for it.

God, though. That kiss. Not her first, clearly, which was a prospect he did not care to contemplate. But however she had obtained the practice, the result—

He touched his lower lip, imagining he could still feel the slight bite of her teeth upon it. When she had pressed against him, her breasts against his chest, her hips rolling forward to push against him . . . He was getting hard at the memory. He'd wanted to pin her against the wall, to let his mouth find all the places she *hadn't* been kissed. To hear her moan again.

He wrenched his thoughts from that path. Charles, first. And the truth of what had happened to Daphne. When he had the proper picture of things, he'd know what to do. How to win her. He could wait. Pure torture as it was, he could wait.